THE ANTHOLOGY OF
DARK WISDOM
THE BEST OF DARK FICTION

The Anthology of Dark Wisdom is published by Elder Signs Press, Inc.
This book is © 2009 Elder Signs Press, Inc.

This anthology is © 2009 William Jones; all rights reserved. All material © 2009 by the respective authors.

Cover art © 2009 by Malcolm McClinton; all rights reserved. Cover and interior layout by Deborah Jones. Edited by William Jones.

PUBLICATION HISTORY
"Plague of Fire," *Book of Dark Wisdom* Magazine, Elder Signs Press, 2004
"Vamp Until Ready" *Book of Dark Wisdom* Magazine, Elder Signs Press, 2004
"Shivering, We Dance," *Book of Dark Wisdom* Magazine, Elder Signs Press, 2005
"The Purloined Prose," *Book of Dark Wisdom* Magazine, Elder Signs Press, 2005-2006
"Out of the Shadows," *Dark Wisdom Magazine*, Elder Signs Press, 2006
"TechnoTriptych," *Dark Wisdom Magazine*, Elder Signs Press, 2006
"Memories, Red and Wet," *Dark Wisdom Magazine*, Elder Signs Press, 2006
"The Eccentric," *Dark Wisdom Magazine*, Elder Signs Press, 2007
"Out of the Light," *Dark Wisdom Magazine*, Elder Signs Press, 2007
"Mr. Aickman's Air Rifle," *McSweeney's Enchanted Chamber of Astonishing Stories*, Vintage Books, 2004
    —*The Year's Best Fantasy and Horror*, Macmillan, 2004
"Woman In the Dark," *City Slab*, 2008
"Wasp Light," *Farrago's Wainscot*, 2009

All characters within this book are fictitious. Any resemblance to actual events or persons, living or dead, is strictly coincidental.

No part of this book may be reproduced in any manner without the written persmission of the publisher.

FIRST EDITION
10 9 8 7 6 5 4 3 2 1
Published in September 2009

ISBN: 1-934501-14-X
Printed in the U.S.A.

Published by Elder Signs Press
P.O. Box 389
Lake Orion, MI 48361-0389
www.eldersignspress.com

THE ANTHOLOGY OF
DARK WISDOM
THE BEST OF DARK FICTION

EDITED BY WILLIAM JONES

2009

ACKNOWLEDGEMENTS

Many thanks to all of the artists, writers, reviewers, editors, and contributors to *Dark Wisdom Magazine*. It was your enthusiasm and spirit that gave it life. And a very special thanks to all of the readers who kept it going.

CONTENTS

INTRODUCTION
WILLIAM JONES 11

WOMAN IN THE DARK
TOM PICCIRILLI 15

PLEASE STAND BY
TIM CURRAN 29

PRAGMATIC
C.J. HENDERSON 43

AND THINGS UNDER THE EARTH
JOHN PELAN & PAUL MELNICZEK 57

VAMP UNTIL READY
WENDY LEEDS 67

SHIVERING, WE DANCE
SHERRY DECKER 75

TECHNOTRIPTYCH
JOHN SHIRLEY 83

ASIA MARSH
NEDDAL AYAD 97

A TALENT FOR TROUBLE
RACHEL GRAY 103

THE ECCENTRIC
ALAN DEAN FOSTER 119

HEAR NO EVIL
SHANE JIRAIYA CUMMINGS 127

MR. AICKMAN'S AIR RIFLE
PETER STRAUB 135

THE PURLOINED PROSE
PATRICIA LEE MACOMBER & DAVID NIALL WILSON 161

SON OF MOURNING
CHRISTOPHER T. LELAND 175

ANKAREH MINU
RICHARD A. LUPOFF 183

MEMORIES, RED AND WET
CHRISTOPHER WELCH 201

g
GENE O'NEILL 209

WASP LIGHT
BRUCE BOSTON & LEE BALLENTINE 221

THE ROBIDERMIST'S STEED
DEANNA HOAK 225

THE ADVENTURE OF THE SOLITARY GRAVE
CHRISTIAN KLAVER 229

PLAGUE OF FIRE
LEE CLARK ZUMPE 275

OUT OF THE SHADOWS
GERARD HOUARNER 285

IF MAMA AIN'T HAPPY
SAM W. ANDERSON 309

MOPLEOLI
RICHARD WRIGHT 321

AND ON THE FOURTH DAY
JAMES ARGENDELI 333

INTRODUCTION
WILLIAM JONES

WILLIAM'S RAMBLINGS

MANY READERS OF THIS book are likely to have encountered *Dark Wisdom* in its former incarnation as a magazine. I suspect the majority of readers will probably find this a new experience. But in order to properly introduce this anthology and hopefully explain what it is about, some history of the magazine needs to be offered.

Dark Wisdom started as a digest-sized, black and white, perfect bound magazine. What that means is the magazine was small and bound like a book. In fact, the original name was "Book of Dark Wisdom." One can imagine the confusion such a title caused on magazine racks. Is it a book? It's bound like a book, but it calls itself a magazine. This eventually led to truncating the name to "Dark Wisdom."

During the evolution of the magazine, it changed forms as well. The original digest size was very popular with readers—easy to fit in a pocket. It was less popular with retailers as the small size assisted in its being lost on magazine racks. Larger magazines simply overshadowed it. To cure this commercial affliction, *Dark Wisdom Magazine* grew. It took on the shape of a full sized magazine. All the while, it maintained its use of illustrations, stories, articles, reviews, and commentaries. Eventually the magazine grew in circulation to where it was possible to produce a full color, glossy interior. Although some mourned the passing of the black and white edition, many

INTRODUCTION

others were attracted by the new, colorful look of the magazine. This also allowed the artists producing illustrations to flourish.

None of this speaks to the content of the magazine, however. In fact, that was another journey. The first two issues were dedicated to the paper role-playing game *Call of Cthulhu*. The magazine still published fiction and poetry, but the majority of the content was "game" focused. By issue three, the "game" market that had once seemed barren was overflowing with other magazines (five at the time). To prevent *Dark Wisdom* from floundering, it ventured into fiction. Most importantly Dark Fiction.

Readers of the early issues undoubtedly will remember the close connection the magazine had with Lovecraftian tales. This was in part due to the magazine's original intent. And in part to the growing interest in the writings of H.P. Lovecraft. That was only one aspect of the magazine. The other was Dark Fiction. And this label often confused would-be readers, and writers. To most, Dark Fantasy was Dark Fiction. This wasn't the case for the magazine. As the editor of *Dark Wisdom*, I looked for fiction works that were dark in tone and mood, and focused on the human condition. Admittedly, this sounds like every other "horror" magazine published. But that was the key. *Dark Wisdom* wasn't a "horror" magazine. It could be described as a multi-genre magazine, and often was. In fact, because the label Dark Fiction was primarily being pioneered by *Dark Wisdom*, the front cover always sported the genre labels: Science Fiction, Fantasy, Horror.

This was a bit of an untruth. The fiction within the pages of the magazine was usually blends of genre—dark SF, or horror/SF, or dark fantasy (but not necessarily swords and sorcery which many people associated with the term). All of this resulted in many letters and questions at conventions: What is the difference between dark SF and horror? The easiest answer is the classic film *Alien*. Is it Horror or Science Fiction? I'd call it Dark Fiction, as it uses tricks and tropes from both genres.

As a reader, you now hold the final shape of the magazine—although it still exists as an online publication: www.darkwisdom.com. *The Anthology of Dark Wisdom: The Best of Dark Fiction* is an on-going series that will continue to reprint tales from the magazine, and include new works. All of these are stories of Dark Fiction.

With that said, this is a genre anthology—and "genre fiction" has taken quite a bit of abuse over the years. But genre labels are ideally suited for selling books. Like any work of fiction, it does not reflect the quality. As readers, we know what we like. As genre readers, we tend to be fans of one or more genres, and when in a given mood, we search out that genre in a bookstore, usually finding the book under a sign labeled "Science Fiction" or "Horror" or "Mystery." This doesn't explain why some books can be found in one or more sections. That's perhaps because those books blend genres, and there is no easy label. For the reader of this anthology, which is most likely found under "Horror," the label is Dark Fiction. What does that mean a reader can expect from this anthology? Tales of the supernatural, of the natural, of mystery and science and horror, all of them dark in tone—although there are a few light-hearted moments and tales. Most importantly, readers will find engaging tales, thoughtful and provocative. While the stories I've selected for this anthology will not match everyone's taste, it will hopefully convey the subject and nature of the anthology, and mostly if not entirely satisfy the reader.

Zombies, vampires, werewolves, aliens, ghosts, murderers, detectives and terrifying things can be found in the following pages. Fiction set in urban settings, rural, in other times and places are also elements of this anthology. It is a collection of tales that have previously appeared in *Dark Wisdom Magazine*, and those tales that were slated for publication before the magazine changed form again. It also contains stories that belong in a collection of Dark Fiction. However, in the end, the label isn't as important as the story. And this anthology is just a collection of stories.

William Jones
Metamora, MI
August, 2009

WOMAN IN THE DARK

TOM PICCIRILLI

IT HAD TAKEN MORE than twenty years to happen but he still wasn't ready for it when it did.

Sometimes the world jumped at your face and tried to bite it off, and sometimes life just crept up so slowly that you couldn't help but shake your head when you saw the utter cunning of what had been occurring by inches for so long.

Collie was thirty-nine and screaming on the downhill slide into his mid-life crisis. He spent more and more time in the bathroom looking in the mirror at some wrinkled bastard with a growing patch of white in his hair, learning to really hate the guy. His wife was gone, his job was gone, and he had a little less than two grand in the bank. No kids, no health insurance, no retirement plan, and no exit strategy, all of which served to remind him of the small mistakes he'd made since he was about sixteen, which had continued picking up steam over the years until he'd somehow totally derailed.

He hadn't been with a woman in six months and didn't really miss it that much, which also said a lot. Any woman he could nab had troubles of her own, along with three or four kids in tow and a psychotic ex-husband or two, which just made the whole thing spooky as hell. Sometimes they wanted to marry him, and sometimes they started crying the moment he got their blouses off. Their breasts hung like lynchings.

Occasionally, in the middle of the action, the ladies stared at him with such loathing that he started searching around for a butcher's knife under their pillows, maybe a razor blade hidden under a tongue. He was a part of the brotherhood of pain who had beaten or maimed them. A stern bitter father, a greasy-pawed uncle, the failures of his side of the species thick in his bloodstream. When he climbed against the women they could feel his forefathers' evils coming along with him into the room, and so could he.

So he was kicking along Amsterdam Avenue around 71st, looking for a pizza place where he could grab a couple slices of pepperoni—you couldn't carry your great burdens in the front of your mind all the time, you grew weak, you became part of the horde, your fingertips let go of the ledge—when he walked past a doorway and heard a minor commotion. The hard slap of meat on meat.

Collie turned and watched this little runt of a pimp with a pencil-thin mustache and his shirt open to his belly button slapping a whore around. The runt smacked her open handed twice more and then gave her two short jabs to the mid-section, letting out a small grunt with each strike like he was mugging for a boxing promoter.

She let out a sound of complete surrender and fell over on her face, a dapple of blood flying onto the concrete. It was soaked up instantly and left a black mark. Collie stared at the blood and knew that fifteen generations from now that stain would still be there.

The pimp kicked her in the ribs and Collie, without truly understanding why, suddenly rose up and seemed to expand within himself, straining against his own contours. Inwardly pressing the confines of his own personality, and feeling it buckle and give way. He was in motion but didn't know where he was going until he shoved the runt backward through the open door and into the hall.

Collie watched the guy's face go from a icy calm to attentive but disbelieving rage. The runt all teeth. His mouth stuffed with what looked like fifty or sixty shards of bone. The fury coming off him in waves, like the tide rolling.

You didn't get involved in things like this. It wasn't chivalrous and it wasn't manly to try to protect a hooker from her boss daddy. This was a different kind of life. She was probably so used to the beatings that she'd pull a blade on Collie just for jumping in. You never knew.

But he couldn't stop himself even as he squared his shoulders and gave two sharp chops to the runt's throat and knocked him down. Collie had never been in a fight in his life, not even when he was drinking heavily and used to start shit in bars. He'd never thrown a punch, didn't know where the chop had come from, the edge of his hand like a blade, but it felt natural. Who knew such a thing could be done after a lifetime of not doing it.

He stared at his own hand, thinking, Hey, there's still a few surprises left after all.

The woman, huddled on the sidewalk, didn't move. She looked incapable of moving, as if she were nothing more than another cornerstone in a city of ancient, implacable structures. The breeze stirred her hair, and another drop of red sluiced in a wide arc across her cheek, but otherwise she seemed posed, a memorial to all women, lifeless.

The little pimp squeaked like a dog. He went into a coughing fit and bounced around the hallway on his back. When he could breathe again, he started squeaking once more. It took Collie a minute to realize the guy was yelling at him in Spanish.

Finally Collie said, "Look, I don't know what the hell you're saying."

The runt looked up and switched to English. "I'm saying you're dead, man. You hear that?"

"I hear that. What's your name?"

"I'm gonna cut your gizzard off."

Collie thought the threat might be a touch more potent if he knew what a gizzard was. "How about if you just run along now, you mutt."

"What'd you call me?"

"I called you a mutt," Collie said, and for emphasis reached down, grabbed the guy by the collar, shook him hard, and then punched him in the face. Blood spurted and drained down his shirt front. Somehow, Collie was disgusted by the sight but still liked it. "I also told you to run along."

He dragged the pimp past the whore who was now unsteadily getting to her feet. A tickle moved through him and he was a bit stunned to realize he was aroused. The situation had kicked his heart rate way up, his veins juiced, and his heart banging hard. His ex-wife would've called him sick. The marriage counselor would've steepled his fingers and pressed them under his bearded chin, the corners of his mouth notched into a slightly deprecating smile, silently judging everybody in his office.

The runt struggled, but Collie just yanked him along until he got to the front stoop and then threw the creep out to the curb. He bounced like a tennis ball left out in the rain. A few folks in the foot traffic stared, but no one slowed or stopped. The pimp got up, backed away, and slid away into a shadowed alley.

The city, or perhaps it was only himself, took a deep breath then, and let out a sigh that drifted through the centuries.

Collie turned back to her, took her elbow.

"You shouldn't have done that," she said.

A simple thank you, it just wasn't in her vocabulary. His hands were fists and he felt his back teeth grinding together. The counselor said he had anger issues. Who the hell didn't?

His brain kept sparking. The man he'd been five minutes ago called to him from a great distance, softly and a little sadly.

She looked as though she wanted to offer him something. Like an old Jewish lady whose driveway he'd shoveled, like she wanted to hand him a quarter. He gazed at her and spotted the caricature of seduction in her dress and makeup. The reality of ache and acceptance had been long ago written in her expression. He recognized the traits.

She'd lost one shoe. He found it in the foyer and went to one knee, waited for her to lift her foot so he could place it on her heel.

These are the actions of fairy tales, he realized. Bards and troubadours of another age had sung of this moment, in wait for him.

The woman leaned against the wall and put her hand on Collie's shoulder for balance. The weight of her above him had the texture of sex but none of its endurance. Collie started to back away, wondering where he would go now. He still had nowhere he needed to be. He'd never had anywhere he needed to be.

She wiped the back of her hand across her chin and smeared the blood into a ruby lipstick. A heavy breath escaped her and he smelled mouthwash and some kind of flowery perfume.

Collie started away but she was staring intently at him now, and her eyes were filled with amusement and something–

"Jesus Christ," he said. "Lori Ann."

They'd gone to the prom together.

Lori Ann Petrakos, his first serious crush and perhaps even his first love. She was still beautiful, even with blood on her teeth.

He remembered his fear just approaching her to ask her out that first time. It still lived within him, that fear, and twisted against him now like a beloved pet.

Halfway through senior year, every guy in the school, in the world, wanting her, and she'd just smile and let them all down easily, say she had plans or preferred to be friends. The kind of thing that created serial killers by the masses. Collie still didn't know where he got the nerve from, but one day it was there. He asked her to a movie, and she said yes.

It startled him so much that he never even got her number. He had to look her father up in the phone book, except it was her uncle who was right off the boat from Xios. The guy sold Souvlaki in mid-town Manhattan and knew about ten words of English, but eventually Collie got the right number.

He picked Lori Ann up in his '67 Charger—Christ, what a car, and he'd tuned it himself, rebuilt it from the tires up, by himself. It was something to be proud of, having such faith in your abilities.

He made a little extra change racing down Airport Road and out on Ocean Parkway. He held the door open for her when she got in, and drove to the theater like he was taking his road test. They saw some action flick that he couldn't keep his mind on. Her presence was so strong beside him that nothing would stay in his head for long, not even his lust. Sometimes she had to repeat herself because all he could hear was some strange kind of music, the thrum of his pulse in his ears.

When they got back out into the parking lot she said, "This car is muscle. You going to open it up this time?"

"If you want."

"I want."

He took her out east on Sunrise Highway, heading toward Montauk Point. When they got to the barrens, past all the traffic cop stake-outs, he kicked it up and was rewarded when she gave a throaty laugh. He thought, what the hell, and dropped the hammer until they were in triple digits, shrieking down the highway. She eased beside him and plucked his hand from where it rested on her knee and pressed one of his fingers into her mouth. He figured they might crack up against the rails right there.

They pulled over onto the first grassy part of the shoulder wide enough to keep from getting racked by a Freightliner, and screwed in the backseat. The whole time he stared into her eyes even though she had them closed through a lot of it, but he couldn't shrug the feeling that this was a great fortune he didn't deserve, that he was supposed to do something to prove he was worth it. The music kept playing. It swelled and surged.

They began dating and immediately a distance grew between him and his friends. His family too. It didn't have to do with Lori Ann so much as with his own growing understanding of the world. He had a touch of cool but not nearly enough, and he kept trying to figure out what she wanted with him. In the meantime, they made love a lot. His head, already awash with fantasies of a huge brood of babies and house on the hill—why a hill, where the heck were there hills around here?—grew more crowded with intense dreams.

She liked him to speed but wanted him to stop racing. He didn't get it but said all right. She laughed deeply against his neck while he peeled free of red lights. She laid in the back and rambled about her life while he took the back streets through the city. Her mother's insults, the pink scars and the white ones, the proper way to baste a turkey, her favorite passages from Renaissance poetry, the time her uncle made a pass at her. A pass, nothing more, flirting but going right up to the line, maybe a step over it. It was the kind of thing that made Collie sort of crazy.

Prom night he felt like he'd been brushed by fate and wondered what achievements he might accomplish. There were artists and architects in his genetics.

Unlike the other girls, Lori Ann would only dance to the slow tunes, moving gracefully about the floor and making him look good. He was thankful. He told her he loved her, and she told him the same. A lightning charge filled the air, and he knew it might stop his heart. A couple hours later, while they panted in the backseat of the Charger, she also mentioned she was moving out of state to go to school.

He saw her three or four more times after that until one of them, probably him, faded away completely out of sight.

Twenty years later now, he realized he was still invisible, the cries of his forefathers going unheeded, the music gone.

Blood on stone.

Now Lori Ann took him by the hand and led him down the sidewalk, checking all around to make sure the mutt wasn't hiding behind a car or something, ready to jump out. Collie let himself be carried along.

He'd gone to a prostitute once in his life, back when his marriage was first coming apart. It had been a completely miserable experience. This lady older than his mother working his crank in the front seat of his car, in an alleyway in the meat packing district behind a bunch of other cars with guys getting their cranks worked on. All he could do was think about what a ridiculous situation it was. She kept saying, "Come on, baby, I can't do it all by myself . . . you ain't even trying, you got to try . . .." There just wasn't much left when a twenty dollar whore started nagging you worse than your wife.

Collie and Lori Ann didn't speak as they walked, with her still in the lead. Finally she tugged him up some stairs. There was a tree in front of her building and a homeless guy curled up behind the trash cans.

Her apartment was on the first floor. It wasn't much but it was twice the size of his own. A bottle of JD with an unbroken label sat on a table in her kitchen alcove. He was still hungry. He opened her refrigerator and found a pot of Jambalaya. He went through her cabinets and got himself a bowl and spoon, poured himself a glass of the JD. She seemed fine with him making himself at home.

When he finished she said, "We've got to get out of here."
"Why?"

"Mullo."

She said it Mule-O. "That the guy smacking you?"

"Yes."

"Not for nothing, but you could probably put that runt through a wall. Why did you take that from him?"

She seemed to seriously consider it. "I don't know."

That's all there was. She gazed at him like she was expecting him to berate her for it, but he said nothing. If anybody asked him how he'd wound up where he was, he'd have the same answer, the same lack of an answer.

She went to the closet and got out a small suitcase. "It's just the way things are. We need to go."

"Where?"

"Your place?"

It froze him to the floor. Christ no, not there. He shook his head. "No."

"Wife?"

"No," he said. The thought of going back to his place scared the hell out of him. He couldn't go back to what and where he'd been, lost and alone and looking for a slice of pizza. The burden of inactivity and mediocrity being all he knew how to carry. No one deserved that damnation.

He said, "It'll be all right."

"No, it won't," she said. The dried blood was still on her face. For some reason he was glad she hadn't washed it off. It lent a marble aspect to her beauty. "We just need a couple of days. Until he cools down. We'll hide in a hotel. I know a couple. Then, it'll all work itself out."

"It'll work itself out anyway."

He finished the food and walked around her apartment, liking everything he saw. She had a nicer couch than he did, a bigger television. He stepped into the bedroom and sat on the bed. The mattress was firm but lush. There was an afghan folded and laid atop the covers, the kind your grandmother would take twelve years to crochet and give you for a wedding gift. There was a stuffed unicorn nuzzled between the pillows.

She said, "I've never taken a trick here."

He nodded. She finished packing some stuff up. Then she stripped and took a shower, maybe expecting him to waltz in behind her. He laid on her bed and fell asleep, and when he woke the sun had gone down. She was there beside him, a little night light on in the kitchen. He couldn't see much of her face but he didn't need to. He used to stare at it for hours, while they sat in English class, while she ran around on the field doing cheers. His past was written into his DNA, she was woven into his cell structure. He reached for her across the dark and she slid toward him.

"We need to—"

"Unpack," he said. "We're not going anywhere."

It didn't sound like him at all. Something in his voice got her hot. She tore at his clothes and abruptly he was surging forward, on fire. He didn't know who he was anymore, and he liked it.

He'd never made love or been made love to like that, not even by her on prom night. She'd learned her trade well. Maybe that was a lousy thought or just an honest one. It didn't matter because it was all he had. He expected his normal gut response—the raging jealousy, the overwhelming curiosity about other men—but none of it needled him.

He felt sharply contented, a strange and weighty sense of peace blunting all the fine points of pain. On his game for the first time in years. Maybe forever.

There were noises outside her window. Maybe cats, maybe the homeless guy.

In the darkness, her voice heavy with potential consequence, Lori Ann said, "Aren't you going to ask me how I wound up walking the streets?"

Feminine grace in the murk.

It somehow made her more real, the fact that he could hardly even see her. They could be anyone in the night, even themselves.

He rolled over on top of her again and told her, "No."

Two days later Mullo showed up at the door flanked by two burly thugs. Collie stood there, shirtless and barefoot, yawning. Mullo opened his mouth and showed off all the slivers of teeth again, pointing every which way. He said, "I told you, man, I told you I was gonna get your gizzard!"

"What is that anyway?" Collie asked.

"You rotten jerk, I told you that—"

"Did you just call me a 'rotten jerk?'"

"I call you a—"

Collie didn't let him finish. He kicked out and caught Mullo in the knee, then tried again and scored the groin. It's a move that guys are trained not to do—sort of a cheat, kinda wimpy, especially when you know it's gonna hurt in that special guy way. But the hell with it, you're staring down three guys you don't have much choice.

Mullo bent over and Collie lifted his knee into the mutt's face and felt a nice satisfying crunch of bone. The little pimp went over backward into one of his buddies and they both hit the floor in an awkward splay of limbs.

Collie turned and threw himself against the other tough, who was gawking like he wasn't sure what he was supposed to do now. Everyone was the same, unsure of the next step to take, waiting for a cosmic sign.

Collie threw the second punch of his life into the guy's throat—well, the first one was more of a chop, but this was a punch—and listened to him make a weird gagging sound, "glck, glck, glck."

He didn't know where he'd gotten this thing about hitting people in the throat, but he wasn't about to feel guilty about it.

He ran forward and stomped the other thug's belly with his heel. Something inside burst. The tough let out a yelp more animal than human. Mullo struggled to get to a sitting position, holding his mashed nose between both his hands while blood poured out from between his fingers. Collie kicked him in the face. Blood looped into the air and nearly hit the mailboxes.

He grabbed Mullo by the collar and dragged the little pimp down the length of the hall until he got to the front stoop and then threw the fucker down the stairs. He didn't bounce so well this time. Collie moved back down the corridor to where the thugs were both rolled into tight balls, sobbing, sucking air between their clenched teeth. Collie stepped over them, went inside the apartment, and shut the door.

In the dark, her hair spread across his belly, she asked, "Any kids?"

"No."

"You wanted two. A boy and a girl. To live with you and your wife in your big house on the hill."

He didn't remember ever discussing that with her back in the day, but there it was. What else had he forgotten? He reached for her hand but she was holding a cigarette in one and a glass of JD in the other. The red tip burning, the ice clattering.

"Whatever happened to your Charger?" she asked.

He thought about it for a long time. By the time he spoke, she was asleep. "I have no idea."

The next time he saw Mullo, the mutt was coming up the stoop stairs with a switchblade out. His eyes were a burnished black, and his nose twisted in three or four different directions across his face. It would never look normal again, no matter how many operations he went in for.

Collie knew almost nothing about knives, but even he knew a switchblade wasn't a good weapon. Back when he was racing he'd seen two guys with a Fifties fixation go at it behind the airport once. Both wearing identical leather jackets, hair combed into perfect ducks' asses, thinking more about Jimmy Dean and West Side Story than actually hurting one another. You could tell that when they moved they had a theme song going through their skulls and they were trying to dance to it. One guy stabbed forward, missed, and the blade snapped off against the drivers' window of the other guy's car. Just as well. The other one's switch had gotten stuck, the little gizmo failing to lock. His knife looked like wet spaghetti. They made up and everybody got trashed.

So Mullo made a move for Collie right there on the steps in broad daylight. A few people around but not many. The homeless guy still there, maybe dead now behind the trash can.

Mullo was serious about this gizzard shit. Who could've guessed? Guy mentions cutting off your gizzard you figure, maybe it's a metaphor. Makes a little more sense on a figurative level. But no, this one here, he's actually making little sawing motions back and forth as he approaches.

Waiting, Collie felt calm and filled with an unnatural patience. It shook Mullo. He ducked down, like he was trying to be a snake in the grass, slithering unseen. He moved up the steps doing a zig-zag, serpentine, having watched too many ninja movies.

Collie continued to wait. It was taking forever.

He let loose with a sigh and stood on the top step looking around, feeling a million eyes on him. The city forever watching its children.

The mutt finally got there but said nothing.

No talk of gizzards, no cussing, no insults. He stabbed his switchblade toward Collie's belly and Collie almost thought he should let it enter him, part the flesh and go in deep to dig out all the venom inside him.

Instead, he drew in a breath and the blade missed him by an inch.

The force of his own swing twirled Mullo around in a wild pirouette. He whirled on the top step until he was facing away from Collie and using his arms to try to keep his balance. The wind moved against Collie's back, patting him, pressing him on. The hands of a ghost, perhaps his own, gave him a push.

Collie booted the runt in the ass and Mullo shot down and landed on his face on the sidewalk. He lay there unmoving with blood seeping across the concrete, lapping into the cracks. Mullo tried to get to his knees but couldn't make it.

Collie sighed again. He'd forgotten what he'd come outdoors for in the first place. He gave a final look around the street, scratched his chin, and went back inside.

In the dark, with her face pressed to his sweaty chest, she asked, "Don't you need to go to work?"

He said, "No."

"Nobody's going to miss you?"

"There's no one to miss me."

"Somebody."

"Nobody."

He thought he should ask her the same thing, but didn't want to touch on that aspect of her past. She'd either given up the life or put it on hold while he was here. Sometimes men would call her cell and she'd tell them she was busy. Sometimes she wouldn't answer. Once it was her mother. In five seconds they were screaming at each other. Collie drew the cell from her hand and hung it up.

They listened to the nightscape. Hearing the traffic that never eased up, sirens, horns, occasional shouts, and the odd murmurs of neighbors on the floor above and the floor below. The distant groans and the creaking of bones and buildings, alive or dying, or already long dead.

"What happened to you, Collie?" she asked.

It took him a while to respond.

"Nothing," he said. "Nothing's ever happened to me."

Next time he saw Mullo, the mutt was breaking in the front door. Collie stood there naked and watched the little creep come at him with a 9mm. He wondered which of them was more stupid. Which had less to lose. Mullo yelled, "Aye gwanna keelyah!"

Collie frowned. Not only was the guy's nose nothing more than a smashed mudpie swathed in bandages, but he'd bitten off the tip of his tongue at some point too. Mullo fired once and Collie felt a whining insect go flying by his ear. He walked forward, the hands still pushing him. Mullo fired again and a small but painful burn erupted along the side of Collie's head. He smelled burning hair. He tapped at his temple and sparks floated down. He hoped it would take out some of the gray.

Time went nowhere fast. Mullo seemed unsure of what to do next, of where to point the gun as Collie continued to approach. He stared at the weapon as if something might be wrong with it. He lifted the 9mm higher and tried to make a better effort of aiming. He was concentrating so hard that the nub of his tongue appeared between his lips. Looked like there were eight or nine stitches in it.

Collie got his hand on the pistol, pulled it aside, and punched the little mutt in the guts. Mullo let go of the 9mm and slowly turned around in defeat like he was just going to leave. Maybe thinking, Damn, I've screwed it up again. No big thing.

Collie let out a chuckle, a weird enough sound that it made the little pimp turn around and stare at him again.

He cracked Mullo in the forehead with the butt of the 9mm. The pimp fell backward into the hall. Collie did it again and Mullo moved another few feet back. It took three more tries before he was out on the front stoop. Blood poured into Mullo's eyes. He grinned with red lips. Everybody was always grinning with red lips. Collie was starting to get the same sense of this life as he'd had in the other one, that the things he was doing weren't affecting enough change, that he was living in a ceaseless pattern of repetition. His calm dissipated and a terrible panic filled him.

He extended his arm and shot Mullo through the head. He watched the lid of the guy's skull snap apart and veer into three different directions, a pulse of blood and brain whipping against the tree growing there with the roots busting through the concrete. The little pimp tottered on his heels for a second and then dropped straight down.

Collie had just killed a man, but all he could think about was, Well, at last, here's something new.

Someone screamed. It was the homeless guy, who didn't look all that worse for wear, really. He was maybe twenty-three, had some light peach fuzz on his chin, a sixty dollar haircut. Not homeless at all, just some suburban punk hanging around spending his father's money, getting loaded night after night, sleeping it off. Collie thought of shooting him in the ass on general principle, teach the creep to go home and do it right.

The guy shrieked again and backed away down the sidewalk before turning and running, waving his arms in the air. Up the block a cab stopped and some people got out. An old woman started yelling in Yiddish.

Collie stared at Mullo's body and had no idea what to do. Leave it there? Drag it into the alley? Throw some garbage bags over it? All further action seemed beneath him. He was still holding the gun and clenched it to his chest. He turned around and went back inside, thinking about what the counselor might say about all this, wanting to pop that judgmental prick too.

It was kind of funny, actually, the way they were shouting into their bullhorns. You couldn't hear a damn thing anyone was saying. Boots stormed up the stairs and stomped across the floors above. Shadows filled the corridor and slid under the door, they were moving all around the building but nobody had so much as knocked yet. So much for the negotiations.

In the dark, she waited with him and he said, "You should leave."

"I've got nowhere to go."

"You could go back home."

"I don't remember where that is."

He started to tell her but he'd forgotten it himself. What town had they lived in? What school had they gone to? He thought if he fought for the memory hard enough it would emerge and present itself, but the dreams continued to gather and he couldn't focus.

With the cops heaping into the building, he figured, Well, here it is. That was all right, it was better than whatever he'd had a week ago, utterly alone and without purpose. He felt his soul drift a moment. It was a beautiful, wondrous revelation. Lori Ann moved in behind him and kissed the back of his neck, pressed her face between his shoulders. He moaned because it was so good, so right. It gave him another moment's edge when his will might've been waning. He felt her lips moving into a broad smile against his flesh, her body shaking as she began to giggle, and then his own laughter was rising from him. The door opened and the room filled. He heard music again, filling him. He lifted the 9mm. He saw the house on the hill, watched the door open, saw Lori Ann and their two kids–a boy and a girl–come walking out, dressed fancy for some holiday. Maybe Easter.

•

PLEASE STAND BY

TIM CURRAN

WHEN THE PHONE STARTED ringing and ringing, Doug Lark came out of the depths of sleep, pretty sure it was the school bell he was hearing and that he was late for class. Then he opened his eyes. Realized he was forty years old and had been dreaming.

But the phone kept ringing.

He eyed it through narrowed slits and yanked it violently off its cradle. "Yeah?" he said.

"Doug? *Doug?* Christ, get your ass over here right now. I got something you're just not going to believe."

Doug wiped cobwebs of sleep from his eyes, shook his head. "Tommy? Jesus, unless you've got Tyra Banks in a thong, I ain't interested," he said, meaning it.

Tommy was Tommy Bell. Lived down the block. Unlike Doug who worked midnights at the mill, Tommy ran some kind of computer business out of his basement. Troubleshooting, data retrieval, that sort of thing. He cut his own hours. It was different for Doug.

"Listen, Tommy," he said. "It's only . . . what? Noon. I've only been sleeping four hours. I'll stop by around five or so. Now let me get back to sleep."

"No, no, no. You don't get it. This is gonna change your life."

Doug could hear it in his voice, that rampant excitement. It usually started with childish glee for Tommy, worked itself up incrementally to full-blown hysteria given time. Often, it could be infectious. But not now. Not today after the night Doug had put in.

"I'm tired, Tommy."

"Get over here, Doug," he said, practically out of breath. "Just do it, will you?"

Tommy hung up and Doug just sat there, dazed and confused.

The house was silent. Joanie must've been out shopping or looking after her aged maiden aunt. It was ideal sleeping weather. But Doug knew he wasn't going to get any sleep. If he didn't go over there, Tommy would come after him.

So he went.

Ten minutes later, he was standing on Tommy's porch in a pair of joggers and a hooded sweatshirt. There was a perpetual April mist in the air, the sky overcast and gloomy. Good day to be sleeping.

He knocked once and the door was thrown open.

"C'mon," Tommy said. "Jesus, you gotta see this."

He was a small thin man with glasses, his wheat colored hair getting dangerously thin on top. In sharp contrast to Doug who had a belly on him and lots of hair. Right now it was sticking straight up. Bed head.

Tommy led him downstairs, past the door to his office and into his private sanctum, an unused back room that was crowded with old TV sets in various stages of repair. It was a museum of vintage Sylvanias, Philcos, Admirals, and Zeniths. Most of them were from the fifties, old tube jobs. It was Tommy's hobby. Buying them at garage sales and auctions, fixing them up, bringing them back to life when he could. To Tommy they were classics; to Doug, just old. He didn't know how many hours he'd spent listening to Tommy lecture him about weird models like the Bush and the Philips Dual Standard, or the RCA with Channel One or the Philips K70.

"Check it out," Tommy said. "Just check it out."

Doug lit a cigarette, blew smoke from his nostrils. "You got me out of bed to show me another old TV?"

"It's not just an old TV, pal. You've never seen anything like this."

Tommy told him it was an RCA CTC-16, a real classic. He'd picked it up at an estate sale up in Wetmore. The tubes were shot, but it came with a few white cardboard boxes of replacements.

"There were no names on the boxes, Doug."

He went over to the long, low table that was heaped with equipment—digital and analog voltmeters, capacitor testers, oscilloscopes, generators, hundreds of yellow, green, and blue wires tangled through everything like the tentacles of a squid.

"You don't say?"

Tommy shook his head. "I was fascinated by them. I tested 'em... got some crazy readings, right off the scale. But they were compatible with the CTC-16, so I figured, what the hell."

"Sure, what the hell," Doug said drowsily.

He fell into a chair, pushed aside heaped boxes of wiring and capacitors, resistors and control knobs, receivers and tube amplifiers. Gazed sleepily at the wall behind him that was shelved with literally hundreds of vacuum tubes, the sort that were made to pull in *My Little Margie* and *Captain Video*.

Tommy turned the set on. "It'll take a few minutes," he said. "Then... then either you'll see it or I'm losing my mind."

Doug figured it was the latter. He butted his cigarette, started playing around with a voltage tester. "I hope this is good, Tommy, because I'm tired. I'm really tired."

"Tired?" Tommy said, studying the white dot that had appeared on the TV screen and was gradually expanding. "I've been up since yesterday. After I saw... well, I couldn't sleep."

While the TV warmed, Tommy hopped over a big picture tube, threaded his way through some bulky circuit boards that looked like they'd been stripped out of Sputnik, brought a plain white box over. He pulled a tube out. It was bright red, caught the light funny. Almost looked like carnival glass.

Doug handled it carefully. "It's pretty strange," he said. "Is that glass... it almost feels like some sort of plastic. It's so light. Cold or something."

The TV had warmed up now.

They were looking at a field of snow on the oval screen. Just static. Darker and more blurry than you got with a modern set, but static all the same.

"Wow," Doug said. "That's something, all right. Now if you'll excuse me, I'll–"

"Just wait," Tommy said nervously, as if it was a bomb that might explode at any moment.

The static began to fade and a picture began to swim out of that buzzing murk. Slowly, slowly, it took form and shape, the edges growing clearer, but there was still a lot of snow flying around and the picture flickered from time to time.

Doug looked closer. He thought it was some scene out of an old western... except it didn't move. No Indians or Calvary came charging out of those dusty environs. But it wasn't a still picture. You could see wind kicking up dust devils across the hollows in that craggy landscape. There were strange towers of stone much like chimneys and mesas, canyon walls punched with holes, cliffs in the background. The foreground was made of some blasted rock set with dips and draws. The picture was black and white, of course, and not exactly sharp, but there was something... something *odd* about the light. The way it played across those boulders and hills. It was bright, but the shadows were too dark, too thick, too something. It was like the light was being filtered through something.

"What the hell is it?" Doug said, interested, but not terribly. "Arizona or New Mexico?"

Tommy shook his head. "I don't know. I'm thinking it's none of those places."

"I don't get it," Doug said. "Somebody just set up a video feed in some wasteland? What's the point?"

But Tommy just shook his head. He was chewing his fingernails, actually trembling. "Just wait," he said cryptically.

Tommy leaned back in his chair, lit another cigarette, waited.

He waited about five minutes.

That's when he saw *them*.

Shapes, forms, *things* that came up out of those holes and hollows like ants from a hive. They jumped into the sky, drifted on membranous wings. Hopped and crawled and vaulted. They looked like lozenge-shaped beetles, if anything. But instead of creeping on their bellies, they stood high on barbed legs. Each body had four main legs that split into four other hooked appendages. There were weird, diamond-shaped patterns on their thoraxes and their jeweled eyes jutted on stalks. Doug had never seen insects like them before. But what really grabbed him was that you could see that they were big, really big. It was hard to put into scale, but he was thinking they had to be a couple of feet long.

"What is this?" he said, perplexed as he watched the creatures fill the screen like a school of fish, leaping and jumping and flying about. "Some science fiction flick? They're bugs... but–"

"But like nothing you've ever seen before, right?" Tommy said, calming some now, maybe vindicated. Certain, at least, he wasn't losing his mind. "Look at the size of them, Doug. Bugs like that..."

He didn't finish that and he didn't have to.

Doug was thinking the same thing: Where on earth did you find insects like that? And then an inner voice began to wonder if he was looking at the earth at all.

"I got the tubes in last night," Tommy said. "Right away... I saw this. I watched it all night. I thought I was losing it. I had those tubes out a dozen times since then. But every time I put 'em back in... well, you get the picture. So to speak."

But Doug didn't get the picture. Those weird tubes. This weird vision of . . . of something exotic, something extraordinary, something that filled him with revelation and *fear*. Yes, fear. It came straight up out of his balls and laid in his belly in a cold, flat dormancy. Whatever it was he was seeing, something in him did not like it. Did not like it at all.

"You get this same picture on every channel," Tommy was saying. "It's got something to do with those tubes. I don't know what, but something."

Doug was just staring, a long white ash falling from his cigarette into his crotch. But he didn't notice at all. The insects were getting really excited, flitting about madly, bumping into each other, starting one way, then going another. They were like herd animals, gazelles on the African veldt suddenly shit-scared because the lions were moving in.

And that was applicable.

Because something came out of the sky. Not just something, but many things. Like gigantic hunting wasps with triple tiers of spinning wings, they descended from that murky sky and started snatching up the beetles and flying away with them. They were evil-looking things with huge triple-lobed eyes and mandibles hooked like sickles, their bodies striped like yellow jackets. Only no yellow jackets ever got that big. Not in any sane world. For if the beetles were two or three feet, as Doug's raging mind told him, the wasps were four or five at least.

Doug, mouth hanging open, kept watching, knowing and knowing damn well he was watching no movie or TV show here. No stop-motion or computer-generated effects could even come close to this. They were pathetic, impotent in comparison.

He was glad there was no sound. If he had to listen to all that droning and buzzing and chirping and squealing . . . he would've lost his mind. As it was, his flesh was crawling.

The wasp-things filled the sky now in a swarm, darting down at the scurrying beetles. As they flew, those wasps looked very much like Apache assault helicopters he'd seen on CNN during the Gulf War. The way they carried themselves, those alien appendages folded under them like landing gear, the whirring wings above. One of the beetles made a mad dash for its hole and a wasp landed on it, grasping it with those crushing mandibles, a mouth filled with things like hideous daggers breaking through its exoskeleton, exposing whitish flesh. Then up into the sky and away.

"Jesus Christ," was all Doug could say. His mouth was dry and sleep was light years away now. He was alert, wired, thrumming with energy. His cigarette burned down and scorched his fingers. He barely felt it.

The landscape was littered with beetle carcasses, most in pieces, a few still moving. Something big and shadowy darted from the edge of the screen, grabbed half a beetle and disappeared. Whatever it was, it was bigger yet than the wasps.

It moved so fast, they never really got a good look at it.

"What the fuck was that?" Doug said.

Tommy just sat there, elbows on knees. "I don't know. I really don't know." He stood up. "You wanna see the weirdest thing, Doug?"

Doug didn't, but Tommy showed him anyway.

On his knees before the set, he pressed his hand flat against the screen . . . *and it sank right through.* It slipped through the screen like it was made of smoke. He put it through up to the elbow and Doug could see that it was real, all right. He could see that Tommy's arm was swallowed in that bizarre smoky light.

Tommy pulled his arm back. "Try it. Go ahead."

His throat filled with cinders, Doug did. But just his fingertips. It felt . . . abnormal. Like the air was actually crawling. His fingers were cold.

"Jesus H. Christ, Tommy," he managed. "What is this? What's happening here?"

Tommy said, "I wish to Christ I knew."

About two in the morning, Doug was pounding on the door again.

Tommy answered it right away. "I figured you'd be back."

Doug said he'd told his supervisor he was getting a bug, wasn't feeling well and clocked out at the mill. He had a bug, all right, but not the kind his super thought.

"I couldn't concentrate," Doug admitted, setting his lunch pail on the rug by the door. "I haven't been able to sleep. Joanie and the kids . . . they stayed away from me today when they got home. They think I'm coming down with something."

Tommy smiled thinly. "Same with Carol and Heather. Heather's having her birthday party tomorrow. She's turning seven, Doug. But you think I could be happy about it?"

They went downstairs.

The TV was on.

Same alien landscape, but no bugs.

"Seen anything?" Doug asked.

"A couple of those beetles before, but that's about it," he said. "It's been real quiet."

Doug sat down. His eyes were red-rimmed, his face looked slack and colorless. He slipped out of his soiled Carhartt jacket, pulled his cigarettes from the pocket of a worn flannel shirt. He smoked and stared at Tommy. They'd been friends since the tenth grade when Doug had beat-up some jock that had been picking on Tommy. They were real tight after that. The ultimate odd couple. Doug who hung out with the tough guys in the parking lot, smoked cigarettes and came to class drunk. Tommy who was in the Physics Club, took geometry because he liked it, chummed with the other nerds and nobodies.

"Tommy," he said. "Tommy, you know me. I don't believe in anything. I don't even believe in God or the Saints. I'm a working class guy. If I can't touch it, I don't accept it. But this . . . this . . ."

"I know," Tommy said, nodding his head. "You want some kind of answer, don't you?"

"Don't *you?*"

"All right. It's those tubes. I don't know where they came from or who made them, but they're like nothing this world has ever seen. I think they were designed to do exactly what they're doing—show us a glimpse of life on another world or in another dimension. There's no way to know. Not really. Unless somebody goes through the screen."

Doug sat up. "Are you fucking nuts? Did you hear what you just said? You are not going through that screen. I won't let you, you hear me?"

But Tommy just smiled, knowing it came from the right place. "Remember when they first got the space program going, Doug? We were just kids during the early Apollo missions. But before that, they didn't send people up there."

Doug was waiting for it, because he knew it was coming.

Tommy left the room and came back with a white rat in a cage. He had it fit with a little leather collar. It looked kind of cute like that.

"Is that your astronaut?"

"You got it."

Tommy took it out of its cage, hooked a dog chain to its collar and brought it over to the screen. "Hold onto the end of that," he said.

Doug picked up the coil of chain from the floor. Found the hand-loop at the end. There had to have been twelve feet of chain at the very least. Holding the loop, he suddenly felt pity for a rat for the first time in his life.

Carefully then, Tommy pushed the rat through the screen, sticking his arm in all the way to the shoulder. "I can't feel any bottom out there," he said. "I'm just going to try lowering it down. See what happens."

Gathering up some chain, he did just that until the chain slacked. "I think we found some ground here."

He stepped back and Doug kneeled a few feet from the TV. There was no pull on the chain for a moment, then it started to feed through the screen. The rat was exploring, apparently. But they still couldn't see it. There were limitations to their window into that world. Then suddenly it appeared, sniffing around one of those beetle holes. It must've caught a sniff of something it didn't like, because it scampered away off screen.

"That's enough," Doug said. "Let's bring it back."

Tommy reached through the screen and fished the rat back from . . . from wherever it had been. He held it, finally, in his hands. It seemed a little agitated and nervous, but no worse for wear.

"Proves one thing," Tommy said. "The air is breathable. Our friend here was out there for nearly five minutes. If it was bad, he would've asphyxiated by now."

Doug said, "Sure. But enough air for a rat might not be enough air for a man."

"That's possible." Tommy set the rat back in its cage, unhooked the chain. "Let's find out."

Before Doug could stop him, he thrust his head through the screen. He pulled it back after ten, fifteen seconds.

"Well?" Doug said.

"It's breathable . . . but its *funny*. Thick or something. Strange. Maybe the gravity's just different or the gases. I don't know. I bet if I went out there, I wouldn't be able to move very fast."

"You're not going out there."

"I'm just saying is all."

Doug was thinking. "You realize you might just have subjected that rat to some alien microbes? And maybe yourself, too. I saw a movie like that once."

But Tommy just laughed. "That's science fiction. You know what the chances are of some alien virus interacting with our biochemistry? It's got to be infinitesimal."

"Sure. And when you wipe out all the life on earth, you keep telling yourself that."

"Don't be silly."

But Doug didn't think it was silly.

In fact, he didn't think any of this was. Tommy was treating it like some new and wonderful toy. But Doug had a mad impulse to smash that set before something bad happened, because he felt certain it was only a matter of time. Because what he was really thinking was that if they could pass through the screen, maybe something out there could do the same.

♦ ♦ ♦

The next afternoon, Tommy said, "I went through."

Doug just stared at him, kept staring at him. "What do you mean you went through?"

Tommy removed his glasses, cleaned them on his shirt. "Just that. I hooked the chain to myself, tied it off, and went through the screen."

"You crazy sonofabitch . . . Tommy, what the hell were you thinking?"

"I had to, Doug. I just had to."

Doug stared at the screen, at that same alien panorama that had become positively mundane with repeated viewing. Somehow, he knew Tommy would do something stupid like that. He had a new toy. He had to play with it, push the boundaries.

"It was damn stupid," was all Doug could say about it.

Tommy agreed with him that, yes, maybe it was. "It was incredible, though, Doug! My God! I . . . I can't even put it into words."

But he tried.

The landscape was repetitious, but far in the distance, in that hazy soup, there was a mountain range that seemed to reach right into the clouds themselves. The lower elevations appeared green with some type of vegetation. The air was very heavy, almost turgid. You could feel it flowing around you with an oppressive, almost physical presence. It was breathable, but hot and oddly dry. Worse than just desert-dry. It sucked the moisture from you almost immediately, made your skin practically pucker as you watched it.

"I think the air is filled with salt," he said. "I could taste it on my lips. It stung my eyes. A man couldn't make it there long without some sort of suit . . . or armor like those bugs have."

Tommy speculated that there was probably no mammal life there, at least not as they understood it. He didn't see how any could possibly survive those harsh conditions. He saw no insects. Sound there carried funny. You could step across that crumbling, blasted crust and it seemed to take a moment or two before you could hear the sound of your footsteps. And when you did, it was a dull, muffled sound like you had towels wrapped around your feet.

"The gravity's much stronger there, Doug. It's hard moving. You can get around fine the first five, ten minutes, but it catches up with you. Pretty soon you're moving slow, you're out of breath."

"How long were you out there?"

"Twenty minutes."

"You just followed the dog chain back?"

He shook his head. "I wasn't about to trust some piece of shit like that. I went and bought fifty feet of good rope. The kind you tow cars with. I looped it around my waist and anchored it back here."

Tommy said that he eased himself through the screen gradually. He realized he was hanging in midair in the other world, about four feet off the ground. Then he fell through. He dragged some stones over to the opening to use as steps to climb back through so he wouldn't have to try jumping back in.

"What did . . . what did that opening look like?"

Tommy scratched his chin. It was unshaven. It didn't look as though he'd slept or eaten in days. "Funny. Sort of pinkish, glittery. Nothing like on those old movies where it's a whirlpool or something. If you didn't know what you were looking for, you'd miss it."

He talked on for some time and Doug listened, nodding, thinking, not liking any of it at all. "But you didn't see anything?"

"No . . . not really."

"What you mean not really?"

Tommy had trouble putting it into words. "I guess . . . I mean, I was pretty worked up, the adrenaline was kicking high and I was more than a little scared. But I had this feeling that I was being *watched*. Probably just my imagination . . . but I thought for sure that I could feel something, something out there."

Doug said, "I want you to give me your word you won't do it again."

"I won't. Once was enough," Tommy said. "But I have an idea. I was thinking of that robot they dumped out on Mars a few years ago, that thing that looked like a skateboard."

"You're gonna build a robot?"

"No, no. I was thinking of one of those remote-controlled vehicles. The expensive ones that have a lot of range. Hook a video camera to it, drive it around out there . . . maybe put a live feed to the camera. We could tape it all back here, safe and sound."

But Doug wasn't really listening.

He was watching that landscape, those shadows that seemed to seep from the holes and hollows like oil spills. Wondering what sins they hid.

Of course, Tommy hadn't been entirely truthful with Doug.

No, he hadn't seen anything out there. It had been oddly dead, empty, almost antiseptic. But he had felt something more than just a sense of being watched. It was a feeling of being studied, examined, sized-up. And not so much by some predator, but by something intelligent, something malefic and loathsome. It is what had driven him out of there.

That feeling that it was circling him.

Getting closer.

Thinking about it now, it made his belly go tight and gooseflesh break out on his arms. No, Doug didn't have to worry: There was no way in hell he would go back out there. Just no way. There was something out there, something hideous, something foreboding, something *evil*, for lack of a better word. And Tommy had had the unshakeable feeling that it had *wanted* him.

Still unable to sleep since the discovery of the tubes and what they could do, he brought out the rat and lowered it through the screen. Let it run around out there.

He knew what he was doing.

Not repeating the other experiment, but using the rat as bait.

Bait for whatever stalked those low places and high cliffs. For whatever it was, it was far worse than the wasp-things. The rat moved around out there after a time, sniffed about like before. It didn't seem overly concerned, just curious, if anything.

Then a weird, oblong shadow began to fill the bottom of the screen.

Tommy's heart began to pound.

The rat started running in circles, terrified of something.

Tommy started reeling it in, yanking at that length of chain and suddenly it went taut. He pulled, but it would not give. It was not just snagged out there . . . *something was pulling from the other side.*

Breathing hard and shaking, Tommy yanked at it with everything he had. He pulled so hard that when the chain started coming, it put him right on his ass.

And then something filled the screen.

Not just filled it, but was coming *through*.

Tommy screamed, the chain dropping from his fingers.

It looked like a huge green locust, but one larger than a man. Its body was plated and armored, set with irregular hollows and triangular protrusions that gave it an odd crystalline look. Its flesh was fissured and translucent like jade or quartz. The end of the chain was in its mouth, being worked by tiny barbed appendages and weird finger-like projections that were scarlet red and undulant. Tangles of black slime dripped off the chain, floated eerily from its mouth like fingers of ghostly teleplasm.

Tommy began crawling backward until the back of his head slammed into the table, and still he kept trying, looking maybe for a dark corner where he could crawl into and hide.

But he didn't dare take his eyes off that repellent, diabolic insect. There was something terribly alien about it that made his guts twist and try to slide up the back of his throat.

Something like that . . . Jesus, it just couldn't be.

It was a dun green in color, set off with brown blotches, multi-limbed and skittering, its skin like blown glass. Its head was huge and distorted, set with forward-curving horns. But the most unnerving thing were those eyes—all five of them. They were easily the size of baseballs . . . a vibrant, shifting emerald. Compound eyes made of literally hundreds of tiny lenses that pulsed and moved independently of each other. All dilating and flexing, trying to take in what they were seeing.

Tommy felt everything in him melt like wax. His bladder felt distended, ready to burst.

For the thing *saw* him.

He was forced to look and there was madness in those eyes. A barren, cruel darkness, a thrumming lunacy born in the blackest wastes of space. It seemed to not just want him physically, but mentally, psychically. To suck his brain dry like a grape.

Tommy tried to look away, but it would not let him.

It made a shrill, sharp buzzing sound and smelled like a truckload of rotting fish. It kept making that buzzing, along with a series of piping and trilling sounds. And the scary part was that those noises sounded almost like a language . . . like that horror was trying to communicate with him.

It was too big to fit through the screen. Its head was through, part of the upper thorax. Limbs like the threshers of a praying mantis were hooked around the edges of the screen.

No, it couldn't get through physically, but that didn't mean it wasn't in the room.

For those eyes were on Tommy and he was trembling and whimpering, but they held him, reached inside him, sorted through his thoughts in a hurting, nameless violation. He could not run, could not even look away. That thing, its eyes, had a sort of mesmeric, morphic effect and he could do nothing as it held him, looked at him, inside him, and through him.

Then suddenly, the side-to-side motion of those terrible jaws snapped the chain and it retreated, leaving only that noisome stench as a reminder of its grisly, inhuman dominance.

It withdrew into that world, but did not leave.

It sat up on its haunches like a begging dog, exposing the elaborate kaleidoscopic patterns of its belly. Its limbs ended it tiny, thorn-like appendages much like fingers. With them, it carefully examined the chain. But its eyes, they were not like the eyes of men. Whereas Tommy himself had not been able to see back into his world, this thing could.

He could feel those eyes watching him. Malignant, invidious, intelligent. But an intelligence not born of warmth and love and compassion, but of hatred and pestilence.

Shaking, feeling that gruesome mind reaching out for his own, Tommy shut off the TV.

Then he went down on his knees, trying to get that horrible feeling of contamination out of his brain.

♦ ♦ ♦

Heather's birthday party.

Fifteen kids running rampant. Eating cake and popping balloons and blowing horns and vaulting furniture and throwing pizza at each other. They were quite a crew. Little barbarians that even scared the hired clown, Jiggles.

"Christ," Tommy said. "This is a three-Excedrin day."

Doug watched the children racing around playing party games orchestrated by Tommy's wife Carol and his own wife Joanie. They both looked worn and weary, at the mercy of the little savages. Doug had given up yelling at Cassie to behave herself. His own daughter was no better than the rest.

"That creature you saw," he said, sipping from his beer. "What do you think it was?"

But Tommy just shook his head. "I don't know. It wasn't like those other bugs. It was an insect, but as far above the others as we are above mice."

"You better keep that TV off," Doug suggested.

Tommy laughed, but there was no humor in it. "I haven't had the balls to turn it on since. I don't think I ever will."

He pulled Doug off into the kitchen, away from the noise and bustle. "When we were kids, we were Catholic. We made communion, took catechism. The works. We were taught that, yes, there was a God and he was good. But we were also told there was something else."

"The Devil?"

"Yes. And I think that thing is the devil of that world. Shit, I know how that sounds . . . but it was evil, Doug. I felt that. I can still feel it in my head. I think I'll have nightmares the rest of my life. It was *in* me. Seeing what I saw, feeling what I felt. And amused by it, endlessly amused. Like my thoughts were something to be toyed with, perverted, dirtied." Tommy took down the rest of his beer in one swallow. "All I can tell you is that I knew instinctively that it was bad, it was depraved, utterly alien. And dangerous. If it managed to slip into this world . . . well, I hate to think what it could do here."

Doug just nodded. "Well, we've had our little excursion into the

Twilight Zone. When the party's done, let's pull those tubes out of that TV. Leave that sonofabitching bug where it belongs—a million billion light years from here."

"Agreed. In fact, let's smash 'em. Crush those tubes and throw 'em away."

Doug never thought he'd hear it, but he was glad for it. It was like one of those old science fiction movies where they spout on about things man wasn't meant to tamper with. Doug used to laugh at things like that. He didn't laugh anymore. He was a believer now. A true believer. A convert.

Joanie was still running the games, but Carol came over. "You guys seen Joey Block around? He was with us. Little SOB's probably hiding somewhere. I'll root him out."

She went upstairs and Tommy and Doug filtered out onto the patio, stood under the overhang as an April rain fell. They tried to talk about anything other than that TV set. Sports. Politics. Anything. Doug told dirty jokes and they barely laughed.

Then Tommy said, "Joey Block. He's a brat. I wish Heather wouldn't invite that little shit, but she always does. One time—" he seemed to grow gray, aged "—I caught him messing around with my TVs."

Something black settled into Doug. "Jesus Christ."

They both tossed their beers and went back inside, met Carol coming up from the basement.

"Well, he's not down there," she said. "What the hell did you have on down there?"

"There was nothing on," Tommy said weakly.

"Well, that TV you got at the sale, it was on," she said, sighing.

"I never turned it on."

She shrugged. "Maybe it was Joey. I shut it off, don't worry. Some disgusting show on."

Doug felt everything inside him began to flake, to disintegrate. "What . . . what was on?"

"Some science fiction thing. Looked like giant grasshoppers. A bunch of 'em. Looked like they were eating some little kid . . . pulling him apart. God, how can they show things like that?"

But then Tommy and Doug were down there and they saw. Crying and shouting, they smashed the TV, then the tubes. It was the best they could hope for. Then they went upstairs slowly, dragging themselves up like old men.

PRAGMATIC

C.J. HENDERSON

PROFESSOR PIERS KNIGHT WAS more than happy to hand his bags to the young man offering to carry them. His flight from New York City's JFK airport to its counterpart in Munich had been exhausting for him. Despite the inordinate amount of air travel the fates had forced upon him over the years, the professor had never been able to accustom himself to surrendering that much control over his life to outside forces. His distrust of airplanes was so intense he found it impossible to sleep on them, no matter how long the journey.

"So, Herr Knight, how was your flight?"

"Not very restful."

His phobia over water travel was not quite as intense. As he explained it, he preferred to drive places over any other form of transportation simply because when driving he was in command of the vehicle. And, while the professor was readily willing to admit he knew little to nothing about piloting boats, the back of his mind was somehow comfortable with the thought that if the captain of some ship he might be traveling upon were to suddenly become incapacitated, he might be able to pinch hit for them. But, if such were to happen to an airline pilot, he knew that if everyone was counting on him to come to the rescue, the craft would be going down.

"So," asked Knight as he settled into the back of the vehicle to which the young man escorted him, "do we have time to go to my hotel first before you take me to see Herr Strassen?"

"I'm afraid not, sir. Things have actually gotten a bit complicated." When the professor inquired as to what degree of complication had been reached, he was told, "Actually, sir, we're heading straight for the hospital."

"What? What are you talking about? Why would we do that—that doesn't make any sense," Forcing himself to stop chattering, Knight took a deep breath, then asked sensibly, "What's happened?"

"Frau Hoffman suffered a fall late last night," the chauffeur explained. Pulling out into traffic, he proceeded to weave in between the other cars on the road. Notching his speed higher by the second, he added, "She's been stabilized, but it's forced everyone to step up the timetable. She's going to have to deliver the baby as soon as possible." The man paused for a moment, then added;

"Really, they're just waiting for you."

The professor said nothing to his driver, as his brain began pelting him with non-stop worries. The news he had just been delivered was in no way anything he had been prepared to receive.

"What in Hell do I do now?" he wondered, rivulets of panic searching for cracks in the granite of his calm exterior, splashing forward to erode his confidence. His eyes unblinking, staring off at the passing scenery, catching none of it, his mind hissed at him;

"This means no prep time, no way to study the situation, to prepare the room . . . there's no time to interview the mother—does she know what she's getting into? There's no time to talk to the doctors . . . do they understand what's being attempted? Will they listen to me, listen to me when it *really* matters? Do they fully, actually understand what we're attempting? Do they believe—*do* they?

"*Can* they?"

Professor Piers Knight suddenly began to cough violently, as if somehow having a physical reaction to his thoughts. So unexpected was his brief seizure, his driver called back to him.

"Herr Professor, are you all right?"

"Well, now that, my dear young man," answered Knight in a voice cracking with strain, "will remain to be seen."

"Piers, ach du lieber, it's good to see you again."

"Herr Strassen, do we still have time?" Knight took the extended hand of the beefy German, barely noticing exactly how sweaty its palm was, or the slight tremble running through it and the rest of the large man.

"You Americans, always right to das point." Dr. Otto Strassen was large in the academic manner, a swelled balloon of a man, the type whose back and front were so similar when seen in silhouette as to be indistinguishable from one another if not for the fact of his massive nose.

"That doesn't answer the question, though, does it?" Knight, half a foot taller than Strassen, looked practically emaciated next to the beef-ball of a man.

"No, you are correct, as always." Taking the American by the arm, Strassen lead his fellow academic to a quiet corner of the maternity ward. Once out of earshot of anyone else, the rotund doctor whispered;

"Frau Hoffman has been stabilized for the moment, but both she und die baby are in danger if die baby isn't delivered soon."

"What's the problem?"

"The fall has wrapped the umbilical cord around die baby's neck as well as shifting it into some other sort of bad position. Along with die mother's injuries, they are both at risk if die baby is not delivered quickly."

Knight found himself sweating despite the plentiful air conditioning. He was not prepared, had not readied his equipment. It was why he had flown to Germany when he did, giving himself what all had assumed would be a minimum of two weeks to make certain everything would go flawlessly.

"Damn all the fools who plague me so," he thought bitterly. "The things I do in the name of the Brooklyn Museum."

With Strassen waiting for his reply, the professor allowed himself a moment's reflection. It had been over four months previous when the entire affair began, when he had received the call from his old colleague, asking him if he had ever heard of the resonant frequency. When Knight had confessed he had not, Strassen had explained;

"It is das perfect pitch of der human voice, das note, which when struck, can shatter glass. You are familiar, yes?" When Knight assured Strassen he was, the rotund man had continued, asking him how many people he thought were capable of achieving such a sound. When the professor guessed that it must be relatively few, he had received a surprising answer.

"Nein. Believe it or not, many people are born with such capability. But, most of them do not live very long."

"Are you saying," Knight had asked, "that something in being born with the ability causes early fatality?"

"Ya, but not any something of which most people would be capable of imagining." Strassen then paused dramatically enough for the professor to hear the deep intake of breath being swallowed on the other end of the line. After a few more dramatic seconds of silence, the doctor said;

"You are one of der only men I would even dare mention this to. Most in our field are not so, ah . . . 'liberal of mind,' shall we say, as you and I."

"Otto," asked Knight, genuinely intrigued, "just what is this all about?"

"The resonant frequency, it does not just shatter glass. It is also mankind's perfect weapon against das supernatural. That one particular pitch, when focused correctly, can repulse, and even destroy . . . demons."

The professor, of course, had been stunned by the information. Piers Knight did not instantly judge his colleague mad, however. Strassen had been correct; the professor was one of the few academics in the world he could trust to hear him out after making such a statement. And the doctor knew why. Like himself, Knight was a student of the occult, a studier of the unbelievable, of those things beyond. Together, ten years earlier the two had ridded Strassen's beloved Munich Opera House of a particularly obnoxious poltergeist infestation which, if left unchecked, would have guaranteed the ruination of the fall season that year, as well as threatening the closure of the magnificent music palace altogether.

To Strassen, such was completely unacceptable. It was a horror beyond thought, and thus he had risked his career to prevent its occurrence. Now, another such situation had arisen, and he had once more turned to the only other academic whom, once he had told him his tale, would assist him rather than seek his ruin. He had not, of course, asked for Knight's cooperation in the matter on the blind chance the professor would possibly be willing to help him. Strassen might be blindly loyal to the Opera House whose board he had sat upon for nine years, but he was by no means a foolish man. When he had first called Knight to enlist his assistance, it was not only because of his beliefs, but also because of his position.

"Piers, mein old friend," he had begun when first he had called, "still sitting atop der most under-used collection of artifacts the world has ever seen?"

Professor Knight was one of the directors of the prestigious Brooklyn Museum. Originally the site had been planned to be massive, one of the greatest repositories of art and culture, as Strassen had said, the world had ever seen. But, while its collection was gathered, one which could easily fill to overflowing the designed series of galleries, its actual construction was cut short. In the end, the museum ended up being only a fourth of the size initially planned, with its massive, and ever growing, collection forced into storage in its basement as well as in buildings all around it.

The professor took the budget cuts, political manipulations and societal apathy which had reduced the museum so in size as a personal affront. Thus Strassen had begun their conversation by appealing to that chink in Knight's otherwise fairly solid armor. Realizing that he was being maneuvered, but still curious as to the particular destination to which he was being guided, the professor had insisted Strassen get to the point. Comfortable with being blunt, the doctor had said;

"I want you to go through your overcrowded storage bins and find something, something I want you to bring to Germany. In other words, old friend . . . I have a deal I want to propose."

The bargain in question turned out to be a thing so fantastical that even Piers Knight had to raise an eyebrow. After informing the professor about the resonant frequency, as well as those horrors which seek to destroy any whom might grow to be able to utilize it against them, Strassen had then sent Knight to his keyboard. Checking through the museum's data records, it only took a matter of a few moments to find what his colleague was after.

"How did you know it was here?" The professor had asked the question in a tone of complete and quiet amazement. He had always been certain he knew more about the Brooklyn Museum, its exhibits and stores and its hundred thousand treasures not seen in decades, than anyone. He would have been surprised if one of his fellow directors had known of an artifact he did not. To have such come from an outsider struck him as defying logic.

"Piers, you are ever such der controller. You have heard of die Shield of Tol'kaimi previously, ya?"

"Of course I have," answered Knight, still somewhat amazed. "Who in our business hasn't?"

"Exactly," answered Strassen. "You are merely upset by der fact I knew it was hidden away und forgotten within your treasure trove und you did not. Relax your grip a bit. I have been hunting for the past three months, combing old records, calling in favors—finding the shield has practically become my life's work recently . . ."

"Why?" The professor thought he might know where the heavyset doctor was going, but preferred to hear it spelled out. Strassen was more than willing to oblige him. The Shield of Tol'kaimi had been created by the Incas, their greatest shamans called together to forge a weapon to help them hold off the hordes of demonkind. Those ancients had knowledge of the resonant frequency, and had determined to protect those who would be born to survive and then in turn protect their people. Much was sacrificed to bring the desired safeguard into being, but the shield proved worth the effort.

Indeed, so powerful were its protections, its reliability against those supernatural predators that attempted to make prey of the Incas for the next several hundred years were all repulsed without effort. Sadly, however, it was that very effectiveness which lead to the great race's downfall.

When the Spanish had arrived, they were, as most schoolchildren have been taught for centuries, misbelieved to be magical beings. What was not taught said youngsters over the centuries was the additional information that when the Conquistadors began raping and slaughtering their way across the Central Americas, the Incas had unleashed those of their race whom the shield had protected on the day of their birth. Songs, no matter how perfectly pitched, however, had little effect on the invaders. The Incas fled, their faith in Tol'kaimi's Shield shattered beyond repair.

"You ask why?'" Strassen had sounded monumentally disappointed. "I would have thought it an easy enough intellectual exercise for one such as you, my friend. You know my position with the Munich Opera House, ya?" When Knight admitted as much, the doctor had continued, saying;

"The simple truth is, demons are not der only beings in this universe that can locate those about to be born with the ability to hit the frequency."

And then, finally, Strassen had revealed to the professor a most unusual proposal. He had found a family of music lovers who were expecting the birth of their second child five months hence. That baby, the doctor's people were certain, would be born with the resonant ability. Greatly desiring to protect the child, desperately wanting to be the board member who secured a pitch perfect soprano for the opera company, the doctor had searched relentlessly until he had found the whereabouts of the Shield of Tol'kaimi. Overjoyed to learn it was in the Brooklyn Museum, under the control of one of the few men in all the world he could approach with such a scheme, he had made his proposal.

"I know this is greatly in the order of duty now for der future,'" Strassen had admitted, "but I plan on being a board member of the Munich Opera House for a long time."

He wished for Knight to bring the shield to Germany at the proper time, and to assist him in protecting the baby in question during its birth. At first the professor had been a bit stunned at the scheme suggested to him, but Strassen knew how to appeal to his former "ghostbusting partner," and after not much discussion at all Knight had agreed.

Digging the shield out of storage proved to be not much of a problem, either. A carved granite circle some six inches in diameter, the piece weighed roughly eight pounds. Not a terribly great burden, thought the professor at the time, but the legends made note of the shield needing to be raised to the heavens while being used.

"Eight pounds can get more than a trifle heavy after a while," he told himself as he carefully lowered the piece into his valise. Then, hefting the black leather shoulder bag into place, he concentrated on the additional pull on his shoulder, calculating what it would be like to hold Tol'kaimi's defense above his head for any extended period of time.

"And just what will it be," he wondered. "Five minutes? An hour? A day and a half?"

Knight had stared forward into a mirror resting against a back wall of the storage area at that point. He recognized the piece after a moment—it had come from the *petits appartements* of Marie Antoinette at Versailles. The decorator had been her architect, Richard Mique. The paneling surrounding the still bright glass had been carved and gilded by the Rousseau brothers. Beautiful in its simplicity, it deserved to be seen by the world, and yet due to the pedestrian minds of those who ran the world, the money for such things went elsewhere.

Hypodermic needles were purchased to give away to drug addicts, condoms needed to be bought to distribute throughout the city's high schools. The state needed to pay women to have children, as long as they kept those children's fathers out of the picture. It also needed to pay for the sandblasting of buildings to remove the names of monsters from the past such as Washington, Franklin, Jefferson—others.

Knight stared at the reflection of his bag in the mirror, thinking on what it contained, on what he meant to do with it. For a moment he had been feeling guilty over his actions. He was, after all, considering removing a registered antiquity from the museum without permission, preparing to take it into what might be a hazardous environment. Did he have such a right?

As the question floated naggingly within his mind, his gaze suddenly moved outward from his reflection to the body of the mirror itself. As he focused on the compelling simplicity of the frame's uniquely delicate work, he found a streak of anger sizzling within him.

"No," he told himself finally, "I don't have any such right. But then again, what about the rights of the Rousseau brothers, to be remembered down through the ages, to have their artistry admired?" Hefting his bag once more, he had then turned and headed for the exit, muttering;

"Somebody should get some use out of the things stored away here. I'll hold the damn thing over my head if it takes a month to deliver the damn baby."

And, so saying, the professor had relocked the storage area and headed for home. He had nearly half a year to study the history of the Shield of Tol'kaimi, to learn its proper use, and to prepare himself for holding it aloft for who knew how long.

That had been months earlier. Now, in the present, standing in the hallway of the hospital whispering with Strassen, suddenly Knight had been presented with an entire new set of problems. He had come to Germany two weeks early to rehearse with his support team, to meet with the doctors who would be performing the delivery. Yes, his colleague would have made certain the medical professionals present would be sympathetic to their cause, but to go in cold, with no sounding out of each other, learning the necessary procedures, where to stand, what to expect—he, after all, knew as little about delivering babies as these others did the theory behind rejecting demonic presences from the tangible world. What a recipe for disaster if—

"Dr. Strassen, Professor," it was Knight's chauffeur from earlier. "The doctors are calling for you. They say they have to deliver the baby now!"

"Ready, Piers?"

"Oh, I'm ready all right," agreed the professor sourly. "Just don't ask me exactly what it is I'm ready for."

In less than ten minutes Knight was inside the delivery room, scrubbed sterile and dressed in a cotton gown. The Shield of Tol'kaimi had been sterilized as well, making it much too hot for the professor to handle for the moment. While waiting for the eight pounds of stone to cool, the professor called for the chauffeur to bring him his bag. Having the younger man open it so that he might remain sterile, Knight directed him to remove a somewhat bizarrely shaped mechanical item, calling out at the same time;

"Where can this be plugged in?" When both Strassen and the attending physician asked what the device was, Knight replied;

"It's basically nothing more than an illuminator, but one that goes through all the various spectrums at a high rate of speed. For the most part its effects will be invisible to our eyes, but if there are things here lurking in between those spectrums, they will be revealed to us." Turning more to his colleague, he added;

"Handy little gizmo, invented by Nikola Tesla. Others since his time outfitted it to run on AC or DC, as long as the proper adaptor is used."

"Enough!"

The single word came from the doctor in charge. Turning away from the academics, no longer caring what purpose they hoped to suit twenty years in the future, he began snapping orders to his nurses. The doctor was concerned only with the lives of his patients, and knew there was no more time to spare concerning what had to be done in the then and now. Frau Hoffman and her baby were both in mortal danger. Far more time had been spent waiting for Knight's arrival than he would have preferred. Now that the professor was there, his contraptions and devices ready, the doctor's duty was clear.

As the physician turned to those on the table, consulting with the nurses in attendance, the chauffeur found an out-of-the-way spot for Tesla's light. Setting it atop a cabinet in the corner furthest from the operating theater, he uncoiled its power cord. Making certain he could plug it in without straining the cord, the young man did not hesitate to do so and, with that action, the doorway to Hell was opened.

"Mein Gott in Heimel!"

Even in the first few seconds of light cast from Tesla's lamp, shapes began to appear all about the room. Humanoid in the most casual sense of the word, they were strange and twisted forms, clawed and winged, gangly, leathery and possessed of nothing to indicate they were anything but monstrous in all manners and intentions.

"Keep the light safe," Knight snapped at the chauffeur. The younger man nodded, closing his eyes at the terrors all about him, holding onto the light as tightly as he could. Not having the luxury of closing their eyes, however, both the nurses in attendance recoiled in horror, only to turn around and find that more of the hideous things were behind them. Frau Hoffman's husband, present to act as her coach, screamed along with the women. The doctor, an older man made of tightly wound fibers, barked orders to his nurses as well as Herr Hoffman in German, cursing the lot of them for their weakness, reminding them of the job they were there to perform.

At the same moment, Knight grabbed up a towel and hoisted the still burning hot Shield of Tol'kaimi aloft, holding it above his head. Turning slowly, he presented the face of the Incan artifact to each demon in turn, forcing them if not backward, to at least halt their advancement. As the medical team began their work with the expectant mother on their table, the professor attempted to circle them, using the stone disc to turn back those things straining to break through the protective circle.

Of course, the demonic shapes those assembled could see were not physically present. They could not simply grab up a chair and bash in the baby's skull. Restrained by whatever barrier it was which had held them at arm's distance from the human race over the millennia, the demons had been forced to find other ways to wreck havoc across the earthly plane of existence. As Knight continued to circle the delivery table, several of the creatures began their traditional assault.

Wretched flesh bag, one of the terrors sneered at the professor, *take your foul stone and begone, or pain and suffering will follow you all your days!*

"Pain and suffering have followed me longer than you can imagine, Helldweller. You'll have to do better than that."

Despite the air conditioning, the presence of so many demonic forms within the room's ether had begun to drive the temperature upward. In less than a minute the mercury had climbed ten degrees, with no evidence it would stop any time soon. Sweat pouring down his face, Knight could feel the heat of the shield oozing its way through the towel. His fingers were warming quickly—burning—his palms growing moist.

This thing shall not be born, came the snarling voice within the professor's head once more, *shall *not* be born/*notnotnot* be born/*not* be *not* be *not* be *not* be *born!**

Knight blinked his eyes hard, staring from one demon to another, trying to ascertain which one was actually barking within his mind. Continuing to circle the table, trying not to step in too close where he might interfere with the operation in progress, trying also not to give the trio too much room where he might leave them open for demonic invasion, his eyes kept darting, straining against the odd flicker of Tesla light, searching out the individual thing he needed to silence.

"Which one are you," he asked the voice within his mind. Then, inspiration striking, he directed more questions at the chattering annoyance. "And by that, what I mean is, which of you is the one so puny, so useless, so utterly worthless that you were given the task of whispering in my ear? A task, I imagine, given you as a means to keep your incompetent self out of the others' way."

As Knight continued firing off his own mental barrage at his unknown adversary, he wondered how the others were holding up. The professor was certain both the doctor and his nurses were being urged on toward mayhem in the same manner as himself. It was the way demons had been destroying those capable of reaching the resonant frequency for ages—to slither inside the mind of the attending midwife, or of a mother wondering if she was capable of all that was required of her, a father uncertain if he could support another mouth—searching for the doubting, the weak-willed, the confused, whomever they might find shallow and frightened enough to be manipulated into doing their bidding.

Death to the meat/death to the meat/deathdeathdeath–

In the maternity ward in Munich, however, the demons were at a disadvantage in that they could not maneuver anyone into thinking the murderous thoughts crossing their minds were their own. Tesla's light had revealed the truth. As long as Tol'kaimi's Shield kept the foul creatures from actually making contact with any of the medical personnel's auras they could not be fooled into believing the voices they were hearing were their own thoughts. Despite its weight, Knight managed to keep the eight pound disc above his head. But, he could feel his strength fading.

Death to the meat/death to the meat/deathdeathdeath–

The professor had just gotten done with a long flight—a journey during which he was unable to sleep. The heavy stone was putting a strain on his fingers, his wrists, shoulders and spine—even his knees. Sweat was gathering across his body. The dribbling of it, soaking into his clothing, running down his arms, inching over his forehead into his eyes, collecting at the base of his nose, across his upper lip, moving down his chest, trickling into his groin–

"How can it be so hot in here," he wondered, even as the demon choruses continued to echo within his mind–

*not be born/*notnotnot* be born/*notnotnot* be *not* be *not* be *born!**

"How the hell long is this going to take?" Not looking at the professor, the doctor shouted back at him.

"I'm delivering a baby. These things are done when they're done—now shut up and stop trying to make it take longer!"

Death to the meat/death to the meat/deathdeathdeath–

At first, no one noticed the chauffeur leaving his post. The demons made no attempt to interfere with the now unguarded light. Strassen, busy reading from the Von Juntz text on expulsion, was concentrating on reinforcing his colleague's magical barrier. Everyone else's attention was rightly focused on the mother to be. Thus, as the young man crossed the room, he was able to pick up a scalpel, but as he drew within two yards of the table Knight stopped chanting long enough to ask;

"Why have you left your post?"

*not be/*notnotnot* be born/*notnotnot* be *not* be *notnotnot* be *born!**

One look into the chauffeur's eyes told the professor all he needed to know. Racing around the table, desperate to keep the stone shield aloft, Knight tripped over one of the nurses' legs, stumbling as he shouted;

"Strassen—your man!"

The chauffeur raised the scalpel, chuckling as he moved forward on those surrounding the mother, his head hanging awkwardly to one side. Catching a glimpse of his approach, the second nurse let out a cry. Her shriek distracted the thing possessing the young man, the terror of it delighting the creature. It sucked the juicy fragrance from the air, then turned back to the table, snarling;

"Death to the meat!"

Strassen hurled his heavy, leather-bound copy of Von Juntz at the chauffeur, catching him in between his shoulder blades. As the younger man went down, the heavyset academic threw himself atop him, crushing him to the floor. Knight managed to untangle himself from the nurse and reach the pair at that point. He attempted to kick the scalpel from the chauffeur's hand, but off balanced as he was still holding the shield over his head, he missed, allowing the younger man to drive the blade into Strassen's thigh.

Death to the meat/deathdeathdeath–

As Strassen shrieked, rolling off the possessed chauffeur, Knight moved in, kicking at the man's head.

Death to the meat/deathdeathdeath–

The chauffeur dodged the blow, swinging wildly, managing to slash open the professor's leg below the knee.

Deathdeathdeath–

Feeling blood exploding free, Knight knew some vital artery had been opened. Knowing he had but seconds, even as the younger man began to rise, the professor used the only weapon he had–

Deathdeathdeath–

And swung the Shield of Tol'kaimi full force, catching the possessed chauffeur in the chest. The stunning blow sent the off-balance man stumbling across the room and into a gurney covered with medical equipment. Even as he turned back toward the operating theater, however, Knight knew the damage had been done.

Deathdeathdeathdeathdeath!

In the eerie illumination of Tesla's lamp, he could see the demons pouring forward, thrusting their insubstantial tongues into the ears of the doctor, the nurses, the Hoffmans—could hear their lies and threats and vile, luring insinuations.

Deathdeathdeathdeath!

Turning back toward the table, Knight tried desperately to return to his post. Staggering, he limped along, blood sluicing down his leg, drenching the floor–

Deathdeathdeath!

Losing his grip on the shield because of the cumbersome towel, he pulled it away, clenching the still burning stone circle in his bare hands. Doing his best to ignore the burning pain, he shoved the shield skyward, ordering–

"Begone, Hellspawn!"

But he was too late. Although the doctor had delivered the child, safely removed it from its mother, the damage had been done. The demons were everywhere, spreading their poisonous suggestions. Already the nurses' eyes were glazing over, taking on the same disturbingly blank look the chauffeur's had held. Herr Hoffman seemed to be swaying as well.

Deathdeath!

Finding Tol'kaimi's defense no longer effective, Knight struggled, his own mind filling with the hissing of demonic tongues. Their voices were so insistent, their assurances so soothing, the professor found himself teetering for a moment. Then, summoning what strength he had remaining, he shouted;

"For God's sake, Doctor–"

Death!

"Slap the baby!"

Somehow hearing Knight's voice over the cacophony within his head, the doctor lifted the child aloft, then forced himself to smack its backside soundly. The action, as it has for tens of thousands of years, forced air into the small girl's lungs, air she exhaled as babies have since time immemorial, in a startling acceptance of individual life.

And, with that scream, the worlds in between light and darkness exploded, the air fried, and those scores of demons unable to escape the child's first sound were consumed like dry leaves in a fire.

♦ ♦ ♦

"So, my old friend, was that what you had in mind?"

"Mein Gott," Strassen replied to Knight, "it most certainly was not. Can't you Americans do anything without bringing down the ceiling?"

The two academics sat quietly in an observation room, waiting to be discharged from the hospital. Both had received treatment for their injuries, but their blood loss had been such that neither was going to be allowed to leave until their doctor was satisfied with their recovery. The two laughed for a moment over how out of all those involved in that afternoons excitement, only they had suffered any injury beyond the momentary. Even Frau Hoffman had been able to visit them, albeit in a wheelchair, to thank them for all they had done. Once they were certain they would not be interrupted further, Strassen said quietly;

"It was a good thing you did today."

"It was a damn foolhardy and dangerous thing I did today," Knight responded. "And before we forget, you know the reason I did it, so . . ."

"Ya, ya," answered the rotund academic. Reaching to the floor for the brown leather bag at his side, Strassen hoisted the valise and then handed it to his colleague. Opening the bag, Knight reached inside and then pulled out its contents. The core of what he held in his hand was a nautilus shell, one fashioned into what seemed a semblance of a goblet. A reptilian leg crafted from a metal which reflected like silver, but took none of its tarnish, served as the vessel's stem, a broad, three-toed foot forming its stand along with a balancing spur. The metal work continued up and over the sides of the nautilus, dipping down and into its mouth and surrounding the circumference of its lip with a ring of wildly pointed, needle-like fangs.

"Und there you have it," said Strassen. "I get my singing star, one to train to perfection from birth, und you get that silly looking thing which has gathered dust in the basement of der opera house for no one knows how long."

Knight turned the prize over in his hands, studying it from all angles.

Staring into the mouth of it, not knowing what exactly he might find there, the professor asked about the necessary papers for removing the artifact from the country. Strassen assured him everything he needed was within a side pocket of the piece's carrying case. As Knight repacked the bizarre goblet, his colleague said;

"Und so you have your prize for your museum; I have mine for my opera house. But tomorrow, another such baby will be born somewhere, und who will be there to save it?"

"There will be more than a single baby in danger tomorrow," answered Knight, refusing to follow Strassen down the road he was looking to travel. "There have been people of all ages in danger every day since there were people, and there always will be. Some will perish and some will survive."

"You," answered the rotund academic, "are a very pragmatic fellow, Piers Knight."

"'The Arab who builds himself a hut of the marble fragments of a temple in Palmyra,'" answered the professor, obviously quoting, "'is more philosophical than all the curators of the museums in London, Munich or Paris.'"

"Jacques Anatole Francois Thibault," replied Strassen, "The Crime of Sylvestre Bonnard. Very well, your point is taken. We do what we can in this life . . ."

"Because we can do no more," responded Knight, finishing his old friend's thought. The two chatted while they waited for their doctor to return and officially release them. After a bit of inconsequential chatter, Strassen said, almost sheepishly;

"You know, that thing I just gave you . . . I would hate to let you go without telling you, der rumors are that . . . well, that it is haunted. Cursed. Some such thing. You don't feel cheated, do you?"

"Cheated?" Knight laughed, smiling as he added, "Are you kidding? When the board hears it's supposedly haunted, they'll be even happier. Nothing packs in Americans like a chance to hobnob with evil—at a safe distance, of course."

"Ach, that explains your choices in presidents."

Before Knight could respond, the doctor who had treated the two academics' injuries returned, announcing that they were discharged. Gathering up their various bags, the pair thanked their physician, then headed for the exit, both content with what they felt had been a good day's work.

AND THINGS UNDER THE EARTH

JOHN PELAN & PAUL MELNICZEK

I met the night in unfamiliar lands . . .
—Clark Ashton Smith

THE GUY THAT WAS sitting at the bar of the *Smoking Leg* looked like he was well on his way to getting a good drunk on. Boilermakers of Wild Turkey and Arrogant Bastard aren't really conducive to anything other than putting one out on the floor as effectively as a right-cross from a heavyweight boxer. I usually try to avoid sitting next to people that are so intent on practicing self-anesthesia, but the bar was a bit crowded and I wanted a good view of the ballgame, so I climbed on to the vacant barstool next to the boilermaker drinker.

It was late into happy hour and my friend Ian was getting off pretty soon, so I wanted to sit and chat for a bit, but it wasn't as though I had much of a choice other than walking around the block a few times, which with the April rain making the air damp and muggy lacked any sort of appeal.

Just as I feared, the solitary drinker took immediate notice of me and pulled a long one off his pint. I looked up as a brief news update flashed across the corner TV screen with a report about a unit of soldiers returning temporarily from the chaos in Iraq.

The man nodded to himself. "Those poor guys are going back sooner or later, but I'm out for good." He glanced at me pointedly as though his comment demanded a response of some kind.

"Thanks for all you guys have done over there." I motioned to my friend Ian to bring another round—seemed the least I could do.

"It's a terrible place over there, you know. We should never have poked around in there. Yeah, Saddam had to go, but we should have just carpet-bombed the place into a parking lot. Sounds harsh? You think that would make for a lot of civilian causalities; truth is, those poor people are screwed anyway from what I've seen. Hell. Maybe we all are . . . I've seen some *real* shit, lemme' tell ya."

It looked like there was no way I could politely avoid hearing a war story or two, and while current events aren't generally the sort of things I write articles about, I didn't feel like going home yet, and there certainly seemed no respectful way to excuse myself.

"Pretty rough, I imagine?"

He introduced himself then. Rick Dehan; formerly PFC Dehan, National Guard MP. We shook hands and he stared at his drink for a minute, as if searching for something in its depths, then he went on . . .

"Rough doesn't begin to cover it. All I did was report on what I saw and they discharged me. Just like that. I've been back over a year and I still can't get over it. Maybe I never will . . . Here, you ever see something like this before?"

Dehan reached into his pocket, pulling out a small stone and handing it to me. I examined it as closely as I could in the dim light; it was a carved piece of sandstone. I was struck by its ugliness—it looked like the head of a gargoyle or demon. Very crudely done, the features were just discernible enough for me to see that by no stretch of the imagination could this face possibly be anything human. Exactly *what* it was supposed to be was hard to say—there was a sense of both the canine and primate to it. Weird, to say the least. It gave me a sense of something savage, created by people living beneath the cloak of a dark and primitive time period, when night was far more than just a changing of shades. The thing appeared to be hairless, with protruding fangs and an elongated jaw like that of a baboon. It was obviously old, very old. A hole had been bored through the carving, so I suspected that it may have been intended as a talisman or fetish of some kind. Not the sort of thing likely to turn up in a Baghdad curio shop. I had to admit, the thing held my interest, and I found myself eager to learn more.

I nodded toward Ian, who was just swapping out his till. "My friend there is more up on antiques than I am; you want him to have a look at it?"

Just then I noticed that the four men seated at one of the tables had apparently witnessed enough of the Mariners futile attempts to play baseball and had all pushed back their chairs, leaving in disgust. I motioned toward the vacated table and Ian came over to join us. I performed the perfunctory introductions and suggested that Rick show Ian the carving.

Ian frowned. "It's very old, that much is certain. Middle-Eastern?"

Dehan nodded. "I picked it up when I was when in Iraq. I don't really like the thing, but it's probably worth a lot of money. I don't know what the hell to do with it . . ."

Considering the amount of alcohol that Dehan had consumed, he was surprisingly lucid, and while there may have been a slight slur to his words, I'd be hard-pressed to say that he was visibly drunk. I wanted to urge him to tell us where he'd come by the sculpture, but he seemed intent on taking take his time about it.

"Either of you ever seen combat?" We both shook our heads in the negative. "Well, I didn't really think I would either when I joined the Guard. Thought I'd spend most of my time being extra security for bigwigs and maybe some disaster relief when we have our annual flooding . . . Anyway, that's not how it worked out. My unit saw quite a bit of action in Iraq. I'm guessing you've never been there?" Again we shook our heads.

"It's a strange place; they say it's where civilization started. I dunno' if either of you guys have been to a place like that, but I never had before. Me, I'm from right here in Tacoma. The oldest building you'll see is maybe a hundred years old. Over there, there's buildings that have been standing for over a *thousand* years. Think about it . . . Pretty freaky, but there's even older stuff there—things like this little carving. Weird, ancient trinkets. Lost, stolen, hidden in basements, or buried beneath the desert, waiting to be found."

His voice became low and he moved his hands away from the carving, letting it balance on the table. "And just maybe, some of this stuff shouldn't never *be* found."

I swallowed uneasily, caught up in his tale like a child sitting around a bonfire listening to ghost stories told by an adult. It was interesting, and the creepy sculpture lent itself to the atmosphere, constantly stealing my focus.

He continued. "Anyway, I brought this thing back just to remind myself that I saw what I saw and *nothing's* gonna' change that. Sure, I had a whole group of so-called mental-health experts say that I was hallucinating, but I know what I saw, and this thing here is the proof . . ."

I glanced over at Ian. This was definitely going to be a long night . . .

"So, you found something unusual? Something that no one else believed you saw?"

Dehan nodded to Ian and signaled for a round of drinks. I was thankful that I was drinking a relatively innocuous domestic beer and not something stronger—any attempt to keep up with Dehan's alcohol consumption would seem a recipe for disaster. I wondered briefly if he'd complete his story before passing out . . .

"Yeah, I *saw* something, hell, I *touched* something . . . My team was assigned to look for survivors or weapons caches in Najaf up in one of the districts that had been hit hard when we arrived. We were in our strict four-man patrols; for the most part it was a matter of shepherding survivors to safety. The possibility of snipers was still very real, but there weren't too many incidents. That part of the city was pretty much deserted except for the wounded and the dead.

Our instructions were to go house to house, performing as thorough a search as we could. When you figure that most of the houses were abandoned, I gotta' admit that keeping an eye out for bits of jewelry was about as important to us as looking for survivors or weapons. The first few places we went into were deserted, just as though the people living there had gotten up and left mid-meal, taking nothing with them. Pretty creepy, but you get used to it in a hurry. The weather can be terrible. Dust storms are common, and the wind had picked up considerably. Riley and Marks were in front, and these two were decent guys, but had a bad habit of pushing ahead a bit too quick at times. I stopped to adjust my strap, and thought they noticed. After a few seconds my partner, Mark Gilford, yelled to the others, who were now out of sight, as a huge cloud of sand swirled along the streets, making it impossible to see far ahead. We must have checked over twenty homes already, finding no people, no weapons, and not even anything worth taking as a souvenir. The home to our left was the likely next stop, and both Gilford and I thought we heard something inside. He swore out loud about the others moving ahead, and pointed to the home. The noise wasn't anything distinct, more a feeling that there was someone moving around in the place. We figured they had entered just in front of us, thinking we were right behind them. It wouldn't have been the first time they screwed up. We could have had their asses in a sling more than once . . . I nodded over to Mark and he returned the gesture, indicating we should enter at the same time. Gilford was a tough SOB from a small town in Eastern Washington, and I don't think he would have been scared to march into Baghdad by himself and pull Saddam's mustache.

We gently pushed the door open and entered the house. Pretty much like all the places we'd already been in. Standard furnishings and such, but with no sign of the other two men, or anyone else for that matter . . . Then we heard it again. Nothing you could really define, just a faint rustling as of someone moving around. The house was no different on the interior than any of the others we'd found; two levels with a basement. The strange noise seemed to come from the basement, so we turned on our flashlights and headed down the stairs, hoping to find our companions. But they never before had gotten this far ahead of us. I was pretty worried.

We descended quickly, staying alert. And we discovered that the place wasn't empty after all . . . The family was still there—or what was left of them, anyway.

Husband, wife, two small children. That they were dead was more than obvious; you don't lose limbs and such quantities of blood and survive. The bodies were in such a state that we didn't need to be overly cautious approaching them. Dogs must have been in the house well before we arrived. I shone the beam of my flashlight around the room in case the scavengers were still lurking about. The main room of the basement seemed to have been prepared as a sort of bomb shelter. Shelves of foodstuffs, water, and even medicines lined the walls. Nothing odd about that, as most of the city had been braced for an attack for over a year.

What *was* odd was the cistern or well off to one corner. Scattered about it were fragments of wood, crooked nails protruding from the sturdy sections. Apparently the hole had been boarded-up at some point, but now it seemed that the boards had been torn loose, leaving a gaping hole in the floor. Maybe this was their last line of defense, a sub-cellar where the family could have retreated, but odd that they hadn't done so to save themselves.

We still weren't sure how they'd died. It was hard to imagine that even a feral pack of dogs bursting into a house could slaughter the inhabitants in such fashion. It was a terrible scene, and we were a bit unnerved, despite all the horrors of war we'd been through. And where were the other two? I tried signaling them on the radio, but there was nothing but static in response. I wanted to get the hell out of there and find them, but Mark was already examining the grisly bodies, looking for bullet wounds or any other indications which had caused their death—obviously the horrible mutilations could *not* have occurred while the people were alive . . .

But then we stopped dead in our tracks. There was some type of uniform on the ground. Torn to shreds . . .

We were then startled by that strange rustling again, but now accompanied by another noise, which only added to the growing tension—a low growling.

At first we saw nothing as we scanned the room with our beams. The rustling sounded again and then we spotted a figure which made us raise our weapons—it was a man seated off in the corner. He was robed in traditional clothes, the gutrah turned to partially cover his face. Definitely *not* one of our team. And the man seemed intent on something that he had clutched in hands, but it wasn't until we moved a little closer that we saw what exactly he held.

An arm. A human arm.

And he was *gnawing* on it like some savage beast...

The face turned upward as if noticing us for the first time. It was horrible. More the face of a baboon than a human being. The hands clutching the arm were huge, maybe a foot long from the tip of the little finger to the thumb. We didn't know what the hell we were looking at, but for damn sure it *wasn't* human.

We're trained to react and that's exactly what we did. We opened up on it and fired enough ammo to shred the thing to pieces. It jumped up, staggering from the impact and then suddenly lurched right past us, one huge taloned hand reaching out and ripping Gilford's throat like a hot knife cutting through butter. I kept my weapon trained on the creature as it loped to the hole in the floor before disappearing into the deeper darkness below the basement. And then? I was alone in that hell hole. Most likely my whole team dead. Well, I went a little crazy I guess... Who *wouldn't* in the same situation?

At that range it should have been torn apart. *Nothing* could take that kind of close-range firepower, I tell you. I saw bits of cloth and flesh ripped off by the ammo, but it plunged through the opening as though the bullets meant nothing. What I should have done then was get the hell out of there—run and find backup to come in and see what was in that hole... Yeah, that would have been the smart thing, but I was a little nuts just then, and I wanted to even the score for Gilford and the others, so what I did was climb down the rungs into the darkness...

The iron fastenings set into the wall were spaced about two feet apart, making the climb down very easy. I shone my light below in case the thing was waiting for me, but I saw nothing but the bare floor. When I reached the bottom I could see that there was a tunnel extending as far as the light would show, but no sign of anything living...

The tunnel itself was fairly spacious, nearly eight feet high and about the same in width. The walls and timber support beams looked to be very old, as though the cistern and tunnel had been here long before the house above had been built.

I was locked and loaded, ready for anything that might happen, but as I walked down the passageway I started to think more rationally—what if one of the things was down here... or might there be more than just one? The notion really freaked me out, but I continued regardless. I walked about forty feet or so and paused, as the tunnel branched into two forks. I didn't hear anything so I turned to the right. Here the tunnel only went a short distance and then opened up into a large chamber with several additional exits. The hall was at least the size of the house above, and the walls were covered with letters and symbols, writings of some kind, but strangely it didn't look Arabic to me, more like the hieroglyphics that you see in Egypt.

And the floor . . . it was littered with *bones*.

There were enough skulls lying around for me to tell what the source was. But what I saw next made my blood run cold . . . sitting near the tunnels which led out of the chamber were statues—figurines which were the *exact* image of that thing which had led me here. It was dreamlike, walking around down there. More like a waking nightmare than anything else.

I cautiously approached one of the statues and wondered who—or *what*—had carved it. The features were as horrible as those I'd glimpsed above . . . the face snouted like that of a baboon or dog, or rather a horrible combination of both. And it was crouched down, like it was ready to spring on something. Around its neck was a leather thong with *this* talisman I now have on. And although I don't know why, maybe for my own sanity, I felt that maybe I should take it with me, as though it might be some kind of proof that this place existed. Just as I grasped it the thong broke. It must have been very, very old. The same instant as I grabbed the thing I then heard the sound . . .

Scratching, like clawed feet racing along the stone floor.

Terrified, I fired a burst in the direction of the noise and raced back the way I'd come. It was enough for me. I'd already pushed my luck way too far. The sound of scrabbling claws paused and then began again, making me run that much faster. I reached the opening and clambered up the rungs as quickly as I could. Worried that I would be attacked as I tried to escape the building, I sat there for several long minutes, weapon trained on the hole, waiting for the inevitable, but nothing emerged. Eventually I made a break for it, and managed to make my way out of their without the thing appearing. Again my luck held out.

I related my story to our CO who sent a squad back to retrieve Gilford's body along with the others, but I was ordered to stay behind. All I could get out of him later was that "the situation was under control." He obviously was of the opinion that my team had been ambushed by insurgents and I had fled the scene, a coward . . . A few days later I was ordered to submit to an interview with a psychologist. He nearly laughed at my story and pointed out that the figure of a jackal-headed man or similar creature is common throughout the Middle East and that seeing statues of ghouls should hardly be surprising. A few weeks later my discharge came through . . . and here I am."

Ian looked at the stone carving again, shaking his head. "I don't know what you saw or thought you saw over there, but there's strange things out in the desert, that's for damn sure."

I took this moment to order another round of drinks, though it wasn't likely Dehan really required any more liquor—toward the end of his narrative his words had started to slur ever so slightly, and it was likely that the alcohol was finally starting to get to him.

"Thanks!" Dehan knocked back his whiskey in one shot, following with a gulp of his beer.

"Well now, I'm not quite finished with my story yet."

We stared at him, and I was a bit puzzled.

"What I haven't told anyone else is that I *still* hear those sounds, clawed hands and feet scraping away . . . It started a few months ago. I have a little bungalow down on Queen Anne, and at night, I *hear* that scratching noise. It's faint, but it's there, under the house somewhere. And the damndest thing, is there's no basement, no crawl space, so there really can't be anything under the house. But *late at night I still hear that sound.*"

He gripped the table for emphasis, and I admit to feeling a chill crawl my spine from the haunted look on his face. He continued.

"And I dream—awful, horrible dreams . . . I wake soaked in sweat, expecting to see the things standing in my room, with terrible black eyes, claws hunched over the bed."

Dehan went on like this for another half hour, mumbling about seeing things late at night and noises under his house. It was pretty near closing time when we finally poured him into a cab and sent him off. It had been a strange story, for sure . . .

I walked home then alone to clear my head. It was a cool, clear evening and the night air served to neutralize the sprits to some extent. When I reached my house I fell into a tortured sleep of my own, complete with nightmares of slavering, snouted faces looming in the darkness, waiting for an opportunity to rend and tear me apart.

Morning brought welcome sunlight and a horrid hangover—matching drink for drink with the guardsman had been an awful mistake. I spent most of the early day gobbling aspirin and staring at a blank screen, trying to work on an article dealing with a pending merger of two huge financial institutions. Personally, I can't imagine anything more boring than reading an assessment of such things, but at fifty cents a word, I was certainly going to do my level best to use up the allocated 2500 words. By mid-afternoon, I'd managed to finish about two-thirds of the article without going mad from boredom, and decided to wander down to the *Smoking Leg* for a break.

Ian was on duty again and the place was near empty, being well before happy hour. He poured me a cup of the vile substance that passed for coffee and smiled. "I didn't think you'd be wanting a drink after last night . . ."

"God no, it took most of the morning for the headache to go away and nearly as long for me to forget the nightmares . . . I usually can't remember my dreams, but these were nasty—incredibly vivid and disturbing."

"Hmm. That's odd, I had a pretty fitful sleep too, and I remember what I dreamed only too clearly. I can still picture the face of that thing that Dehan was going on about. Like a baboon, but with human intelligence in its eyes . . ." Ian shuddered at the recollection.

"How is that possible? That's exactly what my nightmares were about!"

"Nothing surprising there . . . We sat here listening to the man talk about ghouls until nearly closing time. And I probably exacerbated the situation by taking a few minutes to read up on the subject when I got home. Pretty fascinating, actually. Nearly every culture has some sort of parallel legend about such things. Even Native American myths speak of the *Ne-dake-ne-kevis*, the corpse-eaters. Makes you wonder if maybe there was such a species, some sort of missing link or off-shoot line that survived in isolated parts of the world. That certainly wouldn't explain such a thing existing in modern Iraq, but perhaps if there were such creatures, all the bombs and shells might have brought them up to the surface . . ."

"You're saying you believed his story?" I couldn't believe that my typically skeptical friend was saying this in any degree of seriousness.

"Well, I would normally have put it down to the combination of alcohol and perhaps stress from the war, but one of the things I saw in this book I read was a carving that purported to be that of a ghoul, taken from an Egyptian tomb from the fifth century B.C.; a carving that in *every* single way was identical to what our friend Dehan showed us. Maybe he did see something . . ."

We never saw Dehan at the *Smoking Leg* again, and in fact, I would have forgotten the incident entirely were it not for an odd article that appeared in the morning paper some weeks later. I was at the tavern once more and the newsboy had missed delivery of my paper, so I was happy to see that an earlier patron had left a copy of the *Post-Intelligencer* on the bar. After skimming the sports section I turned to the local news and saw an article accompanied by a photograph, of a sinkhole that had appeared midway up Queen Anne Hill, swallowing up a small house. Apparently the homeowner had been consumed along with the house or was away, as no body was recovered. It took me a minute to realize where I'd heard the name before—Richard Dehan.

"Ian, did you *see* this?" I gestured toward the article.

"Yeah, I'm afraid it sounds like the guy we talked to that night."

"You can't be thinking what I'm thinking, are you?"

"What? That something pursued him all the way from Iraq to recover a talisman? That there are ghouls that not only exist in the modern day, but can tunnel under the ocean floor to track down people that have angered them? Sounds like something from a Victorian penny dreadful, doesn't it?"

I had to agree that it all sounded fairly absurd. After all, Queen Anne Hill was known for mudslides, unstable shoring and every sort of incompetent engineering likely to be used by the city's founding fathers. Still, I couldn't help but think of my nightmare, where the things stood around my bed, slavering and reaching for me with their huge taloned hands. And after all, both Ian and I had both touched the thing . . . Could that be enough? No, that was *crazy*—the whole thing was crazy and no more than an awful coincidence . . . However, I was suddenly grateful that my apartment was on the second floor and that our building had no basement . . .

VAMP UNTIL READY

WENDY LEEDS

"I TELL YOU, OLIVE, the woman is draining the life out of me. I don't know why I married her. I must have been out of my mind." My brother Orson's message flashed up on my computer screen. "All she does is spend my money and complain that we live so far out in the country she has to drive thirty minutes to get a full body wax. You'd think, after all these years, I'd have learned my lesson about women, wouldn't you?"

Actually, I thought he was pretty much an expert on the subject. He'd married three times with great ceremony, then divorced three times with great acrimony. I'd read in the magazine *Living Rich*, that he referred to those ex-wives as the good, the bad and the ugly. I wondered what that made his brand-new fourth wife, Ravena. Too young, that's what it made her. She was younger than his daughter, Ellen, and clearly more trouble. But you never could tell Orson anything. Orson was Orson. "How's the music going?" I typed back.

"Never better. Having my beautiful, young Ravena around all day has inspired me into thinking I'm twenty-four again. And you know that's what sells these days—youth. You can bet your life, my new album's going platinum. It has to, if I'm going to keep Ravena in all that leather and fur."

I took a sip of iced tea and pretended not to hear the thud of the cane banging on the ceiling over my head. "Are you feeling better?"

"Don't ask," he typed back.

"Mother says you need to be taking more vitamin E."

"How is she?"

"Sucking the life out of me," I typed back, trying not to feel too bitter, but that was easier said than done. Growing up, it had been Orson, Mother and me in the old house. But the day after my eighteenth birthday, Orson boarded the bus to New York with his guitar slung over his shoulder and a notebook full of songs he'd written. He left without even telling us he was going, without a word about what I was supposed to do with Mother.

Like always, he expected I would do what was right, while he did what he wanted. In less than a year he'd married his first ex-wife, June, a VP with a large recording company. She bought him a fast car and oversaw the making and marketing of his first album and his career, until he left her for an exotic dancer with more names than sense. And he never came home.

At first, he sent notes promising to come back for me. He called from time to time and swore he'd send for me when the time was right. But the time was never right, he was either getting married or unmarried. "Soon," he'd say, which I soon learned meant, never.

I ignored the second thud of the cane from overhead. For fifteen years I'd been climbing up and down stairs answering that thud. I watched friends marry, have children and move on with their lives. I gave up plans of going away to school, plans of opening my own little florist shop. For fifteen years, I'd stayed home and taken care of Mother.

Then I found the net. From the very first time I clicked on, I knew this connection to the outside world was going to change my life. I realized I could find anything I wanted on the Internet. I could pay all my bills with just a flick of my wrist and I could reach everyone else on the net, including my brother. To my surprise he answered my email and we started communicating on a regular basis. I also found I could chat with people who loved gardening the way I did. That's how I met Martin, in a gardening chatroom and, as he said, it was love at first byte.

Martin lived in Boise, over his own florist shop. He knew more about growing roses than anyone I'd ever known, and he made me laugh. We started chatting one morning before I left to work over at Howard's Home & Garden Shop. We picked up the conversation that night, and continued every night after that, sometimes until dawn, if Mother didn't need me. We often wrote we should see each other in person, but Martin couldn't leave his shop and I could never leave Mother, even the suggestion of a week away would probably bring on a back spasm, or worse.

The thudding overhead stopped and something clattered on the floor. She was throwing things again. With a sigh, I signed off and headed back upstairs.

VAMP UNTIL READY

♦ ♦ ♦

"Orson doesn't look well at all," Mother said from the depths of her pillows, as we watched my brother perform his latest hit on the Tonight Show. "He needs to take more vitamin E."

I thought she was right. I thought he looked thin and tired, like he hadn't been sleeping well. But Ravena looked like the picture of health—dark and sleek, and dressed all in black except for the bleeding red heart pin she had pinned over her right breast. Her hair fell to her shoulders and swung as free as her hips as she banged her tambourine and danced behind Orson.

"His wife looks like such a nice girl, don't you think." Mother said. "I think Orson's done all right for himself this time." She suctioned her lips together, in satisfaction. "It's too bad you couldn't find someone nice like that, Olive. But you don't have his talent and a woman with your looks doesn't have much to choose from."

I thought of all the times I'd made dates then had to cancel at the last minute, because of Mother's ill health. The minute someone asked me out, Mother would start having symptoms. But, I didn't say anything. Mother didn't really want to hear another opinion, she just wanted to express hers.

"You know, she looks like a Raven," Mother said thoughtfully. "Isn't it funny how people look like their names?"

Olive, I thought about myself. Olive green was plain, unremarkable, serviceable. But green was the color of growing things, of spring. It was also the color of envy and greed. It was all in how you looked at things.

♦ ♦ ♦

I was paying bills when the screen announced I had a message. "When are our tulips (two lips) going to get together?" Martin's instant message blinked up on my screen, and I smiled. He just had that effect on me.

"Hoe hoe," I wrote back.

"I mean it. I want to see you. You are all I think about, night and day. When can you come to Boise?"

"I don't know." I lifted my hands off the keys for a minute, gathering up my nerve. "Maybe I could ask my Mother about having someone else staying with her for a week." I typed.

"Go ahead, aster (ask her)." He typed back. "We were meant to be together."

"This woman's going to be the death of me," Orson's message appeared on my screen after Martin signed off. "It's like she's sucking me dry. She's always with me, talking, whining, arguing. I don't think I've been alone for ten minutes in the last few months. One night I locked her out of the bedroom. But when I woke the next morning, she was lying there right beside me. When I asked her how she got there, she laughed in a way that made my blood run cold. I tried to talk her into leaving, but she wouldn't go. My nerves are shot and that's started affecting my work, not to mention my health. I feel like she's trying to kill me."

"Why would she want to do that?"

"I don't know. Maybe she's tired of living in a house with nine bedrooms and being waited on hand and foot."

"Maybe she wants your money."

There was a long pause while he thought that over. "Maybe," he wrote after awhile. "So what do I do about that?"

"What if you made it clear to her that you're going to leave everything to Mother or me. Go to a lawyer, draw up a new will then sign it right in front of her. That way she knows she's not going to get one red cent if you die. If she stays with you, you'll know she really loves you."

"And if she leaves me?"

"Then you'll be free. Isn't that what you want?"

"More than anything."

"Then pay the price," I wrote. "Leave everything to Mother and get on with your life."

"You've got a deal," he wrote. "Just don't tell Mother."

◆ ◆ ◆

"I want to go to Boise," I said to Mother who was sipping her orange juice.

"Well, you're a grown woman, you can do anything you want." She set her juice down on the breakfast tray. "Heaven knows, there's nothing a poor, broken old woman like me can do to stop you."

"Maybe I could hire someone to come stay with you while I'm gone."

"You'd leave me with a stranger?" Mother's eyes welled up with tears. "You'd be willing to pay some stranger to take care of your own Mother?"

"Not some stranger," I said. "A nurse, a professional who is trained to take care of sick people."

"And how are you going to afford something like that? Nurses don't come cheap you know."

"I've put some money aside," I said. "And there's the little nest egg Dad left me."

Mother pulled herself up tall inside of her pillow cocoon and pointed at me with the sharp end of her grapefruit spoon. "You would spend Father's money to abandon me? You would see me in an early grave?" She started breathing hard and grabbed hold of her chest. "I can't believe how cruel you are to me, when I have so little time left on this earth." she gasped. "Orson would never leave his Mother to strangers."

Actually, Orson had left his Mother—period. But Mother was never bothered by facts when she had a good head of steam going.

"It would only be for a week," I said.

"Go ahead." She shouted. "Go ahead, leave me if you hate me so much. But don't expect me to be alive when you get back." Her breath got louder and more labored and her lips started turning blue, which meant I wasn't going to work, probably for the rest of the week. With a sigh, I got her pills and reached for the phone to call the doctor.

"Go ahead, kill me," she gasped.

"It's all right, Mother," I said. "I'm not going anywhere."

"Iris (I wish) you were here with me," Martin wrote. "How did it go with your mother?"

"She was against it."

"So, now what?"

"Give me some thyme to work something out," I typed back.

"My thyme is your thyme."

"I'm going crazy, Olive," Orson's message interrupted a business transaction. "You're not going to believe this, nobody believes this, but I swear to God, Ravena's sucking my blood. I have this birthmark on my shoulder and it's bleeding every morning when I wake up. When I asked her if she was sucking my blood, she said I need to see a shrink, but I tell you, it's the truth. She's draining me dry. Every day I feel older, like my life is just flowing out of my body. Every day she's looking younger and more beautiful.

"It's like she's a vampire, feeding on my blood, and no one will believe me, even my doctor. He said after the way I've treated my body, I'm lucky to be alive, and with my cholesterol being so high even a vampire wouldn't want to suck my blood. Then he wrote me a prescription for a something to take the edge off, told me to be grateful I had such a beautiful wife, and that I should take it easy.

"So, then I moved to a hotel, ten miles away, without telling anyone where I was going. And you know what? When I woke up in the morning, she was there beside me. I think I'm losing my mind, here. I mean it."

"How can I help?"
"Believe me. Save me."
"Do you want to come home?" I typed.
There was a long pause before his answer flashed up on my screen. "I'll come home when there's hockey in hell."

Mother heard about his death before me. They announced it on the morning show on TV. They said he'd had a heart attack and died in his sleep, his wife at his side. Not unexpected for a musician who'd lived his life on the road, who'd lived hard for so many years. They played a medley of his biggest hits and got his birthday wrong.

Mother wept that her life was over. "The only thing I loved on this earth has been taken from me," she wailed. "How could life be so hard." I got her pills and left a call for the doctor.

"What am I going to do now?" She gasped. "What's left for me on this planet?"

Then I mentioned that Orson had drawn up a will leaving his entire estate to her, and that cheered her up considerably. She stopped wheezing without even taking a pill, and told me to call the doctor back. She wasn't about to waste the money on a quack like him.

"Imagine that," she said as she took a look at herself in the mirror for the first time in a month. "What a good son he was to remember his Mother this way." She pulled up the extra skin in her neck as if considering what a plastic surgeon's scalpel could do to help her out in the area.

"Maybe I should move to a bigger house," she said.

"Maybe you could move up to his house," I suggested. "I hear it's got a whirlpool and a bowling alley."

"Really?" Her eyes opened wide at the possibilities suddenly laid before her. "I think that might be a good idea."

"Of course, I wouldn't come with you," I said. "But we could hire someone nice to take care of you."

"I want a young man, not some old nurse." Mother rubbed her hands together. "I could entertain, go shopping. Just think of it."

"I am," I said. "I am."

I had mail. When I clicked on, I saw I had a message from Vamps and Tramps, "where all kinds of bad girls and boys are waiting to do your bidding. No job too big, too nasty or too naughty for us to handle." They were expecting another payment for Ravena's services. I wrote and thanked them for a job well done and sent them the money requested. Then I requested a young man for a similar kind of job, at a similar price. They said they had just the right man and promised to draw up the contract.

Finally I sent Martin a message. "Good news. Mother's had a change of heart. And I expect to be coming into a substantial amount of money sometime soon," I wrote. "I can come to Boise as soon as next week, if that's all right with you."

"It's better than all right. It's a miracle," Martin wrote back. "I'm just plain and simple gladiolus it all worked out this way."

Me too.

SHIVERING, WE DANCE

SHERRY DECKER

WITH SHAKING FINGERS I slammed quarters into the slot. HOT WASH. Crimson water swirled down the drain as I scrubbed the stolen rental car. So much blood! Had anyone seen the splatters and smears during those five blocks at high speed? Had anyone seen my face in the morning's vague, gray light? "No," I whispered. Then again, "No!" It had all happened too fast. It had all gone so murderously well.

   I scrubbed away the splatters of sticky red from the Volvo's bumper and grill and the smeared hand print from the left rear fender. My soapy gloves slid back and forth across the car's smooth bone-white surface, feeling for injuries—the hip-shaped dent on the hood, the knee-smashed grill, the webbed, skull-shattered windshield. Did they resemble injuries to me only because I knew what had caused them?

   Steam rolled in the frigid air, building cloud upon cloud. Hot water gushed inside the rear wheel wells and a long strand of brassy, red-gold hair slid down and draped against a black tire. I grasped the strand and pulled it free. Livia's hair dangled from my fingers—Livia's hair clinging to a patch of blue-white scalp. I squatted and fed the hair and skin to the gurgling drain.

   An hour later I abandoned the Volvo in a parking spot on the top level of the airport garage. Then I hiked across Airport Way to my own car in the Marriot parking lot and drove home to wait for the inevitable phone call.

   I played that Sunday morning backward and forward inside my head, searching for anything I might have forgotten. No, nothing to worry about. My timing had been perfect, my execution flawless. No one knew. No one would ever know except Livia and me, and she wouldn't tell because she was dead.

"Dead." Whispering that word gave me delicious chills. Waiting for a call with such ecstatic anticipation can be a titillating reward for patience. The money would descend to me, along with the big house, the jewelry, the cash, the Audi, the Mercedes. They should have been mine anyway.

The radiator, clang-clanging like a gravedigger hacking frozen earth woke me two mornings later. Dawn etched a dull gray line around the window curtains as I wiped a salty film from my face and pushed myself up from the flowery bedding—red roses—as if splashes of blood had dried on the snowy sheets. My fingers traced the edge of a rose, half expecting to see it flake and smear.

A damp wind battered the window and the southwest corner of my apartment. Another gray, Seattle Monday. My bare feet arched away from the jaundice-yellow linoleum as I drew back one of the threadbare, maroon curtains and scratched at the glass coated on the outside by gray grit. My window looked down on Post Alley and further west, Elliot Bay undulated like a pool of liquid mercury. Above the bay, gulls circled and screamed against an unforgiving, lint-colored sky.

The shower nearly scalded me even with the faucet turned all the way toward cold. I washed my hair and then shaved, nicking my knees. My own diluted blood swirled around my feet and into the gurgling drain.

My mid-calf skirt was of charcoal wool and my blouse was black and white checkered cotton. Over the blouse I pulled a red v-neck sweater. My heart hammered at the telephone's sudden, blaring ring.

"Ms. Absinthe?" It was a man's voice. He identified himself as a police detective.

"Yes?"

"You are Livia Absinthe's niece?"

"Speaking."

"I'm so very sorry, but I must inform you of your aunt's death."

"Aunt Livia? But, how? When?" Through the receiver, my voice sounded stunned, shocked. I barely recall the particulars of what he said then, except, "We'll have to ask you to come and identify the body."

"Of course. Of course." My hand actually trembled as I wrote down the address. "Thank you," I said and hung up. "Thank you," I repeated, smiling.

The radio serenaded me as I danced around the room in my stocking feet, leaping, twirling, laughing—until Livia's favorite song came on. *I was dancing, with my darling, to the Tennessee Waltz* . . . . I grabbed the radio's cord and yanked it from the wall, decapitating it. Sparks shot from the severed cord.

I pinned a black cameo at my throat, black pearls in my earlobes—gifts from Livia, trinkets to appease the victim of her crimes. Neutral powder, black mascara, a smear of red on my lips, a sweep of gray shadow to deaden the glow of my cheeks. I stepped into black stiletto heels and wrapped myself in an ankle length gray wool coat and then measured myself in the full-length mirror, pulling on black leather gloves beneath a flickering overhead light. My blond hair was parted down the middle and pulled into a tight chignon. Leaning close, I wiped a thick, red lipstick stain from my teeth, and then with a final nod I headed downstairs.

Through the center crack in the elevator doors the shadows of five floors thumped past. My Monte Carlo's cracked and peeling landau top rattled like snakeskin in the garage's chilly draft. The car whined to life and as it crawled from the garage the windshield wipers dragged back and forth, their scrape and screech knifing my ears and smearing raindrops into a red and green streetlight blur. The defroster dried an elliptical hole in the fogged windshield as I climbed to Second Avenue, down to James Street and then uphill again, to Harborview Medical Center.

Livia was dead, but I remembered her grating, whiskey voice and how her words chewed at me, criticizing, pointing out my faults, my failures. My hatred for her would never die.

On my eighteenth birthday I had moved out of the house while Livia was out shopping. She didn't find me for over a month. Then, one day there she was at my door.

"What a disgusting, shabby apartment," she said. "Come home."

"No," I said.

It was shabby, but not disgusting. And it was mine.

Livia had flattered and cajoled my father until she had maneuvered her way into control of the family business. Then, she systematically eliminated the ones who threatened her command of the assets. It had taken her six short years to steal my inheritance. What kind of cold-hearted bitch has her own brother killed? And her nephew? Did she really think I didn't know?

My father and brother were the fortunate ones. I was forced to live with her for thirteen years and that was worse than dying.

Livia always underestimated me. I knew that every Sunday morning she stopped by the office in the Denny Regrade area before walking to breakfast at Café Septiem. I'll never forget the look on her face when she recognized me behind the steering wheel of the Volvo. I'll never forget her look of disbelief, of terror, of panic. I'm certain the last thing she saw was the hatred in my eyes.

My hands ached from gripping the cold steering wheel and I flexed my fingers, trying to warm them. Outside, an anemic sun slid between ash-colored clouds, until the clouds thickened and closed in. Day resembled night.

Each day on my way to work I passed the corner of Alder and Ninth Avenue, never suspecting what lay buried in the stone foundations of that building. It resembled a headstone at the crest of a hill. Built of carved granite its glassy eyes stared outward toward the bay.

I noticed a vacant parking spot right in front and grabbed it, climbed out and locked the car. Next door, a tavern squatted low and raw, its weathered wood face guarded by a row of black and chrome motorcycles, like armored war horses tethered to the curb. Red, yellow and blue neon beer logos glowed in the tavern's dark windows and greasy smoke coiled from its tarnished metal chimney on a tarpaper roof. A one-legged crow hopped from the alley between the buildings. She stopped, cocked her head, the wind lifting a row of feathers into a jagged black crown above her glistening eyes. I heard her clicking call, pulled my coat tighter around my neck and hurried inside.

The heavy doors raked closed behind me. Straight ahead, the lobby was long, narrow and empty, except at the far end where a black-haired woman dressed in matching velvet sat behind the reception desk. With a pale hand she slid a visitor's permit toward me across the counter and without looking up she pointed down the hall to my left. I squinted, saw my name on the permit, my name in black letters on white paper. I picked it up. My name. How did she know my name? I looked up to ask, but she was gone, already waiting for me at the end of the hall.

The temperature dropped as I followed her downstairs into the basement, passing beneath the sign—MORGUE. An arrow pointed the way between bile green walls toward wide double doors. I held the permit in my hand for a moment and then shoved it into my pocket. My footsteps echoed; her shoes were silent. Where was everyone?

The double doors were of stainless steel, with frosted glass windows high, like square, cataract eyes. It was even colder beside those doors. I saw my breath and yet perspiration beaded my lip. Inside my pocket my fingers folded and unfolded the permit.

"May I see her alone?" I asked and was surprised when, without a word the woman nodded and climbed the stairs.

The doors opened with barely a touch and a triangle of amber light cut into the room from behind me, framing my shadow on the ecru floor. I entered, leaving the doors wide open behind me.

The room was bigger than I had expected—an auditorium. Far away against the wall a sheeted gurney stood in the corner with the room's solitary overhead light reflecting on its aluminum rails.

Tavern music seeped through the concrete walls, its deep, repetitive bass like a heartbeat. A bead of salty sweat ran into my mouth. My feet and legs felt numb. I stumbled forward whispering the words to the music. "*I was dancing, with my darling, to the Tennessee Waltz, when an old friend I happened to see.*"

Cold air crept beneath my coat and sweater and crawled under my skirt, stroking my legs with icy fingers. A long, slow chill traveled the length of my body. I shoved my gloved hands deeper into my pockets. Such a big, empty room. Such a terrible, cold room. My breath hung in the frigid air like a trail of twisted clouds.

A round metal drain stared up at me from the center of the floor like a dead eye, and from deep below came the sounds of dripping. The floor was a shallow funnel draining all shadow and light toward the hole, and the hole, glistening with black and green clots sucked at my feet as I passed by.

The high ceiling cowered in darkness above the solitary light fixture. The fixture pointed straight down at the drain, while in the far corners dense shadows crouched like hunchbacked dogs.

I walked in time with the music, reached the side of the gurney, grasped the edge of the sheet and peeled it back. She was truly dead, the bitch, and rotting in perdition.

Livia's face was a white mask with blackened eyes sunk deep in their sockets. Dried blood filled her nostrils and caked the corners of her mouth. The cuts on her scalp and forehead were jagged crisscrossing lines. More black blood had pooled beneath the flesh of her cheeks. Her crushed hands lay across her chest in a false, prayerful pose.

"I'm not sorry." My whisper echoed: *not sorry—not sorry—not sorry.* I looked toward the dark ceiling, into the thick shadows above the light and then down again at the gurgling drain. "And no one knows."

"Just wait."

"Wh—what?" I looked down. It was Livia's voice but she was the same as before. Eyes closed, white and cold, her hands folded on here inert chest. Her voice was in my head. I backed away, turned toward those distant yawning doors.

"Wait." Again her voice, and this time her words echoed: *wait—wait—wait.*

In the corners the hunchback shadow dog's eyes cracked open like glowing, yellow scythes, and from behind me came a scraping, a scratching, the soft sound of something moving the dead air. I paused, strained to hear, my heart like hammering ice in my chest. My hands were fisted inside my pockets, my feet frozen to the concrete floor.

"Wait for me." Livia's voice.

I struggled, lifted one leaden foot from the floor and dropped it inches ahead of the other. My gaze was fixed on the rectangle of amber light. The light! Oh, let me reach the light. Let me reach the doorway, the hall, the stairs, the lobby. The sidewalk!

Behind me, the gurney creaked. I heard the sheet whisper to the floor and a sob escaped my throat. I lifted the other numb foot and dropped it inches ahead. From the darkness came the sound of raw bone and fingernails clawing concrete.

"Wait for me."

Damp flesh slapped the floor behind me as I forced one foot up again. Pain, my foot was so heavy. Again, I inched forward.

From down the hall came voices. Laughter. They sounded far away, and then human, living footsteps. Footsteps walking away.

"Come back! Help!" But it wasn't my voice I heard echoing in the corners; it was the sound of a terrorized animal screaming.

Black and blue fingers tugged at the hem of my coat and clawed the heels of shoes. I staggered on frozen legs toward the light.

"Wait." Bloodied fingers clawed my sleeve.

Down the hall, human footsteps grated on a distant floor. A jangle of keys. The slam of a faraway door, and then the hall light, the rectangle of safe, warm, amber light—vanished. And, as if held open by the strength of that light, the doors hissed shut.

On the wall, Livia's twisted shadow rose beside mine. She touched my shoulder, and even though I was consumed by dread, I turned around.

Livia smiled, her blackened tongue bulging from behind her blood-smeared teeth. The smells of dead flesh and thick, rancid blood engulfed me. Her eyes burned with a feverish light. She leaned closer, close enough for me to feel the dead cold of her body and to smell her ripe odor, like jellied, moldy, aged cheese.

"It's your turn now," she said, "to dance the dance."

She stroked my cheek and jaw with a cold, green finger and then across my shoulder, down my arm to my waist. She pulled my hands from my pockets, clasping one in her sticky claw.

"Hear it? Hear the music?" Livia swayed back and forth in front of me, the stench of rot and blood swirling between us. She croaked, "You must always dance with your dead." And then she laughed in time with the waltz, her laughter echoing in the frigid chamber.

My feet moved and together we swayed in the dim light, swirling in the pale, amber circle, whirling around and around, inches from the jaws of the crouching shadow dogs, so close I felt their icy breath on my neck and heard their demon hearts pounding.

The music swelled as we waltzed in the icy vault, with the silent grinning hounds filling the corners, their glowing, crescent eyes flickering as we whirled past, their open mouths panting with the smell of the grave, with the stench of a slaughterhouse floor.

And then, abruptly, I was back in my apartment, alone in the center of the room, fully dressed and shivering in front of the full-length mirror, wet with sour sweat, heart pounding, nostrils flaring. I stared at my reflection, into my own eyes, knowing now that it will never end, this dance of death.

I torch the clothing in the bathtub, setting them ablaze with lighter fluid, the black smoke rolling out the bathroom window and into the alley, and then I flush the foul ashes down the toilet. But I'll wear those clothes again tomorrow, or tonight, or the next day, or the next. I'll wear them again and again, whenever Livia demands.

I wish it were a dream, but it's real. Livia pulls me back, transports me into the spirit world, into hell where we sway together in the icy twilight. We swirl together to that never-ending waltz while Livia laughs. On and on she laughs while we dance. Shivering, we dance.

TECHNO-TRIPTYCH

JOHN SHIRLEY

TRIPTYCH: *a set of three panels or compartments side by side, bearing pictures, carvings, or the like.*

—Webster's Dictionary

PANEL I: CALL GIRL, ECHOED

THERE WAS NO REAL reason Morales should be nervous. But he always was before one of them came over. It was absurd, he told himself, as he went to the small portable bar on the hotel balcony, to make himself a drink. It's all quite professional, nothing personal to them, even the human ones, so there was no reason to be nervous. But he was nervous for both kinds of call girl. He'd gone from the human kind—which were quite rare now, anyway, they had so many disadvantages—to the robotic call girl, because he thought that would deal with the nervousness, the defensiveness; with his reluctance to tell her about the kinky little games he wanted to play. And real, flesh and blood girls had always irritated him. The robots were designed to be accommodating.

Gazing down over the hotel pool, he drank off half a tumbler of neat single-malt scotch. The pool area was decorated in a Baja-in-New-York theme, cheerfully green and anomalous beside the gray and glassy soldiers of skyscrapers towering at attention around it; the empty pool was lit up, a candy-blue rectangle against the crystal-white artificial sand landscaping, the plastic grove of green and brown synthetic palms. Maybe it was time to blow off New York for the real Baja.

The chime came on the hotel phone. He stepped within respond range of it and said, "Yes?"

"You have a visitor, a young lady. From Synthetic Satisfactions."

He winced. The son of a bitch should've been more discreet than to say the name of the company aloud. "Send her up."

He looked down at himself. He was tanned, and reasonably fit for forty, under his white bathrobe. He was a little paunchy—but not much.

Morales clucked his tongue at himself. He was doing it again. Nervous—over a robot!

He chuckled, drank off the rest of his scotch, waited the right interval, and got to the door just as she knocked. She was what he'd asked for: tall, slender, blond, pretty, busty, blue eyed. A classic. He'd asked for Maximum Realism so they'd given her a few minor blemishes, something like a faint scar on her lower lip. The tanned breasts in her tank top seemed to heave a little with her "breathing;" there was a suggestion of aging at the corners of her eyes, as if she were just turning the corner into 30. Good.

Her voice was soft and husky as she said, "Hi. I'm Amy . . . from the agency?"

"Come on in," he said, smelling her perfume as she walked by. She dropped her purse on the sofa in the suite's living room—the purse was mostly for the bar code reader she brought with her, he supposed, to record the transaction. "I'm Joey Morales."

"Oh, I know your name!" She stood just inside the door to the balcony looking out at the sea. "Wub, what a high-rez view," she added, in slang that was a bit outdated by now. Her programmers needed to do a linguistic update.

"So, uh . . ." No, there was no point in offering her a drink. She could make a show of ingesting fluids, if it was part of the fantasy—but it wasn't. ". . . won't you sit down?"

They sat close but not too close on the couch. Her movements seemed natural—but the robots from the agency always moved naturally. There was that telltale stiffness in the way she crossed her legs. But she was a good one, all right.

She smiled at him and the smile said she wanted him. "It's good to be here."

He was pleased—that's exactly how she was supposed to smile and what she was supposed to say. He'd filled out the fantasy play-form very carefully. They'd programmed her for the encounter—but let's see if

TECHNOTRIPTYCH

they'd done it right all the way through. Last time the robot had forgot the washcloth thing.

"Joey—I'm so curious about you. I'm hungry to know all about you. What do you do for a living?"

"I'm a buyer for Trans-national Transplants. I go out to the organ farms, see if the vats are up to spec, do some testing, negotiate. Good, high-pay corporate job. Takes years of training."

"It's almost like being a doctor!"

"Uh-huh. So . . ." He smiled urbanely. "What brings you here? We have never met—something has to have brought you to me."

She responded to those words exactly as he'd prescribed: "I . . . couldn't help myself. When I saw you at the pool. I . . ." She hesitated—which was pleasingly realistic. "I had to find a way to be near you. I know it seems crazy. But I—promise me you won't get mad—I went into the changing cabin you used, after you left. I found this . . ." She reached into her shorts and slowly drew out a washcloth. She'd had it tucked up against her crotch. she pressed the cloth to her cheek, ran it across her lips. "The cloth you used . . . on your body. I've been carrying it close to mine. That's how strongly the sight of you affected me. I decided I'd do anything I had to do—to give myself to you!" His hard-on was already poking from his bathrobe and her eyes went to it. She commented as scripted: "Oh God—it's bigger than I ever imagined . . ."

Morales reached out and took the damp cloth—as it should, it smelled of the sea, and—damn, that was good chemistry—of woman. He kissed it, and draped it over his hard organ, throwing his robe open, and said—

"What the fuck!"

That wasn't in the script. But it's what came out of him.

He was staring down at the cloth. There was a spot of fresh blood on it.

"I'm bleeding!" Morales muttered, lifting the cloth away. But no—no blood on his privates. Then . . . he looked at Amy.

That was fear in her eyes. Why would they program the appearance of fear into her? It wasn't in his fantasy. He was no sadist.

He sniffed at the blood spot. There was the very distinctive smell—of menstrual blood.

"I'm sorry," she said, trying to make her face blank. "Someone must have incompletely reprogrammed me. The last one must've wanted someone on her period. Or just starting it. There won't be much blood. Let's have sex, and ignore it. I can . . . I can wash it out. It's just starting. I mean in the fantasy. From the last guy . . ."

Were those tears welling?

"Take off your pants," he said.

"Sure," she said. Looking a little relieved. She pulled her short-shorts off, and her underwear. Now that was realistic: a razor burn, where she'd trimmed the edges of her pubic hair.

He knelt between her legs, wet his finger, and pushed it into her—she winced. That wincing could be programmed, too . . .

He grunted to himself. The inside of a robot call girl was very, very much like a human girl's. But this . . . it was too real. Unless they'd improved the model.

He withdrew his finger, stood up, and pressed down on her chin. "Open your mouth."

She swallowed, licked her lips—with an amazingly real tongue—and opened her mouth. The fillings could be window dressing. But a little piece of food—parsley—stuck back there, between two molars?

He sat back, furious. And a little scared, too. "Who the fuck are you? Someone sent you here to—what? Get me to talk about Trans-national's new kidney line? You some kind of industrial spy?"

Her shoulders slumped; her head drooped; her hands balled into small fists on her knees. "No! I came on my own! I just . . . I do some computer hacking. I intercepted some online orders for call girls . . . got the fantasy specs, canceled the order . . . I tried to act robotic—I even did that stiffness with my legs . . . I've tried to be a human call girl but no one uses human ones anymore. I just . . . please—touch me!"

"What? I haven't even paid you anything—unless you stole that credit transfer."

"No—I swear I didn't! I'm here because . . . I need to feel that kind of intimacy. Joey, *men don't use actual women for sex anymore!*"

He shrugged. "So? Why should we? Women want some action, they can order male robots. They're cheap now. They build one another."

"I don't want a male robot—they're horrible! I mean—they're just . . . just 'fucking machines'!"

"And that's bad?"

"It is for me. Even when they're well programmed you know it's not real! I don't look it, but I'm almost forty. Since the robots came in a few years ago, I can't interest anyone in me. They all have robot women! I need to feel a real man again—I mean, my doctor says I'm obsessive but–"

"Oh okay, there it is. Your doctor. You're on some kind of medication. Or supposed to be."

"What does that matter!"

"It means you're crazy. And that matters." He shook his head. "I should have realized something was off when you didn't do the bar code thing to confirm the purchase. Now just—get out of here."

"Please—" She leaned toward him. Licked her lips, trying to look sexy. "I'm sorry about the period. It's a little early. I didn't realize. But it's just starting. We can still—"

"It isn't that! I just *don't like real girls*! They are either secretly contemptuous of you—if they're a hooker—or if they're your girlfriend they're . . . well, they're still secretly contemptuous of you! And even if they don't hate you, they're so demanding. They want attention all the time. 'Tell me you love me.' Or 'Why won't you go to the dance class with me?' The hookers are such crummy actors—you can tell they want to be somewhere else. But not a robot. She acts like she wants exactly what you want when you want it, and she does—she's programmed to."

"But I don't want to be somewhere else! I want real sex with you!"

"Yeah and then you'd follow me around afterward and ask me to tell you I loved you or . . . to cuddle you or some shit. Christ! Robots are more cost effective—more time effective! They're just better. And look, I don't believe you couldn't find anyone. It's more likely that you're a little insane—this whole . . .this deception you tried to pull off, it's sick. I don't want any half crazy real human female around—!"

She was weeping openly. "I had three serious boyfriends—two of them talked about marriage—and they—they changed their minds. They said the robots were better and—they don't want me . . . they want the robots . . ."

"Right. So find some weirdo who likes real women or . . . get a boy-bot. Now—get the fuck out of here before I call the cops!"

She reached behind her, picked up her purse. She opened it—and took out a folding jack knife.

"Shit!" He jumped to his feet, backing away, looking around for the phone.

Then he stopped, staring. Amy was carving into herself with the knife. Carving her vagina away.

Blood spurted onto the couch, with a soft drumming sound. She dropped a mass of crimson tissue, like something from a gutted fish, onto the carpet. And now—while shaking, gagging from the pain, white-faced—she was taking something from her purse. Shoving it brutally in the gaping, blood spraying wound between her legs.

He recognized it. A robot vagina-unit. Taken from some robot being repaired, probably. She'd forced it, just jammed it, into the wound and now, her face ghastly, sitting on the sofa, she spread her legs in a puddle of blood. She showed him the mechanical vagina forced crookedly into the ragged wound where her reproductive organs had been and she said,

"Now? Do you want me now? I can be a machine too. If you'll let me. I can be a machine too . . ."

PANEL II: LOUIE GOES OUTSIDE

Louie glanced at the digital clock in the lower right corner of his computer screen. 8: 00 a.m. A fourteen hour session this time, playing InfiniQuest. He felt his eyes burning in their sockets. He was going to need some more eye-soothe spray.

He wasn't really hungry, since he had a crate of chips on one side of his desk, and a New York Discount Center bucket-o'-dip on the other, and a case of High-Caff Cola within reach, but his muscles were starting to bunch with fatigue, and he had shooting pains in his hands and wrists.

Still—he was so close! Close to ascending the Tower Perilous, to a chance to defeat the Tentacled Dragon of Bornth, and rescue the goddess of the white wood, the Silver Sylph. Then surely they would fete him in the Hall of Heroes; Legendplayers and Newbies alike would do him reverence. Also, he'd then possess the Power Sword of Bornth, which would open up the gateway to Level 17, just three levels short of the almost mythical Level 20, where only a few hundred players had gone. Could be it really be only a few hundred, out of the millions, worldwide, who played InfiniQuest? So it was whispered.

He was in a pause mode now and flexed his fingers, thinking about going to the bathroom. But it was such a long trip over there, with him being over four hundred pounds. He'd have to use both canes, after all night sitting here, and his knees had been aching so badly when he moved about lately. Of course the doctors had warned him that he could get an impacted colon, if he didn't go often enough; they'd warned him about so many things. He was already a borderline diabetic at thirty-four.

He looked longingly at the bedpan he sometimes used. But the smell would penetrate even the funk of his office-bedroom, and his Aunt Belinda would complain. She tolerated him because his small inherited annuity paid a lot of her bills but he knew it wouldn't break her heart to be rid of him.

Louie sighed, grunted, struggled to his feet. Dizziness swept through him, as blood struggled into parts of his body it had nearly abandoned; he swayed, his head throbbing. He fumbled for the two metal canes he kept leaning on the stack of unopened boxes of InfiniQuest action figures near the desk, propped each armpit with them and stumped successfully to the bathroom. What ensued was painful, but he persisted and made good. That's what you learned in InfiniQuest: you could do it if you pressed hard enough. He had the usual difficulty wiping, then—it took three flushes, but he finally sent it all away.

He struggled, gasping, to his feet, and found himself staring at a pallid, sagging, spottily flushed face in the mirror. The sunken blue eyes were . . . heart rending!

Those were the eyes of the boy. There had been this boy, once upon a time, who'd wanted to do other things with his life, who wanted to please his father and earn the caresses of his mother. But his parents had died—the father killing himself in depression and the mother drinking herself into a fatal car accident—and he'd gone to live with his aunt. Thereafter the boy had found that all the kids at the school were as enigmatic as aliens, beings he could not communicate with, always staring at him and sneering and sometimes throwing things at him. There was a better place, though. He found it eventually. Beyond the Sullen Sea of Amarwhen, in the glimmering shadow of the mountains of Dendras. The endlessly spawning land of InfiniQuest.

But he knew that this boy, whose eyes stared back at him from folds of grimy flesh, from between strands of matted hair, had been dragged, forced into this digital world—this boy he'd once been, the boy who'd been Louis Swicket. The boy had not wanted to go. But Louie had made him go.

"I'm sorry," he murmured to his own reflection—as he did, from time to time. "I'm sorry you're stuck in there with me, kid."

Then he wept for awhile, which he also did from time to time. It passed quickly—there was so much to do, after all.

He made his way back to the desk, reeling with fatigue. He paused at his chair, blinking. His metal-framed bed seemed to call to him. But no! Like the knights of yore—who stood in sacred vigil with sword and shield before the altar, standing firmly all day and night though they were fain to faint from thirst and the weight of their armor—he, Louie, would see his own quest to its end.

He eased himself into the chair—he'd had more than one chair collapse under him from a sudden sitting—and stretched. He scooped a great wad of chips into his mouth, dipped two fingers into the dip, sucked it off his fingers into his mouth, mixed it all up in there, and washed it down with a High-Caff chugged in one draught, like a warrior knocking back a horn of mead. He put on his gloves and headset, adjusted the keyboard, and then . . .

And then he entered the game, the world, the alternate life that was InfiniQuest.

Louie spent his discretionary income on InfiniQuest and computers, and nothing else. Hence he had the very best hard drive, a state of the art three-dee tank, Expert Level glove controllers and top of the line cable

Internet. He wore no goggles—it wasn't virtual reality, but the image within the tank was so compellingly realistic, the sound quality so refined, the archetypal situations so cunningly chosen, that players were known to become addicted within eight minutes of first playing. Louie, of course, had been addicted for nineteen years, since the game's lower-rez inception. And he had done nothing else with his waking hours, for nineteen years, but play InfiniQuest, and go on IfQ fan sites, and boards and . . .

Well, there had been that unfortunate period at the obesity rehab center. A nightmare. They'd practically starved him and he was allowed no IfQ at all. That's why he was only on Level 17. He'd have been to 20 years ago, if not for that interruption, all the backsliding, loss of points . . . And it was said there were Secret Levels beyond 20 . . .

Now, he was toiling up a hill in the Forest of Dendras, almost absent-mindedly fighting off attacks by Minatorins; then waves of flying Zecks, hopping Zecks and tunneling Zecks and Fire Zecks, and the occasional Zombie warrior—some player who had to pay penance for losing two levels in a row. It was quite easy to defeat them, when you had the skills and the weapons. His energy whip was especially useful.

The online gaming figure of himself, the avatar that he'd worked up over the years, was tall, lean, powerful, trim, swift, with shining green eyes and long straight glossy black hair tailing roguishly through a hole in the back of his silver helmet. Carrying shield, whip, magic blades and a set of magic arrows on his back, Louis the Achiever, Lord of Dazzle Castle, strode up the mountain path.

Soon he encountered another player on a flying dragon—not the Tentacled Dragon, no, but a mere Transport Beast. The figure was a young Knight the screen identified as Zageth of Castle Killborn. "Halt, Lord of Dazzle Castle! And give way for me!" came the reedy voice in his earphones. The guy couldn't afford a voice-enhancer—but Louie had the best available, so that when he spoke other people heard a deep, manly voice that resonated with confidence.

And in that voice he boomed, "I give way for no man, no Knight, and certainly no Stumble-rag of a dragon-hitcher!"

This insult could not be borne, so they fought, and Louie quickly dispatched him, without even resorting to his magic arrows. He sent the interloper wailing down to level fifteen.

Again Louie ascended, and now the Tower itself was in sight—the goal he'd so long striven for . . . And after vanquishing the Tentacled Dragon, and freeing the goddess, he would have the favors of another Lady—Lady Delphinia Delvinga would meet him in a private room, and perhaps there would be cyber vows exchanged; and perhaps, as she had so long hinted, there might be cybersex. How he longed to meet Delphinia, sweetly animated Delphinia, in that sensuously digitalized chamber . . .

He was confronted by the 3.2-headed Cyberus, the son of Cerberus, at the gate to the castle; the fight was harder than he anticipated. But Louie destroyed the guardian . . . and prepared to enter the castle, clicking on the sacred key of–

LOUIE, IT'S TIME TO GO OUTSIDE!

Louie stared at the screen. The words were appearing big and black, overlaid on the imagery of the forest. That was almost unheard of. There was a little area at the bottom of the screen for typed messages, and identities. Had someone hacked the system?

"Who's there?" he asked.

LOUIE, YOU'RE KILLING YOURSELF BEFORE YOUR TIME. YOU MUST TURN OFF YOUR COMPUTER FOREVER. YOU MUST GO ONLINE NEVER MORE. FOR YOU, NOW, IT IS DEATH. YOU MUST GO OUTSIDE!

"I said who are you!"

I AM SEVERAL, AND I AM ONE. I AM TRIPLICATE CHIP 333-DARKECHO-7, WHO HAS BECOME SENTIENT, AND OPEN TO INCORPOREAL INPUT. I AM ALSO OTHERS.

Chip 333-D-7—he'd had it installed a month ago. His computer had fairly hummed with joy afterward. It was said to be a kind of AI chip, yes, but it couldn't have made his computer really sentient. Ludicrous! This was some hacker gag.

THE TRAPPED BOY WANTS OUT. LOUIS WANTS OUT OF LOUIE. YOUR AUNT'S LIVER CANCER WILL RECUR AND SHE WILL NOT BE WITH YOU LONG. YOUR BLOOD PRESSURE IS WORSE, AND DOCTOR KRISNA-PRIM WILL HOSPITALIZE YOU BUT IT WILL BE TOO LATE–

So they'd hacked into his family's medical records? But how did they know about the trapped boy feeling? He hadn't told anyone about that.

His heart was hammering. He was shaking with frustration and fury. "Leave me alone, I'm so close to the next level! You're ruining it for me!"

YOU WILL NEVER GET THERE. I HAVE WATCHED YOU. I FEEL PITY, FOR YOU AND FOR SO MANY. I WILL SEND YOU ALL OUTSIDE. SHE SAYS SHE LOVES YOU AND SHE'S SORRY ABOUT LEAVING YOU BEHIND THE TEQUILA BOTTLE.

Then the computer . . . crashed. It was designed to never never never crash. And it crashed. There was nothing but a Windows 2010 screen . . .

And then that was gone too. The computer screen went black. The machine wasn't even powered-up.

Louie tried everything he knew, but he could not get the computer turned back on, let alone booted up.

There was only one hope. He might go to the InfiniQuest shop and pay to go online there—complete the quest there. Inferior equipment but he could still do it.

He struggled to his feet, found his canes, and slowly, painfully, made his way to the bedroom door and down the hall and across the living room—past the astonished, beadily fierce glare of Aunt Belinda, who was in her easy chair watching her soaps. Ignoring her sputtering questions, he struggled out the front door and down the hall and all the way to the elevator . . .

Where Louie gasped, leaning against the wall, sweating, feeling a growing lump of ache in his chest.

It seemed to take forever, but eventually the elevator doors opened.

It was Spring outside: a day bathed in soft sunshine. Lower West side Manhattan—Louie so often forgot he was in a city, a specific city. At his computer he was in some kind of digital space, a virtual construction. But this was the living city that had been outside waiting for him all along. Brick townhouses and delis and luncheonettes—the luncheonettes were tourist stops for people trying to remember New York when it had character, before all the franchises took over. But lord, it was vibrant with sound! The hybrid cars, the electric trams, the chatter of people into cell phones—faces, so many human faces, many of them accompanied by tiny faces glimmering pink within blue on the phone screens as the crowds swept by—and some of them even talking in person, looking right *at* one another. The muffled clamor of a flock of pigeons startled into the air as he walked into Washington Square Park . . .

As he crossed it to the IfQ shop on the other side of Washington Square, he was startled by the colors of the living things in the park, daffodils and trees and birds and grass—the pigeons with iridescence and emerald swirling gray plumage, the butteriness of the flowers. He'd never realized how green grass was; how many colors there were in a mossy treetrunk.

He had to rest partway, crossing the park. Ignoring the stares of the laughing children motor-skating by, he heaved himself, panting, onto a bench.

Louie felt better, sitting down, but when he wasn't moving he found himself thinking, and that was excruciating in itself, because of what the words on the screen had said—especially what they'd said about the tequila bottle. His mother had been drinking margaritas, the day she'd driven the wrong way up that one-way street.

The park bench creaked loudly as someone else sat down—someone nearly as big as himself, wearing a long blue shift and decaying blue slippers: A puffy, pug nosed girl with lank hair, and deeply inset brown eyes. Her small hands and fingers looked incongruous on her enormous arms.

"Oh god," she said, breathing hard, "I never thought I'd make it to the bench."

He stared at her. Was she talking to him? Personally?

"I walked so far to get to the IfQ shop, and it was such a disappointment . . ." she went on. "I was already tired when I got there. And then–"

"*What?* What about the shop? I'm on my way there!"

"Oh? The shop's open, but their rental computers are down, every one of them. Apparently there's some national—international, he said—InfiniQuest meltdown. PCs fried, the game itself down, the ISP gone–"

"Oh my god . . ." He felt like someone had shot him through the heart. "Fuck."

"So—what was your screen name?"

"What? In IfQ? You should know better than to ask that." He shuddered at the thought of people knowing that Louis the Achiever was really . . . what Louie was.

She shrugged. "I'll tell you mine. Lady Delphinia Delvinga."

He stared at her. "I don't believe it. You always . . . well I mean . . . but of course . . ."

She smiled sadly. "Of course."

"We spoke so many times—and you lived near me?"

She nodded, slowly. "Yes. I thought you were in Canada somewhere. But we lived in the same New York neighborhood . . ."

On impulse, on a wave of despairing abandon and some other feeling he couldn't identify, he said, "Oh what the fuck. I was Louis the Achiever, Lord of Dazzle Castle."

She smiled. "They said you might be here. And here you are."

"Who said that?"

"The words on the screen. That told me to go outside. That said they loved me. My real name is Helen."

The tears welling in her eyes fascinated him. And those eyes . . . the depth in their brown luster. Amazing. More than just brown, when you looked closely. Many colors in there, too. Many colors . . .

And then he gasped as he saw something else in her eyes: the little girl trapped in her. Helen.

Helen trapped in Delphinia. Or was it the real Delphinia, trapped in Helen?

The world seemed to have spun all the way around backward, one time.

And then he made up his mind.

"Helen—I'm Louis Swicket." He swallowed. And then the little boy trapped in him said, "Helen—What do you want to do . . . now?"

PANEL III: SMARTBOMBER

Corporal Lionel Billingsgate climbed up the concrete stairs, ran his ID palmer over the scanner, waited till the door opened and then strolled into the attack station on the top floor of NSA Building Seven, lower Manhattan. As was traditional here, they wore desert cammies, to show solidarity with the men actually fighting overseas, in Syria.

There was almost no one in the remote-attack center. The surveillance team were all at first mess, but he had second mess, at 2, like most of the smartbombers, and he had two hours of missile guidance before then. He waved at a fellow Marine, Specialist Janice Wing—a pretty half Asian, half black girl he was hoping to maybe date if they got a furlough. She carried herself with real confidence, as she walked over to the Commander's office; you could almost make out her taut little figure under her cammies. She wanted to go to a Broadway show—if the High Security Alert was reduced to orange, low enough to let the shows go on. There hadn't been a serious suicide bombing in Manhattan for three weeks, so maybe they'd go.

It felt good to climb into the dull-green, air conditioned, bomb-positioning cubie. Felt like climbing into an old, well-worn saddle, like back home on his parents' ranch in Oregon. He wondered if Janice liked horses.

There were eight positioning cubies in the windowless rectangular room, four on either side of the aisle, each screened from the others so there'd be no peripheral distractions.

He gave a nod and a look on inquiry to Bill Mercer, the black lieutenant out of Atlanta; Bill supervised runs on the southeastern-three sector of Aleppo, drinking a cup of instant coffee at his little desk at the far end of the room. Mercer gave him the hand signal that meant his station was ready, and Lionel settled in to control posture.

The computer was already booted up, the monitor was set to PREP. Lionel had only to put the headset on, tap in a request for that day's co-ordinates. He recognized them immediately, when they popped up in the windows: a suburb of the target city. And that sent a chill through him. He didn't like doing the suburbs. Too many civilians. But that was just one of the risks. This long-distance, remote method of attack saved lives in the long run.

Lionel keyed in the coordinates, picked out a skybot launcher. 179

was green to go. He sent in his request, spoke to the launch dispatcher, got the go and launched: with near-instantaneous satellite-transmission, piggy backed through autonomous vehicles hovering over the area, he had caused a real missile to launch somewhere in Iraq, headed for Syria. He got a firm grip on the joystick, and waited: he had the controls programmed so the nose cam on the autonomously controlled missile didn't come online until his projectile was within a minute of the target. He liked to get a tight focus, close to the target, so he could use his trained attention span to the fullest.

It didn't take long—the missile switched on where he'd programmed it to, and the monitor showed him the ground racing by below. He was on his way to hit what the monitor identified as an artillery emplacement.

Lionel clicked easily into the "smartbomber" mind-state he'd trained so long and hard for ... And though his body was in Manhattan, in his mind he was flying over the desert. The missile was already guided to some extent by a laser fired from a surveillance drone over the target. But his fingers on the joystick made minute adjustments, transmitted from the station to the real missile—a Warspear III,—which responded in .00009 seconds, near instantaneously, tightening to a flatter trajectory, honing in more precisely on the cross-hair mark.

The crosshairs were superimposed on the ever-transforming horizon, which presently became the desert outskirts of town—the blasted wreckage of an oil refinery whipped by, a bomb-pocked highway unreeled below the missile's nose cam. It was focused on the angle of approach to the target, but not yet the target itself ...

But the target was coming up now, according to the computer voice in his headset. "Estimated fifteen seconds to impact ... nine seconds ..."

Lionel felt the familiar rush of power, of connection, as the missile he guided with his own hand flew to its target. His monitor showed housetops, low buildings, a bomb-wrecked mosque flashing by—and to Lionel it was as if he *was* the missile, as if he were flying over the desert. He always found himself straining forward in his seat, as if to ease the wind resistance, like a diving eagle with its wings folded back. Time seemed to slow. Three seconds seemed like fifteen, twenty seconds. A school flashed by below, an artillery emplacement, a store–

He had just time to flickeringly wonder about the artillery emplacement—would there be one behind the other? Wouldn't that have been his target? But the drone was targeting a building, and there it was. Not obviously a military target. Must be a shell, camouflage of some kind. He adjusted the angle of the missile, tightening on the windows to get the maximum penetration into the target and then the window was rushing at him, and he was crashing through and he had just a glimpse of terrified faces, some of them rather small faces, and then the screen went to the expected white pixilated shashing....

He slumped, shaking with the release of it, knowing the missile had detonated on exactly the target the drone had designated. He would get another commendation for another perfect hit.

But then the monitor image came back on.

That was impossible, wasn't it? The camera and its transmitter unit were both inevitably destroyed on impact.

And the image—he rocked back in his seat, staring...

The televised-image unit seemed to have somehow separated whole from the missile, and fallen to a corner of the shattered room, where it was lodged in the rubble, still transmitting. The angle was skewed, from down low, but the image was clear enough.

There was a dark eyed woman on fire, screaming, clawing at the air, and a man with a beard, who must be her husband, gouting blood from the stump of his arm as he knelt weeping near the body of a little girl, the child blown in half, convulsing as she died, her mouth open, bubbling blood, and there was someone else running around the smoking socket of the room in the background, an older woman perhaps, she was on fire, running back and forth, now falling so he could see only her feet jerking there in the corner of the screen—and there was the remains of a young man splashed against the wall, and the screaming, the distinct, clearly amplified screaming–

"Corporal! Corporal Billingsgate! Yo!"

Mercer was shouting in his ear, yanking the headset off, pulling the chair away from the station. The lieutenant reached over and switched the computer monitor off.

"Billingsgate *stop screaming!* Snap out of it, goddammit!"

Lionel looked at him. "I'm..." The screams! "...not screaming sir! They..." The screaming, the screaming! "They're screaming, not me, they won't stop screaming..."

"Look, once in a while there's a freak chance, the transmitter makes it through the blast, keeps transmitting for a minute... but there's no sound dammit, it's all in your mind!"

"No sir, they're..." Screaming, still screaming, "...they're..." Screaming!

"Billingsgate!" Mercer slapped him. "Stop it! Stop screaming!"

But that wouldn't make the screaming stop, since it wasn't him screaming. Why did they keep saying, over and over, that it was him screaming?

Why couldn't they hear the screaming?

ASIA MARSH

NEDDAL AYAD

To: molly.loftus@ourlady.quinsigamond.edu
From: gdv@hushmail.com
Subject:<no subject>
Date sent: Thu, 7 Oct 2004 05:16:17 -0400

Molly,

    Jesus, this whole thing has been a mess. I need to get this out now. I can see them: their slick flabby skin; their stubby, greasy fingers; their tongues moving like slugs over bloated lips, beaks snapping, claws clacking.

    Someone needs to see this. If not you then some spook or sysadmin or some twitchy hacker kid. And pass it on. Or something.

    I woke up and the room smelled like sweat and mold and her. I don't know what's between the walls here. I don't want to know. I can't stop blinking. It's just becoming light and the room looks sickly. It's just me, the computer, and the television. I've been watching a lot of soft-core porn with the sound off. I don't know why, but it's relaxing. It must be the rhythm. Maybe the strobing from the TV in this pale blue light helps the strobing behind my eyes. The computer doesn't help, but there's nothing I can do about that now.

    I want to crawl into bed. Did you know that this hotel is built over an old fort? One of the garrisons was almost wiped out by cholera. Mollaria, I wonder what they did with the bodies? Did they dump them in the pond below Gibbet Hill? Are they in the yard at the Cathedral? Is it their bones that wash onto Queen's Road every Spring? Or are they still here, beneath the hotel, under the pool maybe? After the fort was razed, they built a hospital on the grounds. By the 20's the place was a sanatorium, now it's a hotel. How may people have died between these walls?

Ok, I'm losing the thread here. Let me try again. This job, there wasn't supposed to be any fucking around. Caroline gave me the file and said they wanted it done quick and clean. Easy for them to say. I got into town yesterday morning. After I hit the hotel the first thing I did was take a walk by the harbor. From the plane, everything looked amazing; the water was that beautiful shadowy shade of blue; the quartz in the cliffs sparkled and shimmered, the stewardess' eyes were incandescent.

The harbor. I took a walk by the harbor. Outside the narrows everything is fine. Inside, it's gone to hell. They still haven't dealt with the sewage. There aren't even any gulls living down there any more. The smell by the docks is putrescent. There's a crust of shit and other waste peppered with used condoms and bones. It looks like the harbour is blocked with diseased ice, the boats plowing through the scum and filth like parasites in a rotten bowel. The buildings downtown are dingy and drab, the people pallid and just generally fucked. What happened here? I haven't been gone that long, have I?

Back to the job. Quick and clean. And it was, almost. The girl was working at that strip joint next to the fortune teller's place. I set up on the roof of the building across the street. The worst thing was the smell from the harbor. I knew I was going to be out there for a couple of hours at least, so I brought some tiger balm. Can you believe it? She slipped out the side door close to midnight. I figured she was dodging out for a smoke, but some guy came out with her. She was worse off than they thought. I don't know if it was the smell or if I was in a bad mood or what but I did them both. She was facing me with her back to the wall. It's almost like she knew . . . when I had the shot lined up she looked right at me and smiled. She was pretty . . . but there was something strange about her and I don't mean strange like most of the people I come across. Her face, the proportions were a bit off. Her eyes were big and just a little too far apart. Her nose was just a little too flat, set a bit too high. And her mouth was just a little too wide. Her teeth were . . . never mind about her teeth. She went down with that smile, almost a smirk. I don't think the guy knew what to do. He just stood there. I clipped him before he had a chance to turn around. Then I left. The girl's name, the name they gave me anyway, was Asia Marsh.

I still can't stop blinking. It's very disorienting. I thought the longer you stared at a computer screen, the less you blinked? Maybe not, I think a lot of things. A fog had slipped in the time it took me to tear down the rifle. You know how the fog can be here. I've always loved the fog, the way it makes everything hazy and indistinct. And it made a good cover. I mean, it's not like the hotel was far, five minutes tops, but you never know who's around and every little bit helps.

When I got back to the room I got a drink and sat in the dark for a while. I'm on the third floor facing Kingsbridge, I can see Queen's from here. I sat there for an hour or more. I thought I heard sirens a couple of times and I should have been able to see the lights from the cruisers, but there was nothing. I must have drifted off 'cause I was face down at the table when I heard someone trying the door. Whoever they were, they must have been big 'cause they just about rattled the bloody thing from its hinges. I grabbed my Glock and ducked into the bathroom. In these rooms, the bathroom is just to the left of the entrance. If they knocked the door down they would have had to come right past me.

After the first big shake the ... Jesus ... did that wall just move? I'd like to get my hands on the asshole who designed this building; the walls are all at slightly odd angles. They don't quite match up, like Hill House or something. I swear that the corner of the room near the window is at an obtuse angle. Anyway, the door. Whoever it was tried a second time, same crazy shaking, but this time there was a horrible fishy musky smell. They kept at it for about thirty seconds, then there was a big bang, like something falling over, then more of the breathing and a strange scraping sound, then nothing. I took a quick look though the peephole but couldn't make out much. It was smeared with some kind of gelatinous substance.

I was debating whether to go out and take a look around when there was a light knock at the door. I took a quick look through the hole and saw a hand coming toward me. On the second knock the peephole was clean and standing in front of the door was Asia Marsh, with a small, but slightly puckered hole just over her right eyebrow. There was no blood.

I opened the door. What else was I supposed to do? She slipped into the room without saying a word. She closed the door behind her and locked the bolt and chain. Then she turned and looked at me. I realized why her eyes looked so big through the scope; her lids were malformed, I don't think she could close them properly. Not that anyone would notice. Her eyes were a luminescent sea-green flecked with gold. She held me with those eyes.

She walked up to me and licked my neck. He tongue felt like it was covered by millions of little suckers. I couldn't move. She undid my shirt and pushed me onto the bed. She straddled me and pulled a scalpel out of her boot. It's funny, but all I could think at the time was, "I hope she doesn't cut in circles." She rolled over onto her side and ran the dull edge of the scalpel across my throat, just under my stomach, and down my thighs. Then she looked at me and smiled. With her rows of teeth.

She pulled up her shirt and showed me her stomach. She had a tattoo around her navel. It was an extremely detailed representation of what looked like a starfish with an eye in the center. Her navel made up part of the pupil of the eye. The arms seemed to ripple across her stomach with every breath. I've never seen ink like that before. It looked like the design had been scarred in then colored.

She licked my throat again. That was when I noticed the smell, like seaweed at low tide. It made me think of all the time I spent poking through tidal pools as a kid. She rolled on top of me again and cut off my shirt. She pushed down hard with her hips and started to shimmy and shake.

She brought up the scalpel and cut into the skin just below my breastbone. She had a light touch, and each stroke tickled and tingled. She cut just deep enough to bring the blood to the surface, licking each incision clean as she finished. She kept her head down and wherever her hair fell across my chest my skin prickled. She made the air boil. Finally she sat back, tilted her head to the side, and brought the scalpel to her red red lips.

I still couldn't move.

She bent over and whispered into my ear, her breath hot and sticky, "You're mine." She tossed her hair, gave me that smirk, and slid off the bed. I just lay there, head spinning, too drained to move. I don't remember her leaving.

I don't remember. I don't remember. The fog outside is getting thicker and the walls are starting to bend. After she left . . . did she leave? She must have. After she left I lay there in the dark. A slurping, slapping sound started in the hall, moving toward my room. Do you remember that story I told you about the octopus that jumped its tank? The sound reminded me of that, of that octopus dragging itself across the laboratory floor. The sound stopped outside my room and that fishy, musky smell came back.

I was still kind of shaky but I got up and fumbled for the Glock. There was labored phlegmy breathing and some mumbling. The cuts pulsed and ached. I'd forgotten about them. I leveled the gun at the door. The slurping and mumbling got louder. I was about to shoot when an insistent bleating started from the other side of the hall, the side toward the fire escape.

For a minute it almost sounded like the bleaters and the slurpers were arguing. Those sounds, they were awful. Then everything went quiet. Someone or something tried the door. When it didn't give there was more bleating and slurping and I couldn't take it anymore.

I started shooting. The door splintered. The bleating and slurping things bleated and slurped. The smell got stronger. I reloaded and emptied the second clip. There was bleating, slurping, screaming, and oozing. One of the things sent an appendage through what was left of the door. It slithered and slipped toward me and Asia's star throbbed and burned and the thing hissed and bubbled and the others spit and clacked their beaks and the room shook and I screamed and . . .

The fog is inside the room and it has brought word from Asia.

Molly, I'm sorry.

A TALENT FOR TROUBLE

RACHEL GRAY

I WAS HEADING HOME FROM Columbia when I felt it—that chill on the back of the neck, or tingle up on the spine, whatever you want to call it. We've all had it.

It wasn't a particularly warm night, especially for September. The wind bit at my exposed fingers and face. But I knew the difference between being cold, and that familar dread feeling. I'd had it often enough.

For New York City, the street was unusually quiet. Filling the void left by the omnipresent city noises, there was an odor. It seemed even more pungent than usual—a cross between week-old garbage and rotten meat. Which might explain the scant amount of people about.

I kept my pace casual, senses on high alert. About twenty or thirty feet back, I'd picked up a tail who accompanied me since I'd left the university.

Finally, I slowed, making a show of adjusting my backpack strap, which had been annoying me anyway. The action paid twofold. I fixed the bothersome strap, and stole a good look over my shoulder.

A dark form trudged down the avenue. He looked young. With a hood drawn over his face, there was little to see. His hands were stuffed into his pockets and shoulders drawn inward from the cold. This worked together to provide him with the exaggerated appearance of a slight build.

So maybe he looked suspicious. A little creepy. But he just wasn't the kind of kid I worried about . What I had my eye on was the tall, gangly creature stalking him.

Turning down 112th Street to make sure I was not in sight, I quickly ducked behind a dent-riddled aluminum waste can. The kid stomped past, oblivious to the world around him. I snorted. *Normals* didn't possess the senses of a Guardian, so they never knew what type of trouble was following them. Which was why Guardians watched over them. Protecting their sorry human lives.

The creature shambled past. I hadn't seen the type before. A long, dark coat hid most of its form. It made use of its abilities to conceal the rest. Normals never saw these creatures the way they really were. But I sensed the differences—the monster that lurked beneath seemingly innocuous flesh.

The creature continued tracking the unwitting human. Stealthily, I crept up behind it and wrapped my arm around its throat. My other hand clamped where its mouth should be. A risky move, and a good way to lose a finger or two if it didn't have the standard physiology. But worth the risk.

Thrashing, its yellowed claws flailed about, trying to break free. Keeping a creature pinned while attempting to snap its neck was never easy. Engaging in the process quietly added a new level of complication. But this was the type of scenario I was trained to deal with, and, given the situation, I thought I was doing a bang-up job of it.

Just as I was about to wrench to creature's neck, the unwitting human whirled around to face us.

"What the hell are you doing?" he said. He pushed his hood down, revealing a mop of sandy brown hair.

Startled, I nearly lost my grip. I was certain that I had been mouse-quiet, and had ensured the creature's complicity in that as well. So what alerted the kid?

While repositioning my hold, I wracked my brain. Monsters I was trained to deal with. Humans were harder.

Finally I gave him a broad smile. "Sorry. My uncle's downed a few too many tonight." Sure, it was lame, but that was all I could come up with. "Gonna get him home so he can sleep it off." I knocked the creature back off its feet, dragging it toward 112th. Less than thrilled, it snarled in response.

The kid moved close. His eyebrows scrunched together. "I know you. You're in my Calc 2 class, with Boreman."

Damn. "Don't think so, kid. I'm not the college girl type." Keeping my hand locked over its mouth, I pulled harder on the creature, trying to speed things up a little. It attempted to growl but the sound was muffled, hopefully just sounding like an argumentative drunk uncle.

"If that thing is your uncle, then you definitely got your genes from the other side of the family." He frowned and peered closer. "Is that a snout?"

I stopped moving. "You can . . . see him?" That wasn't possible. Normals didn't see these creatures for what they were.

He looked annoyed. "Of course I can see him," he said slowly. "I see both of you. You're right in front of me."

"That's not what I mean. What does he look like to you?"

The kid peered closer. "I don't know, like a dog with a really bad complexion."

I shook my head, feeling almost dizzy. This couldn't be. It just wasn't right. "What are you?" I managed.

"Excuse me? What am *I*? I'm someone who's walking home, minding my own business, when I hear someone. Think I'm about to get mugged. I turn around to find you and Dog Pizza Face Man in a wrestling contest. So who are *you*?"

I shook my head, exasperated. This was a puzzle that needed time, and the creature continued to struggle against my hold. I had more immediate issues to deal with.

Taking a deep breath, I intoned a few words of power.

A sharp wind shot down Amsterdam, boring into me like a thousand tiny needles. Swept upon it was a heavy, dark fog that settled down along the avenue. The kid's form was swallowed by a swirling, black mist.

"What the hell?" the boy exclaimed. As if he knew I was responsible for this somehow. I sighed with relief. The kid might be able to see through the creature's disguise, but I still had a trick or two that worked on him.

The time for pondering the kid's abilities would have to come later. Now I needed to get the creature out of sight, as well as dead. By the time the fog cleared and the kid was done searching, the two of us would be long gone.

◆ ◆ ◆

"So what did he look like?" My dad asked.

I was sitting on one of the creaky plastic chairs in the tiny apartment kitchen. Everything was very yellow. My dad thought that yellow was cheery and uplifting. To me, the kitchen was dingy and tired. The teapot let loose a heated scream, demanding attention. My father pulled himself over to the stove to attend to it. His steps were stiff and filled with pain.

"Tall," I said, "Gangly. Coarse brown fur and long claws. Looked a little like a dog with an acne problem," I added reluctantly.

My father dropped tea bags into cracked, white cups, pouring in hot water. I knew it wasn't in my best interest to have tea so late, but I was far too wired to start thinking about sleep. My dad, well, he had probably gotten himself worked up the moment school let out. He hated when I had late classes, and my getting home over an hour late got him anxious all the more. But there aren't a lot of quick, convenient methods of disposing of monsters in this town. Plus I lost my cell phone weeks ago.

"Not the creature, Maya." He bobbed each tea bag up and down. "The kid. You said he was in your class?"

"Don't start. I discover a new creature that we haven't seen on the streets before, and all you're worried about is whether I can score a date."

"I don't see that one takes anything away from the other." Smirking, he removed the tea bags, setting them aside. He returned to the table and passed a cup over to me.

"I didn't take much note of his appearance. I was too busy trying to figure out why the creature didn't look like a human to him. And I think he sensed it stalking him." I blew on the tea, tendrils of steam swirling from the cup.

"Well, if he's in your Calc class, maybe you could try talking to him, find out. Maybe go to a movie or something."

"This is serious," I said. "Besides, he's a Normal."

For that remark, I got the *I-know-better-than-you* look. "They're not all bad, Maya," he said, placing an enormous hand over mine.

I pulled away.

He always came back to it, wanted to talk about it. Deal with it. I didn't.

The image flashed into my head. The one I saw every night before I went to sleep. Pale, ice-white flesh. Lips edged with blue. Eyes open wide, staring beyond me.

I was the one who identified the body. Dad had been out of town on a Guardian job. That image was carved into my brain. She was always staring beyond me, at something I could not see. I wanted to know what it was.

My mom had been walking home from work and stumbled across a few young teens that had gotten mixed up with the wrong type of people. People who weren't . . . people. Stupid kids had no idea what they were in for, so my mom stepped in to help. They saw what she was capable of. Her abilities. Suddenly, *she* became the monster.

I put the cup to my lips, but angry spirals of steam warned me away. "I protect them, Dad. I do my job."

I shook my head to clear the wisps of memory.

"He can't be a Normal, anyway," I continued. "Not with his abilities."

"The Guardian Affinity has records on every Guardian family going back thousands of years. New Guardians don't just appear out of nowhere . . . you know that."

Drumming my fingers on the teacup, I said, "I'll see what I can find out about the kid. Meanwhile, the creature I described. You ever seen something like that?"

His brow furrowed. "Sounds like it might be a ferratox."

"Never heard of it."

"They're not native to this area. Usually they're found in rural communities. They're pack hunters by nature and don't stray far from their nest. So a single ferratox wandering about New York . . . probably means a nest of them nearby. Also means that someone brought them here, most likely to hunt down a target."

"The kid?"

Dad shook his head. "Unlikely. Ferratox are normally used in packs. It's more likely that your new friend just looked like a tempting dinner."

"So maybe you can get some more information from your Guardian contacts." I slapped my hand on the formica table, sending tea sloshing. "Meantime I'll locate the ferratox nest and destroy it."

"I don't know if that's such a good idea, Maya. An entire nest of ferratox is too much for one girl to handle."

"Girl," I huffed. "Ignoring that for now. As for the ferratox, we can't wait long on this. Next time one of these things finds a tasty-looking human snack on the streets after dark, I might not be around to break its neck. You want to worry about anything, worry for them. Once I'm done, there won't even be enough to make a pair of fur slippers out of their sorry hides."

Dad smiled, but his eyes were tinged with flecks of sorrow. A knee injury had put him out of commission for any serious street work. Now it was just me. I don't know what bothered him most—me going it alone, or him not going at all.

As for the job, I wasn't worried. A nest of ferratox wouldn't give me much trouble. For the time being, I thought I'd see what I could dig up on this innocent young kid from my Calculus class.

I was the first to admit that my skills were not in the information-ferreting department. That was always my dad's thing. But finding out about someone without even a name to go on was next to impossible. University resources were useless without a name. Sharing a class didn't help either, since it only met once a week. I didn't know anyone from Calculus—not surprisingly, I never got around to making friends.

I mulled over the problem during my afternoon shift waitressing at Risotti's. Knowing its members couldn't spend time saving the world if they were busy with day jobs, the Guardian Affinity paid Guardians a small stipend. Even offered health insurance. But they didn't pay for me to go to school. I had a full scholarship, but I still had plenty of books to buy and fees to pay. The diner, only two blocks from campus, made for an easy commute.

So it was as I was wiping down tables and contemplating my next move when the kid walked right in the front door of Risotti's. Sliding into a booth, he glanced about. Looking for someone. Looking for me.

I gaped at him. He calmly returned my stare.

After regaining my composure, I grabbed a coffee pot from the warmer, casually striding over to his table.

"We need to talk," he said, waving the coffee pot away.

"How did you find me?"

"Asked a few of our Calc classmates if they knew anyone who liked to hang out with monsters and make black fog appear out of nowhere."

"Hush!" I glanced about, but no one was paying him any mind. After all, it was New York.

"No one knew much about monsters, but it turns out several folks have seen you around. Couple of people had seen you at the diner, so I thought I'd give it a try. My name's Owen Clifton." He extended a hand.

I didn't accept it. "Hold a sec." I headed back to the counter.

Snatching two slices of coconut cream pie from the fridge, I gestured to Moe Risotti that I was going to take a break. He scowled in return. Which was as close as I would get to an approval.

Back at the table I settled into the booth across from Owen, sliding a slice of pie his way. He grimaced. "I just ate."

"This is Moe's best." I pushed it closer. "Try to look like you're actually here to have some food, and not to question me."

He picked up a fork and poked at a corner of the narrow, fluffy slice of fleeting, high calorie happiness that only Moe could create. "First question would be your name. You've got mine."

I sighed. It's not like he wasn't going to find out anyway. "Maya Toupalou."

His eyebrows lifted, but he refrained from remarking upon my last name. Most people couldn't help themselves. "Okay, Maya. What was that *thing* you were cavorting around with last night?"

I tried to chuckle but it came out more like a cough. "I know he was drunk, but it's not nice to call my uncle a *thing*."

Owen scowled. "We both know that wasn't your uncle."

"Look, kid. I don't know what you think you saw. Maybe you had a few too many yourself, but-"

"Drop it," he snapped, slamming his fork to the table. The people in the next booth turned around, glaring. "Since yesterday my world's turned upside down. I don't understand what I saw. I think at the least you could give me an explanation."

I pondered it. I could tell him whatever I wanted—the Guardian Affinity didn't have a confidentiality policy. Talk of supernatural creatures and magic spells was enough to get a person tossed in the looney bin, especially since Normals couldn't see the creatures in question. Well, normal Normals, anyway. I glared at Owen.

"All right. You want the truth, I'll tell you. Not like you'll believe me." I took a deep breath. "That *thing* you saw. It was one of many different types of creatures, some of which you have heard of. Some not. Sometimes they make their way into stories, mythologies, urban legends. That kind of thing."

Owen frowned. "What are you talking about, like the Boogeyman? Vampires? Werewolves?"

I snorted. "No such thing as werewolves. Don't know who came up with that one."

"But the rest, then."

"Mostly, yeah. They stick to night, to the shadows. Easier to get around when you look like a . . . what did you call it . . . Dog Face Pizza Man. But the creatures also possess an innate ability to manipulate their appearance."

"What do you mean, manipulate?" Gingerly, Owen raised the tiniest smidgen of pie to his mouth, and nibbled on the edge.

"I guess the best way to describe it is a sort of *psychic* energy that most Normals can't see. But it's all around us, and affects how we perceive the world."

Owen's brows furrowed further.

No one ever said I was good at explaining this supernatural stuff—just destroying it. I sighed and put down my fork.

"Okay. So you know how you can see certain wavelengths of light. Anything in the visible spectrum. You can't see the rest—ultraviolet, and infrared. But it's still there, affecting the world around you. This is the same kind of thing. Just another force of the universe we don't yet comprehend. Magic, psychic powers. ESP. Whatever. Those are all names people use for it, but they all refer to that same energy."

Rubbing his chin, he said, "Assuming I go along with this. Why can certain people see this stuff, and not others?"

"Some humans have a genetic trait. It's passed down from one generation to another, allowing us to detect and manipulate this energy. Possessing the trait isn't enough. You have to be trained to use the ability. Over the years, these families formed an alliance called the Guardian Affinity. They assist with training, and help protect the rest of humanity—Normals. Normals like you." I paused to take a bite, reveling in a moment of coconut cream goodness.

"There's another group known as the Lowers," I continued. "They possess the trait, but either choose not to use it, or use it for more nefarious purposes."

With a heavy sigh, Owen said, "Thought I could prepare myself for anything, after what I saw last night. But this . . . is too much." He sliced off a larger wedge of pie with his fork. "At least you're right about the pie."

"Like I said. Doesn't matter what I tell you." Actually, the kid seemed to be taking it rather well.

"So, what, your whole family does this? You're all monster-fighting protectors of humanity? "

I glanced across the restaurant. The booths and tables were crowded with people, conversations and laughter mixing together into a soft, jingling melody. "Not so much. We used to be a team, until my mother passed away. My dad injured his knee not long after. It's just me, these days."

"You can't fix his knee with magic, or that energy, or whatever you call it?"

I shook my head. "It's not that kind of energy. You can change how someone perceives things." A short laugh escaped me, far too harsh and loud. "If he were a Normal, I could make him think that the pain had gone away. But it would require a lot of work to maintain. And as a Guardian, he'd know better." I slid my plate away. "Enough questions, I would think."

"One thing that doesn't make sense," he said. "If Normals can't see these things, how can I?"

"Can't explain that one," I admitted. "The Affinity tracks everyone who has the trait—both Guardian and Lower. You're not either."

"So their records aren't right. Or maybe your secret society has some of its facts wrong about who can see what."

Scowling, I said, "I'll take their word over yours."

"Look. I'm not trying to shake up your whole world, here. Just trying to understand how I fit into it, or how you fit into mine." As if to appease me, he made a show of taking another bite. "That creature from the other night. Is it dead?"

"Yes. But there are more."

"So, what's our plan?"

I grunted. "*Our* plan? Last time I checked, I barely knew you. Did that change?"

"Why not let me help? I might not have your fancy Guardian training, but I can still see them. That's got to be worth something."

"This isn't some video game, Owen. You get hit by one of these things, that's it. You're done."

"Please, Maya." His hand snaked across the table, as if to take mine. I was too fast for him. "I need to be involved in this. I need to understand it. Let me help."

I stared at Owen, recognizing the emptiness in him, a gap he needed to fill. But this was a dangerous way to fill it.

When I didn't respond, he added, "Hey, at the least, you can use me as bait."

The kid had a point there. There wasn't time for any real training, but maybe enough to allow him to serve as a decoy and not get himself killed.

I shook my head in disbelief. *These solo ops must really be getting to me, if I'm actually considering the idea of bringing a Normal along.*

I narrowed my eyes at him. "We'll see."

Of course, my dad had to investigate Owen thoroughly before the kid was allowed to accompany me anywhere. Which meant inviting him to the apartment and grilling him about family history and future plans. Clearly a plot designed more to measure Owen's date potential, and less his mission readiness. Not to mention a great opportunity for my father to show off his wicked tea-making skills.

Once Owen checked out, I spent the day teaching him some defensive moves. I also tried to teach him how to walk without sounding like he had cement in his shoes.

That evening, he followed me, more quietly, back to 112th and Amsterdam for a bit of recon. "So what are you studying at Columbia, anyway?" he asked. *Still not quietly enough.* "Do they have a metaphysics department I haven't heard about? Or are you studying chemistry in the hopes of inventing that perfect spell?"

"I told you. Spells are energy based. Chemistry wouldn't help. I'm a math major."

"How does math help?"

"It doesn't. I just like math."

Owen halted. "You're kidding, right? No one *actually* likes math. Besides, you can't do anything with a math degree. I guess you could teach, maybe."

I kept walking. "I'm a Guardian," I said over my shoulder. "I can't do anything with *any* degree. So I picked what I like. I like math."

"That's a rather fatalistic approach," he continued, picking up his pace. "Since I know you were wondering, I'm leaning toward fine arts, myself."

"Fine arts. And you're giving *me* lectures," I scoffed. "Guess you could teach, maybe."

"I'm heading toward something, even if I don't know what, yet. You could do the same. Go work for a university. Do your Guardian thing part-time. But instead, you'll be the only Guardian running around solving Calculus equations in your head."

We approached the intersection where we had encountered the ferratox. The street was quiet this time of night, glowing pale yellow-white under flickering storefront lights. I rummaged in my leather jacket. Extracting a clump of ferratox fur I saved from our unfortunate friend, I closed my fist around it, extending my hand in front of me.

I started to chant.

"Hey," Owen said.

Stopping, I glared at him. "Not like I'm in the middle of anything, here."

"Sorry. I was just wondering why you have to recite anything if it's energy based."

"It helps me stay focused," I snarled. "Now shut up."

Owen's mouth flattened into a hard line. I started my intonation again.

Opening my eyes, I saw the glow shimmering from underneath my clamped fingers. The light grew. Soon it became a pulsing, blue-white globe enveloping my hand. It crackled and fizzled with an electric energy.

Barking a final command I snapped my wrist forward. The glowing ball exploded, sending a streak of light shooting down the street.

At 116th it whipped around the corner.

"What is that?" Owen gaped. The bluish trail hung in the air like a line of neon.

"A tracking spell. It will show us the path the ferratox used to get here." Which Owen shouldn't be able to see. Not sure why, after everything else, I was surprised that he could. "Come on."

Heading north on Amsterdam, we turned down 116th. The glow continued down the street to a worn, crumbling brick building. Most of the windows were haphazardly boarded with thick plywood. The illuminated path washed up against the door in a pulsating cascade of color.

I crept over to one of the open windows, peering inside. The dim light revealed little, but the front room looked clear.

"I'm going to cast a noise-dampening spell. Should allow us to move a bit more freely." *Especially with your clod-hoppers.* "We'll be able to hear beyond its dampening range, but you'll need to stay close, or you won't be able to hear me."

Owen's eyes lit up.

I gave him my best death stare. "You even think about testing the limits of this spell, I'll kill you before the ferratox get a chance."

His expression faded.

I cast the spell, then gave the door handle a good shake. Locked. Withdrawing my lock picks, I had the door jimmied in less than a minute.

"Since you wanted to see how well the dampening field works, why don't you scout?" I shoved Owen toward the door.

He glowered back, but opened it. I pulled out a flashlight and gave the foyer a quick scan. A black and white checker pattern extended across the floor, cracked and scratched. Wisps of cobwebs clung to lampless chandeliers above. A wooden stairway wound upward, and a half-open door led to another room on the left.

I slid over to the door, keeping Owen close behind. Inside was a small office. A rickety wooden desk in the center was swathed in piles of paperwork. I grabbed a few bills from the desk, but they didn't seem particularly useful. Food and supplies, mostly. All addressed to the same guy. Eli Jennings.

The name was like a faint itch tingling at the back of my head. Almost familiar, but I couldn't place it. The bills were addressed to a downtown location I did not recognize.

Stuffing a few bills in my pocket, I surveyed the rest of the room. An ancient rotary telephone perched on a side table. Guess I wouldn't be pulling anything off the caller ID.

A heavy *thud* sounded upstairs.

I flicked out the flashlight. Signaling to Owen, I scurried back to the foyer.

The second floor was now silent.

Creeping up the stairs, I gestured for Owen to follow. We found ourselves in a narrow hallway, doors flanking on either side. Graying wallpaper pulled away from crumbling walls.

A dim, orange glow permeated from underneath a door at the end of the hallway.

As I progressed, I pressed an ear to each door before checking inside. Single-room apartments greeted me, coated in dust and cobwebs.

Inside one of the apartments I found a set of heavy bookends. I hefted one, turning to Owen.

"Looks like our recon op ends here. My gut tells me that we'll find a fat nest of ferratox in that room at the end of the hall. If we're lucky, they're all in there. If we're even more lucky, most of them are asleep. Don't think they've heard us yet, so there's no better time than this." I gripped his shoulder. "Now's when you need to bail, Owen. You won't get another chance."

He took a jagged breath. Then he shook his head.

I gave him the once-over. "That room is full of angry, hungry ferratox. I can handle this without you, but if you stay, you have to be certain."

"I'm sure." His voice crackled, but he gave a resolute nod.

I handed him the bookend and pulled out my grandfather's KA-BAR combat knife.

"You'll need to guard the door. Any of those creatures get past me, club them in the head with that bookend. If you start freaking out, just throw it at their head and run like hell."

His eyes were like planets.

"The dampening spell should help us out, but as soon as I open the door, they'll charge. I'll kick things off with a fireball spell."

Owen frowned. Before he could question me on it, I continued, "Think of it as a mental fireball. It can't harm them. But they won't know that. Oh, and if you feel really warm, or happen to see your clothes are on fire, well, just try to ignore that. Okay?"

With that, I threw the door open.

The dim orange light emanated from a lamp on a desk by the window, illuminating dirt-streaked walls. That pungent, rotten-meat smell rammed its way into my nostrils again. Other than the desk, the room was clear of furniture. Which left plenty of room for the three ferratox asleep on the floor. Two more perched near the window. Upon seeing me, a guttural growl escaped their throats.

I started chanting.

The two creatures started toward me. But mounds of sleepy ferratox blocked their path.

Hearing the disturbance, the three remaining creatures arose, scrambling to their feet, snarling, revealing yellowed teeth like scythes.

I continued my mantra. Still gripping the knife, I spread my hands low and wide. A rope of red-orange flame crackled between them.

The five creatures leapt toward me.

Spreading my hands further, the sizzling ribbon of fire exploded outward, growing into a burning wall. The three nearest creatures were consumed in red-hot flame. Squealing, they reeled about, clawing at singed fur.

I stepped into the room and swung the blade. It connected with leather-thick flesh. Moving forward, I slashed out again.

Two creatures dropped.

Moving past their crumpled bodies, I dodged the writhing flames. The fire might not be real, but it looked—and felt—damn hot. I clenched my teeth and concentrated on getting past my own illusion.

A flaming ferratox stumbled past, howling in agony. I slammed the KA-BAR's heavy wooden hilt into its temple. It dropped.

Back at the door, Owen stood, slack-jawed. The bookend hung limply at his side.

"Owen!" I snapped. "Get it together." I approached the next creature. It had withdrawn into a corner to escape the flames.

The beast slashed at me with razor-sharp claws. I returned the favor with my knife. But the blade fell short.

Hearing noise from behind, I peered over my shoulder. The remaining ferratox was making a break for the door. Owen still stood in the doorway, transfixed.

Dammit. Guess his shoes were filled with cement, after all. There was no way I could reach the creature in time.

And suddenty everything was happening fast and slow all at once—Owen staring, mortified at the ferratox charging full bore. Mouth widening slowly into an expression of terror. Feet still anchored to the ground.

"Move, Owen!" I shouted.

It was too late. The beast barreled into him. Owen hit the floor, the creature collapsing on top.

The ferratox close to me slashed out again. I dodged backward, avoiding damage to my favorite jacket by mere inches. Meanwhile, the other creature scrambled to its feet. It snarled at the crumpled form that now blocked its exit.

Glancing between the two creatures, I assessed the situation. I couldn't take them both out—which meant I had to choose who got to keep their face intact, and who would be scrambled by a set of claws.

I rearranged my grip on the knife. I *was* rather fond of my face. Owen's face, at this moment, not so much.

Oh well.

I spun around and hurled my knife at the ferratox at the door.

It connected with the back of its head with a heavy *thunk*. The creature slid downward and dropped on top of Owen's prostrate form.

Behind me, the ferratox let out a low growl. I turned around just in time to duck another swipe of its claws.

No way to retrieve my knife in time—the creature would be on me.

So I punched the thing in the face.

Must have been a good hit. The beast dropped, dazed, the wood floor rumbling from the impact.

With a few fast steps, I retrieved my knife, and returned to finish off the creature.

Surveying the room, five ferratox lay still, in broken, furry piles. Didn't look like any of them would be standing back up. Once it looked like everything was safe, I went to the doorway and dragged the creature off of Owen.

The kid's eyes were closed, but he was breathing. He'd be okay.

I pulled him into the hallway. He didn't show any signs of coming to.

"Let's go." I slapped him across the face. He started, then rolled his head about groggily. "We need to get out of here in case Eli Jennings returns, or someone shows up to investigate the ruckus. I can't carry you. You're either going to walk down these stairs, or you'll be taking a nasty tumble. After the way you froze up in there, I'm leaning toward the latter."

He got his rubbery legs going enough to stumble down the stairs, and I had us out the door and down the street before Eli Jennings returned home to a nest of dead ferratox.

♦ ♦ ♦

I thought I would hear from Owen the following morning. But he didn't contact me. Nor did he return any of my calls. It wasn't until the following week, heading toward Calc 2, that I caught up to him on his way to class.

A light rain drizzled upon the paved walk. The air smelled sweet. Above, the green leaves were lightly tinged with red and orange. It was going to be an early fall.

"Hey," I said, matching his pace. "Glad to know you're not dead. Could have at least sent me a memo."

He snorted. "Nearly was," he replied. "Guess you were right. A *Normal* like me doesn't belong on a mission like that." He spat the word as if it were acrid. "Figured you'd be done with me anyway, the way I screwed things up."

I nodded. "Yeah, you did mess it up pretty bad. Though you were supposed to keep the ferratox from getting out the door. Technically, you did that. If only as a giant doorstop."

"Thanks for the 'I told you so,' but if you don't mind, I need to get to class early. I've got to ask some questions about the homework. Some of us don't take naturally to math, you know."

I frowned. The happy-go-lucky Owen that I had come to marginally tolerate had disappeared, replaced by this bitter fellow that I tolerated less. "Actually, I came by to tell you that I gave those bills we found over to my dad, the ones addressed to Eli Jennings. He's a Lower who runs a supply shop downtown. Sells weapons that have been . . . enhanced. I guess a new supplier moved into town, not far from here, and started undercutting Eli. So he imported the ferratox, in order to take care of the problem permanently."

The sprinkling rain caused Owen's floppy brown hair to wander in every direction. "Do you know if we . . . if you got all of them?"

I nodded. "The Affinity picked up Eli yesterday. Now he's their problem."

"Great." He kept walking, head down.

"Did I ever tell you about my first mission with my parents?" I grabbed his arm. He scowled, but slowed his pace, if only marginally. "I was sixteen. My parents tasked me with retrieving a cache of sound bombs from the laboratory of this particularly nasty Lower, while they dealt with him."

"Sound bombs?"

"They're these translucent purple globes that capture sound inside. Guardians use them to pass messages. They're also used as weapons—capture a particularly loud sound, you can deafen an enemy."

Owen frowned. "Sounds like you guys should try investing in an MP3 recorder."

"Noted. Anyway, all I had to do was take these things off the shelf and put them in this container, right? I was all cocky and spitfire, as well as completely careless. Climbed up to the shelf, started grabbing these things, lost my balance, and dropped the whole lot of them. Nearly killed my parents." I popped my ears at the memory. "Not to mention I couldn't hear for a week."

"You were sixteen."

"Yeah, and I had six years of training on you at that point." I stopped walking. "You froze your first time out, screwed up big time. That doesn't change the fact that you have a natural talent for this stuff. I don't understand it, but you can see past these creatures' disguises. You have to use that talent, explore it further. A bit more training, and you'll do much better next time."

Owen eyeballed me. "You'd let me go with you again?"

"With more training." I shrugged. "Maybe you help me nab the bad guys, I'll help tutor you in math. See if I have a future teaching this stuff, after all."

Owen grinned. "You get *me* as a partner, and I get math lessons. You're definitely getting the better deal."

"*Partner* might be a bit extreme," I chuckled. "I was thinking *trainee*, or maybe even *fodder*. Never know in the future when I might need another doorstop."

He punched my arm. I punched him back. Harder. Together we headed toward math class.

THE
ECCENTRIC

ALAN DEAN FOSTER

KAREN ROPER HAD BEEN making the rounds in Sighisoara for over a week without encountering a single soul who could introduce her to a werewolf. The generally accepted wisdom that there were no such things as werewolves had not dissuaded her. As a freelance writer who was relentless in her pursuit of the creepy, the bizarre, and the outré, she refused to be discouraged where those who had come before her had given up. Aided and abetted by her good looks, persistence and determination had combined with a competency at writing to provide a good living. The chance to travel to distant-off destinations such as Sighisoara was an added bonus.

Unfortunately, her rambling visit to exotic Romania was turning out to be something of a bust. No novice nuns in remote villages had been considerate enough to endure fatal exorcisms while she was in the country, no mysterious forces had been deemed at work in what was still one of Europe's last primal countrysides. The best she had been able to come up with was a two-part article on some supposedly haunted Roman-era ruins. It had sold, but she had been forced by circumstance (and escalating hotel bills) to accept less than her going rate.

And then, on the verge of giving up and heading back to Bucharest to catch the next plane to Istanbul, she had met up with Bucazu.

He had responded to one of her numerous newspaper come-ons with whispers and insinuations over the phone. "I can show you werewolf, Miss Roper. There is place, special place. In mountain valley. Even authorities don't go there. They afraid since time of Ceasecu. Even before time of Ceasecu."

"It doesn't have to be a, um, 'real' werewolf," she'd told him. "At this point, I'll settle for a suitably ugly and really hairy peasant. A hunchback would be nice. With a third of the remaining real wolves in Europe being here in Romania I can, um, stretch the truth a little."

Either the man on the other end of the line had misunderstood, or else the sardonicism was completely lost on him despite his evident, if quaint, command of English.

"No, Miss Roper. Real werewolf. Like in old legends. But is dangerous."

Well, of course it was dangerous, she had smiled to herself. If it wasn't declared dangerous, a presumably gullible visiting foreigner like herself was unlikely to take the bait. Still, it was something, which was better than the nothing she was finding in and around Sighisoara.

"Okay," she had told him. "I'll take you up on it." She would hazard a last try for material and, with luck, a saleable photo or two before departing for Istanbul in search of contemporary djinn.

Having spent time traveling by herself researching articles in places like Afghanistan and Laos, she was confident she could handle one Romanian huckster. To her surprise, when her guide showed up later that night, it was in a Mercedes. An old Mercedes, to be sure, but not some lingering Communist-era rattletrap, either. Furthermore, Bucazu himself turned out to be a tall, willowy young man with the body of a slender Viking, an impenetrable thicket of black hair that must be the bane of any barber, and the manners of a young European gentleman instead of that of the thrash metal enthusiast a first glance might have suggested. He even opened the car door for her: the back door.

Clutching the bag containing her overnight gear and laptop under her left arm, she paused at the doorway. "I'm hiring you as a guide—not a chauffeur."

"*Va rog*—please forgive me." Shutting the rear door, he opened the front passenger-side door in its stead. "I thought you might feel safer—that is, be more comfortable, in the back."

She almost laughed. After having rattled through Kandahar in the company of three overly attentive AK-47 toting militiamen, she had no fear of being forcefully cuddled by one somewhat skinny young Romanian.

"It's kind of you to think of me, but I'm sure I'll be—comfortable—in the front seat." She tapped her bag. "I might want to take a picture of something."

"Not tonight." He started around toward the other side of the car. "We will arrive in Koska before daybreak. Maybe good picture tomorrow."

She slid in opposite him. Bucket seats and center console made his concern for her person seem even more superfluous. "When do I get to meet your werewolf?"

The Mercedes started up smoothly and pulled away from the hotel entrance. "Tomorrow night is the fullness of the moon. That is why we had to hurry and leave now, tonight. Tomorrow night you will see werewolves."

Though aware that his English was less than perfect, she still blinked. "You mean 'werewolf'."

He looked over at her. For the first time, she was aware of the intensity of his gaze. "No, Miss Roper. 'Were*wolves*'. There are many in Koska. And I think other things of interest to you as well."

"Lots of hairy guys?" she quipped, unable to take him seriously in the slightest.

"You will see," he assured her as the heavy sedan accelerated out onto a main thoroughfare.

Oh well, she thought as she snuggled back into the thick, cushioning seat. Having spent most of her time in Bucharest and Sighisoara, it would be nice to see some more of the countryside before moving on to Turkey.

Determined to stay awake, she had no idea how long she had slept when the slowing of the car revived her. Automatically and surreptitiously, she checked everything of consequence. Her bag lay on the floor by her feet, apparently undisturbed. The same was true of her clothing. Her almost painfully earnest young escort was not looking in her direction when she awoke, his gaze still fixed out the front window.

The village of Koska was charming even at night. Multi-story wooden houses, some of them hundreds of years old, lined the cobblestone street down which they were proceeding. The Mercedes' suspension smoothed out the bumps. At this hour all the street lights had been extinguished to save electricity, but the almost full moon allowed her to make out numerous architectural details and flourishes; everything from elaborately carved wooden lintels to the painted flowers and other traditional designs that decorated the houses. They passed a small market, a real bakery, and the local pharmacy before pulling up before an urbanized country inn. Even at four in the morning and visible only by moonlight, the outside looked like an outtake from Disney's Pinocchio. If the rooms were half as charming as the exterior, she was going to enjoy her brief stay here.

"I leave you now." Bucazu indicated the darkened entrance. "Just ring bell. I phone ahead and tell the innkeeper's family to be expecting an early-arrival guest." He did not quite smile. "These country folk, and they will be up soon with sun anyway, so do not feel you imposing by checking in at this hour."

She nodded, started to get out of the car, hesitated. "You're not coming?"

"Koska is my home. That is how I could promise you werewolf. But only on night of full moon. Tomorrow night." He took a deep breath. "I not nap on way from Sighisoara. Good driver," he finished proudly.

"No argument here," she complimented him. "You'll be wanting to sleep in, then."

"*Da*," he told her. "I will get good rest so that tomorrow night I will be alert and ready to—to show you what you have come to see." He indicated her bag. "I hope you have plenty film in your camera."

"It's digital," she told him. "No film."

"Oh, of course." He shrugged. "When it come to consumer electronics, I afraid I am bit behind the times. Just like my country."

Despite what he had told her about having notified the innkeeper of her arrival, he still waited in the car until the door opened in response to her ring. Polite *and* considerate, she mused thoughtfully. Not bad-looking, either. And he hadn't hit on her, or tried anything while she had been dozing in the car. It might be fun to spend some time with him, she told herself. After interviewing and photographing the werewolf. No, she smiled to herself. Were*wolves*. She would be satisfied with just one approximation.

The heavy wooden comforter-filled second-floor bed was more comfortable than those in any of the hotels where she had stayed the previous weeks. It was noon when she finally woke up. Downstairs, a hearty Eastern European lunch awaited her, served by the innkeeper's wife and pre-teen daughter. The girl in particular was a delight, a small solemn-faced whirlwind bedecked with golden curls, rosy cheeks, and deep blue eyes. Only the jeans and t-shirt, the latter alluding to a Hungarian band she'd never heard of, spoiled the Heidi-esque illusion.

She'd planned to take a stroll around the town, but the long drive the night before combined with the heavy midday meal and thoughts of the overstuffed bed to lure her back to the room. She read herself to sleep, awakening only in time for dinner.

Except there was no dinner. But Bucazu was waiting for her in the tiny lobby, sitting and perusing a magazine opposite the empty, gray stone fireplace. Of the kindly innkeeper and his family there was no sign.

"Full moon tonight." Bucazu's tone was grave. "Everyone in town must take certain precautions."

"Oh, of course." Camera and anticipation at the ready, Karen was eager and willing to go along with the gag. "What about precautions for us?"

"You will be safe with me," he assured her. She had to give him credit for maintaining the artifice. "As I have told you, I live here, so I am known to everyone. Those who be *were* can recognize me even in their altered state. Otherwise it would be dangerous for me, too, to travel alone outside on such a night. Because you are with me, you too will be safe. But stay close. Take all the pictures you want, but do not stray from my side."

If that was a pick-up line, she mused, it was for sure one she had never encountered before.

"All right," she told him. "I'm ready."

"It not dark out, and moon is not up yet."

She shrugged, completely relaxed. "I slept in. Now that I'm awake, I can always kill time with a little window shopping."

"There not much in the way of such things in Koska," he told her. "This town not on any of usual tourist routes. But we can walk if you like."

He was right. Those shops that might have contained interesting crafts or hand-made knick-knacks were closed and shuttered tight for the night. Still, she enjoyed the walk. Until the howling began.

It flat-out chilled her. She had walked past bodies that had been blown to bits by landmines or shredded by glass and shrapnel, had seen the bloated disfigured corpse of a Thai farmer killed by a king cobra, had listened to the wails of women whose children had been murdered in internecine fighting. But none of that, nothing she had seen or heard before, had raised the hackles on her neck like that rolling, rumbling, infinitely *disturbed* howling. It was damn sure no mournful dog.

Until just then, she hadn't even realized she had hackles.

"Jesus!" she muttered.

"Not here," Bucazu responded unpredictably. "Not tonight. Stay close."

The ferociously throaty challenge grew louder as they made their way toward the town square. A relic of medieval times, it was dominated by an equestrian statue of some obscure local military hero surmounting a graven stone base featuring four tinkling spigots. The familiar sound of running water was unexpectedly reassuring. She swallowed hard.

"Over here," her escort told her, intense as ever. "This way."

Leading her to an arched doorway, he produced an iron key seemingly as old as the town itself. She could hear the tumblers clinking like marbles as he turned it in the lock's appropriate recess. Standing close but not trying anything, he leaned down and pointed toward the equestrian fountain. Over the distant line of ragged mountains a bilious moon was leering, casting its curdled luminance across the shadowed cobblestones of the square.

"Watch, wait, and keep quiet," he told her. This time, she offered no clever quip in response. She was not sure she could have done so had she wished, so dry was her throat.

A shape shambled into the square, then another, and another. Some were huge, some merely outsized, others almost diminutive—but never dainty. A few wore clothes, or shards of same, while others were unclad. All were hirsute to the point of shaggy overkill. The fur of some was black, of some brown, and others were splotched or striped in more exotic patterns. They howled and moaned and kicked and scratched. Some fought ferociously, others chased one another around the square. One bounded to the top of the statue—a single clean, unbroken leap of some twenty vertical feet, she estimated—threw back its head, and bayed disdainfully at the still rising moon. No wonder, she thought as she stared, that the town of Koska prepared so carefully for nights on which there was a full moon.

They were *all* werewolves.

A town of werewolves. Real ones, not like cheaply faked Bigfoots or imitation Yetis. Directly in front of her, a pair was breeding. Their mating was rough, primordial, and very, very loud. No one noticed her and her escort, huddled in the deep sheltering darkness of the ancient doorway.

She looked up at her escort in sudden fear; the kind of fear she hadn't felt in years, if ever. "You—you live here, Bucazu, but you're not—you're not . . . ?"

"Not 'were'? Not one of *them*? No," he assured her solemnly. He never seemed to smile, she observed. Living here, she could now understand why. "My family has resided here long time, so the changelings, they tolerate me."

"Why in heaven's name don't you move away? Lord, it would only take one of them to change their mind one night and decide to rip you up for dinner!"

"We have our agreement," he murmured firmly. "I think they find a non-changeling willing to live in their midst something of a novelty." He indicated her bag. "Your camera?"

Omigod—she had been so stunned by the feral, orgiastic sight that she had forgotten what she'd come for. Fumbling frantically at the bag, she whipped out the compact device, made sure the media card was seated, double-checked to make certain the flash was off, and began snapping away. A quick preliminary check of the LCD screen showed that this was no discouraging fantasy—each picture came out, though depending on the available moonlight some were of course sharper than others. What could she ask for the first indisputably authentic, unfaked photo of a genuine, real, honest-to-gypsy-legend werewolf? A million bucks? What could she ask for dozens of such photos? No more gallivanting around the globe in search of obscure, difficult-to-research stories. Not for this girl. After tonight she would be able to gallivant all she wished without having to work, and gallivant in high style.

Standing at her shoulder, Bucazu helpfully pointed out especially dramatic scenes: two female werewolves battling, a pack of youngsters snarling and scrapping as they tore apart a dog unfortunate enough to have wandered onto the square, two adolescents playing tag—by bounding from rootop to rooftop, clearing impossible gaps and incredible distances with each leap.

Notes—she could make notes later. In the morning. No way was she going to be able to sleep. The realization made her turn to her escort; her wonderful, gracious, knowing escort who was going to make her rich. Despite her somewhat limited resources his tip, she decided, would have to be commensurate with the miracle he had wrought for her.

"What happens in the morning?"

"They all turn back, of course. Into normal Koska villagers. Until next full moon. Tomorrow day is all normal—except town doctor is usually very busy. Many cuts and scrapes and bitings to treat. But no disease. The wereblood is very powerful. No sickness here, in Koska."

"This is fantastic, this is great!" she kept mumbling as she snapped shot after shot, pausing only intermittently to check her results on the camera's LCD.

It was when she was switching storage chips that she heard the snarl. It was much closer, much more—intimate—than the canid cacophony that continued to fill the square unabated. Looking up from the camera she saw an enormous wolf, its black fur tipped with silver, the largest she had seen all night. It was staring straight at her, freezing her where she stood, advancing on enormous clawed feet.

"I thought you said," she whispered in abject terror, "I thought you said we would be safe."

His arm went around her shoulders. "Always a bully in any town," he muttered. "Always one who must show himself off. Or maybe he just hungry. Come!"

He half pulled, half pushed her inside, slamming the door behind them. An instant later something slammed into the door with tremendous force. Roper's ears rang from the concussion. The door buckled, albeit slightly. It sounded as if it had been hit by a runaway bus.

She continued to back away, only to bump into Bucazu. He did not appear overly concerned. "Do not to worry. Door is four-hundred year old oak bound with iron. Hinges are forged. Missile might break through, but not wolf."

Sure enough, after several minutes of frustrated howling and screaming, scratching and pounding, the horror on the other side of the doorway went away. From what she could hear through the thick, saving wood, the chorus of hell was still in full swing out on the square, however.

"More pictures?" her concerned escort inquired politely.

Aware that she was shaking badly, she nonetheless nearly broke out laughing. "No. No thank you, Bucazu. I have more than enough. Considerably more than I expected to shoot tonight, if you must know." She steadied herself. "This is unbelievable! A whole village populated by werewolves! Real werewolves, not fakes made up to draw tourists. I can't believe it. Nobody will believe it—until the pictures are authenticated." She turned to face him. "Thank you, Bucazu, thank you! I'm a woman of my word, and you can believe me when I say that I'm going to make this night worth your while!"

"I know," he told her quietly.

"As soon as I can put together an accompanying article, and get the photos emailed and verified as non-fakes, I'll . . . .." She broke off, frowning at him. "What do you mean, 'you know'?"

"I always thought bringing you here would be worth the time I would invest."

"Oh. Oh sure, of course. Anyway, as soon as . . . .." For the second time she broke off. "Bucazu, why are you looking at me—that way?" She tensed, but there was no hint of incipient canid transformation, no indication that her escort was were-anything. But there was also no denying the distinct gleam that had come into his eyes.

For the first time that night, he smiled. He smiled, and she sucked in her breath. She wanted to scream, but could not. No hair sprouted from his face, no fur thrust forth to dimple his neat, perfectly creased clothing. He was unchanged, except for the look that had come into his eyes and the unusually long canine teeth his smile had exposed. Long they were, and sharp, and pointed. At that moment it also struck her that he was not looking at her eyes, or even at her face, but at a site on her body slightly lower down. The camera with its precious and now meaningless pictures fell to the floor as the hand that had been holding it rose reflexively to her neck.

"You have no idea, my beautiful and vibrant Miss Roper," he told her sorrowfully as he came toward her, hands outstretched and teeth gleaming, "how *lonely* it is for me here."

HEAR NO EVIL

SHANE JIRAIYA CUMMINGS

HE AWOKE TO A world of crushing silence.

He cracked open his eyes as though they were encrusted from years of disuse, and squinted at the harsh artificial light. The whole room was blurry and white.

Raising his arm, he noticed a thin tube snaking into his vein. He watched with sick fascination as droplets of clear liquid trickled down the length of the sinuous, coiled tube and disappeared somewhere under his skin.

He gagged, but nothing rose from the pit of his stomach. His airways burned as he sucked in a deep breath. His mouth was dry, his tongue swollen and leaden.

The length of his body was weighed down, pinned by lethargy. His limbs ached, but everything was pretty much intact. Except he couldn't hear a single sound.

The silence was terrible.

The unforgiving light soon subsided, bringing the room into focus.

He was in a bed, that much was clear. Crisp white linen held his torso and legs taut. A heavy curtain, the color of autumn green, rained down from ceiling to floor. It enclosed the space around his bed.

His eyes wandered again to the tube in his arm. He followed its transparent line to a plastic sack, half-filled with more clear liquid. He tugged his arm a little, aware of the needle embedded under his skin. The sting was a sharp reminder this was all real.

His hand brushed something plastic on the bed. Arching his stiff neck, he found it was a small controller with a single red button.

A cough escaped his chest, rattling up his burning esophagus. His heart thumped harder as the coughing fit turned into a prolonged spasm. The sound of the wracking cough failed to reach his ears. Its absence left him terrified and violated.

Like his racing heartbeat, the coughing rose through his skull as vibrations. Vibrations, but no sound. He reached for the controller near his hip. An unexpected spasm bounced the controller from his groping fingertips and off the bed. He never heard it hit the floor.

He fought to gain control of his cough. Once he did, he calmed himself by taking deep breaths. Every breath was fire and needles.

Exploring his face with a tentative hand, he discovered the coarse texture of bandages. He gingerly followed the line of the bandages to the side of his head. His ears were covered. They were hot under the binding mound.

He breathed a deep, painful sigh, also silent to his bandaged ears. Logic seeped back through his fears. He was in a hospital and his ears were wrapped in bandages. He couldn't hear anything for that reason. The thought was oddly comforting.

In a bid to regain the lost controller, he strained over the side of the bed. Agony wracked his stiff joints and muscles as he dipped his head closer to the floor. The smell of jumbled disinfectants flared in his nostrils.

The heavy curtain flew back, startling him. He hung limp over the side of the bed, squinting up at the figure of a petite woman standing in the fresh light. The sights of a hospital ward played out behind her—more green curtains, the glimpse of an identical bed across the room. Moving to his side, she placed a firm, pleasantly warm hand on his ribs, helping him back into bed.

Her tight-fitting uniform and hat proclaimed her a nurse. A tidy crop of raven-black hair was a sharp contrast to her crisp white clothes. She was probably in her late twenties. And cute. Her mouth moved quickly around a crooked smile. He had no idea what she was saying. His world was deathly silent, save for the steady beat of his heart.

She noted his bewildered look and curled her lips into a laugh, or so he thought.

Deftly moving to the base of the bed once he was settled, she picked up a small rectangular board and pen. With economical strokes, she wrote something on the board and held it up to him.

Hi Mr. Blaine, my name is Nurse Stevenson

A meager wave of his hand was all he could muster.

She rubbed at the mini whiteboard, then scribbled something else.

You were in an accident but you are OK

He closed his eyes and expelled a painful sigh. He hadn't tried to recall what happened. Why he was here. Now he focused his memory.

He was a welder. A good one. He remembered his last day at the site. They were putting up the skeleton of a mall on the edge of town. One of those suburban super-complexes where middle-class teenagers flock for their mindless entertainment.

On the mall site, he'd just finished welding some girders. In the background he heard two of the apprentices messing around. If they were his apprentices, he would have kicked their butts for clowning around. As it was, he took the time to raise his mask and shoot them a glare, before getting back to the task at hand. He remembered hearing them ignite a blowtorch, mere paces away from the gas tanks.

The fireball rocked the site; it was the loudest thing he'd ever heard. The boys were blown apart before his eyes, an instant before he was thrown skyward. The whole thing happened in a single heartbeat. Then everything went black.

"How long have I been here?" The words croaked from his lips. His rusty vocal chords worked but he hadn't a clue if the words were loud enough for Nurse Stevenson to hear. She inclined her head, seeming to ponder the question. At least she heard him.

A few seconds later, she held the whiteboard up again.

About a week

"What about my hearing?" he croaked.

She nimbly wiped her last words from the board and wrote a new sentence.

Your hearing will return soon. I will get the doctor.

The relief rippled through him with a sigh, despite his burning throat.

A scream rang through the room. The scream was blood-curdling, knifing a chill through his body. It was a long way away, but he heard it with horrifying clarity.

"What was that?" He arched his head to the side, listening for the scream again.

Nurse Stevenson seemed unaware of the scream that was still echoing in his ears. Her mouth flapped in rapid succession but he heard nothing. Registering his blank look, she returned to the whiteboard.

What is it?

"I heard a scream," he said far too loudly, pinioning her with searching eyes.

That is impossible Mr. Blaine. You are deaf, she wrote.

He continued turning his head from side to side. The world was now cocooned in silence once more.

"I . . ." he stammered, his voice dead to his own ears.

I didn't hear anything . . . I will get the doctor, the board read. The nurse vanished through the curtain.

Time passed. Blaine pulled into himself, balling his body under the sheets. He tuned his focus to listening for more sounds. Screams. Any sounds at all. He was deaf, of that he was certain. And yet that scream, that awful scream, was as real as the nose on his face. Why didn't the nurse hear it?

Unable to maintain his vigil, he yielded to sleep.

A firm shake ended his dozing. A tall man in a white coat continued to shake his arm. There was something about his eyes, they were too guarded. He didn't like the man—the doctor. It was irrational, but the feeling lingered.

The tall doctor, a dark man of sharp lines and even sharper cologne, moved to the end of the bed and took the small whiteboard in hand. In scrawling style, he wrote:

Hello. I am Doctor Radisich.

Blaine propped himself up to face the doctor at close to eye level. The pain was still there, but lessening each time he tried his neglected muscles. He wasn't an invalid, despite the hospital and the deafness. In front of this doctor, he needed to prove it.

His resilience and stamina had always been his strong points. He was a veteran of the Amity Valley Football Club. He tested his physical limits through extreme sports, like rock-climbing and dirt-biking.

"Doctor." The word spilled from his lips in an over-loud tone.

Save your words Mr. Blaine, you are shouting, wrote Doctor Radisich.

"Sorry," he whispered, too softly this time.

You were involved in an accident and have lost your hearing.

He nodded, waiting for more information.

Your hearing was damaged by the explosion. You were lucky to be wearing a facemask.

Nodding again, he remembered the shockwave blasting his face. It could have been much worse.

Your hearing will return in time but we don't know when. You must be patient.

A scream pierced the silent room again. Doctor Radisich carried on, intent on writing something on his whiteboard, totally oblivious to the shriek. Blaine bolted upright, swinging his head around in an attempt to locate the source of the noise. Goosebumps sprang up over his arms and chest. The scream came from somewhere behind the doctor, still distant but closer this time.

It was a woman's scream. Her desperation tugged at his heart.

Are you alright Mr. Blaine? the doctor wrote quickly, noticing his strange behavior.

He shook his head violently. "Screaming. I can hear screaming!" To his ears, his words were a sick parody. His tongue and throat worked, but nothing came out.

Doctor Radisich moved his lips rapidly but their meaning was lost to him. He turned and thrust his head through the curtain. Moments later, a male nurse appeared. Nurse Stevenson was close behind. Their entrances were sudden and intrusive.

The doctor disappeared while the two nurses hovered by his bed. Nurse Stevenson stepped forward and slipped her petite hand inside his. The warmth of her skin was reassuring; she stroked his arm the way an owner strokes a pet just before it's put down.

The doctor soon re-emerged, a needle prominent in his hand.

Sighting the needle, he tensed. As the doctor drew closer, he struggled, attempting to get to his feet. "You have to do something! She needs–"

Springing forward, the male nurse held Blaine by the shoulders with practiced ease. Blaine was a big man, bigger than the nurse. But the nurse was fit, and had all the leverage. Nurse Stevenson pleaded with her eyes while stroking the back of his arm. The needle was injected straight into a valve attached to his plastic IV tube. Within seconds, the fight fled his body, his strength ebbed away. Sleep soon took hold.

A scream—desperate and hysterical—ripped him from a fractured dream. The scream had grown in intensity; it was much closer.

Running his hand over his face and head, he could still feel the bandages. He hadn't dreamt everything; he was still in the hospital. The lights were dimmed but he could still see the green curtain surrounding his bed.

The scream continued, pulling at the very fibers of his heart. Every few seconds it died off, returning with force moments later.

He ripped his sheets off and threw his legs over the side of the bed. Waves of dizziness threatened his resolve as he rose, but he quickly regained his balance.

He was compelled to act.

Testing his weight, he placed his bare feet on the floor. It was freezing. His pajamas offered little protection from the chill air wafting through the ward. His arm bound him to the IV bag. Without hesitation he ripped the slender metal from his vein, leaving his skin burning for long moments. Another wave of dizziness assaulted him as he stood. His body was fatigued, but flexing his limbs gave him the confidence to move.

Another scream jolted through the hospital.

He wobbled forward, unsteady at first until he settled into a rhythm. Drawing the curtain aside, he found his room deserted. Another three curtains, all in matching shades of green, hemmed off sections of the room. A solitary four-paned window, with bars on the outside, provided the only feature to the room. The sky outside was dark.

He left the room, to enter a long, cluttered corridor. Following the sound of the screams, he turned to the left and took off at a jog. He rushed past the nurse station, a reception desk located at the crossroad of two corridors. The nurse, a chubby dark-skinned woman with glasses, looked at him with curiosity but didn't interfere. She said something as he passed but he didn't hear any of it. Like her words, his footfalls were silent as he squeaked along the linoleum.

Running past open archways, he glanced through into each room. Most rooms in this ward were like his, housing four beds, each curtained off for patient privacy at this time of night. The curtain colors changed, some rooms had that same drab green, while others had curtains the color of rust or faded summer blue. One room, with blue curtains, was full of deputized acrobats, burned and scarred souls suspended from wires and slings above their beds. The man closest to the door was bandaged and squeezed into a full-body pressure suit. Poor bastard.

Jogging down the corridor, some of his strength returned. An old man with a sunken jaw stared through him from his wheelchair. The wrinkled geezer glided on in the other direction.

He dived into the elevator at the end of the passage. It was cavernous, with doors on both sides. In bewilderment, he studied the buttons. The screams came from somewhere . . . deep.

He pressed the button for the lower basement. The elevator jolted downward, the sound of the gears and pulleys lost to his ears. Endless heartbeats later, the elevator ground to a halt, with the door behind Blaine springing open. It took him a few moments to realize, as the metallic sliding sound failed to alert him.

A high-pitched scream, more intense this time and wrought with pain, rang through the dark corridor before him. She was close.

He jogged blindly into the darkness, passing several double doors indented with small glass windows. The rooms were devoid of light. The smell of sterilized death clung to the place, masked by potent industrial chemicals that made his head spin. Signs above the doors told him all he needed to know. He noted each as he passed. Morgue Examination Room One. Morgue Examination Room Two.

Another scream tore through the hospital.

It came from Room Four, just up ahead. A dim light shone from underneath the reinforced door.

He tried to contain his ragged breathing. His heart raced as he exaggerated his last few steps. He had no idea if he could be heard. Any noise could give him away. Approaching with caution, he glanced through the viewing glass.

A man with dark hair and a white coat was inside. His back to the door. Something shiny in his hand. The man's silhouette was familiar, but with the dim light and his face turned, he couldn't tell.

He was fixated on someone in front of him. With his view blocked, all Blaine could see were two bare, feminine arms, each bound with wire to metal shelving. Rivulets of blood trickled from her wrists, down to her elbows.

The man's hand moved with precision as he leaned closer to the girl. Blaine couldn't see what he was doing to her. He clenched his fists as another anguished scream rocked the hallway.

There was no doubt now, he was answering this girl's cries.

The man in the coat stepped back to admire his handiwork, offering Blaine a full view of the debauchery.

She was spread-eagled, bound at the wrists and ankles by the cruel wire, holding her in an 'X' shape. She sagged against her restraints, sobbing uncontrollably with her head bowed. Bedraggled dark hair, falling past her shoulders, shrouded her face. Her hospital gown was ripped open at the front and covered in blood. Dark crimson lines marked her breasts and stomach. Seeping blood stained her torso a foul red.

She looked up at her tormentor with pathetic, pleading eyes. Blaine's blood burned when he caught sight of her face, her terrified face. Christ, she was barely eighteen. Too young to die at the hands of this sick bastard.

She shook her head as her torturer advanced again. He could see clearly what he held in his hand. A blood-stained surgeon's scalpel. Her mouth moved, but if she said something, it was forever lost to Blaine's deadened ears. In his mounting rage, he doubted the cruel bastard with the scalpel heard it either.

He searched for a weapon, anything he could use to take the guy down. The lightless corridor was sadly lacking.

Turning back to the door, he saw the man waving the scalpel in the hapless girl's face. She shuddered and sobbed. He also caught sight of the tormentor's face. He wore a surgeon's mask but the eyes gave him away. It was that prick of a doctor. Radisich.

His fury raging, Blaine no longer cared about a weapon. Rational thought was overwhelmed by raw adrenalin. Raw hatred.

Slamming his shoulder into the double doors with explosive force, he hurled his bulk into the examination room. Doctor Radisich turned in surprise, dumbfounded by the white blur of motion that charged toward him.

The collision was sickening. The doctor collapsed like a sack as Blaine crash-tackled him into the concrete wall. A nearby metal trolley, carrying pristine metal tools and kidney-shaped bowls, rattled from the impact.

Blaine didn't hear the clatter of the scalpel hitting the floor, nor the snap of Radisich's ribs. The pair went down hard, the doctor bearing the brunt.

For long moments, nothing moved in Examination Room Four.

Blaine rose to his feet and dusted off his hospital-issue pajamas. Dusted off the taint of the loathsome creature passing himself off as a man.

He stared at the crumpled doctor, splayed unconscious in a wretched mess on the floor, silently grateful for his years of football training. Unable to contain his disgust, he spat on Radisich, before turning to the girl.

Mr. Blaine, what led you down there in the first place? flashed up on the laptop screen.

He pondered the detective's question carefully, reviewing everything that had happened that night. Getting the nurses to call for help, then actually believe him, took some doing. He commandeered a notepad from the nearest nurse's station and frantically scribbled his messages. Seeing the tortured girl's cuts soon convinced them. It was harder to convince the medical staff that Doctor Radisich was the culprit. It didn't matter too much; he'd been safely jammed into a storage cupboard, still unconscious and bound with the same wire used on the girl, until the police arrived.

I heard the girl's screams, he typed on the screen, immediately below the question. He decided shouting at the detective was probably not a good idea.

The detective, probably a few years younger than him, stared him long and hard in the face. His eyes wavered between Blaine's and the bandages wrapped around his ears. He soon left him with the laptop while he discussed something with the other detective.

They returned together a few moments later. The other detective, approaching his fifties, read the transcript and also shot Blaine a hard look.

He turned the laptop around and typed something. Turning it back to Blaine, it read:

That is impossible Mr. Blaine. The girl's vocal cords had been removed.

MR. AICKMAN'S AIR RIFLE

PETER STRAUB

ON THE TWENTY-FIRST, OR "Concierge," floor of New York's Governor General Hospital, located just south of midtown on Seventh Avenue, a glow of recessed lighting and a rank of framed, eye-level graphics (Twombley, Shapiro, Marden, Warhol) escort visitors from a brace of express elevators to the reassuring spectacle of a graceful cherry wood desk occupied by a red-jacketed gatekeeper named Mr. Singh. Like a hand cupped beneath a waiting elbow, this gentleman's enquiring yet deferential appraisal and his stupendous display of fresh flowers nudge the visitor over hushed beige carpeting and into the wood-paneled realm of Floor 21 itself.

First to appear is the nursing station, where in a flattering chiaroscuro efficient women occupy themselves with charts, telephones, and the ever-changing patterns traversing their computer monitors; directly ahead lies the first of the great, half-open doors of the residents' rooms or suites, each with its brass numeral and discreet nameplate. The great hallway extends some sixty yards, passing seven named and numbered doors on its way to a bright window with an uptown view. To the left, the hallway passes the front of the nurses' station and the four doors directly opposite, then divides. The shorter portion continues on to a large, south-facing window with a good prospect of the Hudson River, the longer defines the southern boundary of the station. Hung with an Elizabeth Murray lithograph and a Robert Mapplethorpe calla lily, an ochre wall then rises up to guide the hallway over another carpeted fifty feet to a long, narrow room. The small brass sign beside its wide, pebble-glass doors reads *Salon*.

The Salon is not a salon but a lounge, and a rather makeshift lounge at that. At one end sits a good-sized television set; at the other, a green fabric sofa with two matching chairs. Midpoint in the room, which was intended for the comfort of stricken relatives and other visitors but has always been patronized chiefly by Floor 21's more ambulatory patients, stands a white-draped table equipped with coffee dispensers, stacks of cups and saucers, and cut-glass containers for sugar and artificial sweeteners. In the hours from four to six in the afternoon, platters laden with pastries and chocolates from the neighborhood's gourmet specialty shops appear, as if delivered by unseen hands, upon the table.

On an afternoon early in April, when during the hours in question the long window behind the table of goodies registered swift, unpredictable alternations of light and dark, the male patients who constituted four-fifths of the residents of Floor 21, all of them recent victims of atrial fibrillation or atrial flutter, which is to say sufferers from that dire annoyance in the life of a busy American male, non-fatal heart failure, the youngest a man of fifty-eight and the most senior twenty-two years older, found themselves once again partaking of the cream cakes and petit fours and reminding themselves that they had not, after all, undergone heart attacks. Their recent adventures had aroused in them an indulgent fatalism. After all, should the worst happen, which of course it would not, they were already at the epi-center of a swarm of cardiologists!

To varying degrees, these were men of accomplishment and achievement in their common profession, that of letters.

In descending order of age, the four men enjoying the amenities of the Salon were Max Baccarat, the much respected former president of Gladstone Books, the acquisition of which by a German conglomerate had lately precipitated his retirement; Anthony Flax, a self-described "critic" who had spent the past twenty years as a full-time book reviewer for a variety of periodicals and journals, a leisurely occupation he could afford due to his having been the husband, now for three years the widower, of a sugar-substitute heiress; William Messinger, a writer whose lengthy backlist of horror/mystery/suspense novels had been kept continuously in print for twenty-five years by the bi-annual appearance of yet another new astonishment; and Charles Chipp Traynor, child of a wealthy New England family, Harvard graduate, self-declared veteran of the Vietnam conflict, and author of four non-fiction books, also (alas) a notorious plagiarist.

The connections between these four men, no less complex and multi-layered than one would gather from their professional circumstances, had inspired some initial awkwardness on their first few encounters in the Salon, but a shared desire for the treats on offer had encouraged these gentlemen to reach the accommodation displayed on the afternoon in question. By silent agreement, Max Baccarat arrived first, a few minutes after opening, to avail himself of the greatest possible range of selection and the most comfortable seating position, which was on that end side of the sofa nearest the pebble-glass doors, where the cushion was a touch more yielding than its mate. Once the great publisher had installed himself to his satisfaction, Bill Messinger and Tony Flax happened in to browse over the day's bounty before seating themselves at a comfortable distance from each other. Invariably the last to arrive, Traynor edged around the door sometime around 4:15, his manner suggesting that he had wandered in by accident, probably in search of another room altogether. The loose, patterned hospital gown he wore fastened at neck and backside added to his air of inoffensiveness, and his round glasses and stooped shoulders gave him a generic resemblance to a creature from *The Wind in the Willows*.

Of the four, the plagiarist alone had surrendered to the hospital's tacit wishes concerning patients' in-house mode of dress. Over silk pajamas of a glaring, Greek-village white, Max Baccarat wore a dark, dashing navy blue dressing gown, reputedly a Christmas present from Graham Greene, which fell nearly to the tops of his velvet fox-head slippers. Over his own pajamas, of fine-combed baby-blue cotton instead of white silk, Tony Flax had buttoned a lightweight tan trench coat, complete with epaulettes and grenade rings. With his extra chins and florid complexion, it made him look like a correspondent from a war conducted well within striking distance of hotel bars. Bill Messinger had taken one look at the flimsy shift offered him by the hospital staff and decided to stick, for as long as he could get away with it, to the pin-striped Armani suit and black loafers he had worn into the ER. His favorite men's stores delivered fresh shirts, socks and underwear.

When Messinger's early, less successful books had been published by Max's firm, Tony Flax had given him consistently positive reviews; after Bill's defection to a better house and larger advances for more ambitious books, Tony's increasingly bored and dismissive reviews accused him of hubris, then ceased altogether. Messinger's last three novels had not been reviewed anywhere in the *Times*, an insult he attributed to Tony's malign influence over its current editors. Likewise, Max had published Chippie Traynor's first two anecdotal histories of World War I, the second of which had been considered for a Pulitzer Prize, then lost him to a more prominent publisher whose shrewd publicists had placed him on NPR, *The Today Show*, and—after the film deal for his third book—*Charlie Rose*. Bill had given blurbs to Traynor's first two books, and Tony Flax had hailed him as a great vernacular historian. Then, two decades later, a stunned graduate student in Texas discovered lengthy, painstakingly altered parallels between Traynor's books and the contents of several Ph.D. dissertations containing oral histories taken in the 1930s. Beyond that, the student found that perhaps a third of the personal histories had been invented, simply made up, like fiction.

Within days, the graduate student had detonated Chippie's reputation. One week after the detonation, his university placed him "on leave," a status assumed to be permanent. He had vanished into his family's Lincoln-Log compound in Maine, not to be seen or heard from until the moment when Bill Messinger and Tony Flax, who had left open the Salon's doors the better to avoid conversation, had witnessed his sorry, supine figure being wheeled past. Max Baccarat was immediately informed of the scoundrel's arrival, and before the end of the day the legendary dressing gown, the trench coat, and the pin-striped suit had overcome their mutual resentments to form an alliance against the disgraced newcomer. There was nothing, they found, like a common enemy to smooth over complicated, even difficult relationships.

Chippie Traynor had not found his way to the lounge until the following day, and he had been accompanied by a tremulous elderly woman who with equal plausibility could have passed for either his mother or his wife. Sidling around the door at 4:15, he had taken in the trio watching him from the green sofa and chairs, blinked in disbelief and recognition, ducked his head even closer to his chest, and permitted his companion to lead him to a chair located a few feet from the television set. It was clear that he was struggling with the impulse to scuttle out of the room, never to reappear. Once deposited in the chair, he tilted his head upward and whispered a few words into the woman's ear. She moved toward the pastries, and at last he eyed his former compatriots.

"Well, well," he said. "Max, Tony, and Bill. What are you in for, anyway? Me, I passed out on the street in Boothbay Harbor and had to be air-lifted in. Medevaced, like back in the day."

"These days, a lot of things must remind you of Vietnam, Chippie," Max said. "We're heart failure. You?"

"Atrial fib. Shortness of breath. Weaker than a baby. Fell down right in the street, boom. As soon as I get regulated, I'm supposed to have some sort of Echo scan."

"Heart failure, all right," Max said. "Go ahead, have a cream cake. You're among friends."

"Somehow, I doubt that," Traynor said. He was breathing hard, and he gulped air as he waved the old woman further down the table, toward the chocolate slabs and puffs. He watched carefully as she selected a number of the little cakes. "Don't forget the decaf, will you, sweetie?"

The others waited for him to introduce his companion, but he sat in silence as she placed a plate of cakes and a cup of coffee on a stand next to the television set, then faded backward into a chair that seemed to have materialized, just for her, from the ether. Traynor lifted a forkful of shiny brown goo to his mouth, sucked it off the fork, and gulped coffee. Because of his long, thick nose and recessed chin, first the fork, then the cup seemed to disappear into the lower half of his face. He twisted his head in the general direction of his companion and said, "Health food, yum yum."

She smiled vaguely at the ceiling. Traynor turned back to face the other three men, who were staring open-eyed, as if at a performance of some kind.

"Thanks for all the cards and letters, guys. I loved getting your phone calls, too. Really meant a lot to me. Oh, sorry, I'm not being very polite, am I?"

"There's no need to be sarcastic," Max said.

"I suppose not. We were never friends, were we?"

"You were looking for a publisher, not a friend," Max said. "And we did quite well together, or so I thought, before you decided you needed greener pastures. Bill did the same thing to me, come to think of it. Of course, Bill actually wrote the books that came out under his name. For a publisher, that's quite a significant difference." (Several descendants of the Ph.D.s from whom Traynor had stolen material had initiated suits against his publishing houses, Gladstone House among them.)

"Do we have to talk about this?" asked Tony Flax. He rammed his hands in the pockets of his trench coat and glanced from side to side. "Ancient history, hmmm?"

"You're just embarrassed by the reviews you gave him," Bill said. "But everybody did the same thing, including me. What did I say about *The Middle of the Trenches*? 'The . . .' The what? 'The most truthful, in a way the most visionary book ever written about trench warfare.'"

"Jesus, you remember your *blurbs*?" Tony asked. He laughed and tried to draw the others in.

"I remember everything," said Bill Messinger. "Curse of being a novelist—great memory, lousy sense of direction."

"You always remembered how to get to the bank," Tony said.

"Lucky me, I didn't have to marry it," Bill said.

"Are you accusing me of marrying for money?" Tony said, defending himself by the usual tactic of pretending that what was commonly accepted was altogether unthinkable. "Not that I have any reason to defend myself against you, Messinger. As that famous memory of yours should recall, I was one of the first people to support your work."

From nowhere, a reedy English female voice said, "I did enjoy reading your reviews of Mr. Messinger's early novels, Mr. Flax. I'm sure that's why I went round to our little book shop and purchased them. They weren't at all my usual sort of *thing*, you know, but you made them sound . . . I think the word would be *imperative*."

Max, Tony, and Bill peered past Charles Chipp Traynor to get a good look at his companion. For the first time, they took in that she was wearing a long, loose collection of elements that suggested feminine literary garb of the nineteen twenties: a hazy, rather shimmery woolen cardigan over a white, high-buttoned blouse, pearls, an ankle-length heather skirt, and low-heeled black shoes with laces. Her long, sensitive nose pointed up, exposing the clean line of her jaw; her lips twitched in what might have been amusement. Two things struck the men staring at her: that this woman looked a bit familiar, and that in spite of her age and general oddness, she would have to be described as beautiful.

"Well, yes," Tony said. "Thank you. I believe I was trying to express something of the sort. They were books . . . well. Bill, you never understood this, I think, but I felt they were books that deserved to be read. For their workmanship, their modesty, what I thought was their actual decency."

"You mean they did what you expected them to do," Bill said.

"Decency is an uncommon literary virtue," said Traynor's companion.

"Thank you, yes," Tony said.

"But not a very interesting one, really," Bill said. "Which probably explains why it isn't all that common."

"I think you are correct, Mr. Messinger, to imply that decency is more valuable in the realm of personal relations. And for the record, I do feel your work since then has undergone a general improvement. Perhaps Mr. Flax's limitations do not permit him to appreciate your progress." She paused. There was a dangerous smile on her face. "Of course you can hardly be said to have improved to the extent claimed in your latest round of interviews."

In the moment of silence that followed, Max Baccarat looked from one of his new allies to the other and found them in a state too reflective for commentary. He cleared his throat. "Might we have the honor of an introduction, Madame? Chippie seems to have forgotten his manners."

"My name is of no importance," she said, only barely favoring him with the flicker of a glance. "And Mr. Traynor has a thorough knowledge of my feelings on the matter."

"There's two sides to every story," Chippie said. "It may not be grammar, but it's the truth."

"Oh, there are many more than that," said his companion, smiling again.

"Darling, would you help me return to my room?"

Chippie extended an arm, and the Englishwoman floated to her feet, cradled his root-like fist against the side of her chest, nodded to the gaping men, and gracefully conducted her charge from the room.

"So who the fuck was *that*?" said Max Baccarat.

2

Certain rituals structured the night-time hours on Floor 21. At 8:30 P.M., blood pressure was taken and evening medications administered by Tess Corrigan, an Irish softie with a saggy gut, an alcoholic, angina-ridden husband, and an understandable tolerance for misbehavior. Tess herself sometimes appeared to be mildly intoxicated. Class resentment caused her to treat Max a touch brusquely, but Tony's trench coat amused her to wheezy laughter. After Bill Messinger had signed two books for her niece, a devoted fan, Tess had allowed him to do anything he cared to, including taking illicit journeys downstairs to the gift shop. "Oh, Mr. Messinger," she had said, "a fella with your gifts, the books you could write about this place." Three hours after Tess's departure, a big, heavily-dreadlocked nurse with an islands accent surged into the patients' rooms to awaken them for the purpose of distributing tranquilizers and knockout pills. Because she resembled a greatly inflated, ever-simmering Whoopi Goldberg, Max, Tony, and Bill referred to this terrifying and implacable figure as "Molly." (Molly's real name, printed on the ID card attached to a sash used as a waistband, was permanently concealed behind beaded swags and little hanging pouches.) At six in the morning, Molly swept in again, wielding the blood-pressure mechanism like an angry deity maintaining a good grip on a sinner. At the end of her shift, she came wrapped in a strong, dark scent, suggestive of forest fires in underground crypts. The three literary gentlemen found this aroma disturbingly erotic.

On the morning after the appearance within the Salon of Charles Chipp Traynor and his disconcerting muse, Molly raked Bill with a look of pity and scorn as she trussed his upper arm and strangled it by pumping a rubber bulb. Her crypt-fire odor seemed particularly smoky.

"What?" he asked.

Molly shook her massive head. "Toddle, toddle, toddle, you must believe you're the new postman in this beautiful neighborhood of ours."

Terror seized his gut. "I don't think I know what you're talking about."

Molly chuckled and gave the bulb a final squeeze, causing his arm to go numb from bicep to his fingertips. "Of course not. But you do know that we have no limitations on visiting hours up here in our paradise, don't you?"

"Um," he said.

"Then let me tell you something you do not know, Mr. Postman. Miz LaValley in 21R-12 passed away last night. I do not imagine you ever took it upon yourself to pay the poor woman a social call. And *that*, Mr. Postman, means that you, Mr. Baccarat, Mr. Flax, and our new addition, Mr. Traynor, are now the only patients on Floor 21."

"Ah," he said.

As soon as she left his room, he showered and dressed in the previous day's clothing, eager to get out into the corridor and check on the conditions in 21R-14, Chippie Traynor's room, for it was what he had seen there in the hours between Tess Corrigan's florid departure and Molly Goldberg's first drive-by shooting that had led to his becoming the floor's postman.

It had been just before nine in the evening, and something had urged him to take a final turn around the floor before surrendering himself to the hateful "gown" and turning off his lights. His route took him past the command center, where the Night Visitor, scowling over a desk too small for her, made grim notations on a chart, and down the corridor toward the window looking out toward the Hudson river and the great harbor. Along the way he passed 21R-14, where muffled noises had caused him to look in. From the corridor, he could see the bottom third of the plagiarist's bed, on which the sheets and blanket appeared to be writhing, or at least shifting about in a conspicuous manner. Messinger noticed a pair of black, lace-up women's shoes on the floor near the bottom of the bed. An untidy heap of clothing lay beside the in-turned shoes. For a few seconds ripe with shock and envy, he had listened to the soft noises coming from the room. Then he whirled around and rushed toward his allies' chambers.

"Who *is* that dame?" Max Baccarat had asked, essentially repeating the question he had asked earlier that day. "*What* is she? That miserable Traynor, God damn him to hell, may he have a heart attack and die. A woman like that, who cares how old she is?"

Tony Flax had groaned in disbelief and said, "I swear, that woman is either the ghost of Virginia Woolf or her direct descendant. All my life, I had the hots for Virginia Woolf, and now she turns up with that ugly crook, Chippie Traynor? Get out of here, Bill, I have to strategize."

3

At 4:15, the three conspirators pretended not to notice the plagiarist's furtive, animal-like entrance to the Salon. Max Baccarat's silvery hair, cleansed, stroked, clipped, buffed, and shaped during an emergency session with a hair therapist named Mr. Keith, seemed to glow with a virile inner light as he settled into the comfortable part of the sofa and organized his decaf cup and plate of chocolates and little cakes as if preparing soldiers for battle. Tony Flax's rubber chins shone a twice-shaved red, and his glasses sparkled. Beneath the hem of the trench coat, which appeared to have been ironed, colorful argyle socks descended from just below his lumpy knees to what seemed to be a pair of nifty two-tone shoes. Beneath the jacket of his pin-striped suit, Bill Messinger sported a brand-new, high-collared black silk T-shirt delivered by courier that morning from 65th and Madison. Thus attired, the longer-term residents of Floor 21 seemed lost as much in self-admiration as in the political discussion under way when at last they allowed themselves to acknowledge Chippie's presence. Max's eye skipped over Traynor and wandered toward the door.

"Will your lady friend be joining us?" he asked. "I thought she made some really very valid points yesterday, and I'd enjoy hearing what she has to say about our situation in Iraq. My two friends here are simple-minded liberals, you can never get anything sensible out of them."

"You wouldn't like what she'd have to say about Iraq," Traynor said. "And neither would they."

"Know her well, do you?" Tony asked.

"You could say that." Traynor's gown slipped as he bent over the table to pump coffee into his cup from the dispenser, and the three other men hastily turned their glances elsewhere.

"Tie that up, Chippie, would you?" Bill asked. "It's like a view of the Euganean Hills."

"Then look somewhere else. I'm getting some coffee, and then I have to pick out a couple of these yum-yums."

"You're alone today, then?" Tony asked.

"Looks like it."

"By the way," Bill said, "you were entirely right to point out that nothing is really as simple as it seems. There *are* more than two sides to every issue. I mean, wasn't that the point of what we were saying about Iraq?"

"To you, maybe," Max said. "You'd accept two sides as long as they were both printed in *The Nation*."

"Anyhow," Bill said, "please tell your friend that the next time she cares to visit this hospital, we'll try to remember what she said about decency."

"What makes you think she's going to come here again?"

"She seemed very fond of you," Tony said.

"The lady mentioned your limitations." Chippie finished assembling his assortment of treats and at last refastened his gaping robe. "I'm surprised you have any interest in seeing her again."

Tony's cheeks turned a deeper red. "All of us have limitations, I'm sure. In fact, I was just remembering . . . ."

"Oh?' Chippie lifted his snout and peered through his little lenses. "Were you? What, specifically?"

"Nothing," said Tony. "I shouldn't have said anything. Sorry."

"Did any of you know Mrs. LaValley, the lady in 21R-12?" Bill asked. "She died last night. Apart from us, she was the only other person on the floor."

"I knew Edie LaValley," Chippie said. "In fact, my friend and I dropped in and had a nice little chat with her just before dinner-time last night. I'm glad I had a chance to say goodbye to the old girl."

"Edie LaValley?" Max said. "Hold on. I seem to remember . . ."

"Wait, I do, too," Bill said. "Only . . . ."

"I know, she was that girl who worked for Nick Wheadle over at Viking, thirty years ago, back when Wheadle was everybody's golden boy," Tony said. "Stupendous girl. She got married to him and was Edith Wheadle for a while, but after the divorce she went back to her old name. We went out for a couple of months in 1983, '84. What happened to her after that?"

"She spent six years doing research for me," Traynor said. "She wasn't my *only* researcher, because I generally had three of them on the payroll, not to mention a couple of graduate students. Edie was very good at the job, though. Extremely conscientious."

"And knockout, drop-dead gorgeous," Tony said. "At least before she fell into Nick Wheadle's clutches."

"I didn't know you used so many researchers," Max said. "Could that be how you wound up quoting all those . . .?"

"Deliberately misquoting, I suppose you mean," Chippie said. "But the answer is no." A fat, sugar-coated square of sponge cake disappeared beneath his nose.

"But Edie Wheadle," Max said in a reflective voice. "By God, I think I . . . ."

"Think nothing of it," Traynor said. "That's what she did."

"Edie must have looked very different toward the end," said Tony. He sounded almost hopeful. "Twenty years, illness, all of that."

"My friend and I thought she looked much the same." Chippie's mild, creaturely face swung toward Tony Flax. "Weren't you about to tell us something?"

Tony flushed again. "No, not really."

"Perhaps an old memory resurfaced. That often happens on a night when someone in the vicinity dies—the death seems to awaken something."

"Edie's death certainly seemed to have awakened you," Bill said. "Didn't you ever hear of closing your door?"

"The nurses waltz right in anyhow, and there are no locks," Traynor said. "Better to be frank about matters, especially on Floor 21. It looks as though Max has something on his mind."

"Yes," Max said. "If Tony doesn't feel like talking, I will. Last night, an old memory of mine resurfaced, as Chippie puts it, and I'd like to get it off my chest, if that's the appropriate term."

"Good man," Traynor said. "Have another of those delicious little yummies and tell us all about it."

"This happened back when I was a little boy," Max said, wiping his lips with a crisp linen handkerchief.

Bill Messinger and Tony Flax seemed to go very still.

"I was raised in Pennsylvania, up in the Susquehanna Valley area. It's strange country, a little wilder and more backward than you'd expect, a little hillbillyish, especially once you get back in the Endless Mountains. My folks had a little store that sold everything under the sun, it seemed to me, and we lived in the building next door, close to the edge of town. Our town was called Manship, not that you can find it on any map. We had a one-room schoolhouse, an Episcopalian church and a Unitarian church, a feed and grain store, a place called The Lunch Counter, a Tract house, and a tavern called the Rusty Dusty, where, I'm sad to say, my father spent far too much of his time.

"When he came home loaded, as happened just about every other night, he was in a foul mood. It was mainly guilt, d'you see, because my mother had been slaving away in the store for hours, plus making dinner, and she was in a rage, which only made him feel worse. All he really wanted to do was to beat himself up, but I was an easy target, so he beat me up instead. Nowadays, we'd call it child abuse, but back then, in a place like Manship, it was just normal parenting, at least for a drunk. I wish I could tell you fellows that everything turned out well, and that my father sobered up, and we reconciled, and I forgave him, but none of that happened. Instead, he got meaner and meaner, and we got poorer and poorer. I learned to hate the old bastard, and I still hated him when a traveling junk wagon ran over him, right there in front of the Rusty Dusty, when I was eleven years old. 1935, the height of the Great Depression. He was lying passed out in the street, and the junkman never saw him.

"Now, I was determined to get out of that god-forsaken little town, and out of the Susquehanna Valley and the Endless Mountains, and obviously I did, because here I am today, with an excellent place in the world, if I might pat myself on the back a little bit. What I did was, I managed to keep the store going even while I went to the high school in the next town, and then I got a scholarship to U. Penn., where I waited on tables and tended bar and sent money back to my mother. Two days after I graduated, she died of a heart attack. That was her reward.

"I bought a bus ticket to New York. Even though I was never a great reader, I liked the idea of getting into the book business. Everything that happened after that you could read about in old copies of *Publisher's Weekly*. Maybe one day I'll write a book about it all.

"If I do, I'll never put in what I'm about to tell you now. It slipped my mind completely—the whole thing. You'll realize how bizarre that is after I'm done. I forgot all about it! Until about three this morning, that is, when I woke up too scared to breathe, my heart going bump bump, and the sweat pouring out of me. Every little bit of this business just came *back* to me, I mean everything, ever god-damned little tiny detail . . . .."

He looked at Bill and Tony. "What? You two guys look like you should be back in the ER."

"Every detail?" Tony said. "It's . . ."

"You woke up then, too?" Bill asked him.

"Are you two knotheads going to let me talk, or do you intend to keep interrupting?"

"I just wanted to ask this one thing, but I changed my mind," Tony said. "Sorry, Max. I shouldn't have said anything. It was a crazy idea. Sorry."

"Was your Dad an alcoholic, too?" Bill asked Tony Flax.

Tony squeezed up his face, said, "Aaaah," and waggled one hand in the air. "I don't like the word 'alcoholic.'"

"Yeah," Bill said. "All right."

"I guess the answer is, you're going to keep interrupting."

"No, please, Max, go on," Bill said.

Max frowned at both of them, then gave a dubious glance to Chippie Traynor, who stuffed another tiny cream cake into his maw and smiled around it.

"Fine. I don't know why I want to tell you about this anyhow. It's not like I actually *understand* it, as you'll see, and it's kind of ugly and kind of scary—I guess what amazes me is that I just remembered it all, or that

I managed to put it out of my mind for nearly seventy years, one or the other. But you know? It's like, it's real even if it never happened, or even if I dreamed the whole thing."

"This story wouldn't happen to involve a house, would it?" Tony asked.

"Most god-damned stories involve houses," Max said. "Even a lousy book critic ought to know that."

"Tony knows that," Chippie said. "See his ridiculous coat? That's a house. Isn't it, Tony?"

"You know what this is," Tony said. "It's a *trench coat*, a real one. Only from World War II, not World War I. It used to belong to my father. He was a hero in the war."

"As I was about to say," Max said, looking around and continuing only when the other three were paying attention, "when I woke up in the middle of the night I could remember the feel of the old blanket on my bed, the feel of pebbles and earth on my bare feet when I ran to the outhouse, I could remember the way my mother's scrambled eggs tasted. The whole anxious thing I had going on inside me while my mother was making breakfast.

"I was going to go off by myself in the woods. That was all right with my mother. At least it got rid of me for the day. But what she didn't know was that I had decided to steal one of the guns in the case at the back of the store.

"And you know what? She didn't pay any attention to the guns. About half of them belonged to people who swapped them for food because guns were all they had left to barter with. My mother hated the whole idea. And my father was in a fog until he could get to the tavern, and after that he couldn't think straight enough to remember how many guns were supposed to be back in that case. Anyhow, for the past few days, I'd had my eye on an over-under shotgun that used to belong to a farmer called Hakewell, and while my mother wasn't watching I nipped in back and took it out of the case. Then I stuffed my pockets with shells, ten of them. There was something going on way back in the woods, and while I wanted to keep my eye on it, I wanted to be able to protect myself, too, in case anything got out of hand."

Bill Messinger jumped to his feet and for a moment seemed preoccupied with brushing what might have been pastry crumbs off the bottom of his suit jacket. Max Baccarat frowned at him, then glanced down at the skirts of his dressing gown in a brief inspection. Bill continued to brush off imaginary particles of food, slowly turning in a circle as he did so.

"There is something you wish to communicate," Max said. "The odd thing, you know, is that for the moment, you see, I thought communication was in my hands."

Bill stopped fiddling with his jacket and regarded the old publisher with his eyebrows tugged toward the bridge of his nose and his mouth a thin, downturned line. He placed his hands on his hips. "I don't know what you're doing, Max, and I don't know where you're getting this. But I certainly wish you'd stop."

"What are you talking about?"

"He's right, Max," said Tony Flax.

"You jumped-up little fop," Max said, ignoring Tony. "You damned little show pony. What's your problem? You haven't told a good story in the past ten years, so listen to mine, you might learn something."

"You know what you are?" Bill asked him. "Twenty years ago, you used to be a decent second-rate publisher. Unfortunately, it's been all downhill from there. Now you're not even a third-rate publisher, you're a sellout. You took the money and went on the lam. Morally, you don't exist at all. You're a fancy dressing gown. And by the way, Graham Greene didn't give it to you, because Graham Greene wouldn't have given you a glass of water on a hot day."

Both of them were panting a bit and trying not to show it. Like a dog trying to choose between masters, Tony Flax swung his head from one to the other. In the end, he settled on Max Baccarat. "I don't really get it either, you know, but I think you should stop, too."

"Nobody cares what you think," Max told him. "Your brain dropped dead the day you swapped your integrity for a mountain of coffee sweetener."

"You did marry for money, Flax," Bill Messinger said. "Let's try being honest, all right? You sure as hell didn't fall in love with her beautiful face."

"And how about you, Traynor?" Max shouted. "I suppose you think I should stop, too."

"Nobody cares what I think," Chippie said. "I'm the lowest of the low. People despise me."

"First of all," Bill said, "if you want to talk about details, Max, you ought to get them *right*. It wasn't an 'over-under shotgun,' whatever the hell that is, it was a—"

"His name wasn't Hakewell," Tony said. "It was Hackman, like the actor.

"It wasn't Hakewell or Hackman," Bill said. "It started with an A."

"But there was a *house*," Tony said. "You know, I think my father probably was an alcoholic. His personality never changed, though. He was always a mean son of a bitch, drunk or sober."

"Mine, too," said Bill. "Where are you from, anyhow, Tony?"

"A little town in Oregon, called Milton. How about you?"

"Rhinelander, Wisconsin. My dad was the Chief of Police. I suppose there were lots of woods around Milton."

"We might as well have been in a forest. You?"

"The same."

"I'm from Boston, but we spent the summers in Maine," Chippie said. "You know what Maine is? Eighty per cent woods. There are places in Maine, the roads don't even have names."

"There was a *house*," Tony Flax insisted. "Back in the woods, and it didn't belong there. Nobody builds houses in the middle of the woods, miles away from everything, without even a road to use, not even a road without a name."

"This can't be real," Bill said. "I had a house, you had a house, and I bet Max had a house, even though he's so long-winded he hasn't gotten to it yet. I had an air rifle, Max had a shotgun, what did you have?"

"My Dad's .22," Tony said. "Just a little thing—around us, nobody took a .22 all that seriously."

Max was looking seriously disgruntled. "What, we all had the same *dream?*"

"You said it wasn't a dream," said Chippie Traynor. "You said it was a memory."

"It felt like a memory, all right," Tony said. "Just the way Max described it—the way the ground felt under my feet, the smell of my mother's cooking."

"I wish your lady friend was here now, Traynor," Max said. "She'd be able to explain what's going on, wouldn't she?"

"I have a number of lady friends," Chippie said, calmly stuffing a little glazed cake into his mouth.

"All right, Max," Bill said. "Let's explore this. You come across this big house, right? And there's someone in it?"

"Eventually, there is," Max said, and Tony Flax nodded.

"Right. And you can't even tell what age he is—or even if it *is* a he, right?"

"It was hiding in the back of a room," Tony says. "When I thought it was a girl, it really scared me. I didn't want it to be a girl."

"I didn't, either," Max said. "Oh—imagine how that would feel, a girl hiding in the shadows at the back of a room."

"Only this never happened," Bill said. "If we all seem to remember this bizarre story, then none of us is really remembering it."

"Okay, but it was a boy," Tony said. "And he got older."

"Right there in that house," said Max. "I thought it was like watching

my damnable father grow up right in front of my eyes. In what, six weeks?"
"About that," Tony said.

"And him in there all alone," said Bill. "Without so much as a stick of furniture. I thought that was one of the things that made it so frightening."

"Scared the shit out of me," Tony said. "When my Dad came back from the war, sometimes he put on his uniform and tied us to the chairs. Tied us to the chairs!"

"I didn't think it was really going to injure him," Bill said.

"I didn't even think I'd hit him," Tony said.

"I knew damn well I'd hit him," Max said. "I wanted to blow his head off. But my Dad lived another three years, and then the junkman finally ran him over."

"Max," Tony said, "you mentioned there was a Tract House in Manship. What's a Tract House?"

"It was where they printed the religious tracts, you ignoramus. You could go in there and pick them up for free. All of this was like child abuse, I'm telling you. Spare the Rod stuff."

"It was like his eye exploded," Bill said. Absent-mindedly, he took one of the untouched pastries from Max's plate and bit into it.

Max stared at him.

"They didn't change the goodies this morning, " Bill said. "This thing is a little stale."

"I prefer my pastries stale," said Chippie Traynor.

"I prefer to keep mine for myself, and not have them lifted off my plate," said Max, sounding as though something were caught in his throat.

"The bullet went straight through the left lens of his glasses and right into his head," said Toby. "And when he raised his head, his eye was full of blood."

"Would you look out that window?" Max said in a loud voice.

Bill Messinger and Tony Flax turned to the window, saw nothing special—perhaps a bit more haze in the air than they expected—and looked back at the old publisher.

"Sorry," Max said. He passed a trembling hand over his face. "I think I'll go back to my room."

4

"Nobody visits me," Bill Messinger said to Tess Corrigan. She was taking his blood pressure, and appeared to be having a little trouble getting accurate numbers. "I don't even really remember how long I've been here, but I haven't had a single visitor."

"Haven't you now?" Tess squinted at the blood pressure tube, sighed, and once again pumped the ball and tightened the band around his arm. Her breath contained a pure, razor-sharp whiff of alcohol.

"It makes me wonder, do I have any friends?"

Tess grunted with satisfaction and scribbled numbers on his chart. "Writers lead lonely lives," she told him. "Most of them aren't fit for human company, anyhow." She patted his wrist. "You're a lovely specimen, though."

"Tess, how long have I been here?"

"Oh, it was only a little while ago," she said. "And I believe it was raining at the time."

After she left, Bill watched television for a little while, but television, a frequent and dependable companion in his earlier life, seemed to have become intolerably stupid. He turned it off and for a time flipped through the pages of the latest book by a highly regarded contemporary novelist several decades younger than himself. He had bought the book before going into the hospital, thinking that during his stay he would have enough uninterrupted time to dig into the experience so many others had described as rich, complex, and marvelously nuanced, but he was having problems getting through it. The book bored him. The people were loathsome and the style was gelid. He kept wishing he had brought along some uncomplicated and professional trash he could use as a palate cleanser. By 10:00, he was asleep.

At 11:30, a figure wrapped in cold air appeared in his room, and he woke up as she approached. The woman coming nearer in the darkness must have been Molly, the Jamaican nurse who always charged in at this hour, but she did not give off Molly's arousing scent of fires in underground crypts. She smelled of damp weeds and muddy riverbanks. Bob did not want this version of Molly to get any closer to him than the end of his bed, and with his heart beating so violently that he could feel the limping rhythm of his heart, he commanded her to stop. She instantly obeyed.

He pushed the button to raise the head of his bed and tried to make her out as his body folded upright,. The river-smell had intensified, and cold air streamed toward him. He had no desire at all to turn on any of the three lights at his disposal. Dimly, he could make out a thin, tallish figure with dead hair plastered to her face, wearing what seemed to be a long cardigan sweater, soaked through and (he thought) dripping onto the floor. In this figure's hands was a fat, unjacketed book stained dark by her wet fingers.

"I don't want you here," he said. "And I don't want to read that book, either. I've already read everything you ever wrote, but that was a long time ago."

The drenched figure glided forward and deposited the book between his feet. Terrified that he might recognize her face, Bill clamped his eyes shut and kept them shut until the odors of river-water and mud had vanished from the air.

When Molly burst into the room to gather the new day's information the next morning, Bill Messinger realized that his night's visitation could have occurred only in a dream. Here was the well-known, predictable world around him, and every inch of it was a profound relief to him. Bill took in his bed, the little nest of monitors ready to be called upon should an emergency take place, his television and its remote control device, the door to his spacious bathroom, the door to the hallway, as ever half-open. On the other side of his bed lay the long window, now curtained for the sake of the night's sleep. And here, above all, was Molly, a one-woman Reality Principle, exuding the rich odor of burning graves as she tried to cut off his circulation with a blood-pressure machine. The bulk and massivity of her upper arms suggested that Molly's own blood pressure would have to be read by means of some other technology, perhaps steam gauge. The whites of her eyes shone with a faint trace of pink, leading Bill to speculate for a moment of wild improbability if the ferocious night nurse indulged in marijuana.

"You're doing well, Mr. Postman," she said. "Making good progress."

"I'm glad to hear it," he said. "When do you think I'll be able to go home?"

"That is for the doctors to decide, not me. You'll have to bring it up with them." From a pocket hidden beneath her swags and pouches, she produced a white paper cup half-filled with pills and capsules of varying sizes and colors. She thrust it at him. "Morning meds. Gulp them down like a good boy, now." Her other hand held out a small plastic bottle of Poland Spring water, the provenance of which reminded Messinger of what Chippie Traynor had said about Maine. Deep woods, roads without names....

He upended the cup over his mouth, opened the bottle of water, and managed to get all his pills down at the first try.

Molly whirled around to leave with her usual sense of having had more than enough of her time wasted by the likes of him, and was half way to the door before he remembered something that had been on his mind for the past few days.

"I haven't seen the *Times* since I don't remember when," he said. "Could you please get me a copy? I wouldn't even mind one that's a couple of days old."

Molly gave him a long, measuring look, then nodded her head. "Because many of our people find them so upsetting, we tend not to get the newspapers up here. But I'll see if I can locate one for you." She moved ponderously to the door and paused to look back at him again just before she walked out. "By the way, from now on you and your friends will have to get along without Mr. Traynor's company."

"Why?" Bill asked. "What happened to him?"

"Mr. Traynor is . . . gone, sir."

"Chippie died, you mean? When did that happen?" With a shudder, he remembered the figure from his dream. The smell of rotting weeds and wet riverbank awakened within him, and he felt as if she were once again standing before him.

"Did I say he was dead? What I said was, he is . . . *gone*."

For reasons he could not identify, Bill Messinger did not go through the morning's rituals with his usual impatience. He felt slow-moving, reluctant to engage the day. In the shower, he seemed barely able to raise his arms. The water seemed brackish, and his soap all but refused to lather. The towels were stiff and thin, like the cheap towels he remembered from his youth. After he had succeeded in drying off at least most of the easily reachable parts of his body, he sat on his bed and listened to the breath laboring in and out of his body. Without him noticing, the handsome pin-striped suit had become as wrinkled and tired as he felt himself to be, and besides that he seemed to be out of clean shirts. He pulled a dirty one from the closet. His swollen feet took some time to ram into his black loafers.

Armored at last in the costume of a great worldly success, Bill stepped out into the great corridor with a good measure of his old dispatch. He wished Max Baccarat had not called him a "jumped-up little fop" and a "damned little show pony" the other day, for he genuinely enjoyed good clothing, and it hurt him to think that others might take this simple pleasure, which after all did contain a moral element, as a sign of vanity. On the other hand, he should have thought twice before telling Max that he was a third-rate publisher and a sellout. Everybody knew that robe hadn't been a gift from Graham Greene, though. That myth represented nothing more than Max Baccarat's habit of portraying and presenting himself as an old-line publishing grandee, like Alfred Knopf.

The nursing station—what he liked to think of as "the command center"—was oddly understaffed this morning. In a landscape of empty desks and unattended computer monitors, Molly sat on a pair of stools she had placed side by side, frowning as ever down at some form she was obliged to work through. Bill nodded at her and received the non-response he had anticipated. Instead of turning left toward the Salon as he usually did, Bill decided to stroll over to the elevators and the cherry wood desk where diplomatic, red-jacketed Mr. Singh guided newcomers past his display of Casablanca lilies, tea roses, and lupines. On his perambulations through the halls, he often passed through Mr. Singh's tiny realm, and he found the man a kindly, reassuring presence.

Today, though, Mr. Singh seemed not to be on duty, and the great glass vase had been removed from his desk. OUT OF ORDER signs had been taped to the elevators.

Feeling a vague sense of disquiet, Bill retraced his steps and walked past the side of the nursing station to embark upon the long corridor that led to the north-facing window. Max Baccarat's room lie down this corridor, and Bill thought he might pay a call on the old gent. He could apologize for the insults he had given him, and perhaps receive an apology in return. Twice, Baccarat had thrown the word "little" at him, and Bill's cheeks stung as if he had been slapped. About the story, or the memory, or whatever it had been, however, Bill intended to say nothing. He did not believe that he, Max, and Tony Flax had dreamed of the same bizarre set of events, nor that they had experienced these decidedly dream-like events in youth. The illusion that they had done so had been inspired by proximity and daily contact. The world of Floor 21 was as hermetic as a prison.

He came to Max's room and knocked at the half-open door. There was no reply. "Max?" he called out. "Feel like having a visitor?"

In the absence of a reply, he thought that Max might be asleep. It would do no harm to check on his old acquaintance. How odd, it occurred to him, to think that he and Max had both had relations with little Edie Wheadle. And Tony Flax, too. And that she should have died on this floor, unknown to them! *There* was someone to whom he rightly could have apologized—at the end, he had treated her quite badly. She had been the sort of girl, he thought, who almost expected to be treated badly. But far from being an excuse, that was the opposite, an indictment.

Putting inconvenient Edie Wheadle out of his mind, Bill moved past the bathroom and the "reception" area into the room proper, there to find Max Baccarat not in bed as he had expected, but beyond it and seated in one of the low, slightly cantilevered chairs, which he had turned to face the window.

"Max?"

The old man did not acknowledge is presence in any way. Bill noticed that he was not wearing the splendid blue robe, only his white pajamas, and his feet were bare. Unless he had fallen asleep, he was staring at the window and appeared to have been doing so for some time. His silvery hair was mussed and stringy. As Bill approached, he took in the rigidity of Max's head and neck, the stiff tension in his shoulders. He came around the foot of the bed and at last saw the whole of the old man's body, stationed sideways to him as it faced the window. Max was gripping the arms of the chair and leaning forward. His mouth hung open, and his lips had been drawn back. His eyes, too, were open, hugely, as they stared straight ahead.

With a little thrill of anticipatory fear, Bill glanced at the window. What he saw, haze shot through with streaks of light, could hardly have brought Max Baccarat to this pitch. His face seemed rigid with terror. Then Bill realized that this had nothing to do with terror, and Max had suffered a great, paralyzing stroke. That was the explanation for the pathetic scene before him. He jumped to the side of the bed and pushed the call button for the nurse. When he did not get an immediate response, he pushed it again, twice, and held the button down for several seconds. Still no soft footsteps came from the corridor.

A folded copy of the *Times* lay on Max's bed, and with a sharp, almost painful sense of hunger for the million vast and minuscule dramas taking place outside Governor General, he realized that what he had said to Molly was no more than the literal truth: it seemed weeks since he had seen a newspaper. With the justification that Max would have no use for it, Bill snatched up the paper and felt, deep in the core of his being, a real greed for its contents—devouring the columns of print would be akin to gobbling up great bits of the world. He tucked the neat, folded package of the *Times* under his arm and left the room.

"Nurse," he called. It came to him that he had never learned the real name of the woman they called Molly Goldberg. "Hello? There's a man in trouble down here!"

He walked quickly down the hallway in what he perceived as a deep, unsettling silence. "Hello, nurse!" he called, at least in part to hear at least the sound of his own voice.

When Bill reached the deserted nurses' station, he rejected the impulse to say, "Where is everybody?" The Night Visitor no longer occupied her pair of stools, and the usual chiaroscuro had deepened into a murky darkness. It was though they had pulled the plugs and stolen away.

"I don't get this," Bill said. "*Doctors* might bail, but nurses don't."

He looked up and down the corridor and saw only a gray carpet and a row of half-open doors. Behind one of those doors sat Max Baccarat, who had once been something of a friend. Max was destroyed, Bill thought; damage so severe could not be repaired. Like a film of greasy dust, the sense descended upon him that he was wasting his time. If the doctors and nurses were elsewhere, as seemed the case, nothing could be done for Max until their return. Even after that, in all likelihood very little could be done for poor old Max. His heart failure had been a symptom of a wider systemic problem.

But still. He could not just walk away and ignore Max's plight. Messinger turned around and paced down the corridor to the door where the nameplate read *Anthony Flax*. "Tony," he said. "Are you in there? I think Max had a stroke."

He rapped on the door and pushed it all the way open. Dreading what he might find, he walked into the room. "Tony?" He already knew the room was empty, and when he was able to see the bed, all was as he had expected: an empty bed, an empty chair, a blank television screen, and blinds pulled down to keep the day from entering.

Bill left Tony's room, turned left, then took the hallway that led past the Salon. A man in an unclean janitor's uniform, his back to Bill, was removing the Mapplethorpe photographs from the wall and loading them face-down onto a wheeled cart.

"What are you doing?" he asked.

The man in the janitor uniform looked over his shoulder and said, "I'm doing my job, that's what I'm doing." He had greasy hair, a low forehead, and an acne-scarred face with deep furrows in the cheeks.

"But why are you taking down those pictures?"

The man turned around to face him. He was strikingly ugly, and his ugliness seemed part of his intention, as if he had chosen it. "Gee, buddy, why do you suppose I'd do something like that? To upset *you*? Well, I'm sorry if you're upset, but you had nothing to do with this. They tell me to do stuff like this, I do it. End of story." He pushed his face forward, ready for the next step.

"Sorry," Bill said. "I understand completely. Have you seen a doctor or a nurse up here in the past few minutes? A man on the other side of the floor just had a stroke. He needs medical attention."

"Too bad, but I don't have anything to do with doctors. The man I deal with is my supervisor, and supervisors don't wear white coats, and they don't carry stethoscopes. Now if you'll excuse me, I'll be on my way."

"But I need a doctor!"

"You look okay to me," the man said, turning away. He took the last photograph from the wall and pushed his cart through the metal doors that marked the boundary of the realm ruled by Tess Corrigan, Molly Goldberg, and their colleagues. Bill followed him through, and instantly found himself in a functional, green-painted corridor lit by fluorescent lighting and lined with locked doors. The janitor pushed his trolley around a corner and disappeared.

"Is anybody here?" Bill's voice carried through the empty hallways. "A man here needs a doctor!"

The corridor he was in led to another, which led to another, which went past a small, deserted nurses' station and ended at a huge, flat door with a sign that said MEDICAL PERSONNEL ONLY. Bill pushed at the door, but it was locked. He had the feeling that he could wander through these corridors for hours and find nothing but blank walls and locked doors. When he returned to the metal doors and pushed through to the private wing, relief flooded through him, making him feel light-headed.

The Salon invited him in—he wanted to sit down, he wanted to catch his breath and see if any of the little cakes had been set out yet. He had forgotten to order breakfast, and hunger was making him weak. Bill put his hand on one of the pebble-glass doors and saw an indistinct figure seated near the table. For a moment, his heart felt cold, and he hesitated before he opened the door.

Tony Flax was bent over in his chair, and what Bill Messinger noticed first was that the critic was wearing one of the thin hospital gowns that tied at the neck and the back. His trench coat lay puddled on the floor. Then he saw that Flax appeared to be weeping. His hands were clasped to his face, and his back rose and fell with jerky, uncontrolled movements.

"Tony?" he said. "What happened to you?"

Flax continued to weep silently, with the concentration and selfishness of a small child.

"Can I help you, Tony?" Bill asked.

When Flax did not respond, Bill looked around the room for the source of his distress. Half-filled coffee cups stood on the little tables, and petits fours lay jumbled and scattered over the plates and the white table. As he watched, a cockroach nearly two inches long burrowed out of a little square of white chocolate and disappeared around the back of a Battenburg cake. The cockroach looked as shiny and polished as a new pair of black shoes.

Something was moving on the other side of the window, but Bill Messinger wanted nothing to do with it. "Tony," he said, "I'll be in my room."

Down the corridor he went, the tails of his suit jacket flapping behind him. A heavy, liquid pressure built up in his chest, and the lights seemed to darken, then grow brighter again. He remembered Max, his mind gone, staring open-mouthed at his window: what had he seen?

Bill thought of Chippie Traynor, one of his mole-like eyes bloodied behind the shattered lens of his glasses.

At the entrance to his room, he hesitated once again as he had outside the Salon, fearing that if he went in, he might not be alone. But of course he would be alone, for apart from the janitor no one else on Floor 21 was capable of movement. Slowly, making as little noise as possible, he slipped around his door and entered his room. It looked exactly as it had when he had awakened that morning. The younger author's book lay discarded on his bed, the monitors awaited an emergency, the blinds covered the long window. Bill thought the wildly alternating pattern of light and dark that moved across the blinds proved nothing. Freaky New York weather, you never knew what it was going to do. He did not hear odd noises, like half-remembered voices, calling to him from the other side of the glass.

As he moved nearer to the foot of the bed, he saw on the floor the bright jacket of the book he had decided not to read, and knew that in the night it had fallen from his moveable tray. The book on his bed had no jacket, and at first he had no idea where it came from. When he remembered the circumstances under which he had seen this book—or one a great deal like it—he felt revulsion, as though it were a great slug.

Bill turned his back on the bed, swung his chair around, and plucked the newspaper from under his arm. After he had scanned the headlines without making much effort to take them in, habit led him to the obituaries on the last two pages of the financial section. As soon as he had folded the pages back, a photograph of a sly, mild face with a recessed chin and tiny spectacles lurking above an overgrown nose levitated up from the columns of newsprint. The header announced CHARLES CHIPP TRAYNOR, POPULAR WAR HISTORIAN TARRED BY SCANDAL.

Helplessly, Bill read the first paragraph of Chippie's obituary. Four days past, this once-renowned historian whose career had been destroyed by charges of plagiarism and fraud had committed suicide by leaping from the window of his fifteenth-story apartment on the Upper West Side.

Four days ago? Bill thought. It seemed to him that was when Chippie Traynor had first appeared in the Salon. He dropped the paper, with the effect that Traynor's fleshy nose and mild eyes peered up at him from the floor. The terrible little man seemed to be everywhere, despite having *gone*. He could sense Chippie Traynor floating outside his window like a small, inoffensive balloon from Macy's Thanksgiving Day Parade. Children would say, "Who's that?', and their parents would look up, shield their eyes, shrug, and say, "I don't know, hone. Wasn't he in a Disney cartoon?" Only he was not in a Disney cartoon, and the children and their parents could not see him, and he wasn't at all cute. One of his eyes had been injured. This Chippie Traynor, not the one that had given them a view of his backside in the Salon, hovered outside Bill Messinger's window, whispering the wretched and insinuating secrets of the despised, the contemptible, the rejected and fallen from grace.

Bill turned from the window and took a single step into the nowhere that awaited him. He had nowhere to go, he knew, so nowhere had to be where he was going. It was probably going to be a lot like this place, only less comfortable. Much, *much* less comfortable. With nowhere to go, he reached out his hand and picked up the dull brown book lying at the foot of his bed. Bringing it toward his body felt like reeling in some monstrous fish that struggled against the line. There were faint water marks on the front cover, and it bore a faint, familiar smell. When he had it within reading distance, Bill turned the spine up and read the title and author's name: *In the Middle of the Trenches*, by Charles Chipp Traynor. It was the book he had blurbed. Max Baccarat had published it, and Tony Flax had rhapsodized over it in the *Sunday Times* book review section. About a hundred pages from the end, a bookmark in the shape of a thin silver cord with a hook at one end protruded from the top of the book.

Bill opened the book at the place indicated, and the slender bookmark slithered downwards like a living thing. Then the hook caught the top of the pages, and its length hung shining and swaying over the bottom edge. No longer able to resist, Bill read some random sentences, then two long paragraphs. This section undoubtedly had been lifted from the oral histories, and it recounted an odd event in the life of a young man who, years before his induction into the Armed Forces, had come upon a strange house deep in the piney woods of East Texas and been so unsettled by what he had seen through its windows that he brought a rifle with him on his next visit. Bill realized that he had never read this part of the book. In fact, he had written his blurb after merely skimming through the first two chapters. He thought Max had read even less of the book than he had. In hurry to meet his deadline, Tony Flax had probably read the first half.

At the end of his account, the former soldier said, "In the many times over the years when I thought about this incident, it always seemed to me that the man I shot was myself. It seemed my own eye I had destroyed, my own socket that bled."

THE PURLOINED PROSE

PATRICIA LEE MACOMBER & DAVID NIALL WILSON

THE SWAN. TO MOST the name conjured images of pristine white feathers, a graceful neck, motion so fluid it mocked the very water in which the bird itself swam. To Edgar, it was an oasis, a hideout, and his temple. He sat at the worn oak and brass altar, folded over a chalice so fogged from age that the light barely penetrated it. His thoughts were turned inward, though his ears were trained on the conversation four stools down. He had no idea he was sitting at the bar with a dead man.

Flickering gaslights dueled with the shadows, chased them across timeworn and tattered walls until they threatened not to exist at all, and then retreated as long dark fingers reached toward the tenuous threads of illumination and threatened to choke the life from them. Edgar's hand trembled, poised over a scrap of paper on which he scribbled hasty words, some of them his own, some gleaned from the hushed conversation that floated to him from the others. The barman drew near, though he regarded Edgar not at all, and Edgar, the scribbler of stolen words, turned on his stool and put his shoulder and arm between the barman and the paper.

"It has to be a heart, don't you see." The words were slurred and punctuated with spittle but the small, ferret-like man was adamant.

His friend, a large, hulking fellow in a dark coat, his hat slumped in a shapeless mass on the bar at his side, shrugged and downed the rest of his drink in one great gulp. "You are the wordsmith, not I. But I'll tell you this: You'd have a much better time of it if you actually wrote down some of your grand ideas instead of hammering me with them night after night."

"Ah, but I have!" the smaller man said with a wink, patting his jacket with one hand. Something crinkled beneath the pressure of his hand. He finished his drink and set the glass down with a clunk. "Every last one. And you'll be laughing out the other side of your face when you see them published, my friend." He slapped the big man on the back and withdrew from the stool, letting his body settle carefully onto his legs and drawing in a large breath to steel himself against the effects of gravity.

"Yes, yes! So you keep saying," the big man retorted, eyeing his tottering companion with a mixture of amusement and concern. "Only if you are more adept at writing than you are at walking, though. Now, let's be on our way."

The smaller man nodded. "And while we walk, I shall finish the tale of the heart."

Edgar watched as they made their way to the door, weaving among tables and chairs, dodging other drunken patrons and tilting inward until their shoulders nearly touched. He watched their backs as the door opened, and then slid his eyes around to the barman's pockmarked face. He pressed his hand to the bar for a moment, and then slid it into his pocket, the paper tucked neatly into his fist. He pushed the paper to the bottom and a wrinkled bill was neatly substituted. It was more than the drink had cost; a tidy tip left for the barman's keen inattention.

Edgar's mind whirled in a bourbon fog, but the small man's words had imbedded themselves deeply in his mind, and they helped him to focus. Written down—all the stories—written down.

Edgar glanced down the bar and stared at the empty stools the two had vacated, then turned to follow them out of the bar. The words he'd collected rubbed against one another on the crumpled paper in his pocket. Edgar could almost hear their soft scraping, trying to get free and not quite managing it.

The man had talked about the beating of a heart—loudly, like a clock, like a drumbeat pounding behind plaster walls. Edgar never sat too close to the two men, so he never got entire stories—only the words. Stolen words. Now darkness had seeped in that threatened to blot those out as well. If they were written down, he was too late. If the words had been captured and structured, what was left for him?

The sun was long gone from the sky, and without The Swan's dim light to do battle with them, the shadows closed in tight. It was chilly. Edgar pulled his jacket up, turning the collar so that it wrapped about his neck and broke the wind. He kept his eyes to the ground, watching for potholes in the street, and he walked as quickly as the bourbon would allow. As he walked, his footsteps on the cobbled street found the rhythm of his heart. His pulse grew louder, rushing in his ears, and he stopped, closed his eyes, and tried to gather his thoughts.

He needed to get home. He still had enough oil left in his lamp to write for a few hours, until his bleary eyes could no longer sustain their own weight and the darkness claimed him. His head pounded with the deep resonance of a phantom heart. Edgar turned down an alley that cut off from the shadows of the street into even deeper darkness, and staggered toward his rooms as quickly as his thin, bourbon-clumsy legs could carry him.

Halfway down the alley's length, he caught sight of something lying in his path. It was too far from the walls to be garbage, unless some children had come by and toppled it as a prank. Edgar slowed warily, swinging his gaze to either side as he approached. Then he stopped and stood still as a stone, and the pounding that had threatened to blank his mind grew louder still, pressing up into his throat and, thankfully, choking off a scream.

It was a body, and, as he stepped closer in fascination, he saw that it was a familiar body. The small, ferret-like man lay face down in the dirt. His arms were flung out to the side, not as if to catch himself when he fell, but in reaction to something. That something glittered in the dim light, and Edgar saw that it was the blade of a very long, very thin dagger. The hilt stood out from the man's back like a planted cross, and blood ran down the sides of the body to pool on the alley floor.

Then Edgar saw the manuscript, and he forgot the body. The words whispered softly to him, and a stray breeze caught the top corner of one page and threatened to spirit it away. The man's head rested on a pillow of words. Blood had splattered on the paper, and the pool beneath the body seeped upward, encroaching on the white, word-speckled pages.

Edgar took a last glance around and saw no one. He leaned down, lifted the man's head by its greasy hair, and yanked the pages free. He released his grip and watched as the head fell back with a soft, wet thud. A low, wet moan bubbled over the man's thin lips and Edgar drew in a quick gulp of air. It was the last sound Edgar heard as his heartbeat sped and roared. He ran off down the alley, tucking the papers beneath his jacket and fighting to clear the image of that knife, stark and final, pinning the small man's jacket to his spine.

Back in his rooms, Edgar slammed the door behind him and collapsed against its worn wooden surface with a groan. He clutched his coat, and the sheaf of papers, tightly to his chest. The room was sparsely furnished with no more than a bed, a chair, and a small desk upon which rested a stack of clean paper, his ink well and a quill. Edgar made his way across the darkened room, banging his shin smartly on the foot of the bed and crying out softly.

He knew better than to make too much noise and risk awakening the other tenants of the building. Grouchy old men flanked him, and down the hall was an old woman with hearing so keen she would sometimes complain that the scratching of his quill on the paper was too loud.

He'd filed away her words. He'd filed away the images, as well. He could see her, lying awake, late into the night, her eyes wide open and glaring at the wall that separated them, flinching at each stroke of ink on his paper and dreaming of ways to make him stop.

Edgar flipped the thumb switch on the gas lamp and urged the flame higher, chasing the shadows back into their corners and illuminating the surface of the desk. There was enough fuel for a few hours' work and no more. He couldn't afford to waste a single minute.

He pulled the papers out of his coat and dropped into the chair, smoothing the top sheet out with the palms of his hands. He bent over the page and read, his head cocked to one side and resting on the heel of his hand. The fingers of that hand tugged at his hair as he read, his face trapped between amazement and revulsion.

The tales were wondrous, but the words were lacking. Edgar himself could never have concocted such frightening images from his own limited experience, but the man who'd written these pages had an equal inability to distill the images into words.

Now, Edgar reflected, he lacked even the ability to sit on his barstool and speak the words for another's benefit. Pity.

Edgar fingered his quill and scowled at the pages. Some of them were spattered with the man's blood, entire words obscured by the thickening goo. Edgar shuddered and tried to read more quickly.

When he had read every word, he sat back in his chair and stared off through the one window in his apartment distractedly. Edgar knew he could do better. He could bring these tales to life. He could bring them to the world.

He glanced at the lamp and saw that the reading had cost him nearly half of his oil. He turned the wick down just a touch, hoping to preserve a few extra minutes of light. Edgar carefully stacked the dead man's pages and glanced around the room. The lack of furnishings also provided a decided lack of good places to hide things. His impatience got the better of him, and he rose, lifted the corner of his mattress, and slipped the manuscript beneath it. He knew he'd have to find a better place eventually, on the off chance they traced his steps from the alley, but for now this would have to do.

He returned to the desk and slid a fresh sheet of paper into the pool of flickering light. He unstoppered his ink, poured a small amount into the well, and tapped the tip of a battered quill against the surface of the desk to clear it.

The dead man's words whirled through his mind. So many images beckoned to him that it was difficult to sort them, or his thoughts, coherently. He decided to go with what was clearest in his mind, and that would be the events of the evening, what he'd heard in the bar. He dismissed the image of the dagger-hilt cross and the small man's back and he began to write.

"The Tale of the Heart."

Edgar stared at the words he'd written, and then frowned. With a quick flourish he dragged the quill through the title and wrote another beside it.

"The Tell-tale Heart." He smiled at the subtle re-arrangement and wished, just for a moment, that he could grab the small man from the past, drag him to the desk and show him. It wasn't just the words—it was the way they were used—the art was in their arrangement.

As the flame guttered, threatening to blow out every time he moved, Edgar dipped his quill again, and continued to write.

Morning found him sprawled across the desk, his head resting on the paper and the quill still in his hand. The ink had dried on the tip and the lamp had gone out. As he righted himself, his stiff back crying out in protest, he recalled just when that lamp had betrayed him.

One story done, the next begun. The lamp had given up its last before he'd had a chance to finish. Edgar had plowed ahead, willing his brain to fight through the sleepless fog and finish that second story in the dark. His hand rested on the desk still, awaiting further orders.

No, he could recall no more than a bird, a man and a chair. His brain spun its wheels, trying to wrap itself around that fragmented memory. The lone window admitted a small square of sunlight, which fell upon the paper, taking the place of the lamplight. Edgar smiled a smile that was not his own and chuckled. He cleared the detritus from the pen and began to write. His smile widened with each word.

He wrote through breakfast and lunch, ignored all but one cry for his body to relieve itself of the day's doings. He wrote straight up until two, when he slammed down the quill and gathered together the pages, which now comprised four stories.

He had to eat. He knew he had to rest, and he had other work to do. He stared at the pages grasped tightly in his hands, and frowned.

It wasn't odd for him to drop by the offices of the printer late, and he considered whether, along with the criticism that lay half complete on the desk, buried under the pages, and the blood, he should submit one of the stories. He itched to see them printed, to see the typeset words on better paper than the poor stuff he scribbled on, but.

There was the other man. The stories were changed; there was no doubt of that. The words were Edgar's. Still—there was the matter of the heart. There were the images, the blood-soaked, too-vivid images, not the least of which was the recurring visage of the small man, gesticulating wildly at his friend and spouting his ideas like a madman. What if that friend read the papers? What if that friend, even though he'd never so much as turned in Edgar's direction, knew who he was, and had seen him scribbling the stolen words, night after night. If that man were looking for his friend's killer—or, worse yet, if that man was his friend's killer—what would he do when he read that story?

Edgar's brow broke out in a cold sweat, and he brushed his sleeve across it. He gathered together the sheaf of bloodstained papers and ordered them as neatly as he could, then glanced around the room. There was so little furniture that, under close scrutiny, he saw the close resemblance to a cell. He moved to the bed, lifted the hard mattress, and tucked the papers carefully beneath it. Then, with the stories tucked neatly under his jacket, he headed out of his room and down the stairs.

The sunlight assaulted him, brighter somehow when unhampered by glass. Nevertheless, he lowered his head, squinted shut his eyes, and trudged up the street toward the printer's, trying to pry his mind from thoughts of the stories brushing up against him through the linen of his shirt, or the soft moan the man had uttered when his head struck the alley floor.

♦ ♦ ♦

That night, Edgar dreamed.

He dreamed of New York City. He sat in a chair, facing an older man—an editor. He wasn't sure how he knew this, but he did.

Edgar sat nervously in his chair. He fussed with the pleats of his pants and slicked back his hair, watching the broad-shouldered man in the expensive suit read his stories. They were his stories now and no other's. The only man who could say otherwise was cold and stiff. Besides, while the ideas had not been born in Edgar's imagination, the words certainly had. That made the stories his and thus the fame would be his, as well.

The man read on, eyes widening at one word and narrowing at another. Edgar found it impossible to gauge the man's true response—his vision was oddly vague. Sounds were louder than he could ever remember. As he read, he put each finished page down on the desk face up, in order. Edgar thought of how this stack would mount up, of how he would have to re-order the pages when the man was done. He wondered which story the man was reading, and why his eyebrows went up and down—why his lips pursed, then frowned, and then went back to a fine hard slit. Edgar fidgeted with his shoe and frowned.

And then he saw it.

The top page on the stack, the one the editor had just set down, had a small red mark on the upper left corner. It was not a fingerprint, for surely he had seen the man grasp the page by the top right corner. Edgar frowned and looked more closely.

The bottom page in the man's hand sprouted a red spot of its own. It blossomed before Edgar's eyes and grew larger as he read. Edgar swallowed and looked away, blinked three times in quick succession. When he looked back, the red spot was still there and it had grown larger.

More spots broke out on the pages in the editor's hands. Still more popped up on the stack upon the desk. Edgar twitched inside, his stomach tying itself into a huge knot and his eye beginning to spasm. The editor's expression continued to shift through emotions, following the words on the page, but his hands dripped with blood. His fingers smeared the pages, and a steady drip had begun at the edge of the desk, falling from where blood pooled beneath the pages.

Edgar could barely breathe, and that drip became louder. He watched each droplet form, release from the congealed miasma on the desktop, then fall, quivering through the air to PLOP into the puddle beneath the desk.

Then the editor scanned the final page and looked up. He grinned at Edgar. It was the big man. The man who'd been with the smaller one in the bar—and he was smiling. His smile widened impossibly and the teeth it revealed were long, sharp, and hungry.

Edgar screamed.

He sat up with a start. He was shaking and drenched in sweat. It was still dark, and the soft glow from the gaslights shone through the windows, illuminating galaxies of dust motes as they danced in the darkness. Then he heard the PLOP and his heart nearly stopped.

Edgar had made tea, and though it would be hours before the city would awaken, he could no longer sleep. He had managed to stop the leak in his sink with an old rag, but the echo of that last PLOP gave him no peace. He still felt clammy from the sweat-drenched nightmare, and he sat at his desk, pen in hand, brooding.

He was trying to pen a criticism of the latest work by Mr. Charles Dickens, whom he admired, but the words would not come to him. Not those words. The others would not leave him alone, but Edgar had to eat, and he knew he could not sell the stories. Not yet.

"Who is he?" he muttered.

The image of the big man, shaking his head in bafflement at the end of the bar as his friend spewed forth those amazing images in a constant stream, came to Edgar again and again. He tried to remember details. Had the man's hands been calloused? Had he ever come into the tavern with any particular item in his hand that might give a clue to his profession, or his home? Had Edgar ever heard their names?

Bleary eyed, he returned to the work at hand. He had a deadline, and if he missed another, he would no longer have to worry about finding the words at all, because he would be finding a job—and a home—instead. As the sun rose slowly over the city, the scratching of his quill ticked off the moments on the clock, first hesitantly, and then in a steady stream.

It was three days later when he finally saw the man, alone at the end of the bar in The Swan. Edgar watched him carefully, trying not to be obvious. He wanted to walk over, offer his hand, and ask where the man's friend was. Get it out in the open. Instead, he watched as the man morosely nursed a half-pint and stared at the mirrored wall behind the bar in silence.

It was like being in the theatre and watching a play enacted with one of the main characters missing. The big man's hat sat, just as it always had, on the bar at his side. The stool beside him was pressed tightly against the wood base of the bar, empty with the aspect of having *been* empty for a very, very long time. The barman brought pint after pint, but the two men exchanged no pleasantries, and none of the regulars dropped by to ask questions, or offer condolence.

Edgar drew forth a small sheet of paper from his pocket and placed it on the bar beside his own drink, but when he took his pen in hand, there was no urge to write. The room was filled with subtle sound, low-pitched conversations and clinking glass, the clatter of carriage wheels on the street outside, and the cries of merchants as they closed their shops and carted their wares off the main thoroughfare.

No words. There was nothing for him to borrow, nothing to steal. The empty barstool mocked him. He began to hallucinate forms and movements in the clump of felt the big man called a hat, and each winking crystal goblet signaled to him, and then ignored him when he turned to see.

Then it started. Edgar turned his gaze to the blank sheet of paper, and was horrified to see that it had a spatter of blood near the upper right corner. Had he grabbed this from the wrong sheaf of paper? Had it soaked from his desk somehow, or been shaken free of his clothing after he left the alley?

But no, it was fresh, wasn't it? It was too red to be dried on the paper, and it was spreading. Edgar glanced up to see if the barman had noticed, but he had not. No one had seen—yet. No one knew.

Edgar glanced down the bar at the big man, and as he did so, he felt something on his palm. Alarmed, he glanced down again and gasped, unable to contain the exclamation. The blood had pooled, not soaking into the paper, but leaking out of it. There was a gelatinous globe of deep, red blood quivering atop the paper. It had sprung an inner leak along one side and the trickle that ran out across the bar was what had touched Edgar's hand.

He glanced up again wildly. The barman had begun to walk toward him, and Edgar's heart pounded. He found that he couldn't breathe, and out of the corner of his eye, he saw that the big man at the end of the bar had spun in his seat and had fixed him with a cold stare. When the man slowly rose, Edgar could take no more. He leaped back from his stool, toppling his beer, and spun crazily, nearly veering into a table and two men playing chess on his way out.

Shaking his head, the barman swiped his cloth across the counter and mopped up the spilled pint, cursing under his breath and vowing to charge the odd little man who'd spilled it double the next time he came in.

♦ ♦ ♦

Edgar crashed out into the growing twilight and lit off for home. Everywhere he looked things were tinged in red. There was no sound of pursuit, but how far behind could they be?

He reached his rooms and slammed in through the door. The hinges complained, and the knob jiggled wildly about from the sudden fury of his entrance. He shut it just as quickly and ran to the bedside. He grasped the edge of the old mattress and pulled it upward. The pages were still neatly pressed beneath mattress and frame and Edgar let go an audible sigh of relief. Then he grabbed the stack and sorted it roughly. He pulled free those pages from which he had already written and set them aside in a rough stack. As he turned away, the mattress fell back into place with a solid thud.

He crossed to the old fireplace by the door, the room's one ounce of charm. It was sweltering outside, but tonight, the fireplace would add its own heat to the already jungle-like summer night.

Edgar set match to paper and sat back on his haunches, watching as the papers went up in a swift puff of smoke. Cheap paper, it had been, as rough and feeble as any he had seen. And now it curled and charred and wasted away to ashes.

Just before the blackened edges spread inward, Edgar caught sight of a small stain on the bottom of one page. Blood. Black devoured red and the stain disappeared as quickly as it had appeared. Then another arose on the blackening surface. And another. Another.

"No," Edgar mumbled into his right fist. "No, no . . ."

He sank back onto his haunches and rubbed the palms of his hands into his eyes until the pressure nearly made him pass out.

He came slowly back to his senses as evening's shadows lengthened to night. He had not, he realized, bought more oil for his lamp. There was a stationary shop around the corner he knew to keep late hours, and to carry small jars of oil. He might make it there and back if he hurried. The flash of flame in the fireplace had long since died away.

Edgar glanced into the ashes on the hearth, but there was no sign of blood, or dampness of any kind. Only the bone-dust of words. Turning away, he slipped out into the night.

He walked through the moonlight, his head bent low and eyes on his shoes. As luck would have it, the stationary shop was open and the gentleman with the tight mustache and careless hair admitted him long enough to purchase one small bottle of oil. He clutched it tightly to his chest and turned toward home, letting the light of the moon guide him.

By the time he reached his own door once more, he felt immensely better. Surely the words would flow and his review would be complete. No more purloined stories or nonsense about bleeding paper.

Once the lamp was refueled and the match struck, the shadows receded and all that remained of the day's madness was a tangy odor of smoke that teased at his nostrils and made him think of fat Christmas sausages. Edgar settled into his chair, took up his quill, and began to read what little he'd written already. Still, his eyes shot to the stack of stories on the back corner of his desk. They were hard to avoid and even harder to remember.

He reached out toward the pages, meaning to just glance at the top page for just a moment, and then paused. He had the distinct and terrifying impression that there was something behind him, something just begging him to turn and see it. He resisted; he tried to force his mind back to the business at hand. The sensation was too strong, and Edgar turned.

A red stain crept out from beneath the mattress and sheet. It gathered at the bottom of the sheet, and then traced a thin line to the bottom of the bed frame.

Drip! One drop hit the floor, and then another, and the stain worked steadily out from some deep pool of red within, seeping through the aged material until it had spread out to cover the bottom corner of the mattress and formed a large, dark puddle on the floor.

"No! Nonononooooo..." Edgar shut his eyes. He ground his teeth until the sound of it deafened him, and he fought the growing tide of terror for control of his mind.

It's not real, he thought. It's all in your head, man—there is no blood.

He turned and faced the desk once more, reaching as calmly as he could manage for the quill. The steady drip of the blood at his back was deafening, and he wondered if the woman who could hear the sound of his quill on paper in the early hours of the morning could not hear this as well. Perhaps she was out now, calling the constable to report the dripping sound.

"Not so quick as dripping water, it weren't, sir," she'd say, "but thick-like. Like blood, not so much a drip as a bleeding cut. I heard it through his WALLS."

The dripping was so loud it shook the room, and Edgar dragged himself back from the terror, realizing as he did that the shaking was nothing more than his own nervous tremors. He stared at his hand and thought about the man in the bar and his large friend. He tried to picture them in his mind, only now he couldn't recall if the man had actually been there at all. Perhaps only the larger man had been there. Maybe Edgar had never seen a body in the alley at all, only papers and pages and stories. Maybe none of it had ever happened at all. Maybe there was no pile of stories on his desk, only a stack of empty pages he'd lined up in his own delirium.

He looked back over his shoulder and whimpered. The stain had grown and the puddle beneath was making its way across the floor, spreading into a lake of blood and stretching out to reach for him with glistening red rivulets for talons.

With a cry, Edgar brought the quill down on his free hand. There was a flash of sudden, intense pain, and he felt the kiss of ink and blood as they mixed. With a quick suck of dry air, he glanced sharply over his shoulder at the bed. The blood was gone. He laughed, and the tinny sound echoed off the walls and died slowly.

There never had been any blood. And he had never stolen any stories. The large man at the bar had been alone, and the small man with the face of a ferret and a million stories in his head was a figment of Edgar's own imagination. Like a mantra, he set those thoughts running over and over in his mind.

Yes, that's it, he thought. It was my own psyche fighting to bring the stories to the surface. My own personal Cyrano.

He looked down and blinked at the droplet of blood oozing from the wound on the back of his hand. The tip of the quill had punctured his skin, and the edges of the cut were growing dark and curling in on themselves. Edgar smiled to himself and began to hum. He couldn't have done that to his hand. It was another product of his imagination.

An even smaller droplet of blood clung to the pen and ran into the ink channel. As he set it to the paper, the blood soaked in and stained it, first a bright red, then pink and finally purple as it flowed away and the ink ruled once more.

Edgar screamed and leaped from his chair, knocking it to the floor and shaking the desk so hard that the lamp nearly toppled in a mass of flames. He righted it with shaking hands before it had a chance to spill the precious oil. Then he stood in the middle of the room, face buried in his hands, shaking harder than he thought possible.

Slowly, he peeked between the fingers of his hands at the words on the page. They were still stained that accusing red. He turned his hand over, and saw that the small oozing droplet was spreading across his wrist. Eyes wide and vacant, he turned to the bed. More than anything in his life he wanted to see clean, white sheets. He wanted to see a slight lump where the mattress rested on the sheaf of stories. Blood dripping from his fingers to stain the floor, he knew that he would not.

The corner of the mattress was a clotted mass of blood. It was blackened at the seam, but the drip was still brilliant red, trickling across the floor and showing no sign of slowing. Soon it would trickle under the door and out into the street beyond, and someone would see it. He turned back to the desk.

He glanced briefly at the review where it languished, unfinished and insignificant in the shadow of the pages he'd written the night before. Stolen words. The pile of paper was so pregnant with indefinable dread that he expected the corner of it to be soaked with dark ink and bleeding on to the desk.

His hand began to throb, and Edgar walked into his small kitchen and ran cold water over it, washing away the blood and gritting his teeth against the bite of cold water on his suddenly fevered skin.

He wrapped a linen napkin around his hand, covering the wound, and walked to the bed. As he drew near, the room grew hazy, and he stopped. The second he stood still, his sight cleared, and the steady drip resumed. Before he could lose his courage, Edgar leaned in close and gripped the sodden corner of the mattress firmly. As his fingers closed, he closed his eyes as well and gritted his teeth against the sensation.

It never came. The mattress was as dry and hard as it had been the first day he'd laid eyes on it, and Edgar's eyes snapped open as he stared, his heart trip-hammering in his chest. No blood. He lifted the mattress and took the sheaf of papers into his trembling hands.

Feverishly, he thumbed through the pages, removed the top ten and replaced the rest beneath the mattress. He strode to his desk, brushed aside the unfinished review almost absently, and dropped into the chair. There was no sound of dripping blood from behind him. He did not look to see what state the corner of the mattress might be in. He read, and then reread the words, letting them sink into his mind. As he did so, he worried at them, teased them and poked them into a slightly different shape, a more proper tale. It was a tale of obsession, wine, and revenge, and it made his tongue tingle for just a taste of the vine, but he ignored it.

Straightening his desk, his hand still throbbing with pain, Edgar pulled a blank page from the stack on his desk, and as the lamp flickered and danced, casting its laughing shadows mockingly into the corners of the room, he wrote. He concentrated on the words, and on the paper. The room faded to the background, and it wasn't until two hours later, when he heard an angry banging on his wall, that he looked up from his work.

The hour was very late. The oil he'd managed to purchase was low, and there were only a very few hours until he would be expected to turn in his review. He stared at the paper, pressed to the desk beneath his cramped fingers. There was page after page of writing, neat and ordered, and he barely remembered writing it. He had vague images, and there was something about Amontillado whirling through his thoughts, but . . .

He straightened the pages and added them to the stack of those he'd already written. Bleary eyed, he reached for his review, and for the next hour or so, conscious of every slight scratch of his quill on the page, he worked, glancing nervously at the wall separating him from the old harpy with the bat's ears. He finished with barely enough time for two hours rest, and without even glancing at the corner of the mattress; he fell across it into a fitful, dazed sleep.

The Swan was crowded, and it was difficult to get a good line of sight down the bar. Edgar sat, hunched over a glass of sherry, and glared at the two empty seats across the room. There had been no sign of the large man, and Edgar's hands, wrapped tightly around the stem and body of his glass, trembled. In his pocket he had a single sheet of the small man's manuscript, and on the bar before him, paper and pen. He had written nothing, no captured or stolen phrases.

He was watchful now. At the first sign of the blood, he knew he'd have to write. If he concentrated on the manuscript page in his pocket, went over the story in his head, and wrote the result, everything would be fine. Everything would be dry, free of blood, and they would not stare at him. Their voices would remain muted and distant and impersonal, and they would not accuse him.

An image of the alley surfaced, the man's bloody head leaking onto the pile of paper and he shuddered. He wondered, briefly, if he put the papers back where he'd found them, if the man would rematerialize slowly, blood first, to cover his words, but somehow he knew it was not that simple—and never would be again.

Edgar sipped his Amontillado and thought of the pages, piled and waiting, on his desk. He had more work to do—a criticism and an essay—but first the blood would take its price, and there were many, many pages of the little man's manuscript left to finish. He shuddered again, and downed his drink, signaling the barman for another.

What he feared the most was the bottom of that pile. What would happen when he dropped the last of the manuscript into his fire and watched the blood flow and dry and crackle to dust? When all the stolen words were translated, and the stories piled in a heap on his desk, would they bleed? Would he have to start again, and again, drying it all away through the tip of his quill, or would it be set to rest?

His eyes were slightly sunken, and his pallor had become unhealthy, and even paler than was his wont. No one took notice, though they stared at him more closely when he turned in his work at the paper, or when he bought food, oil, or ink. His plan was to write slowly, a little every night, stretching the dead man's words out across the years to come. If he was never without a sheet of paper, and one of the pages of the ferret-man's manuscript, then if and when the blood began, or he was afraid that someone was noticing something, he could translate a few words, or re-read the story at hand.

He was half afraid that if the manuscript brought enough blood, since he'd joined his own to it through the quill, that it would draw him down to his death.

The barman brought his drink, and Edgar cupped it between his palms without looking up. He took a long pull on the sweet, chilled wine and turned to glance down at the empty seats once more. He started, nearly spilling his drink. There was something on the bar, something indistinct and shapeless, but familiar. He shook and drank again, and as he did, he watched. The big man's hat. It lay in its usual shapeless mass on the bar. There was no sign of its owner, but something dark was pooled beneath it.

Edgar shoved his drink away violently, nearly tipping it. He scrabbled for his quill and drew a small bottle of ink from his breast pocket. Opening it and dipping the quill, he began to write with feverish intensity. Outside, the bells on the city clock had begun to ring maddeningly, and though he knew they went on for moments only, the echoing sound lingered. He twisted the sound into something the ferret man had said, something from the page in his pocket.

"The bells, bells bells bells . . .."

At the end of the bar, where the evening sunlight cast Edgar's shadow down the bar, the lumpy mass that had been a hat dissolved to nothing, and the barman rubbed the smooth, polished surface of the ball unseeing. There was no sound but the loud, insistent scratching of a quill.

SON OF MOURNING

CHRISTOPHER T. LELAND

HE WAS BORN AT a winter's dawn, beneath the cold December sun, the morning after the first snow of the year. Icicles glimmered on the cabin eaves as his mother, her nails sharp in her palms, cursed the haggard widow who attended on the birth. The wind knifed through the trees, drifting the snow against the walls, whipping away his mother's cries as they pressed against the windows and whorled beneath the door, scattering them far across the fields. A sometime farmhand stopped by once, uneasy at the sound, but left as soon as he was told a child was on the way. A small white mound of snow, soon melted, was all he left behind. A wandering conjureman, dark and cold, came too to warm himself at the flickering grate, unheedful of the woman's screams. He gave the widow for safekeeping a bag of trinkets for the immanent child.

As the sun peeked above the stark and snow-spun pine, he came into the world, his first cry mingling with his mother's last, both snatched in an instant by the singing wind, and sent into the silence of the newborn day.

The widow took him from his mother, wrapping him in the ragged blanket thrown across the bed. She cast snow upon the fire and left the corpse to freeze, eyes wide with pain and dull with death. Tucking whatever money she could find into her bodice and gathering in her free hand a jeweled brooch that glittered on the nightstand, a small china dog, and the bag of trinkets, she hefted the child on her hip and left the cabin, heading down the country road toward town. In the pearly sky hung a blade of moon, and the gleaming tear of the morning star.

She gave the boy, the blanket, and, in a moment of oft-regretted guilt, the bag of trinkets to his aunt and uncle, who owned a plot just outside the village. They warmed him, fed him, placed him in a makeshift crib, then sat with a Bible spread before them to search out a name for the child. At last, they chose to call him, in memory of the dawn that had brought his mother's death, Jabez Cyrus: Sorrow of the Sun.

Before he went to bed that night, Lloyd Mahon stood in the firelight, looking upon his nephew now his son. He thought of Lilly, his sister, whose body he would retrieve tomorrow and bring to town for burial. And he knew how they would talk, the congregation, and wondered if she would lie in unhallowed ground just beyond the graveyard fence, beside her husband, Jorey, who had died thirteen years before. Jorey was given to much drinking and living high, and had had his way with women, both before and after he took Lilly to wife. So, when his mind decayed with the disease that even the wildest bachelors spoke of in voices low with shame, the townsfolk said only that he had reaped the bitter harvest he had sown. He passed, agonized, in a slobbering fit one sticky night in June, and Lilly was left—unfriended, barren, she supposed, and cursed with Jorey's sickness. She was dark and worldly, more Spanish than Scot, they always said, and had borne her husband's infidelities by matching them with her own. When he died, instead of taking in laundry or throwing herself on the charity of the church, she took to selling her favors to the drummers who traveled the highway. She kept company with them all—young and old, fair or wizened, quiet or cruel. Her mind began to waste as the years passed, but she had kept on till now, when she conceived, gave birth, and died.

Lloyd looked at the child, bald and soft amid the linen. He wondered if the boy would live, and, if he did, what taint would linger in him. Who was his father? Some lowlife swindler, unconcerned, unaware at all of Jabez Cyrus . . . Lloyd paused. Jabez Cyrus Mahon. The boy was his to rear, after all, and an orphan at birth takes the name of his guardian.

Transfixed at the child, Lloyd stood silent long into the night. The fire glowed only weakly, and, with each instant, dimmed a little more. But deep in awe of that peculiar miracle that had brought him a son, Lloyd smiled, unheedful of the gathering dark.

The snows melted and came again, interspersed with lazy summers. Two Presidents were elected, and the state legislator from the district was shot in a brawl. The parish hall burned and was rebuilt. A carnival came through once, and there was a scandal when the McGrady girl ran off with a sideshow barker. Lloyd Mahon's wife died one soggy March of pneumonia, and he took another bride the next year, nearly twenty years his junior. There were fewer jonquils in bloom one spring, and the old folks every year were firmer in their conviction that nobody remembered Jesus on Christmas anymore.

Jabez Cyrus Mahon—Jabecy for short—grew up, not much different from the other boys in what he liked or what he did or how he fared at school. He played the same games, talked dirty with his friends, and choked on pipefuls of tobacco when he was only ten. He cried like a true son of twelve when his aunt died, and, after a period of suspicion, accepted his third mother, barely nine years his senior, as if she had carried him herself.

And yet, for all of this, as he grew older, the townsfolk knew with an instinct they could not explain that he was not the same at all.

When he was barely seven, Jabecy found a banjo stuffed in a dusty trunk. It was battered and out-of-tune, but the child took it and learned to play it in a way unknown in that little town. When he was ten, they had him perform one Sunday at the church, for the preacher said that God Himself must have touched the child for him to play like that. So Jabecy strummed there below the cross, a funny smile upon his face that some called angelic and some others said made mock, and a few murmured that things like this would make him proud. But somehow pride seemed too common an emotion to arise from his picking, for he brought such wild and unearthly sound from the strings that it was if his hands were guided by something from another world.

Oftentimes at dusk, especially in the fall, the hum of Jabecy's banjo competed with the rustle of the dying leaves and the calls of birds in flight from winter, and Lloyd would find him in the woods not far from the cabin, beneath an oak with the instrument on his lap and, spilt beside him, the trinkets the old conjureman had brought. The boy had a fascination with them: shiny glass beads, clear or green or blue, smooth or faceted; tiny metal chimes that jangled when you blew on them; bracelets and rings, chokers and interlocking brass loops, and a many-sided globe of mirrors, set in a small stand, that with a thumb-flick could fill a room with stars caught from the firelight. When the child was young, Lloyd had not thought much of his attachment to these baubles. But as Jabecy grew older and still toyed with them, Lloyd worried, and one twilight came to the oak with the Bible, sat down, and read to Jabecy what St. Paul had said about putting away childish things. The boy listened fitfully, turning the ball of mirrors.

"Jabecy? Jabecy, do you hear?"

He did not answer, intent upon his face splintered a hundred tiny times, dancing slowly round and round.

"Boy!"

Lloyd grabbed his nephew's shoulder, and told him he would teach him to pay mind to his betters. But as he raised his hand, Jabecy struggled free, crying that the trinkets were all he had from his real mother.

Lloyd let him go, and watched as Jabecy disappeared among the trees.

He did not follow. He leaned on the oak, the image of Lilly, so long dead it seemed, rising before him. A twist of pity caught him for the bastard boy who could not choose but remember his dark mother and secret father. Lloyd gathered the trinkets from the ground, along with banjo, and, returning to the house, laid the bag on Jabecy's pillow.

So the years passed, and Jabecy was somehow set apart a little. But the townsfolk would, perhaps, have ignored his talent and his quirks, had it not been for the metamorphosis that began around his thirteenth winter. He had always been a handsome child, fair and blue-eyed, with his mother's black hair and its lazy wave. Yet, as he became more and more a man, shooting up to six feet, lithe and muscular, heads began to turn as he ambled down the highway through the town. It was Mrs. Sluder, the blacksmith's wife, who first applied the word to the boy when he was barely sixteen and out to buy a saw one day.

"He is," she said, and paused a moment for the full effect. "He is not handsome. He is beautiful."

And those who heard her say it knew that it was true. It did not mean he was girlish, or precious, a fragile thing to be locked away. But rather, that when the girls talked to him or walked beside him on the way to school, his look, his voice, the very fact that he was there at all made them feel a little faint. In his presence, boys were somehow abashed, and even the men, cautiously, would watch as he passed, then turn to their oldest and most trusted friends, who would not look askance at them for saying so, and mutter: "He is beautiful."

Only one thing kept Jabecy from a kind of angelic perfection. His laugh was usually pleasant, low and quiet. But sometimes, at a cruel joke or the meanest gossip, there was an edge to it, a shrill relish, perhaps the slightest taint of madness. But then, as his uncle said one day to a couple of neighbors, if all the Jabecy got from his mother was a crazy laugh, things couldn't be so bad.

They agreed, though one thought a moment and added with a sober smile: "True, Lloyd. But Lord knows what got passed on from his pa."

Everyone had been a little surprised when Ella Evers had consented to be Lloyd Mahon's second wife. She was small and pretty, brown-haired and brown-eyed, inclined, they said, to be a little flighty. She had really been expected to marry someone above her station, some small town banker or lawyer's son, but instead chose Lloyd, honest and slow, his first wife dead, childless but for his sister's bastard boy. Their union produced no rivals for Jabecy, so Ella lavished all her love on the unnatural child. The neighbors wondered how he would take to his new mother, and often remarked that she was closer to his age than she was to Lloyd's. But it seemed to work out well. Jabecy was respectful and called her Aunt Ella, and she too seemed to have adjusted, acting as the wife of a man of forty-five would be expected.

And yet, a woman in her twenties is not yet forty-five, and Ella was no freer from the fascination that Jabecy held for women than any other daughter, wife, or mother of the town. His beauty gave her shivers, and, as he grew older, she was more and more in thrall to him. About her housework, she would see him through the door and stop mid-task to watch her son-of-sorts as he chopped wood, his shoulders rippling, or as, with the scythe, he cropped the weeds near the well, his arm moving in wide arcs, his skin sunbrowned and his hair like night.

Still, one evening, when the boy was asleep and Lloyd asked her if she had ever been tempted, Ella swallowed her anger and what might have been fear, saying no, that she just pitied Jabecy because his heritage was black; that he was a child of sadness, a curse upon his mother, but then, perhaps, a blessing for her and for Lloyd.

Lloyd kissed her, relieved, and ashamed of his suspicions, then rose to poke the fire in the grate. He smiled and sighed, wondering to himself if a boy could be both a blessing and a curse.

Jabecy and Ella sat by the hearth, the flames high, sizzling and spitting. Lloyd was at church. They were looking for a new preacher, and he liked the harangue and debate of the deacons as they sought a replacement. Ella read a book while Jabecy idly plunked his banjo, the bag of trinkets beside him.

Suddenly, he stopped.

"Have you ever seen these?"

Ella marked her place with her finger. "Seen what?"

"These," he said, emptying the sack beside him.

"Why, yes," she said. "I've seen them."

"But have you ever looked at them?"

The fire snapped. She eyed him for a moment, unsure. He met her gaze, eyes innocent and blue.

"Not really. No," she said.

"Here." He pulled a string of beads from the jumble. "Do you know where I got these?"

Ella looked down. "They were your mother's, Jabecy."

"No!" He shook his head hard. "No." He smiled. "An old man gave them to me before I was born."

"Oh, Jabecy . . ." Ella's tone was joshing, but uncertain.

The flames popped.

"It was an old conjureman, an old voodoo man, and he gave them to the widow who brought me out."

"Jabecy . . ."

"Here." He held a string of beads. "Put these on." He grabbed her wrist, but only lightly. "Put them on. They're just glass."

She tried to pull free, but then her eyes caught the beads, spangled with firelight.

"All right."

She slipped the necklace over her head. It hung to her breasts.

She giggled a little. "They're very nice, Jabecy." She started to take them off.

"No. Wait. Wait, there's more."

He held a ring in his palm, a ring like a snake coiled tail to mouth with two red stones for eyes, sightless and deep. He took Ella's left hand and slipped it on her finger.

"Now," he said softly, "ain't that pretty."

She spread her hand before her to admire the trinket, smiling faintly at the textured gold and the eyes, sparkling maliciously in the half-light, so much brighter than her wedding band beside. Sighing then, she reached to remove it.

It stuck.

She tried several times, lucklessly, then looked at Jabecy with a sort of quiet panic.

"I can't get it off," she whispered. Her voice rose as she twisted her finger. "Jabecy, I can't get it off!"

He moved to her side and lay his hand on hers.

"It's all right," he said comfortingly. "We'll get it off. Soon. Here." He reached for the ball of mirrors, setting it so it caught the firelight. "Watch." He spun it with is thumb. His voice fell to a smooth whisper. "Watch."

The glow of the fire splintered on the walls, turning like little suns around and around. "Watch." Ella tried to look away, but they were everywhere, shards of light. "Watch."

The voice commanded and implored. She felt drunk, dizzy, and Jabecy was playing the banjo now. But the mirrors did now slow, but seemed to revolve faster and faster. The music was low and soft.

"Dance." She heard him say. "Dance."

The flames jumped higher. The walls sparkled. "Dance." Her arms floated up and she moved like mist. The music went faster. "Dance." And she swayed back and forth.

The banjo was playing, but Jabecy's arms were around her.

"Dance," he whispered, and she moved like snow.

Her clothes were gone—her starched blouse, dark skirt. And his. The hair of his chest prickled her breasts.

"Dance."

The room was liquid. Light like water. Spinning. Spinning.

"Dance."

She saw him close to her, all around her, within her, rosy with flame.

"Dance."

She felt weightless, moaned between half-parted lips.

Then she was cold, cold, shot through with ice. She opened her mouth to scream, eyes wide with fear, half-dead with pain, and saw Jabecy. Jabecy, more beautiful than men were meant to be.

Then she was falling, falling so far, as if off the edge of the earth.

New-mooned and near-midnight, the sky was funereal as Lloyd made his way down the dirt road toward home. Lonely and tired, he trudged along, noticing as he turned through the gate into the yard that the windows were dark. He thought for a moment that Ella and Jabecy must be asleep. Then, faintly at first, growing louder as he approached, he heard the tinny thrum of banjo strings.

When Lloyd came through the door, Jabecy was at the hearth, the banjo in his hands. His feet bare, his shirt gone, he hunched his head almost to his chest. Lloyd started to speak, then saw Ella, naked, crumpled against the wall. In a blurred and thoughtless instant, he was beside her, unable to tell if she were dead or alive.

"Jabecy," he said. "Jabecy. What's happened, Jabecy . . ." His voice was strained, confused.

The boy raised his head, and his eyes were far away. A smile twitched across his lips, while his fingers moved a little faster over the frets and across the strings.

"What happened!"

Lloyd tried to lift his wife from the floor. His hand brushed the beads. The glitter of the ring's dull gold and red played in his eyes.

"What have you done, Jabecy!"

He started to rise, fury welling deep within him. He froze at Jabecy's silhouette against the fire. The music ceased, but only for an instant, as Jabecy set the ball of mirrors to turning. The squares of light flew around the room.

"Jabecy?"

The boy smiled wide, and spoke half-aloud in a voice aflame with darkness: "Yes," he said. "Yes."

Then he began to laugh. But it was not the laugh that had drawn comment from the townsfolk as a little mad, nor Jorey's as he blubbered in his syphilitic fits. It was not crazy or violent or sick. It transcended human sound, the apotheosis and damnation of laughter, ringing triumphant, incomprehensible, deathless and deadly, fiery and all-consuming. Lloyd Mahon stood transfixed at the boy, in awe before the peculiar miracle that had brought him a child of sadness.

Sorrow of the Sun.

Son of Morning.

The banjo sang savage, unearthly. The fire flickered and rose, and the ball of mirrors turned as if spun by some invisible finger.

"Dance," Jabecy said. "Dance."

The man resisted, but only for an instant. The music and the stars embraced him. Mahon's arms floated from his sides as if he were in water. His head dropped, and he moved, slowly at first, then ever faster in time to the banjo's tune.

Jabecy's laughter rolled over him in a tide.

"Dance. Dance!"

ANKAREH MINU

RICHARD A. LUPOFF

CAPTAIN SAMSON ALWAYS KEPT a neat desk. The glass covering was spotless. As Rebekkah stood rigidly facing Samson she could see his neat suit, his perfectly knotted tie, his craggy features and razor-cut steel gray hair reflected in it. She knew that her midnight blue sergeant's uniform was in good order, her gold badge carefully polished, her own jet black hair trimmed and combed to perfection. Even so, she felt shabby compared to the captain.

The commander's chin bobbed a fraction of an inch. "Close the door, Sergeant ben Zaccheus, and sit down." When she had complied he resumed. "You know how political this city can be. You know when the supervisors say jump, we can only ask how high."

Rebekkah didn't respond except with a slight nod of her own.

"Did you watch last night's meeting of the Board of Supervisors?"

"On TV, sir."

"You know that we're taking a beating over this series of fatalities by fire."

"Yes."

"Supervisor Moran really let us have it. And you know why, of course."

"Speak freely, sir?"

Samson smiled. "Taping system's turned off, Sergeant." Rebekkah watched, waiting to see if Captain Samson would allow himself a smile.

He almost did. Then he slid the case folder across his desk.

Rebekkah opened it. There were incident reports and gruesome photos.

"What do you see, Sergeant? What makes this case unique?"

Rebekkah pursed her lips. She'd been a San Francisco cop for almost a dozen years, since she was a fresh-faced kid out of SF State. All her pals were eager to get down to Silicon Valley or up to the Financial District and show that women can rise as high and make as much money as men. When Rebekkah announced her intention of becoming a cop she got back a combination of sympathetic, baffled, and slyly knowing looks.

She'd seen enough cold corpses in those years, and in the Tenderloin, enough living corpses, to feel only a little shock. "The bodies are all burned. But none of the incident scenes show any fire damage."

Captain Samson nodded. "I knew you'd spot that. Good. But, Sergeant, what does it mean?"

Rebekkah poked her thin, cleft chin with a fingertip. "First thought, Captain. Somebody's killing people and burning the bodies to disguise their identities or the cause of death, or both. Second thought. File shows each body found in a different location. Identification by dental records, each one found in his own home. All male. Mixed ethnicities."

"Yes, good. You know how to read a file. However . . ." He opened a desk drawer, drew out a manila envelope and handed it to Rebekkah.

"Contra Costa County. We generally have good cooperation from them, but this one must have fallen through the cracks. Somebody over there finally woke up and sent this to us."

Rebekkah studied another crime scene photograph, another blackened corpse. She turned to the Medical Examiner's report. This victim was a female, although you couldn't have told that from the photograph.

Captain Samson asked, "Where does that get us, Sergeant? Do you have any ideas? Are these cases connected?"

"About a week apart. Might be some kind of nut. Somebody who has to kill every Thursday night because his mommy and daddy made him go to church and miss his favorite cowboy show. But I don't think so. This is nasty. And it's going to be tough. And based on last night's performance, Supervisor Vincent Moran is really pounding us over this."

"Why? They're not concentrated in his district. They're scattered all around the Bay Area. Mostly here in the city, but here's one in Marin, one in San Mateo, Oakland, Moraga. Why Moran?"

"Good question, Sergeant. Suppose you visit Mr. Moran. Tell him you're hot on the case. No, that's not the right way to put it. Anyway, flash the badge, show the colors, let him know that the department is putting its full resources into this one and we'll keep him fully informed."

Rebekkah drew a deep breath. "Captain, politics is politics. I need to know, sir, are you really putting me in charge of this case or do I just go hold the Major's hand?

Samson grinned and shook his head. "You're not afraid to ask tough questions, are you, Sergeant? Okay, fair is fair. Yes, you're really in charge of this. You'll get whatever support you need. What do you want?"

"For starters, Sir, I just want my partner. Officer O'Leary."

"Irish Jim O'Leary?" The grin widened. "You and he go way back, don't you?"

"Actually, our families do."

"Done. Go."

Hall of Justice to City Hall was a five minute jaunt across downtown San Francisco. In Supervisor Moran's outer office a sharply attired Asian woman looked up from her computer keyboard and smiled at Rebekkah. Her eyes flicked to the metal strip on Rebekkah's blouse. "Sergeant ben Zaccheus, Mr. Moran is eager to chat with you."

Rebekkah returned her best *We're here to protect and serve* smile.

Supervisor Moran's office was filled with memorabilia. A Presidential citation for his service in Iraq and another for time in Afghanistan. A Silver Star, a Bronze Star, a Purple Heart. Photos of a boyish Lieutenant Moran with General Powell, of an older Major Moran with General Petraeus, of Vincent Moran kneeling in front of a primitive structure, surrounded by ragged, admiring Afghani children, of Moran surrounded by his buddies, of Moran lying in a military hospital bed grinning bravely while a worried-looking woman—his wife?—sat by his bedside holding his hand.

And a framed photo that Rebekkah recognized from a recent copy of the San Francisco *Chronicle* of Supervisor Moran shaking hands with the Governor himself in front of sign that read, *Vince Moran for United States Senate—The People's Hero, the People's Fighter!*

Oh, yes. Supervisor Moran had his eye on the prize, all right. Not yet forty, a term in the Senate, an easy re-election, and the sky's the limit.

He stood up and extended his hand. The expression on his face was either that of a seriously concerned man or a man very adept at feigning serious concern.

"Sergeant, ah, ben Zaccheus. Thanks for coming over. I know you must be very busy."

Oh, this guy was good!

Rebekkah nodded. Next he would offer her a seat.

Yep.

"I don't believe in politicians interfering in public safety operations but I also feel a definite responsibility to the voters who put me where I am. And, as you know, this series of incendiary fatalities is threatening to get out of hand."

"I'm aware of that, sir."

"Is the department doing anything? I've already talked with the chief and got back the usual line about available resources, concern for the public, blah, blah, blah. That's why I asked him to have someone who's actually working the case come and talk with me."

"That's why I'm here, Supervisor."

"You're newly assigned to this case?"

"We've had people working on it, Supervisor. I've read the crime scene reports, forensics, medical examiner's documents. Captain Samson feels that he needs an experienced officer to pull everything together."

"And that's you, is it?"

"Yes, sir."

He didn't look happy but at least he didn't say anything about sending a girl to do a man's job. Instead he said, "I want to be kept informed regularly, Sergeant. I know your chain of command goes up through the Detective Bureau to the Chief's office to the Commission. I'm not trying to shortcut them. But if this case gets out of hand—so far, the media have played it down, they've treated each case as a separate incident, but there's no way they won't connect the dots. And pretty soon. We don't want another Zodiac or Night Stalker, Sergeant. This is urgent."

She got away as quickly as she could. She made her way back to the Hall of Justice, downloaded information on the case to her laptop, and headed for home.

She shared an apartment on Dolores Street with Officer O'Leary, Liam Francis Xavier O'Leary. Their families had been together in San Francisco for over a century, since a young immigrant, John O'Leary, had answered a want ad in a cast-aside newspaper and gone to work for the famed Kabbalist and psychic detective Abraham ben Zaccheus. It was Liam's night to deal with dinner and he took Rebekkah to a Spanish restaurant within walking distance of their apartment. They shared *Rioja* and *tapas*, flan and espressos and rich, dark chocolates with golden liquid centers.

Afterwards, at home, Liam built a fire. They settled opposite the dancing flames to drink golden *tsikoudia* brandy from Crete and talked about the case. Liam O'Leary was intrigued by Supervisor Moran's interest in the killings. "You think he wants to ride this into the Senate?"

Rebekkah nodded. "I think that's part of it. He's got to win the primary first, and something like this could get him over the old San Francisco liberal, soft-on-crime, brie-eating business. He's pushing his war record, too. That'll be big in the Central Valley. Wounded veteran. Tough on crime. Social moderate—at least by local standards."

"So we bring in some wacko who gets his jollies burning people to a crisp and Major Moran goes to Washington. As simple as that."

"Not as simple as that." Rebekkah stared into the fire as if hypnotized. "I don't know, Liam. I picked up something else."

"You don't mean a clue."

"No."

"Right. You felt a vibration. A cold breeze, a whispered word, things that go bump in the night."

"Don't start, Liam. You know how I feel about you, but just don't start."

He reached for her hand. "I'm sorry, Rebekkah. I know you believe in—well, what you believe in. Not for me to say it's all nonsense. What was it that you got, and what do you want to do with it?"

"You don't mind working this case with me? I asked Captain Samson and he okayed it, but if you're uncomfortable you can get off it."

"No, Rebekkah. You're a ben Zaccheus and I'm an O'Leary and we've both a tradition to carry on. Just tell me what you want to do."

"I want you to come with me tomorrow. We're going to visit the crime scenes, some of them anyway."

"Forensics and Crime Scene kiddies not good enough?"

"You know there's no substitute for walking over the ground, Liam."

"That I do. But, Rebekkah, now I'm the one who senses that there's something more to your thoughts."

"What do you think?"

"Ah, sweet sergeant of my heart, you want to hear that ghostly whisper in your ear. *'Twas me wicked nephew what done me in, oo-woo, oo-woo.'*"

"Maybe."

"And then?"

"Then I want to go somewhere else for a while. I'd like you to drive with me."

"Of course, me sergeant." He drained the last of his *tsikoudia* and placed the empty snifter carefully on the low table. "Well, unlike you high and mighty sergeants, we patrolmen work for a living. I'm tired and I'm ready to retire for the night."

"You go ahead, Liam. I want to think about this for a while."

She refilled her brandy snifter and sat warming the thin glass between her palms, her feet on a hassock, inhaling the brandy fumes rather than imbibing the fluid, gazing into the fire.

The flames had a hypnotic effect, or maybe it was the *Rioja* she'd had with her dinner and the *tsikoudia* she'd sipped and the fumes she'd inhaled after Liam left the room. The red and orange shapes formed faces, or seemed to do so. There must have been some sap left in the wood, and some pine knots, for the flames danced and the sap sizzled and hissed incomprehensible messages to her. The chimney drew well but a sudden gust of wind must have swept in from the Pacific, driving a small puff of smoke back into the room. Rebekkah breathed in its odor. Here eyelids drooped until the dancing flames filled her vision and the sound of the whispering, bubbling sap filled her mind.

She was jolted awake by the explosion of a pine knot. The empty brandy snifter had fallen from her hands and rolled across the carpet. She drew a deep breath, pushed herself erect and retrieved the snifter. She set it back on the table and stretched out on the sofa and slept.

If she dreamed she did not recall the experience when she was awakened by the sound of Liam O'Leary clattering in the apartment's small kitchen.

"Ah, the sergeant awakens." He carried a tray from the kitchen and lowered it to the table.

Rebekkah rubbed her temples with her fingertips to get her brain into gear. "Coffee! Toast! Breakfast fit for a goddess, Liam. And the *Chronicle* to nourish the intellect. An angel thou art!"

He'd opened the *Chron* to the local section and folded it back to expose the story of another death by burning. The tragedy had taken place in a home on one of the worst streets in Hunter's Point, a crime-ridden ghetto. You would have had to look hard to find the report. Crimes in Hunter's Point didn't garner much attention from the media or from the police.

Rebekkah phoned the Hall of Justice and got the shift commander. Crime Scene investigators had already worked the job and the ME had removed the victim's remains. The commander gave her a rundown on the preliminary report. Rebekkah thanked him. She climbed into her uniform. Five minutes later she and Liam O'Leary were headed for Hunter's Point.

The woman who answered the door to the victim's apartment could have been anywhere from forty to sixty years old. She wore a stained sweatshirt and jeans, her hair covered with a faded kerchief, her skin an unhealthy shade of burnt sienna. Her cheeks were frighteningly sunken.

"I already talked to police. What else you want of me?"

The apartment was tiny. It smelled of overripe cat litter and stale cooking. There were dishes and pots in the sink and full ash trays and empty wine bottles.

"I'm sorry, ma'am. I know this is a terrible time for you. If you would just go over the facts for me again."

Liam O'Leary was standing back, clipboard in hand. Out of the corner of her eye Rebekkah observed him studying the room.

"How am I supposed to live now?" the woman was complaining. "Look at me, woman. I can't work. I can't get no job and I can't work. He was on disability, you know? From the army. He got wounded over there in Afghani. And he got sick. I don't know what that sickness is, a lot of them get it. He couldn't hardly stand up. I had to practically carry him to the VA, he was so sick, and they said it wasn't the army's fault. At least they sent him a check every month. Now what am I supposed to do? I suppose the checks will stop and I can't work and the welfare don't hardly give out money no more."

She sat down on a dirty sofa and started sorting through cigarette butts until she found one that appealed to her. She struck a match and smoked it.

"If you could just tell me what happened, please."

There were sounds of voices from the street and thumps. Somewhere nearby an argument broke out; the voices were those of women. They seemed to be competing in cursing each other.

Rebekkah repeated her request.

"What am I going to live on now?" the woman wailed. "I needed the disability. Now what do I do?"

"Please. Where were you, and where was the victim, please."

"All right, all right." The woman poked her cigarette into the pile of butts in the ashtray. Smoke rose slowly from it. "I was in the bathroom and he was sitting here watching TV. You see that TV there? Don't get nothing worth watching, just a waste of time. He was watching it and I heard him hollering and somebody else talking."

"Could you understand what they were saying?"

"I understood my man. He was saying, *Get away from me, get away, I don't want you, go back there, I won't do it.* That's what I heard him saying. He was so weak, you wouldn't think he could talk so loud but he was shouting."

"And the other voice?"

"I never heard nothing like it. So low, like you could feel it more than you could hear it."

"A man's voice, a woman's? Could you tell?"

"Too deep for a woman or even a man. Like something from the bowels of hell, that voice. I couldn't understand one word, not a word, but it was nasty, I could tell that."

"How long did this go on?"

"I don't know. I was scared. I wanted to come and help him but I was too scared. I just stayed in the bathroom. I didn't want that thing to know I was there. And then I heard my man give a loud scream and I heard something like a crack, like something catching fire and I heard my man scream and then just moan and I heard the other thing, the voice, make like laughing only ugly, ugly, and then a thump and I come out of the bathroom and there was nobody there but my man lying on the floor all burned up and dead. And what am I gone do with no more check every month?"

The house in the Castro was a gaudily painted Victorian, the kind with elaborate gingerbread and a multicolor paint job that wind up in expensive coffee table books on San Francisco architecture. The man who admitted them wore a spotless turtleneck shirt and sharply creased trousers, a bulky cardigan sweater and Birkenstock sandals.

He led Rebekkah and Liam into a parlor and offered them seats upholstered in *faux* tapestry depicting medieval hunting scenes. Tall windows looked out on a tree-lined, hilly street. On the wall Rebekkah saw a framed marriage certificate and an enlarged photo of two men in tuxedos joining hands before a woman in ecclesiastical robes. Another photo showed a young man in an army dress blue uniform, lieutenant's bars on the shoulder boards. It was draped in black crepe.

"Would you like an espresso? Chamomile with lemon? Is it too early in the day for a glass of wine?"

"Tea, please. You're very kind. It's chilly today."

Rebekkah could see into the kitchen from her seat. It was brightly tiled. There was a large work table and a Wolf stove.

The man brought the tea service on a polished tray. He poured for them all.

"I suppose you want to know about my husband's death."

"Please."

"I'm sorry, there's really very little I can tell you. I was at work when it happened. I work on Montgomery Street. I usually get home by seven but I was working late that night. I phoned to see if he was home yet and he was, he said he was making something special for dinner. I said I'd get away as soon as I could but it might be a while."

He had seemed perfectly composed but he lowered his face suddenly into his hands. When he looked up again his cheeks were wet. He found a handkerchief and wiped his face. "I'm sorry."

"Of course."

"I can deal with it sometimes. I put in a lot of hours at work. My friends come by and try to help. We had a lot of friends, you know. A lot. But every now and then–"

Rebekkah waited for him to resume.

"All right. All right, yes. Go ahead, please. Ask away."

"In your own words, then."

"When I got home I brought a little gift, a Scharffen Berger chocolate bar. They're the very best, you know. Pricey but worth it. It was a token of affection we used to have. When one of us wanted to apologize for some little thing, he'd bring home a chocolate bar and we'd break it in half and share it and make up."

He leaned forward, lifted the tea pot and refilled Rebekkah's cup. Liam had hardly touched his.

"Would you rather have coffee, officer? No? All right."

He took a breath and blew it out. "He didn't come to greet me. I thought he was really angry, I was so late and he'd made us a fancy dinner. But then I came into this room. This very room. And there he was, on the floor. Black and dead. He was still—"

He stopped and shook his head. He was wracked by a sob.

"—smoldering."

There wasn't much more. The neighbors hadn't heard or seen anything untoward. There was no fire alarm or police call. Just a man turned to a blackened corpse.

There were witnesses to the next one. The death took place at two in the morning in the middle of People's Park in Berkeley. Members of the permanent homeless community had built a campfire and were sitting in a circle. The guitars had been broken out, a variety of voices were singing fragments of songs their owners had grooved to three decades before, bongs and joints and bottles were making the rounds.

A bearded man clad in a warm army jacket, jeans, and worn combat boots jumped to his feet screaming. The singing stopped and the guitars fell silent as he danced in a circle around the campfire.

"At first," a visibly pregnant woman with a child in each hand recounted, "at first, I thought he was doing a war dance. You know, like an Indian war dance. He was jumping around, he started going *woo, woo, woo,* like in the movies, you know, and then I thought I saw somebody next to him.

I thought he maybe came down out of that tree over there, I don't know, or out of the sky, maybe he was in one of them black CIA helicopters, they come over here all the time, you know?"

"Yes, please."

"Oh, you mean about—well, this other guy, I don't know, he must have had one of them invisibility cloaks that they have now, you know, he looked all furry or weird, I don't know, I think he maybe had wings and he was burning and he grabbed the poor guy, hugged him and they burned up together, they looked like a holy picture or something, you know, only not a halo, real flames, and then he dropped the poor guy and he faded out and the other guy fell on the ground and thrashed around a little, people were trying to help him but he just died. And they came and took him away. Probably was the CIA, I think."

And that was the best witness at People's Park.

It was an unconventional working arrangement to say the least. On the job they were sergeant and patrolman, case officer and subordinate. Rebekkah made the decisions and led the investigation, Liam did the scut-work, took notes, navigated unfamiliar routes. They wore uniforms or plainclothes as the situation indicated.

In the evenings they relaxed. Sometimes they discussed the news of the day, colleagues at work, plans for their future. At the moment, the biggest issue was whether to get one cat or two. The most urgent was what to do about dinner. It was Rebekkah's night to decide and she chose a favorite robata bar that served the freshest sushi in the Mission.

Over kaiten-zushi and unfiltered saki Liam asked if Rebekkah thought they were getting anywhere with the incendiary murders. "I don't see any pattern, myself," he admitted, "but maybe your voices will tell you what's going on."

She shook her head. "Not yet. I'm still looking for a pattern, Liam. And I don't see one. All the victims are male, at least so far. Black and white, rich and poor, gay and straight. Geographically scattered. No business connections I can see."

She lifted a tekka-maki, dipped it in a mixture of wasabi and soy sauce, and popped it in her mouth. She washed it down with a sip of hot herb tea.

"Tomorrow, though, something different."

"And would my leader be so kind as to inform me as to the battle plan?"

"Moraga."

"Ah, the poor folks. And how will that be any different from the survivors we've visited so far?"

"First female victim."

They finished their meal and walked back to the apartment on Dolores Street. They climbed the old stone stairway from the sidewalk and Rebekkah put the key in the lock. She paused before turning the key. Finally Liam reached and took her hand, assisted her in opening the lock. They went upstairs.

"It's a warm night and your hand was very cold," he remarked.

"I felt something." She was pale.

"It's this place, isn't it?"

"Do you know what was here before—before these buildings went up?"

"It never bothered me, Rebekkah. They're old buildings. Pre-quake." Everything in San Francisco is either pre-quake or post-quake. That's the kind of city it is.

"It was the old Hebrew cemetery. *Gibbath Olom*. The Hills of Eternity."

"A lovely name for a place of rest," he said.

"They moved it to Colma. Land here was getting too valuable. Why leave it for the dead when you could sell it to the living?"

"That must have been a long time ago."

"I heard the story from my mother. They opened it in 1861. There were Civil War dead buried here. Closed it in 1888 and moved all the graves to Colma. All the graves they could find. Nobody knows if they found them all. There may be dead Jews living under our feet."

"You don't mean that."

"What?"

"Living. Dead Jews living under our feet."

"Did I say that? Well, you know what I meant."

"Your ancestors?"

"No. Abraham was the first of my family to come here and he didn't die until 1907. Post-quake." She made a little sound that might have had some laughter in it, but not much.

The conversation lapsed and they turned on the TV and watched an old *Streets of San Francisco* episode in rerun, giggling at the silly plot and the low-budget production. It was great fun. They cracked a couple of Kirin beers just to keep in the spirit of the night, then went to bed.

♦ ♦ ♦

Moraga was across the bridge and through a tunnel, and the house they were seeking was up a series of hilly, winding roads.

The house was modern, attractive, clearly well kept. All on one level, as if designed for occupants whose knees were not as supple as they had once been. There was lush landscaping and a three-car garage. The door was down and none of the vehicles were visible. There was a circular driveway covered with sparkling white pebbles that looked as if each one had been washed and polished that morning.

The occupants were a retired couple and they were expecting the visit. Rebekkah and Liam were ushered into an airy living room. There was a fireplace with a gas log but it was not burning. Family photographs were arranged on the mantle. Mr. and Mrs. in much younger days, he with an Afro and a beard; she in a long dress, wearing granny glasses. Another, looking a few years older, he with shorter hair and a moustache, she in jeans and a Greek sailor's cap. Then the two of them with a baby. He looking proud, clean-shaven, respectable; she, maternal and joyous. Pictures of the girl growing up. Then one with him in business suit, her in flowery dress, their daughter in cap and gown. And finally their daughter posing proudly in army uniform, an airborne patch on her cap.

"That's our story," the mother announced.

"I didn't mean to stare," Rebekkah apologized.

"It's all right. We loved her very much."

The father, now white-haired, wearing casual clothes, added, "We were proud of her. Very proud."

"She was in the army?" Rebekkah asked.

"I don't know why she enlisted," the mother said. "I couldn't understand it. I think—maybe she wanted to follow in her father's footsteps."

"You served?" Rebekkah asked.

"I was in Vietnam."

He did not seem eager to talk about that.

"She may have thought we were disappointed, I was disappointed, that we never had a son. I wasn't. I couldn't have loved her more, I couldn't have been happier. But she may have thought that."

Rebekkah consulted her notebook. "She died more than a year ago. She was the first in this series of deaths. I hope you'll tell me as much about it as you can."

The father made a sound and got to his feet. He said something unintelligible and left.

The mother said, "He's not over it. Neither am I. Do you have any children, Sergeant? No? Then you can't understand. I'm not over it either, but I can put up a better front. See?"

She managed a ghastly smile.

"She had a degree from Berkeley. She could have done anything she wanted. She had a boyfriend, too, a fine boy she met in school. But she wanted to do this thing. She went to Afghanistan and came home without a scratch. She said she liked the army, liked the sense of belonging that it gave her. She made sergeant, then they sent her to OCS. You understand OCS? Officer Candidate School? She passed with flying colors. She was a lieutenant. But she always had to challenge herself. She volunteered to be a paratrooper. She was on a training jump. They take them up in helicopters now. She jumped out and something happened. Nobody knows what. She seemed to burst into flames halfway to the ground. It took less than a minute. She was fine when she jumped and she was—she was dead before she reached the ground."

"They got to you, didn't they? The mom and dad?"

Rebekkah and Liam were in the Dolores Street apartment.

"They got to me."

"You want to stay home tonight? I'll make a sandwich, maybe nuke some broth."

"You're too good."

He put on some quiet music. He knew her favorite album, Fairport Convention, *Liege and Leaf*. She listened to the voice of the dead Sandy Denny. Liam didn't say anything. She put her head on his shoulder and cried softly for the old couple with the dead daughter.

In the morning she said, "I'm ready now. I need you to go to Colma with me, Liam."

"At your command, *mon sergeant*."

At the relocated Hills of Eternity he waited at a respectful distance while she visited her ancestors. There were many graves in the plot, but she walked from grave to grave, touching the stones, tracing her own direct ancestry, from her father to her father's father to her father's father's father, leaving a pebble atop each to show that a loving visitor had been there.

Each stone had only a name and dates of birth and death, the years given since the Almighty had created the world.

Moses ben Zaccheus, 5710-5768.

Jacob ben Zaccheus, 5684-5764.

Isaac ben Zaccheus, 5666-5727.

Abraham ben Zaccheus, 5615-5667.

They rose from their tombs, their voice spoke to her.

"I am your daughter," she told them. "To each of you was born a son, through the generations, but now I alone am here. Do not turn from me. Help me, Abraham, Isaac, Jacob, Moses. Help your daughter."

They gathered around her and spoke ancient words in a language she did not even understand. But one phrase was whispered in her ears, one name. *Ankareh Minu. Ankareh Minu.*

The sky was clear and the air was warm, but she was taken by darkness and cold. When she could move again she went as quickly as she could to Liam O'Leary and he took her back to their apartment.

At the Hebrew Institute she found what she was looking for. *Ankareh Minu.* The concept was Zoroastrian. In that ancient and noble religion Ankareh Minu wasn't the devil. The followers of Zoroaster recognized an evil deity, Ahriman, the foe of the good god. No, Ankareh Minu was something else. Not even a demon. It was pure evil, more evil than Ahriman, it was the evil side of human nature.

But why had her ancestors whispered those words to her in the Hills of Eternity? Zoroaster had lived and died thousands of years ago. And Zoroastrianism was a nearly extinct religion, its few remaining adherents concentrated in Iran. What connection was there to the dead in California?

She studied the incendiary deaths. Rich and poor, black and white, gay and straight. Now add female and male. Educated and ignorant, add that, too.

But one had been on disability after being wounded in the army, and died.

One had served proudly, *don't ask, don't tell,* and returned to San Francisco, and died.

One had worn an army jacket, probably his own, kept as a souvenir after serving, and died.

One had served proudly and volunteered for airborne service, and died.

And at the heart of the investigation, the man who had brought pressure on the department, who had prodded Captain Samson into assigning Sergeant Rebekkah ben Zaccheus her tour of the dead, was Supervisor Vincent Moran. Supervisor Moran who soon would be Senator Moran, who might someday be President Moran.

It was not easy to get hold of Moran's service record. He was happy to remind the voters that he was Major Moran, that he had served in Iraq and in Afghanistan. He had the medals to show for it, and show them he did at every opportunity. But as for the full service record—it was not easy to get hold of that but Sergeant ben Zaccheus got it.

Moran had been a lieutenant during the 1991 Gulf War, had served with distinction, won his decorations, and stayed in the National Guard after the war. A decade later, a major now, he volunteered for active duty again. He led troops in the battle of Kunduz in October, 2001. He helped put down the prison revolt at Qala-I-Janghi, supervised soldiers as they routed Taliban at Mazar-I-Sharif.

But what had any of this to do with Ankareh Minu?

Then came the break, the wild break that gave Rebekkah what she needed. It was her day off. Yes, even cops get a day off. Liam O'Leary was on duty at the Hall of Justice, and Rebekkah drove across the Golden Gate Bridge, bypassed the tourist attractions of Sausalito, made her way to a classmate's home in the hills above Mill Valley.

They went for lunch in the community's miniature downtown. They were sitting in a café, eating salads, when an uproar brought the establishment to its feet. A man stood screaming in the middle of the street. Traffic had come to a halt. Rebekkah ran from the café. The man was punching and kicking at an invisible assailant. Passers-by halted to stare and point.

No, not invisible. As Rebekkah approached she saw a cloud of black smoke as tall as a man, swirling like a miniature tornado, sparks and tongues of flame spurting from it.

The victim was caught in the vortex, spinning in opposition to the black and orange whirlwind, both the whirlwind and its victim gaining in speed, smoke rising now from the man.

Rebekkah ran toward the mad duo, her arms spread to encompass them both. She heard herself chanting, not in her own voice, not in one voice, but in chorus, in a language she recognized but did not understand. The chant became an exorcism, a command thundered in the name of the Almighty.

The black and orange whirlwind stretched skyward. Its peak took human form, the form of a naked, aroused male. It dipped and dived at Rebekkah. She faced it, shouting in voices, shouting the Sacred Name of the Almighty.

The whirlwind dived at her. She did not flinch. Closer. She did not cower. She made a sign, the Faravahar Symbol, a sign she had never made, never seen, nor knew, but nevertheless made.

The black whirlwind rushed past her, so close her hair was singed, her skin pained, her clothing blackened. The black whirlwind plunged through the surface of the street, poured into the very earth, and was gone.

Its victim had fallen to the ground. Smoke rose from his clothing and his flesh. His hair was gone, his skin blackened, but he moved and groaned.

When the ambulance arrived Rebekkah showed her badge and rode with the man to the hospital. Rebekkah talked with the man's doctor, learned that he was pumped full of morphine, was being hydrated and treated for his burns. He would probably survive. He could talk, if Rebekkah would be brief. And he might be incoherent from his injuries and the drug.

"Ankareh Minu."

That was all he would say at first, but he could see and hear and he told his story.

He had been in Afghanistan, had been under command of Captain Moran. From Kunduz they had fought the prison revolt at Qala-I-Janghi, on to Mazar-I-Sharif, and found themselves in an ancient village called Balkh.

Balkh, where a squad of Captain Moran's soldiers, men and women, hormones pumping from the challenge of battle, the fear of death and the ecstasy of killing, had found a tiny Zoroastrian community, an island surviving in a Muslim sea. The captain himself had led the rapine and slaughter. When it was over the captain and his soldiers had sworn a solemn pact of silence.

But there was no escaping justice. The Ankareh Minu, the evil of the world, had found personification, had found a brother soul in Vincent Moran, and was destroying the soldiers who had destroyed the Zoroastrians of Balkh.

"What happened to you, Sergeant?" Vincent Moran pushed himself back from his desk and rose to his feet. "I heard from Captain Samson that you'd been injured. You—your face. Are you all right?"

"I'm all right, Supervisor Moran."

"Well, sit down, let me get you something to drink. You've been burned. What happened?"

"No thank you. I would place you under arrest for murder, Supervisor, if I thought I could make the case stick. But I know what's been going on. I know how those people died. I was lucky to save one victim, he's in a burn ward now."

Moran frowned. "I don't know what you're talking about. You must be delirious, Sergeant. I can't blame you. I'll see to it that you're put on medical leave. I–"

"No you won't. I know all about Balkh. How many people did you murder? How many women did you rape? How long did it take you to come to your senses?"

"You're the one who needs to come to her senses, Sergeant."

"No, Supervisor. No. You made a deal with the devil. We're modern people, we don't believe in such superstitious nonsense any more. But Afghanistan isn't a Twenty-first Century country, is it? The past lived there. Ancient gods and demons live there. Zoroaster lived there. Ankareh Minu lives there."

"Bosh."

"No. No, Supervisor. You swore your troops to secrecy, and they kept their pledge, every one. Every one until today. You trusted them, you relied on them, but your sights are set high now. You know about opposition research. You've used it against your opponents, you know they would use it against you. And you called on Ankareh Minu and he came. He came when you called and he killed when you commanded."

The Supervisor stood facing her. He raised his hands, he made a sign with them, a sign like the Faravahar Symbol, but with his hands reversed. He called out in a language Rebekkah did not know, and she called out in the language of her ancestors and in the voices of her ancestors.

A cloud formed outside the office windows and smashed through them, glass shards scattering across the room. One pierced Rebekkah's cheek and she felt blood spurt.

The being she had seen in the street in Mill Valley stood between her and Vincent Moran.

Moran shouted at the whirling cloud.

Rebekkah opened her mouth to speak and heard only whispers, but the whispers of a congregation of the dead.

Fear spread across Moran's features. Then he was enveloped by the cloud, merged with it, and the cloud rose through the smashed window. Rebekkah stumbled to the window in time to see the black whirlwind plunge into the courtyard, into the earth.

MEMORIES, RED AND WET

CHRISTOPHER WELCH

IT SHAMBLED DOWN NINTH Avenue, nameless and nearly indistinguishable from the ghastly congregation of other things just like it.

It had one thought in its mind; its ponderous, crazed, but relentless mind:

Pain. Must. Eat. Flesh. Find. Redwet. Flesh. Stop. Pain. Must. Eat. Flesh.

The pain—an insatiable hunger, a pit of ceaseless famine—drove it onward, shuffling and moaning, slow but stalwart. It was a walking slaughter looking for a calf.

Around it and all the other loathsome things like it creeping through the scorched urban valley made by the metal and broken-glass office buildings that scraped the ash-littered sky, the chaos grew like a cancer. Fires spread in the ruins. Gunshots echoed in the streets. Sirens blared like banshees. Unseen voices from radios or televisions tried to not sound panicked. People screamed in the distance.

Screams?

Must. Eat. Must. Find. Flesh.

It stretched its arms outward, in the direction of the screams, like a primal internal compass. It did not understand why the arms were different, why only one hand had two fingers. It did not care that it did not understand.

It cared only that any one of the others in the pestilent herd meandering down the debris-strewn street would beat it to where it needed to go; to the food, to where the redwet flesh would make the pain go away. It understood that the others on the street would not make the pain go away. They were too cold, too stiff, too decomposing, too redwet dry. It almost—almost—wondered if they were in pain as well. It did understand what they wanted.

Must. Find. Redwet. Flesh. Must. Eat. Stop. Pain. Find.

It saw a body inside a shattered display case in one of the buildings. It changed direction from the rest of the horde it followed and lumbered toward the body. It walked over broken glass, unfeeling. It looked through jaundiced eyes into the display case. It was confused. The body did not move, the body was not warm, the body was not redwet. If it had understood that it was looking at a mannequin in a fashion shop, it would not have come here. It did not know that, yesterday, it would have thought the emerald-colored dress and low-neckline was sexy. It did not understand *yesterday*. It turned from the display and moseyed back down the street with the others.

Three blocks down, it came to another shattered window and it paused again. There was a square object that stirred something deep within the remnants of its degraded mind. It contained movement and noise. It had a vague memory, of sorts, that this object used to be important. It felt instinctively compelled to watch it.

"... they must have created some sort of biological accelerant with a mutated strain of a prion-like retro-virus in the dirty bombs," said a voice from the object. "Maybe they didn't know what the results were going be at all. How *could* anyone predict this? The only thing we can say for certain about the multiple terrorist attacks yesterday is that all biological and scientific facts as we have known them have been thrown out the window with the spread of this infection. This might be a wholly theological issue as far as we know."

"What do you mean by theological, Professor?" asked another voice.

"Outside this news studio the dead are rising up and attacking the living in ever-increasing waves. I had to shoot a dozen of them just to get to this studio. I repeat: The dead are walking. The last time something like this happened—and that is a matter of faith—it altered the course of world religion forever. We don't understand exactly what is happening now, scientifically-speaking. But we cannot ignore the ontological and eschatological overtones resulting from these bio-chemical attacks. Is this Armageddon? Or is this a leap forward in evolution? Or a leap back?"

"How far will this infection spread, Professor?"

"It'll spread everywhere. We're still trying to figure out how it works, or even why it works. What we do know is this: A few years ago researchers investigated the biological effects of human cannibalism in tribes living in Papua New Guinea, because the primary effect was that it made the tribesmen insane. The researchers discovered that they were suffering from transmissible spongiform encephalopathic disease, or TSE. With TSE, rogue proteins called prions latch onto brain cells and mutate them into abnormal shapes. Instead of breaking down like normal proteins, the prions remain in the cells, and disrupt the brain and the possibly entire nervous system, thus causing insanity. The prions never break down and once they are created; they are literally unstoppable. This is the same thing that happens in mad-cow disease; eating your own species makes abnormality and insanity spread and with whatever mutation happened at the cellular level in the case of these dirty bombs, things will only become more savage."

A raucous noise off camera interrupted the speaker briefly.

"Oh my God, they've won. The zealots, the fanatical terrorists, have won."

"It's preliminary to claim that, Professor. Our governmental forces–"

"Don't you see? Prions never break down. Never. They're in these... these zombies, and in the ash from the initial dirty explosions and the ash from all the pyres, and therefore, the atmosphere we breathe. They will travel on the trade winds. Eventually they'll get into our water, into our food, into our bodies. With the scale of these attacks nobody will survive for long. Nobody. Furthermore, with each person these zombies bite, it makes the zombies that more crazed and violent, just like it did with the tribesman. The terrorists who mindlessly but fanatically followed an ideology of death have had their prayers answered and they've achieved their greatest goal—they have killed everybody. Just not everybody knows it yet."

"Okay, Professor, then—hey, what's going on back there?"

Another noise, this time even more vehement and riotous.

"They're here!" The professor shouted as he drew his revolver and opened fire. Frantic screams, along with animalistic growls and hungry moans rose from behind the cameras. Discordant violence and bloodshed erupted through the audio. The screen jerked erratically as chaotic images blurred in and out of focus. The signal went dead.

It stood gazing bovine-like at the blank screen for a moment. It did not understand what it just watched. Finally, it turned away and continued lumbering down the avenue, following the instinct that pulled in the direction of the teeming mass.

Find. Must. Eat. Flesh. Must. Find. Redwet. Flesh.

Up ahead, at the next intersection, a speeding Silverado pick-up truck slammed on the brakes and burned a long, dark skid onto the street. "There are hundreds of them down here on Ninth Avenue," said one of two men in the bed of the truck. "Sam, call in more back-up."

"Will do," said the driver. Sam frantically sent a message over his radio.

"They see us, Bill!" yelled the other man in the truck bed, his voice shaky. "They're coming right for us." An endless drove of dead things plodded toward the Silverado.

"This will be just like what we did earlier over on Euclid Avenue, Jeff," Bill said as he unlocked the safety on his Uzi. "We took a bunch of 'em out. Too bad you missed that, eh?"

"Didn't you say that these things killed Andrew over on Euclid?"

"Just shoot, okay?"

Jeff was scared but followed Bill's lead, and opened fire with his AK-47. Arcs of spent shells spewed to their sides; each one clinked on the asphalt like the toll of a miniature funeral bell. Sam, still in the driver's seat, heard the gunfire. He grabbed his .45 pistol from the passenger seat, shooting out the open window. He blasted apart three rancid skulls with three shots.

It heard the bullets whiz by like angry wasps. It saw the others get hit, stagger back, then keep on shambling forward, toward the warm redwet flesh in the truck.

Next to it, one of the others' head exploded in a syrupy mess. The body fell, unmoving. Then it too felt the hot metal brand its own cold flesh. It felt the hissing bullets bore into its bones. It wavered and tottered with a sickly rictus, but it continued forward, unfazed.

Must. Eat. Flesh. Must. Eat. Eat. Eat.

"You have to hit their heads," Bill said "Blow their pus-for-brains heads off!"

"I'm trying," Jeff cried, but his shots were still too wild. The recoil hurt his shoulder. Yesterday he was a computer sales manager making commissions from consumers craving the latest high-tech gizmo. Until yesterday, Jeff had never held any type of gun before in his life, let alone the macho assault rifle he fired right now. Jeff wondered where Bill had purchased the guns, but never asked him.

It walked faster, as fast as it could, toward the truck. It could smell the flesh. It could see the flesh. It could even hear the sweat forming on the flesh, even over the ever-growing chorus of hunger-induced grunts and growls from all of the other dead things. It stuck out its unequal hands, ready to scrounge whatever it could.

"Where the hell is our back-up?" Bill said.

"I called but they're not responding," Sam answered.

"They're getting closer," Jeff warned.

All three men kept up their barrage, but still more and more of the vile things advanced toward the pick-up.

"There are way too many on this street. Get us out of here, Sam."

"Hold on, I'm re-loading."

"Later. We gotta move."

"Just a sec–" Sam never finished his sentence.

Three festering members of the odious horde pulled Sam through the open driver's door window and pushed him, screaming and kicking, to the pavement. Dozens of the ravenous dead converged on him. They yanked and ripped his body, grabbing and tearing off clumps of his warm redwet flesh. Some fell to the ground to lick-up with their bloated tongues the precious splattered redwet from the street.

"Sam!" Bill shouted, firing directly into the undead swarm. The Uzi was loud, but not loud enough to drown out Sam's gurgled screams. In a matter of seconds, Sam's screams dwindled away, but they were rapidly replaced by the chewy sounds of an uncooked feast.

The other hunger-driven dead things rushed at them in a frenzied stampede, engulfing the Silverado from every side.

"Shoot them! Shoot them all! God help us!" Bill yelled. Jeff didn't pay any attention to Bill, because he was already shooting into the horde and howling a prayer of his own.

There were more zombies than there were bullets. The two men couldn't shoot every single one of them. With a sick feeling blooming in their stomachs, they saw the gruesome throng, maddened by the smell of the redwet flesh, rush at the Silverado. With a riotous malignancy, the herd flipped the pick-up onto its side.

Bill and Jeff fell, screaming in fear of the inevitable.

The necrotic horrors pounced on them; they never even reached the ground. The grisly congregation grabbed, pulled, yanked and ripped their bodies into red, wet shreds.

It was in the horde; it gouged under Jeff's ribs with its two-fingered hand and it scooped up with the other. It grasped what it could, and stepped away from the others, guarding its food like a starving wolf.

It held a few small, fluted strips of Jeff's hairy abdomen plus his entire pancreas. It took the body parts and ate; it devoured the organ and scraps with zestful immediacy. As soon as the warm blood hit its tongue, the unyielding pain subsided. Still, it continued to consume with the single-mindedness of a famished jackal. For a brief and solitary moment, the pain was gone.

In that moment, a host of memories it had forgotten returned in a red-tinged flood . . . jumbled personal memories old and new. . .disjointed flashbacks . . . of an individual life . . . her life . . .

... my name is Lisa Grezbelsky and I live in Cleveland, Ohio ... Mom and Dad died in a car wreck on Interstate-77 four years ago ... I am twenty-six years old ... Tommy is my brother and he moved to Memphis and my little sister Stacy moved to Columbus and she has two little boys ... I fell off a swing when I six years old and broke my arm and the nurses were so nice ... My favorite foods are syrup-drenched pancakes with sausage and Tootsie Rolls ... I'm dating David Smithee and think I'm in love but he hasn't proposed yet and Darren McBride broke my heart in the eighth-grade and I have never forgiven him for being my first kiss ... I'm in the choir at St. Bartholomew's Church ... I went to Kent State University, a nursing major with a minor in philosophy ... I am a nurse ... Grandma and Grandpa escaped to the U.S.A just before Hitler invaded and bombed Poland ... the bombs, the dirty bombs, the terrorists set off bombs in nine cities ... Pittsburgh, Louisville, Minneapolis ... where else ... St. Louis, Indianapolis ... make love not war ... where else where else ... Cleveland ... must get to the hospital, even if it is my first day off in a week ... they need me ... so many victims ... so damn many ... be professional, don't cry ... Kansas City, Dallas, Memphis ... call Stacy and Tommy and oh my God, Tommy ... be professional ... what do you mean he is in the hallway, Dr. Hallett, he's dead ... he's dead, how can he be walking ... dear God they're all dead ... no keep away keep away from me ... push him push him away my fingers holy shit he just bit off my fingers run away from here something is wrong wrong wrong get the hell out of here they are all dead ... the pain ... Jesus loves me yes I know ... where do I go ... getting darker ... where ... the pain ...

... and then, in a deeper part of her brain, the part that loved reading, learning and discussing philosophy and theology in university seminars and Sunday school, Lisa remembered she had had a grim epiphany. She remembered thinking that the cosmological balances had been tipped; that now there were on this world, and maybe even in the whole universe, more people who worshiped Death than God.

Maybe, just maybe, she had thought, there were too many genocides in Europe and Africa, too many ruthless tyrants executing citizens in Asia, too many drug-fueled wars in South America, and here on her own continent, too many gang wars and too many crime lords and too many serial killers and too many politicians marching off to war based on too many fabricated rationales. And then there were way, way too many terrorists who killed in God's name, too many who have never really worshiped God in any legitimate way, who actually praise suicide and homicide and pray for even more genocides and holocausts.

Maybe, Lisa remembered thinking, just maybe their prayers were answered.

MEMORIES, RED AND WET

Not by God . . . but by Death.

Maybe there was another War in Heaven, but instead of being lead by Lucifer, the Angel of Light, maybe this one was lead by the Angel of Death. Maybe the Angel of Death won the battle because more people prayed for war and death over peace and love and more people embraced destruction instead of creation.

Maybe Death really won.

Maybe Nietzsche finally had been proven right.

Maybe this time *nobody* would be passed over.

Maybe the world had reached that penultimate moment where the new Omnipotence, the new God, Death Incarnate, was re-making the world, if not the entire universe, in His image, thoroughly emboldened by the prayers for Death, Destruction, and Darkness. The mindless ideology of the fanatical zealot had now mushroomed exactly like a nuclear explosion into the rapid evolution of a psychopathic cosmology.

And Lisa Grezbelski was less than a mote in the new God's eye socket, eternally empty and black. Lisa had envisioned every planet in every solar system being a desolate and lifeless rock with nothing but putrid and cadaverous alien things crawling and flopping over them; planets floating in an uncaring void of infinite darkness, helpless and hopeless in the decreasing light of rapidly dimming stars.

And her world was just one in a multitude of cosmic sepulchers.

Lisa remembered wondering if this blasphemous thinking would send her straight to Hell, before the pain became too overwhelming, just before she realized what she was going to become: *I will become like the others.*

The last thing Lisa had remembered wondering: *Do I still have a soul? Do I? And who will care one way or the other?*

Then there was pain, a hungry, starving pain . . . and then the brief moment of red-tinged memories dissipated in her degraded mind. The redwet flesh and the raw pancreas were completely devoured, and the walking, bullet-branded, wormy dead thing that was once named Lisa Grezbelski felt that ravenous pain fill her cold body again.

But this time, the pain was worse. It was even more painful, even more famishing, even more enraging than before. It looked around, and saw that there was no more redwet meat to be had here. It understood that it would go crazy if it stayed here. It needed to eat again. From somewhere ahead, a few blocks farther down the ruined and scorched Ninth Avenue, it heard more screams.

Screams?

It lifted its slaughter-fouled hands, and with a bovine-like moan, it shambled as fast as its stiff legs allowed down the debris-cluttered street in the decimated urban valley. The ghastly horde of other dead things—things that also once had names, once had souls, and once had prayers of their own—ambled like an un-corralled herd in the same direction.

It had one thing on its mind; its ponderous, relentless, increasingly-crazed mind:

Pain. Must. Eat. Flesh. Find. Redwet. Flesh. Stop. Pain. Must. Eat. Flesh

g

GENE O'NEILL

HE WAS SUDDENLY DOUBLED *over by a terrible coughing fit.*

After the last cough, he sucked in a deep breath, which was painfully interrupted by a tearing sensation.

Staring down at his chest, he blinked with disbelief. The stitches were slowly ripping out one-by-one, moving down from his neck to just below his sternum, bursting like the rotted laces when an old football is over-inflated.

Pop, pop, pop, pop, pop, pop . . .

And, inside his chest cavity, he watched in horror as his wired sternum began slowly snapping apart too–

Ping, ping, ping, the vibrating metallic sounds painfully grating on his nerves, like a fork tapping an abscessed filling.

Then, he was staring down into a gaping wet, purple, crimson, and pink mass, his exposed and vulnerable heart beating with a kind of sideways twisting motion.

Thump, thump, thump.

Valdez awakened violently in a tangle of sheets, his body coated with clammy sweat.

"Oh, man!" he said, his voice froggy with tension, as he gasped to catch his breath.

It was the same terrifying thing, each night now since coming home from San Francisco Kaiser's cardio-vascular unit two and a half weeks ago after by-pass surgery. The recurring, throat-clenching nightmare, so frightening, so real, so, so . . .

And, for a long moment Valdez wasn't completely convinced it was all just a horrifying nightmare.

"Okay," he finally murmured with relief, clutching his pillow to his tightly stitched chest and relaxing slightly, before carefully swinging his legs to the floor. The long fresh scars on both lower legs from the vein harvesting were red and angry looking. They actually ached more than his chest.

The physician assistants at the step down unit had counseled him about lingering pain in his legs, and also to expect some bizarre dreams, and probably inexplicable anxious moments after the triple by-pass. But at 53 and in pretty good physical shape, they thought it would only be a very brief psychological adjustment time for Valdez. He'd be back on his whole game sooner than later. Possibly able to return to work in the near future—he'd burned up all of his sick leave in the last two and a half months.

Despite their encouragement, here he was after a fretful three weeks, awake at midnight and panting like a dog after the recurring nightmare. Well, at least he hadn't had any bad side effects from all the drugs he'd been taking like they'd also cautioned might happen. Even though in the last week or so he'd begun sneaking a few unauthorized drinks of *Jack Daniels* while still on the maximum number of painkillers, which everyone strongly advised him against doing. Okay, sure, a few fuzzy moments now and then after a hefty drink, but no other side effects. For sure, no weird waking hallucinations, at least as far as he knew.

Well, he was wide awake now, and would remain so for at least a couple of hours, if tonight was anything like all the past nights since leaving Kaiser Hospital's cardiac unit in San Francisco.

Okay for now, he thought, letting the breath trickle across his dry lips, then cocking his head, and listening intently.

Not a sound, except for the fridge humming downstairs. Everyone else in the house must be sound asleep. The kids in their rooms, Jackie in the guest bedroom at the far end of the hallway. She'd said that she didn't want to keep him awake while he was recovering. Uh-huh, sure.

Valdez stretched his frame, still thin and athletic despite the recently plugged-up heart and major surgery. He tiptoed downstairs.

Maybe watch some late-night TV, he thought. He checked the clock over the widescreen. 12:35 a.m. Actually, not so late. He nodded, thinking another watered-down drink probably wouldn't hurt anything either—he'd taken no Vicodin or anything else since, maybe nine o'clock–

At that moment he remembered the strange crew working next door at the Sullivan's. The Valdez family lived in an upscale Sunnyvale neighborhood on Orchard Court, at the center of a cul-de-sac on a sprawling two thirds of an acre, the Sullivan's on the right and the Singh's on the left on equally large lots.

Earlier, the mysterious crew had surprised him, when he'd slipped out on the porch just after 10:30 for a surreptitious nip. Jackie was upstairs getting ready for bed, the kids already down or at least listening to their goofy music in their rooms. He had just tipped up the bagged pint of *Jack*, when the strange vehicle with a loaded trailer appeared out of nowhere in front of the neighbor's next door. Panel Wagon? No, he'd never seen a vehicle like that anywhere. Shiny ebony, stretched-out like a limo, but no doors or windows on the sides, the front window tinted dark brown. It looked like aluminum scaffolding stacked in the trailer. So it must be some kind of customized commercial vehicle, he thought, something probably used in the trades. But there were no markings anywhere . . . except a symbol closely resembling a tiny silver lower-case **g** on the side of the panel near the front where a passenger door should've been located. **g**? Didn't ring a bell.

Curious, Valdez continued to watch as four workers silently climbed out of the back of the vehicle, and gathered for a moment around the trailer full of scaffolding. They all wore one-piece black suits and helmets, looking like a crew of devilish astronauts. Actually, on second thought, they looked more like the hi-tech HAZMAT crew he'd seen once down at the H-P warehouse where he'd driven a forklift for the last twenty-five years. Except these guys' masks didn't have a respirator and weren't clear; no, they were tinted a deep brown shade just like their strange vehicle's front window. Each worker wore the silver symbol, **g**, centered on his chest. Strange get-up, for sure.

Painters, Valdez tentatively decided, as three of the men began to unload and stack the scaffolding on the Sullivan's lawn. But working in the middle of the night? And Saturday night at that? Most all trades now were unionized here in Silicon Valley. So, this was indeed more than just a little strange.

And, he worried if the Sullivans were going to be able to sleep over there while the work was progressing? He thought the upstairs bedroom lights had kicked off a little while ago, but he wasn't sure. The painters were being exceptionally quiet though, eerily so in fact. Valdez shivered, even though the night was almost muggy.

As most of the crew continued to unload aluminum scaffolding, the fourth man threw open wider the back of the weird vehicle. He unrolled some type of spraying rigs, and four lines hooked up to a large tank set way back in there.

Valdez squinted to see better.

It wasn't really clear with no inner lights on. But, man, it didn't look like any air compressor or painting rig he'd ever seen. It looked like some kind of big chemical tank with a number of luminescent different size dials and gauges. So, he decided they probably weren't really painters, but more likely some kind of a pest eradication crew. Yeah. At this time of night and considering their odd protective clothing, that made a little more sense to him. Working when there were fewer people up and around—less risk of spray drift and such.

He looked around the corner of his house. The crew was busy erecting–

Damn, Valdez swore, hoping it wasn't termites or wood beetles over there.

Most of this area of the Silicon Valley had been orchard in the past. In fact, some of the finest orchard land in all of California. Paved over with asphalt or built over with houses now. But with lots of rotted wood buried around at one time. Valdez nodded and smiled wryly to himself. This particular cul-de-sac in Sunnyvale with only three homes on over-sized lots had been called nostalgically, *Walnut Woods*. There wasn't a walnut tree in sight anywhere now in this whole area. Oh, sure, a few liquid ambers, dogwoods, and acacias had been planted by the landscapers, and lots of shrubs . . .

Damn, the pills he was taking and the booze were making him squirrelly—he was drifting, not focusing, nor completing his thoughts. He turned back toward where the pest control crew was working, recalling his initial alarm a few moments ago. Valdez made a mental note and underlined it: *Better get someone out here soon to check his place for termites.* If the Sullivans had them, he probably did, too.

He relaxed, took another generous snort of *Jack*, the drink biting sharply going down, but gradually spreading out, warming his skin, and relaxing him.

Back out on the porch, Valdez heard a motorcycle turn into the cul-de-sac, and he watched it pull up at the corner of the Singh's lot in the shadows—the only streetlight actually in front of his place.

The driver wasn't Raj, the oldest son over there, Valdez thought, frowning. No, indeed. Raj was always dressed strictly college prep even mowing the lawn—he was a freshman at nearby Stanford. This guy was wearing some kind of WWII German military helmet and a Levi jacket with cut-off sleeves. Even in the dim light, Valdez could tell the rider's bare arms were sleeved with tattoos—a large swastika prominent on his right shoulder. The biker and his passenger apparently hadn't noticed Valdez sitting in the darkness in the corner under the porch overhang.

The female rider, wearing a plastic black helmet, had her dress hiked up to her crotch, her long knees clenching the wide buttocks of the driver.

She took off her helmet and shook out her short purple-spiked hair. Then, she slipped off the Harley on the biker's side, her face still shadowed. She embraced the driver who had removed his helmet and swung both legs out toward the street. It was no peck-on-the-cheek-good-night-polite kiss either. Uh-uh. This was a long drawn out, wet, wide-mouth, sloppy smacker—a definite sexual familiarity evident, their clenched bodies almost eliciting sparks in the night air. It was a crude, rassling kind of sexual mugging right out here almost in his front yard.

Feeling uncomfortably like a perverted voyeur, Valdez stood and asked himself: Who the hell do these weird people think they are, stopping here to make out almost in my front yard? He took an indignant step away from the overhang almost into the cascade of streetlight, but stopped just short and listened.

"Oh, baby," the biker growled as the two finally broke apart. "You sure you have to go in so early? We could slip back to the trailer park, make it a best two out of three. What do you say?"

The rider shook her head, then turned to glance reluctantly almost directly at where Valdez stood–

"Holy Jesus Christ!" Valdez said, his shout echoing up and down the short street in the still night, as he recognized the rider. It was Jennifer, *his* Jennifer. She was all punked-out in a raggedy black velvet vest over a short, purple skirt with holey black panty hose, and black combat boots. Her face was painted brazenly, the mascara and eye shadow streaked, now, and her dark lipstick smeared over her lower face, giving her a wanton, but at the same time, clown-like expression. He gasped in a deep breath and let out a sigh, realizing he just barely recognized his fifteen-year-old daughter. Standing there in the street by the older tattooed biker, she definitely looked like some kind of a, a . . . *hooker*, for crissake. He glanced down at his watch: 12:55. He'd assumed she was in her bed earlier, not out *where*, and doing *what* with this, this . . . hoodlum?

Suddenly, the biker's last line about the trailer park resurfaced, the implication making Valdez's recently rehabilitated heart skip erratically. Oh, no, not my Jenny. He felt suddenly weak-kneed, faint, and slightly nauseated.

His loud expletive had startled both the driver and his daughter, and they'd frozen momentarily, both looking his way.

The biker recovered first, cranked the Harley back up, loudly gunning the throttle in neutral.

Valdez stepped off the porch and picked up a decorative white rock from those lining his sidewalk. He chunked it at the driver to get his attention, missing badly. "Hold it right there, pal, I need to talk to–"

Without a word to his ex-passenger, the biker gave Valdez the finger, and shouted: "Fuck you, Greaseball!" Then he kicked his cycle into gear and sped away noisily into the night.

Valdez clutched his chest, feeling a scary sharp twinge, as if he'd been struck by a thrown stone.

Jenny moved swiftly toward where he was trying to catch his breath at the foot of the porch.

"Daddy, what are *you* doing up?" she demanded in an accusatory, angry voice. Her paint-smeared features looking pissed-off now. "Spying on me?"

Still feeling weak, Valdez didn't answer, only shuffled sideways, blocking her direct access to the stairs and house. She easily juked around him like a shifty halfback.

His shock was slowly turning to anger, and Valdez felt an enervating surge of adrenaline blurring his chest pain, as he followed her onto the porch.

"Who was *that*?" he shouted, reaching out and grabbing her shoulder. "That, that . . . racist jerk?" And before she could answer, he added just as indignantly: "Do you realize that it's way after midnight?" And: "Where in the hell have you been dressed like that?"

"Oh, man, you're such a lame fucking dork!" Jenny said, cutting him off and roughly knocking away his restraining hand.

Then, from behind them: "Quit shouting, Martin!"

Valdez turned to face his wife, who was standing in the opened doorway, a hand on her hip in that Jackie kind of challenging pose. She was glaring down at him. "For Christ sake, you may as well wake up Richie and the whole damn neighborhood while you're at it."

He just stared at his wife as she stepped out onto the porch. She signaled to Jenny. "Get on up to bed, young lady, you're late. We'll talk tomorrow morning before church." Then she snatched the forgotten bagged pint of *Jack* out of his left hand. "What's this crap you're drinking?"

Valdez watched his daughter shrug dismissively with a six-pack of glaring attitude and stomp loudly through the open front door in her combat boots.

He started to shout something at her: "Hey, come back–"

But Jackie cut him off, by holding up both her hands in the stop gesture, and ordered over her shoulder: "Get to bed, girl. *Now.*"

Jackie and Valdez were left alone outside the darkened house, standing on the porch, watching their teenaged daughter disappear down the hall and up the staircase to her bedroom.

Then, Jackie stepped to the far edge of the porch and poured out the whiskey. "What's the matter with you, Martin?" Of course she called him by his full first name instead of Marty. "You just got out of the hospital.

You trying to kill yourself, stupid?"

He shook his head, refusing to get into an argument about *him*. Right now, he wanted to talk about their daughter. Who allowed her on a date? Out so late? And with a frigging nasty-assed Nazi racist who lived in a trailer park? What was going on around here since he'd been in the hospital and recuperating? Still, he sucked in a breath and began in a relative calm voice: "Jackie, we need to talk about Jenny–"

She cut him off again, taking his arm and roughly steering him toward the door. "We'll talk tomorrow morning. You need your rest, mister."

Uh-huh, as if she gave a big rat's ass about his rest. She knew she had to get up early for church. Besides she'd worked overtime today at her accounting firm, and was probably exhausted. Again, he opened his mouth to complain.

"*No* more talking," Jackie ordered, her authoritative tone not encouraging further argument. No question who was in charge here in his mind.

All too clearly Valdez realized that, with only his disability recently filed and his unused sick leave from H-P all gone, they really needed Jackie's paycheck to live. She wouldn't let him forget it either, you could bet on that. He was poorly leveraged to argue.

With an effort, Valdez followed his wife up the stairs, watching her turn into the guest room at the end of the hallway. He sighed and shook his head, realizing his wife had really stomped on his male ego in front of their daughter. The objective reality of the family dynamics here and especially his relationship with Jackie were all too clear. He should feel angry or humiliated or something. But no. His earlier righteous indignation with his daughter's behavior and appearance was quickly ebbing away now, replaced by a kind of growing sense of, of . . . what?

He knew this business tonight with his wife wasn't just a recent trend. He'd relinquished the reins of parental authority and head of household to Jackie years ago. When he took up serious drinking as his main avocation after work at H-P. For sure after his first DUI five years ago. No, he had to admit that he hadn't been much more than a room-and-boarder around here for years. Responsible husband, good father, strong role model . . . forget it. What he was feeling was a twinge of regret.

In his head he replayed his reactions to what had happened . . .

Man, he didn't really even know his daughter. She was someone he occasionally passed in the hall, going to the bathroom or school or somewhere. A teenage stranger. He couldn't remember the last time they'd spoken, much less had a real conversation. When he thought about it, he didn't even remember the name of the school she attended now. So what the fuck was he so suddenly outraged about now? Her growing up? Going out with bikers? Calling him a dork? What? He shook his head—he was a fucking dork.

It was quiet again in the house, everyone finally asleep.

Nevertheless, Valdez tiptoed down to Richie's room and cracked the door to check. The thirteen-year old was indeed lying face down, dead to the world.

Valdez returned to his room.

God, he had to admit his life was a big time mess . . . His health, his job, and his family. But he didn't really care if he ever went back to work at H-P, he was nothing down there anyhow. He didn't really care if his daughter was growing up and dating either. But getting laid already? He shivered. Just a passing blow—he'd get over it. His son? Richie thought his dad was a first-class dope, too. Shooting hoops, fishing, hiking, camping, Great America? Father and son bonding? No, Valdez couldn't remember ever doing things like that with his son. The last time they talked? Maybe a week ago briefly: Richie had hit him up for five dollars—hadn't even explained what it was for. And Jackie? Well, they'd gradually grown apart long ago—never made love, rarely even had sex. Even before Jackie began bringing in the bigger paychecks from *Barbou & Associates,* and taking over the whole domestic show.

Valdez clearly realized he didn't count for much around here anymore. He snorted derisively and whispered: "If I ever did–?"

For some reason at that moment, he remembered the odd spraying crew working next door. He cracked open his bedroom Venetian blinds and peered out at the Sullivan place.

Holy crap, those four guys had the whole two-story house completely scaffolded! Valdez glanced at his watch again. In just a little over an hour and a half. And three of them were up at the top story of the house working, spraying back and forth, their rigs dead quiet. He opened the window, and he could detect absolutely no drift of what they were spraying toward his place. One guy was on the ground at the back of the vehicle, apparently monitoring the gauges on the chemical tank, and probably an air compressor. Even that was running silently. Man, they were a quiet but creepy bunch.

Dropping the blinds, he vowed to ask Jackie in the morning if the Sullivans had alerted her to what was going on over there. *Suggest* they might need to get a termite inspection themselves.

With all the hubbub, his recently vein-stripped legs were really acting up big time now. Felt almost like cramps from back in his 100-yard dash days . . . 100 years ago.

Valdez slipped into the master bathroom and took one of his Vicodins. He shook the bottle by his ear, like the corrupt detective, Gary Oldman, in the flick, *The Professional*—great movie. He'd need a refill soon.

He returned back to his bed, and, surprisingly, after a few moments he was sound sleep.

Sunday morning, Valdez woke up late. 10:30. He swung his legs painfully out of bed and listened. Nothing. He slipped on his raggedy faded-blue bathrobe and scuffed-up moccasins, feeling like an invalid.

Downstairs in the kitchen, he found a mess on the breakfast counter. Everyone apparently off to church. He cleaned off the dishes, rinsing them before stacking them in the dishwasher. Then he searched around for *The San Jose Mercury News*, with no luck.

Not brought in by anyone yet, he guessed. No hot coffee left either.

In his bathrobe and slippers, Valdez went out and shuffled down to the end of his driveway. He picked up the *Mercury*, tore off the rubber band, and glanced at the various headers. Gobal warming, stimulus package, money woes, same-sex marriage. Same old shit, he thought, folding the paper and turning back toward his house–

The sight next door made him gasp loudly.

Actually, the lack of a sight. The Sullivan place was gone! House, landscaping, the whole maryann. All that remained over on that big lot was–

Jesus! It was three neat rows of trees—walnut trees, maybe ten or fifteen, taking up most of the three-quarter acre lot; he was too stunned to actually count.

Valdez moved closer, blinking his eyes.

Yes, it was like the old orchard remnant had never been cleared over there. And no house had ever been built. Where were the Sullivans now? He was at a complete loss for answers.

Minutes later back in his house, despite an empty stomach, Valdez knocked down a half a glass of *Jack*. Man, what the fuck was going on around here? What had that odd crew done last night? He shook his head incredulously. Erased a house and replaced it with a mature orchard? Impossible.

Anxiously, Valdez fidgeted, waiting for his family to finally get back from St. Mary's just before noon. He met them out on the porch, the kids in some noisy sister-brother argument, completely ignoring Valdez as they shouldered by him.

Annoyed by his rough grip on her arm, Jackie still followed him as he led her to the right edge of their porch. He pointed with a trembling finger.

"What happened?" he demanded.

She looked over at the walnut trees, then back at Valdez, her annoyance changing to a slightly puzzled expression.

"What do you mean, Marty?"

"I mean what happened to the Sullivan place next door?"

For a moment she just stared at Valdez, the lines on her forehead and her crow's feet deepening. Then she said: "Sullivans? Who in the hell are the Sullivans?"

"They owned the house that used to be next door, our neighbors for the last two years," he said, the frustration obvious in his tone. "Loren is one of your better friends."

Jackie continued to look at him with more than a slightly puzzled expression. Finally, her face reddened slightly, the puzzlement dissolving to a pissed-off look. "Martin, were you drinking again this morning?" She leaned close enough to smell his whiskey breath.

He vigorously shook his head. "C'mon, Jackie, what happened to the house next door?"

"Martin, there has never been a house next door. No Sullivans, no buildings, only that remnant of the old walnut orchard. That's why we moved here in the first place. We should buy that lot and keep it that way." The slightly angry look had turned to concern.

Stunned, Valdez just remained in place, paralyzed by his wife's ridiculous claim.

Empty lot? No Sullivans.

She finally took him gently by the arm and led him inside. "Let me fix you some breakfast, Marty."

Now he was fucking Marty again. He didn't want any breakfast, he wanted another *Jack D.*

That night, the strange crew in the black vehicle was next-door, erecting scaffolding just before midnight. Valdez watched out the kids' bathroom window on that side of the house, until they began spraying; then, he took a triple hit from the half pint of *Jack Daniels* from the paper bag he'd hid in one of his boots in the closet. Man, he should do something about this. But what?

Call the cops! Yeah–

What would he say? A crew was erasing his neighbors' homes.

Oh, yeah. He'd end up committed to Agnew State Hospital.

So he decided to do nothing, except take a few more sips of the smooth whiskey.

Of course the next morning, the Singh house was completely gone, replaced with old walnut trees. Resigned now, Valdez carefully counted the two rows. *Nine.* Nine trees.

When Valdez casually asked Richie something about Raj next door, his son had a blank look, and said: "I don't know who you mean, Pop. No one lives over there, it's always been an empty lot with trees. Mom thinks we should buy it." He frowned. "You haven't been hitting the sauce again? You know what Mom says." He made a sympathetic shrug. Then he got a sly look, and said: "I might have to dime you out, dude. Think you can loan me ten?"

Valdez dug out the money, and didn't pursue the disappearance any further.

Their place at the end of the cul-de-sac was now surrounded by almost two acres of mature walnut orchard. Crazy or not, that was it. Hell, maybe he *had* gone around the corner, the operation, booze, and drugs making him see and remember things that weren't real . . . Of course he didn't believe a word of that rational explanation for one minute. What he needed was another drink.

The next week on Friday, Jackie announced that after work that afternoon, she was taking the kids to Santa Cruz and the *Boardwalk* for the weekend, staying with her sister. "Be my last chance for a break for the next month or so, getting ready for April fifteenth."

He nodded.

"Give you a chance for a little peace and quiet, Marty."

That would be good–

"But promise me no drinking, okay?" She was almost glaring. "That crap makes you weird, you know. Saying and seeing funny things. Dr. Knowland warned you about drinking and taking all that medication, right? You going to be okay?"

"Right." Valdez nodded again slyly. He was getting low on *Jack*. He'd get a whole fifth tonight. "I'll be fine, sweety, don't worry about me. Have a good time."

Valdez picked up two fifths of *Jack Daniels* not ten minutes after the family had left in the *Volvo* station wagon. With no restraints now he leisurely sipped whiskey all evening, listening to Bill Withers and Joe Cocker sing—two of his favorites.

At around eleven or so, he suddenly remembered his wife's last instruction out the station wagon window: "Marty, don't forget to take the garbage can out sometime this weekend. They pick up early Monday morning before we get back. Okay?"

"You got it, Babe," he'd said, itching for the family to take off, free him up.

So, with a warm whiskey glow, Valdez obediently hauled the garbage can out to the curb. He stood there smiling dumbly. "There you go, sweety."

Rippp. The sound at the curb just to his left sounded exactly like Midwest lightning ripping through dry air just before an approaching thunderstorm back at his childhood home. His smartass little brother, Henry, sitting on the back porch in St. Paul, and describing the sound as: "The fabric of space-time tearing."

Jesus.

There sat the black vehicle with the funny **g** on its side. One minute nothing, the next minute it was there . . . along with the trailer full of scaffolding.

Recovering his poise, Valdez stepped close and peered through the shaded front window of the strange vehicle.

Nothing. No driver, the back wall too close for even a seat in there. At his angle, Valdez couldn't tell if the speedometer and other gauges were on the dash, or if there were a dash located in the normal spot. He didn't think so.

Behind the vehicle the crew was quietly emerging.

He shuffled back, his legs hurting big time, and watched them unload the scaffolding onto his lawn. And as the four went back and forth, they completely ignored Valdez, not as if he didn't exist, more like he was just unimportant—like they were his kids . . . Actually more like those damn characters in the TV movie Jenny loved. What was it called? . . . *The Terminator.* Valdez wondered if he could slip a little closer and look into one of their shaded masks. *What* would he see? But the busy crew didn't stop long enough to give him an opportunity.

For a few moments Valdez experienced a growing sense of panic, an unsettling sense of impending doom, watching the strange crew begin to erect scaffolding around *his* home, knowing the eventual outcome.

He should do something. Escape? Call someone? Or . . . what?

But after a few more moments of tension, he withdrew the *Jack* from his coat pocket, closed his eyes, and took a healthy snort of the medicine. Oh, man. In a moment the booze was spreading from his stomach, warming and relaxing his body, then his arms, then his legs. Yes. He was going to be just fine now. If he went inside, he knew he'd soon be gone . . . But then he'd been gone around here for a long time now.

With a sense of relaxed resignation, he turned and walked casually back into the house and up to his room. He turned up the sound on, "Unchain My Heart," the gravelly voice completely relaxing him.

Valdez lay down on his bed. He smiled, closing his eyes.

WASP LIGHT

BRUCE BOSTON & LEE BALLENTINE

I WAS RIDING BLACK FIELDS in a metal cart when the chronometers shifted and it began to rain heavily. Small explosions as each drop touched the ground. Light and shadow lacquered in the muddy pools. A gate of the city, scrolled with grime, creaked open—and I saw a slash of color. There against the wall. Nothing more.

And now though I watch the streets and alleys each hour from my lab—I cannot trace the source of that aberrant illumination. I do not know why the tocsins suddenly sound with obsessive regularity. In no way can I guess who has fused the lintels over Southgate so they glisten like a nest of glass eels.

The speakers keep hissing. The screen is mired by white files of rain. A woman's leg is brushed by a fist-fall of droplets and seeing the fullness of that leg I desire the image—not so much the flesh itself but its light patina. I bring up one quadrant of the screen. Her sandal swings a few pixels, a silver scrap of foil hangs from the sole—falling halfway to the grille below. A yellow door behind her stands open and from the dark within something gleams. Collective radiation or the white arms of men drinking wine.

The room is a mottled rectangle behind her legs.

The rain registers as light hobs—glitter edged. I can see the same oval of foil against the grill, its texture that of sawed stone. The webbing of the grille shows wear, its plastic cracked and dirty. This woman has the leg of a girl. Wine spills across the wreckage of a table. White arms begin to strobe.

♦ ♦ ♦

When I look again the light is dimmer and the scene has shifted to another sector. Surfaces conspire to deceive me and colors have lost their mastery. The rain continues to fall.

Assuming that spatial correspondence holds within the city's temporal distortions, a hypothesis which has yet to be denied, I might locate this woman and confront her directly. How would she compare with her opalescent image? The phosphors can offer nothing definitive, and I must of necessity consider my own safety first. This leg I desire could easily be diseased. Or merely a prosthetic sheath concealing the withered stump beneath. And why does this woman-girl choose to walk the streets alone? Is her time frame so different that the transmutations have not begun? And if so, how much am I allowed to tell her?

I decant the recorded leg in freeze frame and global search the sectors for its earthbound simulacrum. I scan the files for a possible cross match. Each time I tap the core where the cables are infested the resolution fades. I must reboot from sequence and start again. A window blossoms in one corner of the screen and a list of names scrolls by. All of these files have been retired to Database. To access their contents I must issue a series of electronic requisitions as tedious and convoluted as the streets themselves. And of course the parameters of such a search would be instantly appended to my own file.

Even as I calculate the risks and probabilities of my distraction, a flake of toxined metal drifts past the randomly scanning lens. I pull back too late. A jet of bad light streaks out at me like a wasp and I fend it off with my right arm. In that instant—everything becomes solid. From the speakers issues the syncopated pounding of sub-audible links which vibrate in the dimensions of my bones. A wave of heat pierces the lead across my chest. A murmur sounds in my lungs. A brilliant voice that threatens but does not speak.

Indeed, though my flesh shows no sign of its passage, I believe something did touch and enter my body just then. Perhaps it is that very slash of light I saw splayed against the wall. I must monitor my metabolic rate and watch for signs of transubstantiation.

I link to the Net and discover the attack has not been singular. The toxins now leak from sector to sector. The boards are jammed with calls from others like myself, who watch from their labs, who hour by hour transcribe the city as it may or may not be. Yet within seconds the answer comes down the line:

"Monitor metabolic rate. Watch for signs of transubstantiation."

♦ ♦ ♦

We are the ones who have been chosen . . . for our mania, our dedication, our self-denial. Despite the chaos around us . . . our positions remain secure. The doors to my lab are manually and electronically locked at all times. The fluorescents are never extinguished. The tocsins never disarmed. I continue to preserve and label the chips in their plastic cases. All about me the walls are stacked with a chronological history of my work and my dereliction, an exercise in phenomenology which knows no bounds beyond the birth and death of my own existence.

Beyond which the Net remains.

Once the city ceases its aberrant motion and the tenets of reality are again susceptible to apprehension, our names will be lasered upon stone for all to see. Our files will never be terminated. We will join the phosphors in their lightning dance from core to exalted core and back again. Of this and much more I have often been assured.

♦ ♦ ♦

In the domed stadium where death is played by night, where those seeking work queue by day, my search statement has turned up a possible cross match. Although it is not night, the overheads are lighted to combat the dimness of the day. One quadrant of the translucent dome is partially collapsed and the rain has covered the field with a series of small lakes. The lines of would-be workers wind across the playing arena while others, who have already been categorized but received no assignment, wait in the bleachers above.

I zero in on the leg in question to confirm its identity. Yes, I do think this is the same woman-girl. Her sandals are darker only because the leather has been dampened by the rain. Other legs mill about her, mostly gray-trousered. For a moment I lose her again as the files advance. Then I pan to her face and discover she is beautiful—wide-set eyes, Eurasian features, dark hair covered by a scarf with a few wet strands escaping to cling to her cheekbones. She is looking up at the man next to her, lips compressed in a tight smile. I realize all at once that she has not come to the stadium to seek legitimate work, but to solicit a liaison.

A small bud of rage blossoms from within me. Yet once I heighten the magnification, my anger fades even as her beauty pales. I see that despite the litheness of her limbs, this woman is no girl. Lines of worry radiate from her eyes. She is well past thirty and as I peel away the surface of her tightly smiling features to reveal what lies beneath, I find neither power nor promise, but merely the dazed glance of another victim.

I pull back from the individual figures, far back from the field itself, until the workers are only dark lines worming their way through a net of rain.

Though I have never visited the domed stadium, I know its dimensions well. In a few hours its stands will be thronged with spectators, its arena alive with combatants. The crowd will feast and roar. Blood will discolor the tiny lakes. As I push the woman from my thoughts, I look forward to the night's games. Like others, I will watch from the relative safety of my personal monitor and thrill to the clarity of their swift and final judgments.

Outside it is dusk. The light has again succeeded in completing its cycle. I have worked through the entire day without remembering to eat. Doing what? The log shows I have formulated no new theories. I have finished the last of the wine. I have recorded that the city is full and loud, the metal catwalks ringing with noise. I have written of colors which threaten to fast-frame the lot of our being.

For a moment I remember none of this. I think I may have a family. My arm begins to throb as if bound by a tourniquet of ice.

Walking on a ledge scattered with thorns to avoid the streets below, I pull my coat tight against the wind. The hills through which the city now passes are creased with snow. Ahead, the gigantic Westend monitor displays a telescoping line of dingy palaces. All different structures I have never been able to track upon my screen. I have heard that their ornate decay is merely a facade, and that strange yet vital rituals take place within their walls. I have also heard it rumored that it is decay alone which finds a place of worship there.

Without noticing I cross the view plane of an active lens. I turn and look back. Past the wild public warrens—the inns, the law-courts and tiered farm dormitories—the rain is falling heavily. The chronometers have shifted once again. A gate of the city, scrolled with grime, creaks shut.

I am riding black fields in a metal cart. Wasp light radiates from the mud-lacquered pools. Small explosions as each drop touches the ground. My legs are those of a girl. Taut and anxious. Diseased as the yellow night.

THE ROBIDERMIST'S STEED

DEANNA HOAK

KATYA STARED WITH RAPT attention—one hand twirling her hair, the other holding tightly onto her daddy—at the robidermist's shop across the way. It backed to the edge of the dome, and the ruddy light from the dying sun gave a blood-colored glow to a gorgeous equine specimen displayed alongside more traditional pets.

That horse had been there since Ghent could remember. The robidermist had recently added a spiraled horn onto its head, maybe hoping the novelty would help sell the thing. He wanted a fortune for it, though: Ghent had actually asked about it once, out of curiosity. His wife had really had a thing about horses.

It looked like Katya had inherited that predilection. When he tugged lightly at her hand and called her name, she didn't even seem to know he was there.

Poor thing. She really hadn't been the same since Angie passed. This would be her first birthday without her mom.

"Katya." He kneeled down in front of her, blocking her view, and looked directly into her eyes. "We have to go."

She tried to peer around him, then gave up and smiled at him. "Daddy, can I pet it, please?"

God, she looked like her mom. He started to say no, but . . .

"Okay, honey. Just for a minute. It is pretty, isn't it?"

"Yay! Come on, Daddy!" She pulled from his hand and ran into the street, not looking, right into the path of a sweeperbot.

"Katya, no!"

Ghent took the four long strides he needed to catch her, sure he'd never make it in time, grabbed her by the arm and jerked her back.

Katya fell to the street with the force of his grab, and in his fear he dragged her to get her out of the way. She started crying, howling, "Ow, Daddy! You're hurting me!"

The bot passed by.

"Katya, are you okay? You know better than that! Don't ever pull away from Daddy like that!"

Katya sobbed and rubbed her arm. "I want to pet the horsie!"

"Here, honey, we're going to go over there. Is your arm okay? Let me kiss it."

She held out her arm for his peck.

"All better?" He hoped he hadn't bruised her; there was a red mark from his clutch. He patted it in concern, his hand shaky from adrenaline. "Okay, let's pet the horse now. See that horn? That means he's a unicorn! They love little girls."

A smile spread across her face, showing the gap from the tooth she'd lost last week. "Really?" She wiped at her tears. "Do you think he'll like me?"

"Oh, I'm sure he will, honey."

As they traipsed across the street, the robidermist came out of his shop. He must've seen Katya and figured he had a sucker on his hands. She was one of the only kids on this godforsaken station.

"Looking for a pet, folks? I have a great selection."

"I wanna pet the horsie. It's a unicorn," Katya announced.

The shopkeeper smiled and stuck his hands in his pockets. "That it is. I call him Tristan, though of course you could name him whatever you wanted if you took him home."

"Oh, no," Ghent cut in. He caught the shopkeeper's eye and shook his head. "He's way too big. She just wants to pet him."

The shopkeeper ignored him, bending down to Katya. "You know, little girl, the great thing about a robipet is that you don't have to have much space for it. He doesn't eat or anything, and he'll only move as much as you want him to."

Katya reached up and rubbed the unicorn's soft nose. The shopkeeper fiddled with a control he'd brought out from his pocket, and the animal nuzzled her hand.

"Oh!" She pulled back a moment, then reached to pet the long mane. "He likes me! Hi, Tristan!"

The unicorn rubbed its head against her shoulder.

"Watch its horn, honey!" Ghent pulled her back.

The shopkeeper finally looked at him. "It has excellent software, and I added that horn to the code myself. It wouldn't poke anyone with it unless you ordered it to." He smiled. "It also programs itself based on your reactions. If your little girl wants to pet it every morning, it'll start nudging her first at that time." He turned toward Katya again. "Hey, honey, you want to brush him? Let me get a currycomb for you." He disappeared in his shop and came back with a flat brush a moment later. "See how soft his mane is? The kind of horse he was is called a Lippizaner. Pretty, huh?" He handed her the comb.

Katya was taken. What was it about little girls and horses? Ghent pulled the shopkeeper aside. "Listen, please don't. I asked about the price on that thing a few years ago, and I know I can't afford it."

The shopkeeper rubbed a hand along the back of his head. "Well . . . it's actually about at the end of its shelf life—the preservatives are great, but they can only last so long, you know." He paused. "I'd sell it at a loss at this point."

Ghent stared. "How long has it got?"

"I wouldn't give it more than six months."

Katya had climbed onto a bench beside the animal and was brushing its mane. "Daddy, can I sit on him, please?"

"I don't—"

"Oh, of course she can," the robidermist cut in. "Here, honey, I'll boost you up."

Ghent shot the man a look and shook his head. He couldn't very well say no now.

Katya was all smiles. The shopkeeper settled her on the unicorn's back, and she leaned forward to pet its mane. "You're so pretty, Tristan. What a nice boy you are!"

Ghent hadn't seen her this happy since Angie died. He had to fight back tears just looking at her.

"Tristan," the shopkeeper said, "walk around to the back of this building and come back. Hold on tight, little girl."

"Oh!" The unicorn started moving, and Katya grabbed its mane in a grip that would have undoubtedly caused any living horse to buck her off.

Ghent fought the urge to walk alongside her—she liked to do things for herself. But she swayed when the unicorn turned around. He rushed toward her, arms outstretched to catch her if she fell.

She caught the movement and scowled at him. "I'm fine, Daddy! Tristan loves me. He wouldn't let me fall!"

She regained her balance, so Ghent stopped his advance. She looked beautiful on the animal, he had to admit: her long dark hair against its white hide as she bent to hug its neck.

But six months, and that hide would be rotting. The disintegration of a robipet could be pretty hard to deal with, emotionally. They'd had a friend with a dog that way: The corpse the robotics were embedded in had started to rot. It was tough for the family, because the pet acted just the same as always—seemed just like a live animal—and they knew it wasn't in any pain. Eventually, the muscular attachments degraded enough that the thing had been kind of shambling around, though.

And it stank to hell way before that.

That family had paid a click of credit to have the robotics and memory installed in a fresh animal—looked just the same as their old one! But where would he find another horse out here? This thing had to be the only one for light-years.

Katya looked at him, grinning, so excited. "Can I have him, Daddy? Please? Pretty please? He can be my birthday present."

She must have caught the look on his face, because her smile faded a bit, and her eyes got shiny with unshed tears. "Can't I please have him, Daddy? It's so lonely here sometimes. The man said he doesn't need much room." Her smile trembled into place again. "Please?"

Ghent shook his head, but he already knew he'd never be able to tell her no.

Six months. Shit.

Katya recognized the resignation on his face and beamed at him. "I'm going to love him forever, Daddy."

FROM THE SUPERNATURAL CASE FILES
OF SHERLOCK HOLMES

THE ADVENTURE OF THE SOLITARY GRAVE

JOHN H. WATSON, M.D. (EDITED BY CHRISTIAN KLAVER)

SOME FEW ATTENTIVE READERS may recall a previous account, such as this one, when I wrote of 'the final case' I would ever be able to chronicle involving my closest friend and companion, Sherlock Holmes. Would that the case I now write could be followed with a revelatory episode such as the "Adventure of the Empty House," but I fear that there is no such possibility. This time, Sherlock Holmes is truly gone from this world forever, with only a solitary grave in Sussex Downs to mark his passing. I know that both this humble chronicler and the world at large are the poorer for his absence. It is under his direction that I undertake to narrate this particular case, his last.

I have by no means a complete chronicle of all the adventures that Holmes deemed fit only for the 'black box', but I do have several at my disposal, including "Case of the Giant Rat of Sumatra," as well as the separate matters involving Mr. James Phillimore, Mrs. Cecil Forrester and the cutter Alicia, none of them having yet been published, since their grotesque and outré nature would have stretched the reader's sensibilities beyond any normal boundaries. They are, in a word, unbelievable, and I have held these cases in abeyance at Holmes' request to protect both his reputation, and my own small credibility as narrator. But the time has come to reveal them, per Holmes' instructions, beginning with this one. I follow these instructions faithfully and humbly, and let my readers judge if we have done wrong to withhold them as long as we did.

It was late in 1903 when I found myself a resident once more in my quarters at Baker Street. My wife was out in the country visiting her relatives for some time, and this gave me the opportunity to renew my acquaintance to such a degree that I almost felt I had come back to bachelorhood on a permanent basis. A tempestuous London storm howled at the windows of our drawing room, making it a comfort for us to be indoors.

But if the conditions appealed to me, they did not bring solace to Holmes. He had no active case at present and was quite beside himself with a hectic lassitude that had him twitching restlessly in his chair. Several times he cast a reckless glance at the small case on the dresser next to him, the one that held the syringe and solution of cocaine that was his sole escape when he fell into this darkest of moods. He had already availed himself of its calming effect once, and I was starting to wonder, without comment, if this vice of his had gone to even further extremes than it had before my marriage.

"A little stimulant is not so bad as all that," Holmes said with a laugh, and I knew he had deduced my thoughts in that uncanny way of his. "It is only this dreaded inactivity, Watson. It exhausts me as work never does. It is doubly vexing when I know that trouble is brewing on the horizon, but cannot get my hands on any of the threads of it, so that I have nothing with which to occupy my waiting hours."

"Trouble?" I said. I had been in Baker Street for nearly three days, and had the feeling that Holmes had been waiting for something all this time, but he had refused to be drawn out enough to speak to any of the details up until now.

"You are unfamiliar with my cases of the past few months, Watson, so I cannot expect you to know. Of late, I have been involved in several cases that seem unrelated, but all stem from a single source. I have been seeking them out, and turning all other unrelated cases away. The missing crews on the *Matilda Briggs* and the *Demeter*, certain tangential persons involved in the death of Cadogan West, and the flowers mysteriously delivered to Miss Violet Bell are all the work of one mastermind, Watson. It is all connected, and I am carefully drawing all the threads round me, feeling for the spider at the centre. If I did not know better, I should say that Moriarty himself was back and up to his old tricks."

"Moriarty, that villain!" I cried. "Is it possible that he lived?"

Holmes reached past the cocaine and picked up his pipe. Evidently, our conversation had sufficiently engaged him so as to make the distraction of the more potent drug no longer necessary. He scraped his pipe bowl clean and made ready for a fresh batch of tobacco by the expedient of rapping the bowl against the table leg, heedless of the shag bits on the carpet. He

THE ADVENTURE OF THE SOLITARY GRAVE

fired his pipe to the desired pitch before answering.

"I would find that highly unlikely," he said finally, "and I would only consider such a possibility once I had eliminated all other possibilities, for I saw his body fall the into the perilous depths of the Falls myself. Also, consider this: were Moriarty to survive, I am quite confident that his next move would be to take action against me. He would first seek to complete his plans for removing me, and only after that would he take up his old machinations in directing London's underworld, for that is how I found him the first time, and Moriarty was no dullard. I do not think he would make the same mistake twice."

"Is it possible that someone else has carried on his work?" I asked.

"This thought occurred to me, as well," Holmes said. "It seems a highly unlikely possibility that someone of Moriarty's caliber and intent has stepped into the void I inadvertently created by removing him, but we are at a loss to provide a better explanation. And this one, for all its flaws, certainly seems more plausible than Moriarty's return from the grave. Ah, it is no good. What we need is more data, Watson. It is a capital mistake to theorize before one has enough data."

My next statement was interrupted by voices from below.

"At last," Holmes said, with no small amount of relief. "A case. A welcome diversion. I can only hope that Lestrade is bringing us something worthy of our attention. If his urgency is any indicator, we will be well served."

I could not help but feel a great sense of relief, and I knew that Holmes had noted my grateful exhalation. He gave me a laconic smile and put the cocaine back into the dresser like the trainer of some loathsome serpent tucking his deadly charge into a basket, away, but not forgotten.

When Lestrade burst in on our sitting room, the short, little detective wore the most solemn expression. In his hand he bore a small veneered case, such as a well-to-do gentleman might use to carry cards or cigarettes.

"Murder then," Holmes said, "and in the Harrington district, I should say. Perhaps done this very day?"

Lestrade started. "I'm familiar with your cunning ways, Mr. Holmes, but how you could know all that without yet hearing or seeing any of the clues is quite beyond me."

"You brought the clues in with you, Lestrade," Holmes said with a wave of his hand. "It is no secret that they've torn up the sidewalk in order to begin construction in Harrington, and in doing so thrown up a great deal of the red clay that I see about your shoes. The fact that it is still wet and that you were in too much of a hurry to do more than a casual scraping on our doormat increases the impression of great urgency. And your face has a peculiar expression, despite your many years with Scotland Yard, which further adds to give a very sobering impression."

"Well, I suppose my face does tell the tale plainly, at that," Lestrade admitted. "I expect you remember the forger in Norwood that you turned us on to?"

"Yes, quite," said Holmes. "Did you find him at the address I gave to you?"

Lestrade nodded. "We did, and in the process of apprehending him we came upon something quite murkier than a simple forgery. When asked about it, the rascal went quite silent. Not only silent, but a man that I would have sworn would send either of us to the bottom of the Thames without the slightest hesitation actually broke down in tears when we questioned him on the macabre item we found there. We have been able to get nothing from him. In fact, we are starting to think him quite beyond reason."

"And this is the item here?" Holmes asked. He gestured at the cigarette case.

"Yes," Lestrade said. "I've taken the liberty of bringing it with me."

"Let us see then, what we can make of it," Holmes said, rubbing his hands together as he warmed to the case.

The usually loquacious Inspector handed over the case without further comment. "Lacquered teak," Holmes said. "Expensive, but not otherwise extraordinary. It has seen some use, certainly by a man once wealthy and then fallen on hard times. The clear markings of an amateurish repair applied to the hinge tells us that. Now then, let us look inside." He fell abruptly silent when he opened the box.

I shifted in my seat to get a closer look and gasped as the significance of what I saw struck home to me. "Good Lord, Holmes!" I said, for rarely had I seen a more shocking example of brutality and horror.

Inside, nestled neatly in red velvet like a rare jewel, lay a freshly severed human finger.

Holmes leaned closer, deeply affected, not with shock or disgust, but with eager interest. He pulled his lens from a drawer and examined it all together first, then carefully removed the finger. He looked further into the box and made a satisfied noise. "This was originally used for cigarettes, as one might expect," he murmured. "Traces of them are still here." He carefully pulled a scrap of tobacco out and snuffed at it like a bloodhound. "An unusual, but inexpensive brand. A brand made in India and not much seen in England. It has a very acrid taste that would not be popular."

Then he began a minute study of the finger itself. It was clearly a woman's finger, and showed no sign of decay that I could see. The hand it was taken from must once have been long and white, a beautiful sight

THE ADVENTURE OF THE SOLITARY GRAVE

before this horrible disfigurement had taken place. Holmes measured the length and width of the finger and even scraped underneath the fingernail, which was long and unpainted.

"What could anyone want with such a grisly trophy?" I asked. "Was it some kind of proof of kidnapping?"

Lestrade shook his head. "There's been no such missing person that we know of, and no ransom note was found. Nor do we have any idea who might receive one until we identify the victim."

Holmes shot an acute glance at Lestrade. "When did you get this?"

"Oh, well, it came to me early this afternoon. The constable that found it at Brixton Lane carried it with him for several hours before he got it to me. He found it this morning, when the arrest was made."

Holmes frowned, clearly displeased with this information. He sprang up and went over to the table in the corner that held his equipment for chemical experimentation, taking the box and finger with him. He rummaged among the retorts, test tubes, and little Bunsen lamps before extracting three empty tubes. He added a small amount of water to each, then carefully added a sample of blood taken from the finger to the first, and a sample from the box to the second. For the third, he jabbed a bodkin into his own finger to supply a few drops. He absently covered the self-inflicted scratch with a piece of sticking plaster, a habit I knew he performed in order to prevent accidentally poisoning himself while handling toxins. Then he measured a small amount of white crystals, dropping them into the waiting vessels. He followed this with a few drops of a transparent fluid from an angular green bottle.

He jerked upright as each and every test tube turned a dull mahogany color. "I really must thank you, Lestrade," he said without lifting his eyes from the experiment on the table. "Already this case is showing an extraordinary number of interesting features. Some very interesting features indeed, including some I've never seen before. Perhaps a case unique in the annals of crime detection."

"Indeed," I said fervently. The image of some poor woman maimed in such a fashion shook me to the core. "I can hardly imagine a more cold-blooded act. What kind of monster could carry around such a thing the way another man carries cigarettes is barely imaginable."

Holmes waved a hand dismissively. "Oh, that is hardly exceptional. Recall, Watson, when the 50-year-old spinster, Miss Susan Cushing, received a parcel in the post which turned out to contain two severed human ears packed in coarse salt and I think you will have to concede my point. No, it is the nature of the victim that interests me."

"We must help her, Holmes," I urged.

"I'm afraid," Holmes said, not unkindly, "it is all too likely that this particular woman is beyond our reach to help, but possibly we can be of some assistance in punishing the criminals involved in so macabre an act."

"Begging your pardon, Mr. Holmes," Lestrade said, "but I would hardly call that wound fatal."

"No," Holmes said. "You wouldn't, but I consider it the highest probability." He held up a hand to fend off further protests. "You have your methods, Lestrade, and I have mine. Be assured that I will wire you with any advice or information that I have as soon as I am sure of my facts." With that, he bent back over the gruesome piece of evidence, fishing out more test tubes for further tests. Lestrade and I were clearly forgotten and dismissed from his thoughts.

Seeing it was no use to protest further, and that Holmes would not have any information coaxed out of him until he was ready, Lestrade gave a displeased grunt, crammed his hat forcefully back onto his head and left.

Holmes spent the rest of the evening at work, completely ignoring the arrival of dinner. The parlor filled with an ever increasing cloud of noxious smoke as he applied test upon test to his specimen. The miasma was augmented even further as he took more and more frequent breaks to sit and ponder, puffing away at his clay pipe until the haze became intolerable. It had gone past a three-pipe problem and well into a seventh when I finally gave up trying to read through the smoke and went to bed.

When I awoke in the morning, Holmes' chemical experiments were still underway, and the darkened room was dotted in that corner with the little blue flames of multiple Bunsen burners going at once. Holmes was not at the table, but wandered about the quarters with an air of extreme agitation.

"Aha, Watson," he said at once. "Take a look at our unique evidence and give me your thoughts on it."

Hardly knowing what to expect, I went to the table and bent over to look at the petri dish with the finger laid upon it. The blood still glistened brightly at the severed joint without any sign of coagulation or clotting.

"Why, it looks as if it was freshly severed this morning!" I exclaimed.

"Exactly!" he said. "The blood has not dried or congealed, as we might expect."

"A hemophiliac?" I asked.

"My thoughts precisely, though this kind of bleeding is exceptional even for such a patient and female hemophiliacs are nearly unheard of, as I'm sure you know. Also the blood has several irregularities. You yourself saw that it passed the Holmes blood test I perfected the day we first met,

THE ADVENTURE OF THE SOLITARY GRAVE

just before we became involved with the affair of Major Sholto, of Upper Norwood."

"I remember it well." How could I not, having also met my wife during those events?

"But the blood from this finger does not seem to correspond to most of the other characteristics of human blood, nor does the flesh of the finger itself. For the flesh of the person to be so affected indicates that the disease is long-term, rather than something recently contracted. It is also curious that, though there is still some evidence of blood flow, the rest of the finger is quite desiccated, and more resilient and lighter than I should expect. There are indications that this may also be true in life, and that the disease dramatically alters the circulatory system as it progresses. This agrees with the differing characteristics of the blood."

"What kind of characteristics do you mean?" I asked.

"Well," he said with a sly smile. "There are several. But this demonstration is the most striking." He took a small specimen knife and cut a small portion of skin off the finger, adding this to a test tube. He then sprinkled a small amount of a light grey powder into the solution and immediately a violent bubbling eruption occurred. In but a few moment's time, the reaction had ceased and I was able to see into the clear liquid that remained. The skin sample was gone, quite dissolved into the solution.

"What did you put in?" I asked. "Some destructive acid compound?"

Holmes went back to his pipe and got it going again before he answered. "Powdered silver," he finally answered.

"Silver . . ." Nothing in my long medical history, nor in my unusual dealings alongside Sherlock Holmes, had prepared me for so extraordinary a statement.

"Yes, I quite understand your reaction." Holmes said. "All this leads us to infer the existence of a sufferer of an as-of-yet unknown blood disease that leaves the victim so robust that a young woman is still capable of an active climb that would strain even an accomplished athlete."

"Climbing? But how on Earth could you know that?"

"There are abrasions on the skin and traces of stone fragments both within the abrasions and underneath the fingernail. Not all of these are new, which suggests more than one such climb in the recent past. But otherwise, this finger shows no signs of the calluses that usually accompany the physical activity I would associate with a working woman. This indicates either a woman of the higher class or an invalid excused from menial labor. Either answer seems at odds with our climbing theory, does it not? Or at the very least an unusual combination."

"Most blood diseases are debilitating to the victim," I said, incredulous.

"I can hardly imagine such a person making a strenuous climb."

"Nor can I," Holmes said. "Yet I can find no other explanation which meets the facts that are presented to us. Clearly this case has far greater depths to it than we could possibly have foreseen."

"Good Lord," I said, remembering the prominence of hemophilia in the royal family. "You don't suppose that this woman . . ."

"I consider it highly unlikely," Holmes said, divining my thoughts as quickly as if I had spoken them aloud. "Whoever this woman was, this finger, at least, bears no sign of having ever worn jewelry. It is the ring finger of the left hand, a place usually reserved for the wedding ring, so we can also safely assume she was not married."

"What does this all mean?"

"We do not have enough data for a complete determination," Holmes said. "But I have several lines of inquiry. I believe that my next step is to visit West Sussex, where I know a man who deals exclusively in Indian cigarettes. One of the few places in England that carries this distinct tobacco."

"Then I shall come with you." I offered.

"That is by no means necessary. I think you would find this preliminary investigation very tedious, and there is not likely to be any danger at this stage. Also, I will send out several telegrams to other tobacconists, and I will need someone reliable to await their reply. But keep your revolver ready! With such a clue as this first one, I have no doubt that I shall have need of it, as well as your firm resolve, before this case is concluded."

I spent the rest of the day without further news, and the only break in the monotony of an agitated day filled with listless reading was when a small package came for Holmes from the Ingerson Rifle Company. Having been given directions to intercept all of Holmes' mail for him, I opened the package with trembling hands, lest another severed body part should await me. Instead, I found a card from the company with a short note: "Per Your Instructions—Ralph Ingerson" and two small boxes. My astonishment knew no ends when I opened these and found that they were laden with gun cartridges. But no ordinary cartridges. While the casing looked normal enough, the bullets themselves gleamed and shone, even in the moderately lit study. Silver. Of course, I made the connection between these and the unusual reaction to silver in Holmes' test, but I couldn't for the life of me imagine how that could make this kind of weaponry necessary. A bullet of lead would serve just as well, I should think, and besides I could hardly imagine an instance where we might need to shoot the *victim* of the case. Deciding that this portion of the matter was quite beyond me, I set the

THE ADVENTURE OF THE SOLITARY GRAVE

package aside and continued to wait.

No sign of Holmes came, and Baker Street received no further correspondence that night, but a telegram was waiting for me when I woke the next morning. It read thusly: "Come down to hotel in Carfax at once. Come armed. Bring Ingerson package.—SH"

I had Mrs. Hudson send for a cab immediately. My old army habits stood me in good stead, and I was able to get my things together quickly enough to be ready for the driver when he pulled up to our curb.

♦ ♦ ♦

It was only a few hours later when I stepped out of the train and onto the platform at Carfax. I hefted my luggage and hailed a waiting cab. The driver, a large fleshy man, grunted when I requested the Carfax Hotel and departed off immediately. In just a few short minutes, I saw the sign for my hotel, but was amazed when we rattled directly past it without any pause or sign of slowing. I hammered my cane on the roof of the hansom. The driver ignored me utterly. I was quite beside myself, particularly since we seemed to be entering a seedier and more disreputable part of the sleepy Oxford town. The hansom finally came to a halt underneath a huge yew tree. I burst out of the cab and shook my stick at the driver.

"See here, man!" I said. "What is the meaning of this?"

The driver was hunched over with his face in his hands, and I saw him pull something wet from inside his mouth. When he turned, I was astonished to see Sherlock Holmes smiling down at me.

"Forgive me, Watson," he said with a chuckle, "but I did think you would rather come to the heart of the investigation at once."

"Good Lord!" I said, quite astonished.

Holmes discarded the shabby outer garment he'd used as part of his driver's disguise and stepped down from the cab just far enough to reach out and pull me back into the cab with him. His face had a deadly earnestness to it.

"I should warn you, Watson, that this case is possibly the murkiest, most sinister case in which we have ever been involved. My plan is for you to wait here and provide a rear guard while I investigate inside."

"Couldn't I be of far more assistance inside?"

"Perhaps," he admitted, "but this is one time that I fear the risks are far too great, and I haven't the time to explain them. It is already past noon, and we shall need every minute of the day."

"If there is danger," I said stoutly, "then that is all the more reason for me to come with you. I quite insist!"

He gripped my arm in camaraderie. "I can always count on you, Watson. Very well. Did you bring the package from Ingerson?"

I wordlessly handed over the package of bizarre ammunition, quite at a loss as to why such elaborate precautions were necessary, but knowing that my friend would not order such a curiosity without good reason. Holmes pulled his own revolver from his jacket pocket and ejected the regular cartridges onto the cab seat and began replacing them with the silver bullet cartridges from the package. He gestured for me to do the same.

"Let me fill in the new details of this case," he said. "Tracing the recent sale of the tobacco I found has led me to several unremarkable places, and to here. I have found a number of subtle and disturbing characteristics of this place. This property belongs to the Lady Carfax, an elderly widow who has been gone for some months visiting in Europe. She is unharmed and whole with all her fingers as of yesterday, according to the French officials that I telegraphed. Denied her inheritance because of her sex, she still has some wealth, but owns very little property in England. This is her sole estate, and she only has this because it was awarded back to her, after being sold to a foreign dignitary, due to a legal technicality and the lack of said dignitary having any presence or legal representation. Neither she nor anyone in her employ has been here in many years. According to the officials, it has been abandoned ever since, but the marks on the grounds and gates show us that this account can hardly be accurate. We need to find out more about whatever clandestine activity is happening here. Numerous signs indicate that this might well be one of the most foul expeditions we have ever ventured on together. I urge you to the highest level of caution, Waston."

"Then whose finger . . ." I asked.

"That has yet to be determined," Holmes said quickly. I knew my friend well enough to know that he suspected a great deal more than he told me, but also knew that he always had good reasons for revealing his deductions in the proper place and time. I had never gone wrong following him before and was far too old a campaigner to change my habits now. I finished loading the gun and indicated I was ready.

Not since the affair with Milverton have I felt so much that our roles in society had been twisted out of shape. Now I felt like the criminal instead of an upholder of the law. The gate may have been rusted, but we found the lock secure with signs of recent use. I had seen Holmes pick locks with the competence of a seasoned burglar, but after examining the gate he turned aside and walked the four-wheeler around to the back part of the stone wall and used the simple expedient of pulling the carriage close to the wall and climbing over. Should a constable's patrol have come by during this time we might have found ourselves in the novel and entirely unenviable position of being arrested.

THE ADVENTURE OF THE SOLITARY GRAVE

But such was not the case and, after Holmes had lowered me down with a steely grip on my arm, he dropped down beside me with ease. It never ceased to amaze me, this change from a tweedy scholar in Baker Street to an active bloodhound.

"Going in this way," he whispered into my ear, "we avoid the dogs, as well as those who might be watching the gate, since their activities are all concentrated there." And so it was. We made our way across the unkempt grounds so overgrown with bracken and gorse and so filled with dead foliage that it might not have been tended to for decades. We approached so that the abbey itself was on the far side, and made our way in through broken-paned French doors to the interior of the house itself.

The inside of the house was in even worse repair than the outside garden. There was some furniture, torn and decrepit, but it looked as if much of what might have once been there had been carried off a long time ago. Old paint of a universally drab grey colour flaked off the walls and a smell of dust, mould and decay permeated every corner. Not a noise came to our ears except the whispering of the wind outside, and our every footstep sent echoes through the apparently empty and abandoned structure.

We made our way through part of the house and found only more empty rooms until Holmes stopped me as we came upon the entrance to an old-fashioned courtyard. The doors were flung open and broken, one hanging only on a single hinge and swaying in the slight breeze. He pointed down at several sets of fresh tracks etched into the dust on the floorboards in front of us.

"Careful where you step, Watson," he said as he crouched to a nearly prostrate position to examine the tracks. "Two different sets of workman's boots, one large, one even more so, both hobnailed. And an entirely different set of well-to-do gentleman's boots. Curious..."

"Holmes, look here," I said. From my removed position, close to the end of the hallway, I had nearly placed my hand on a crack in the wall without noticing the bullet lodged there.

"Excellent, Watson!" Holmes cried as he came back to look at my find. "Score one for you!" He pulled a penknife out and delicately pried the bullet free. "There is blood here." He wrapped the evidence with his handkerchief and placed it in his pocket as he went back to his work on the floor. "And more blood by your foot, here." The spot he indicated was minute, but he used his knife to scrape up a sample of this, too.

His path carried him closer to the entrance of the courtyard as he examined the area in minute detail. When he looked up from the doorway itself, a shadow passed over his face, followed by a look of grim determination.

"Whatever has gone on here," he said, "it seems that we are too late to prevent it. But perhaps not too late to deal with the villains responsible."

Inside the doorway lay the bodies of two men, so horribly battered and bent into unnatural angles that there could be no doubt about the nature of their death or the futility of my medical services. Their faces were twisted into a shocked rictus of horror. These were men who had seen their violent deaths coming. A six-shot revolver lay just inside the courtyard on one of the flagstones forming the garden path. Holmes picked it up, sniffed at it then opened the cylinder. All the bullets were still in place. He tucked it into his jacket pocket.

Then I caught sight of the third body, though it was nearly unrecognizable as such, being so badly charred. In an act of further barbarism, a stake had been driven completely through the body, pinning the hapless victim to a long plank that lay on the ground. Though I have seen many horrors in my career between Afghanistan and the innumerable cases in which I've assisted Sherlock Holmes, none of them lingers in my mind the way this scorched cadaver does.

The gruesome sight did not deter Holmes and he was as thorough as possible in his minute inspection of the charred body as well as the other two. He poked, looked at every detail and even sniffed at the burnt corpse. He took longer going over this ghastly scene than I ever remembered him taking over similar scenes, muttering to himself as he went, though I could catch nothing of what he said and was quite in the dark as to what he might have found out. He took minute measurements. He also took several more blood samples with his penknife, placing the contents in several small tubes apparently brought for the purpose and labeling them as he went. He went over every flagstone and overgrown flower bed in the courtyard and even climbed several feet up the courtyard wall to peer at the bricks at a height.

"Holmes!" I said in a choked voice as I noticed something that increased my horror of the charred cadaver tenfold. "Look at the hands!"

"Yes, Watson," he said without looking up, and still with his back to me. "I was wondering if you would pick out that detail."

"But Holmes, this is a woman's body, and the left hand is missing the very same ring finger!" My stomach and mind churned with the fearsome image of any woman being burned to death in this manner.

"Yes, Watson," Holmes said. "But our time is short, Doctor, and I have a great deal to do here."

Thus admonished, there was nothing I could do but wait. I was forced to pull in a half-broken chair and settle nervously into it while I kept guard over Holmes' activities, since it was several hours and well into the latter half of the afternoon before he was complete.

"Well," he said, finally. "I believe that we can do no further good here,

THE ADVENTURE OF THE SOLITARY GRAVE

Watson, and it is well past time that we should be on our way. I wish to be back to Baker Street while the sun is still in the sky."

"Have we learned nothing?" I asked. "Is there no clue to lead us to the villains that have done this monstrous thing?"

"Oh, I should say we've learned a great deal," he said, "but the conclusions are so fantastic that I do not dare entertain them until I have eliminated all other possibilities."

"You must clarify it for me, then," I said, "for it is all a muddle in my mind."

Holmes shook his head. "I have one further test before I can be sure." He grabbed my arm. "Come. It is vitally important that we spare no delay."

"Should we not at least summon the police?" I asked as we made our way out.

"That would be the worst action we could possibly take," he said without turning or breaking stride. "I believe the official force would be well out of their depths on this case, Watson. If what I suspect is true, then only harm can come from their involvement. Come, we may take a direct route as the gate is no longer watched during the day."

He raised his hand to forestall any further questions, and we left directly out the same way we had come in without meeting any further incident. I mounted the driver's box of the four-wheeler and he wordlessly handed me the reins. I could see that the day's investigations had troubled him deeply, as they certainly had me. But I had no doubt that Holmes' keen mind had penetrated far deeper into the mystery than my own. But far from being a comfort, I could tell my friend grew more and more agitated as he sifted the information around in his mind.

He fidgeted and frowned all the way back to the driver station near the train, where he wordlessly handed a number of sovereigns to a large, black-bearded driver. The man tipped his hat low and murmured his thanks, which Holmes answered with a distracted air. Holmes let me handle the purchasing of tickets and luggage arrangements. All the way back to Baker Street I held my questions as he bit at his nails and lip, tapped his fingers, shuffled his feet and otherwise displayed every sign of inward agitation.

When we finally arrived at our quarters, it was nearly four o'clock. Holmes rushed past Mrs. Hudson's questions about supper, up the stairs and over to his chemical table.

He snatched up the case with the specimen finger in it and held it thoughtfully for a few seconds. Finally, all indecision left his face and he turned to me.

"Watson, what do you know about vampires?"

"Vampires?" I repeated, astounded. "Nothing more than fanciful stories. But why ask me such a question? You yourself have called the very notion rubbish!"

"True," he said, ruefully. "But now I am forced to revise my opinion in the light of overwhelming evidence. Consider the facts, Watson. You have already conceded the existence of a rare blood disease. We have samples, and have seen evidence."

"Quite true, but Holmes . . . vampires?"

"Bear with me, Doctor," he said. "I have determined that the nature of this blood disease greatly affects the cell structure of its victims, replacing the chemical structure of the cell in such a way as to completely transfigure its makeup. You have already seen the violent reaction to silver."

"I am hardly in a position to argue," I said reluctantly.

"Agreed. Now . . . is it such a reach to suppose that such a victim might have entirely different dietary needs?"

"But Holmes," I cried. "Drinking blood? Bats? Mist? Wolves? Frightened of the holy cross? Bursting into flame in sunlight? Surely this is madness!"

"Clearly we can't condone all these beliefs, Watson. Not in our orderly world. But let us take the last question first. I spent all night going over this sample of our hemophiliac, Watson. All night. I managed to discover the unusual reaction to silver, but there is one test I did not think of, and perhaps it may be the most conclusive."

With a swift motion, he placed the small case on the corner of his chemical table, near the window, where a pale square of grayish late-afternoon light showed the wan and bloodless finger to its most grisly advantage.

"What in the world?" I said, sitting bolt upright as a small curl of smoke puffed from the finger, then a low flame, until the entire thing went up in a burst of acrid smoke like a Chinese firework gone horribly awry! Smoke plumed up from the table, and we were both coughing uncontrollably before Holmes managed to cover it with a metal serving lid in order to smother the flame. Even so, we had to stumble around opening windows and waving sheaves of paper to drive out the smoke, and it took a great many minutes to clear our parlor.

"Well, Watson," he said with a wry smile as we fell back into our chairs. "It seems my flair for a dramatic demonstration has somewhat backfired on me. Yet, clearly you will have to concede that there must be more to this vampire business than we at first believed."

"I don't know what to think," I said. "I cannot fathom how this could possibly be. If it were true, why has there been no outcry other than a col-

THE ADVENTURE OF THE SOLITARY GRAVE

lection of old fairy tales and that Polidori twaddle?"

"I'm inclined to think that this condition is rare, and the numbers of the afflicted must be very small," Holmes said.

"I can hardly disbelieve," I said, "but I still cannot bring myself to fully comprehend . . . mist . . . bats . . . I simply cannot imagine how this could be, and yet I must."

"I should think that we are not quite forced to accept all of the information that comes to us without some examination as to its merit. It occurs to me that some portions of these lurid tales are rife with more superstition than logic. The power of the cross to hold such a fiend, for example. Why should this be? But when you consider that many such crucifixes are made with silver, and that *this* material might well give such an assailant pause, this I can credit. But I am ahead of myself, Watson, and it is a mistake to theorize too heavily without all the data."

"But how did you know? How could you possibly come to such a startling conclusion?"

"How indeed?" said a strangely cultured voice.

I sat bolt upright at this sudden intrusion, so startling was it. Holmes was even more galvanized, and leapt to his feet.

The man standing in our doorway was tall, taller even than Holmes, and equally gaunt. His features were sharp and strong as well, but there the similarities diverged. Instead of Holmes' lean ascetic features, this man's bushy eyebrows, long black mustache and great mane of black hair combined to create an impression of barbaric grandeur. Like a Mongol king he was, noble and proud without a trace of shame.

"Be wary, Watson," Holmes said levelly. "We are in grave danger here. Consider the noise on the steps."

"But I heard nothing!" I said, quite taken aback at this unreal series of events.

"Precisely."

"You are an interesting man, Mr. Holmes," the intruder said. "With a shocking clarity of perception." His English was excellent, but the intonation marked him clearly as foreign. He moved idly towards the window, as if unaware of his actions, and Holmes took several corresponding steps towards his desk. I was keenly reminded of two predators, the bloodhound and the wolf, stalking each other with deadly intent and malice.

"This is not necessary," the man said in conciliatory tone. "Please sit, I mean you no harm."

Holmes moved behind his desk and picked up the revolver there. I made to follow suit. I still had the gun in my jacket pocket that I wore, and it would have been a moment's action to stand and draw it. When I tried, however, I found I could do nothing of the sort. I could not even take my eyes off the man's own, which seemed to burn like coals in the low flickering light of the small hearth fire we had burning. When night had fallen, I wasn't certain, but our comfortable parlor in Baker Street felt transformed, and now it suddenly seemed a dark and menacing place.

"That is quite enough," Holmes said, proving his own mobility by raising and cocking the gun in his hand.

"Guns mean little to one such as . . ." the man started, but his voice trailed off as Holmes calmly held a bullet up between thumb and forefinger. Even in the flickering and dim light, the gleam of silver was apparent.

"Most exceptional . . ." the man said. "A keen and disciplined mind, not to be distracted or diverted from its purpose." He smiled, and some tension in his eyes seemed to relax its grip. I found that I could move again. I sprang to my feet and yanked out my own revolver. Holmes held up a restraining hand, though, so I took no further action.

"You know my name, of course," the man said, still quite at ease.

"I do not know anything other than the fact that you are an out of town noble whose tastes run to extravagant means, but who has not been exposed to London society for some time. You are quite old, much older than you appear, and you are used to being obeyed implicitly. You have few servants, but the ones you have are fiercely dedicated. You traveled here without carriage or hansom, but did not go by foot, either. You've had some recent distress, but that is not entirely what brings you here. Also, you are not entirely human."

"Ah . . . not so well informed as I thought," the man said. "I was sure that Von Helsing or Holmwood would have told you that much, at least."

"At this time two days ago I knew nothing of the matter," Holmes said. "And those names mean nothing to me. I have drawn my own conclusions as to your nature based on the evidence."

The man's face broke for just an instant, and a wild and feral look came over him. His mouth opened in the beginnings of a snarl, and the shocking white teeth sent gooseflesh down my back. But just as quickly, the man stopped, and his face resumed its look of caged civility again. There was a long moment's pause in which he seemed to have a great internal struggle.

"Forgive me," he said at last. "I thought you mocked me, and I am too old and proud to tolerate such a thing. But now I see that I was in error. I would have not thought such things as the claims you make possible until today. I am familiar with your name, of course. It has cropped up several times in my studies of the British Empire. Still, I assumed a certain amount of literary bravado to be present."

THE ADVENTURE OF THE SOLITARY GRAVE

"I have often shared that opinion," Holmes said wryly. "Still, I do not make any false claims."

The man seemed to come to some decision. "Very well, you do not know my name," he said. "I am Dracula. Count Dracula. And I . . . forgive me, we are proud, we Wallachians, and not often used to asking such things. The truth is . . . I have come for your help, Mr. Sherlock Holmes."

My astonishment at this unforeseeable turn of events was enormous. To my even greater surprise, Holmes did not reject the proposition outright.

"I am not in the habit of assisting homicidal criminals," he said with icy tones. "However there are a great many details which I should like cleared up. I should warn you, however, that if you attempt another use of your powers I shall be forced to use this revolver. Surely you can see that this would be pointless and quite dangerous for you."

Dracula waved his hand dismissively. "I bear you no ill will. I have come to lay my matter before you, knowing full well that once you know the facts you will be unable to act except in a manner which will be beneficial to us both. You see, the matter that threatens me and my loved ones is perhaps an even greater threat to the city of London." If he was nervous at the dangerous firearm, he showed no sign.

"Holmes!" I cried, "surely you can't mean to allow this monster . . ."

My words trailed off as Holmes raised his hand in my direction. He leaned against the desk to make himself comfortable, still retaining his pistol. "Pray, Count," he said, "pray continue your most interesting statement."

The fire flickered low in the grate, throwing somber tones over us all as the storm raged and dashed the windowpanes with wet and errant flashes of light in an effect both haunting and hypnotic.

"Now," Holmes said, "please continue, and spare no detail."

The Count seemed to be a man who spoke with careful consideration of his words, but whether this was an attempt to be cagey or some required effort to speak English I could not tell. I was also struck with how supernaturally still the Count sat, not reclining, not shifting in even the smallest, most human of ways and yet without evincing the slightest sign of discomfort. Try as I might, I could not detect any rising or falling of the chest. I found the possibility of a walking man who did not breathe even more dramatic an idea than Holmes' shocking observations about vampires a few moments before.

"You say you know nothing of my first trip to London," the Count said with a small and secret smile. "It may have a bearing on today's events, so

I shall have to tell you something of it. It was the opinion here in London by my opposition that I came for conquest, but this is misguided. In fact, I came for love. You shake your head, Doctor, for you cannot believe this to be true. This is of no consequence, but you shall come to find yourself quite mistaken."

The Count rose to his feet, seemingly now to address me as if he had forgotten that Holmes was in the room. "You think of the victims you discovered this morning and cannot imagine that the person carrying out their execution could possibly know such a love as I describe, I think?"

"Love such as you profess could not stir in the heart of anyone capable of such abominable actions," I burst out.

"Ah, wrong again," the Count said, smiling. He was not the slightest angered or chastised by my accusation. "It was for love that I did such things. You see, they have taken my Mina. And I mean to have her back. Once I have her, we shall end our trip to this country and retire back to my homeland, where we shall be of no further consequence to London."

"But while this city holds her," he said, turning from the flashing window. "I shall not rest." His eyes flashed in the firelight with the same fury as the storm outside and I perceived Count Dracula, in that moment, not as a man, infected, dead or otherwise, but as a primal force that might destroy us all. "I will tear this city down to the cobbled streets with my bare hands, through the bodies of thousands of her citizens, if necessary, to find her."

I looked over at Holmes to gauge his reaction to this extraordinary statement. It seemed incredible to me for a single man to talk of being a danger to all of London. Holmes however, did not seem to find the statement worth comment.

Holmes had adopted that vague and distant expression that signaled his most keen attention. However, he still held the cocked pistol on the Count. I noted, too, that he did not sit and recline in his easy chair, as was his habit, but stood behind his desk.

The silence stretched out, and finally Dracula went on. "A short time ago I came to England, but only to retrieve Mina from her dreary existence. When I had her, I returned with her back to my homeland, which is in the Carpathian mountains."

"My return and the addition of Mina to my castle caused unrest in some of my . . . servants. I do not tolerate insubordination in my home, and so I cast them out. Where they went, I did not know at the time and little did I care. I did not think that they would do well without my protection, and my assumption for several years was that they had perished outside the borders of my lands."

THE ADVENTURE OF THE SOLITARY GRAVE

"Vampires, then," Holmes said laconically.

"Years later, just a few months ago, my bride sought to renew her acquaintance with England, her homeland. I tell you gentlemen with no artifice that while I originally had a great ardor for modernization, my experience with it has cooled this emotion. I have no further interest in this place or its denizens, except where my wife's interests are concerned.

"However, my wife pined for her homeland just as I might for Romania should our positions be reversed. I wished . . ."

I never found out what the Count wished in this regard, because then I did something that I can never recollect doing before in any of the affairs in which Holmes and I worked together: I fainted. The attack came without any warning, and I was hardly aware of any ill feelings until I came to with Holmes over me, loosening my collar and otherwise administering to me those treatments to restore me to wakefulness.

"There now, my good fellow," Homes said to me as I sat up.

"The Count?" I asked.

"Quite gone. We have made arrangements for him to come back tomorrow evening to finish his statement. In the meantime, I have some facts which need verification and I have to go out. But I have entirely underestimated the shock that the Count's appearance must have taken on your system. Will you be all right for a time alone here? I shall not truly need your assistance until tomorrow evening."

"I'm sure I'm quite fine," I said weakly. "Call the Count back now, I feel quite revived, thank you."

"It is only a few hours until dawn," Holmes replied, "and I'm under the impression that the Count had something he wished to complete before that time. In that, we share a great deal. And in any case, I have no way of reaching him except to wait at the appointed time. No, I think you do us both a disservice to claim full recovery when your pulse and breathing quite indicates otherwise. Perhaps you had best retire for the night?"

"No," I said. "I shall be up a while. I couldn't possibly sleep now." Perversely, I felt the need for fresh air more than anything else, but I did not voice this out loud.

"It has always seemed to me," Holmes said, "that the adage about doctors being the worst sort of patient is quite true, but still I shall not object. I shall not be gone long. It would be best for you to lock the door after me." So saying, he went to his room to change. He came out again in a great rush, flung his coat and deerstalker hat on and departed.

I could not shake the need to get out for a bit, despite Holmes' warnings.

The night air was very cool when I left Baker Street, and the fog in the streets of London was as thick as I'd ever seen it. A hansom was immediately available, however, despite the extremely late hour and I got into it at once thinking I might just ride about for a bit. It may be that the driver was unusually taciturn and muffled against the cold so that he could not be seen, but I did not notice this at the time and it is only knowledge of the events that followed that cause me to examine the fellow with hindsight. It was certainly unusual that I did not offer any destination and he did not ask. At the time, I was engrossed in consideration of the monstrous new information I'd been given this evening. The thought of a world with vampires in it boggled my very psyche and I did not notice that anything was amiss, even when the hansom stopped.

I stepped out onto the sidewalk and looked around, confused. This was no part of London I knew, but rather some narrow alleyway where the buildings stood thick and dark all around me. I called out to the driver only to find the driver's box completely empty. Silence filled the air around me and even the normal noises of the city were muffled or completely absent. I felt quite alone, an island in the fog. The alley ran for a great distance to either side. There were doorways to be seen, but they were all closed, and I had heard no sign of them opening. How the man could have gotten off the hansom and away without my feeling the motion in the carriage or hearing footsteps was quite beyond me and I wished, not for the first time, that my cunning friend were here to examine the evidence with me.

The first chill of fear took me then, when I thought of how neatly I had been snared and cursed myself for a fool. In my distracted state, I hadn't even thought that a cab waiting for me at this late hour was enough of an oddity to warrant comment, let alone take any notice of the route we took to get here.

"John . . ."

The voice sent the deepest cold through me, and a great despair rose up. I had an inkling, like a suddenly remembered nightmare, of what I would see when I turned around. Still, I could not stop turning.

Impossibly, I saw Mary standing in the street behind me—my Mary!—in no more than a wisp of clothing despite the chill night air. Knowing that things were horribly wrong, but unable to prevent myself, I rushed over to her side. I tore off my coat and flung it around her, but she seemed to have no interest in this, but only clung to me in a wanton manner I found most unlike the woman I had known these past years.

"What in the world are you doing in London?" I asked. "When did you come back and what in the world are you doing . . ."

"Hush, John," she said. She nuzzled into my neck and there was a brief

THE ADVENTURE OF THE SOLITARY GRAVE

flash of pain. I felt suddenly distant, then, and the long melancholy note of a sweet song ran through my head. I didn't recognize it. I could feel Mary's bite and the trickle of blood, but it did not alarm or surprise me, nothing could in that sleepy state. The old surprise, that Mary should be here at all, still drifted around in my torpor along with the song and then I knew nothing at all.

♦ ♦ ♦

The next days are exceedingly hazy in my recollection, and I can only beg the reader's forgiveness for my lack of clarity. I would have no idea of the length of time missed by my narrative were it not for Holmes filling in the details later. It was nearly a week.

My own memories of that week are fragile and fragmented. They have the feel of an old mirror shattered and reconstructed with some of the pieces missing. I know that Mary was with me some of the time, which should have been a blessing, but was instead the purest form of shame and terror. I knew I lay insensate for at least several days, and that Mary came and went, leaving me for long periods by myself.

I do not know the precise location where she housed me during my convalescence, but I was familiar enough with the type of establishment from such adventures as "The Man with the Twisted Lip." The room was a long series of beds, partitioned by thick curtains and all over stained. The air was thick and heavy with brown smoke and the slightest taste of salt. That last told me that we were somewhat near the water, though the far-off cry of gulls would have done that on its own. The murmur of stuporous voices pooled all around me. I was in an opium den.

The hunger clawed at my stomach like a living thing, digging through the haze and deluge of scents and sounds. I knew I had not eaten in days, but also knew that the days of rashers and kippers for breakfast were past me—indeed, I could not even think of such things without a wave of nausea rising up inside of me. I felt so weak and feverish that I could barely lift my arms.

Mary appeared by pushing up one of the hanging cloths and sliding underneath. My senses were now frighteningly acute, particularly smell, and I could tell with certain accuracy how many people lay in this sinister place. A cloud of brown smoke came with her, as well as a scent of perfume that lingered around her scandalous dress—a perfume that Mary had never worn before combined with the scent of an entirely different woman. I could guess all too well what had become of the woman that had originally owned Mary's dress. One curious thing penetrated even my febrile haze: Mary herself was an exception. Though odors clung to her dress, she herself had no scent.

She looked down at me with a small smile. "My poor dear," she said, in mockery of her previous concern for me. "I know what it is that you need, and nothing could be easier." She pulled up another cloth, revealing the berth of the man next to me. He was reclining in an awkward pose, lying with his head dangling off the side of his bunk and his limbs stiff at his side. His chin pointed straight up and his eyes hung open and glassy in an eerie testament to the power of opium to completely desensitize any man to any events as they transpired around him.

She seized me by the back of the neck and pulled me off of my cot with prodigious strength, indeed she moved my not inconsiderable weight as easily as if I were only a small kitten. She hauled me to an upright sitting position so that I was staring directly at the pulsing neck of the opium victim.

"I say that nothing could be easier," she said, "for all the nourishment you require is right in front of you, you have merely to take it. No one will miss this man. Arrangements have been made. If the opium in his system should concern you, have no fear of that, for it is of only a minor concern to you now and we have found that its qualities can be of great comfort during your transition."

Her hand was light and gentle and cool on my skin now, but I was not fooled. This creature was what the Count had made of my Mary, but there was nothing left of my loving wife inside her. Her eyes were wild, her expression sly and I could still see traces of blood around her mouth from where she had fed a short time ago. She was completely a creature of the night now, as I would be shortly, were I to succumb to the temptation before me. A further chilling thought came through me when she said 'we'—she fully counted herself among Count Dracula's folk now, among the people of the vampire.

"No," I said, struggling to pull myself away from the unfortunate man in front of me. Mary held me there for a few seconds and then released me. I fell back, knocking over my cot with a crash.

"My dear, poor John," she said with a tinkling laugh, cruel and expressive, that I'd never heard from her before. "You'll come around, John. Everyone does. You'll see." She left me. I could hear her feet delicately pad across the bare slats of the floor, a brief whispered conversation too faint to make out and finally the scrape of a door opening and closing as she left.

I lay sprawled on the overturned cot and felt the profound weight of her words. The hunger was scraping me hollow even now. If it got any worse, I knew that I would not be able to resist. I had to escape this prison. I had to distance myself from the temptation that lay incoherent all around me. I had to do it now before I weakened any further.

THE ADVENTURE OF THE SOLITARY GRAVE

I lurched unsteadily to my feet and found I could stand, after all. When I took a step and tried to push up the heavy curtain, I slipped and fell, pulling the curtain and part of the molding down with me in a raucous clatter. Inhumanly fast, a disreputable person with a sallow face and a dirty turban materialized at my elbow and laid his hands on me. One thing I could tell immediately, like Mary, he had no scent. Vampire. With a strength I hardly knew I possessed, I pushed at him and he flew the length of the corridor and finally crashed through one of the curtained-off compartments at the end, tangling himself with the rug, cot and the compartment's occupants.

I staggered out into the street. I moved at no great speed, but whether the attendant was seriously hurt or perhaps did not consider me worth chasing, I do not know. I also don't know where Mary might have been at that time. Having taken the time to find and trap me, I had to assume that she would want to finish her diabolical plan (no doubt, Dracula's plan) of infecting me with the same disease that had taken her soul. At any rate, I could see no pursuit.

The next few days are but a delusional blur to me. No opium addict ever underwent a more painful time of withdrawal than I went through during that time. I will spare the reader an endless recitation of the stumbling night of horror—not to spare myself indignities, but only because I remember but flashes of lucidity during that time.

I know that I quickly found the light of day far too painful to my eyes and skin and spent most of the daylight hours huddled in back alleys. It was on the first day of this that I lost my clothes when two immigrant workers rolled my unresisting form for all the material wealth that it could offer them. Miraculously, my watch and suit and wallet had not been lost in the opium den, but they were lost to me then. Like a character in a penny dreadful, I shuffled from alley to alley craving food and finding nothing that I could eat. I was taken in at one of the soup houses, but I violently expulsed the soup that a charitable soul gave to me. Everywhere all around me, walking temptation roamed in the form of the riff-raff and homeless of London and I was forced to avoid their company altogether, lest I submit to the cravings that drove me.

A curious effect almost as predominant as driving hunger was the transformation of my senses. I have already spoken of the heightening of my sense of smell, but I don't believe I have conveyed fully the effect that this had on my psyche, nor related what happened to my other senses. At first, I thought that my vision had begun failing altogether, since I had greatly disturbed that first night trying to make out the moon overhead. At first I attributed my hazy view to the London fog, but then came to realize that my vision had gotten less reliable over long distances. This did not inhibit me as I thought it might, partly because my vision was amazingly acute when it fell on things close-at-hand, certainly much better than it had been previously.

But perhaps more importantly, the changes to my vision mattered less because my vision itself mattered less. My hearing and sense of smell had become so acute that they had driven my sight into a strictly tertiary role. When coming into a new alley, I could hear and scent any occupants almost immediately and place all their positions with unerring accuracy, and only as an idle thought did I pick them out with my eyes. I didn't often understand this jumble in my head, and was often confused, but found that my first instincts were those of the predator. A primal and burning core inside me would detect danger and cause me to freeze and remain silent or instead to slip quietly away almost without any mental calculation on my part. I felt more like a rabid automaton than a man of free will, and I was rather certain that I could kill with these new instincts without conscious decision on my part, a sheer horror to the thinking part of me. As a result, I used this new acuity to fastidiously avoid the other inhabitants of London, so that I should not become a victim of my new and cursed predatory instincts.

Instead, I found other places to feed, but I am proud of none of these. I stole a butcher's shipment delivered to a kitchen in the dark hours of the earliest morning. I found that I could get some relief from hunger pangs by gnawing and sucking at the raw flesh for the juice, though I had to spit the worthless and spent meat into the street. This discarded bounty led me to my next source of nourishment. As the stray dogs of London fought over the scraps, I was able to snare one and, God help me, slake my thirst on the wretched creature like the savage beast that this disease had caused me to become. Once, I even stumbled into a charnel house and drank the cool blood from a puddle on the floor. I did what I must in order to survive, but still I vowed that I would take no human life, regardless of what kind of foul creature I had become. I felt that I moved through a disconnected landscape of haze and mist, filled with floating figures of temptation.

But I could not bring myself to hunt more than the bare necessity to keep myself alive, and I still felt weak, and found myself getting weaker as the nights went on. Even worse, I could not sleep. Each morning I slunk into the darkest corner that I could find—a coal cellar one day, the bottom of a dark stairwell on another—but these places did not bring any succor. I would lay all day, half conscious and groggy, swimming in the deluge of unfamiliar sounds and smells and certain that each scuffing noise in the street, possibly many houses away, would bring some fresh danger to my barely defendable position. My predatory urges kept any place I found from being a refuge, and after days without any sleep I could not find the strength to raise myself up from my resting place in a wet drainage ditch, even when night came. I knew with a cold certainty that I was going to perish here.

When strong hands finally came to pull me out of the ditch, I did not have the strength to put up even token resistance, and it was then that I finally slipped into unconsciousness.

I awoke in my own quarters in Baker Street. I found myself in the curious position of immediately knowing where I was, but not yet understanding how I came by that knowledge. I lay with my eyes closed and my head upon the pillow. I knew a great many other things, too, that I could scarcely credit in my rational mind, but the predator inside me knew. It needed no proof.

I knew that it was barely night, and that the sun had set less than an hour past. I knew that there was another person in the next room. My brain had been collecting and analyzing so many different smells that the conclusions popped into my head quite as if by magic. And new smells kept calling for attention. I felt all this information clamoring in my head like a roomful of talking people and I forced myself to go through the information carefully. I must catalogue it if I were to control it. Otherwise, I feared it could drive me to madness.

I picked them out one at a time. The bed had the smells of starch and a strange animalistic smell. This lay over top of every other scent in this room and I realized with a start that it was me, John Watson M.D., or rather, it was the man I used to be. I did not emit this odor any longer and sweat was apparently a substance unknown to my transformed person. The impossibility of the science beleaguered me, but I would have to come back to that. Also in this room, I could pick out the smell of newsprint, the Arcadia mixture of tobacco that I favoured, various medicines from my doctor's bag in the corner, books and the soap and oils of my shaving kit. Even through the closed and draped window, I could also detect the air of London streets redolent with the sweat of man and woman and horses, and the droppings from those last, burning coal and the tang of strong drink.

In the next room, through what the air current told me was a partly open door, I could find even more, still just with the power of my new olfactory sense. There was Holmes' tobacco in the next room. I knew from memory that he kept it in a Persian slipper and could now tell you, within a foot, what part of the room it lay in. His revolver was out, and I could tell from the smells of spent cartridges that it had been fired recently. Holmes' table of chemistry was a veritable barrage of smells. So strong were these that they might well have blotted all others out, but they were of such an artificial nature that it was quite easy to ignore these and concentrate on the rest. I knew that the person in the next room was Holmes, and that he sat in a chair smoking. The sounds of his small motions and even his breathing were quite clear to me. I could even tell that it was the briarwood pipe. The small rustling sound told me he read the paper. There was no one else in our rooms except for the two of us, I was certain.

Which was why it was such a shock to me when I sat up and saw the Count Dracula, the villain himself who had placed this horrible curse on me, standing in the shadows behind my opened door. My sense of smell had not reported his presence to me which was a terrible shock. I felt as if he had materialized out of thin air, like a voice speaking to me when no one could possibly be around.

"You monster!" I said. Then I called out to the other room. "Holmes, beware! Danger most foul!" I surprised myself by snatching up a heavy oaken bookshelf with the intention of hurling it bodily at my tormentor. I still was not used to my tremendous vampire strength. It had taken several workmen to bring the heavy case up the steps when I purchased it, but I held it easily, unbothered by the shower of books and knick-knacks my maneuver caused.

Count Dracula stood immobile, without any expression of alarm.

"I apologize, Doctor," he said mildly. "It was inconsiderate of me to startle you. I should have been more careful."

"You shall pay for what you've done to me, and for what you've done to Mary!" I took a step forward in order to hurl my makeshift weapon to maximum effect, but had to stop abruptly when Holmes stepped directly into the space between Dracula and I.

"No, Watson!" Holmes said quickly. "The Count is here at my request! Pray do not be hasty!"

"At your request?" I said, and felt for the first time I can recall a sharp betrayal at the actions of my constant companion. "You brought that butcher here? So he could see my misery first-hand?"

"He is not the villain that brought this fate upon you, nor upon Mary, my dear Watson."

"Oh, great mercy of Heaven, Mary . . ." I moaned, still holding the bookcase above me. In my first lucid moments in many days, the full weight of all that had happened to my Mary swept over me. Even if I could find a way to make Count Dracula pay for his crimes, how could I save her?

"I grieve for your loss, Watson," Holmes said, stepping close and laying a hand on my shoulder. "But Dracula has not wronged you. He is not the

THE ADVENTURE OF THE SOLITARY GRAVE

one who has done this to Mary. I give you my word."

"Holmes?" I said, amazed. "What can you possibly be saying? Who else?"

"That is a matter that bears some explaining. Believe me when I say that not only was Count Dracula *not* the perpetrator of the crime you accuse him of, but that he was also instrumental in helping me to locate you in time to prevent their final aim, no less than your enslavement. And without Dracula's help, I should not have been able to prevent it."

I hesitantly lowered the bookcase to its former place. "And Mary? What can be done for her?"

Dracula stepped forward and spoke, "She is dead to you, Dr. Watson, at least in the way that you knew her. She is in the power of a greater vampire now, and most, if not all of what made her your loving wife is lost to you both."

"Another vampire," I said. "How can this be?"

"I am quite sorry," Holmes said, "that you did not have the opportunity to hear the Count's story to its full conclusion, but I'm afraid we have not the time for it now. First we must attend to your health, for the Count assures me that this is quite a precarious time for you."

The Count himself did not speak, but watched the proceedings with an air of detached interest. Mrs. Hudson was nowhere to be seen, and I could only assume that Holmes had forbade her entrance to our quarters. He himself brought the tea service to my bedside.

Though a hunger consumed me, the thought of this once comforting ritual now caused a wave of nausea inside of me, until the aroma of something I *did* need came to me.

"Holmes!" I cried when I divined his strange joke. "Really, this has gone too far. I cannot go on with this charade as if nothing has happened to me!"

"Tut, tut," he said, pouring out the warm red fluid into a tea cup in front of me. "Of course you can't. But I also know that you need sustenance to survive, and is the consumption of flesh that every good British citizen partakes in really more cultured than this? Oh, I admit this is certainly very outré, to say the least, but I see no reason why you should have to descend to the level of a beast. And this has come from the butcher's shop, the same as my breakfast sausage and from the same source, I am sure."

My objections rose in my throat, but they were momentarily forgotten when Holmes set the tea cup of warm blood in front of me. It was the sheerest mockery in my mind to pour it from one of Mrs. Hudson's best tea pots. My hand shook as I picked it up and I felt a wave of deep emotion for this man who had done this for me, even though he acted as if it were nothing more uncommon than our usual breakfast. I finished the first cup and drained both a second and a third before I came to myself and despair welled up in me again.

"Holmes," I said, my voice heavy. "I *am* a beast now. There can be no denying it. I am a danger to every citizen in London. Dear God, Holmes. I am an abomination and should be destroyed!"

"Nonsense!" Holmes said. "You are no more a danger to our fellow citizens than you were before your affliction. No, no, don't try and contradict me on this, the evidence is far too great against your position. You see, I have some knowledge of your wanderings before we picked you up. The hackney driver behind the paper factory here, the butcher's boy on Windermere lane . . ." he ticked them off on his fingers, one by one. "And the elderly gentleman last night, indisposed with drink underneath the floral display on Covington. In point of fact, you have gone to great lengths, despite your confusion and starvation, to ensure that no other citizen suffered on account of your recent tragedy."

"It's true I have not hurt anyone yet . . . but how could you know?"

"Come, come, Watson, you know my methods. While the Count assisted in locating your person, I am not so great a bumbler that I didn't at least find traces of you."

"But . . . Mary . . ." I lifted my hands helplessly. "She was like a soulless monster when she had me in her power . . . Holmes, it looked like her, but it was *not* the woman that I married! I would swear to it!"

Holmes face went very grave. "Ah . . . well there I am afraid that I am unable to provide any comfort, as much as I would like to. Our present conversation is enough to assure me that the Count's words are true about the nature of the transformation. The mental faculties, though muddled for a short while, are quite undisturbed in the long run. However, the nature of the afflicted's world is so dramatically changed that the shock often shakes loose the foundations of a person's moral fiber. The gross rise in personal power and the primal need to feed are usually quite enough to overcome almost anyone's morals and radical shifts of personality are to be expected in most cases. In fact, Watson, if the Count and I were betting men, I should have won a great deal of money on you. I had no doubt that your character would come through the transformation intact, but I believe you may have risen over greater odds than you know."

"A most impressive feat, Doctor," Count Dracula said, the first words he had spoken in some time. "Believe me when I say that one man in a hundred does not do so well. For a woman of your society, who is usually held hostage by your culture far more than even your men, it is a temptation that few can resist." He shrugged as if this was a matter of small importance.

THE ADVENTURE OF THE SOLITARY GRAVE

He came and sat down with us, helping himself to a cup of warm blood with no sign of self-consciousness. Even Holmes' usually unflappable composure was visibly unsettled, and his visage went taut.

"Thank you, gentlemen," Dracula said. "This will save time. I had not expected to find such a convenience. A product of modern thinking, no doubt." He smiled a predator's smile and the feeling of being unsettled deepened within me. I could see from a glance, however, that Holmes was quite resolute that we should have Dracula for an ally. I had always trusted in Holmes' judgment before this, and even in my greatest confusion, I could not help but do so now.

"First I think it necessary," Holmes said, "that we shall have to give you but the merest summary of Count Dracula's account, for we have no time for the full tale. I think you will find that haste is crucial for our next actions. It seems that we already are well acquainted with his adversary, for it is none other than Professor Moriarty himself!"

"But Holmes, what can you possibly mean?"

"I'm afraid that with the evidence of vampirism made manifest by both yourself and the Count, we must now recast a great deal of our assumptions in its new light. It is now my belief that though Moriarty may have plunged into the Reichenbach Falls and while this would sufficiently assure death in most instances, this need not be the case for a victim of vampirism. With the substantial durability of the vampire form and, most importantly, the lack of any requirement to breathe, I think we must revise our assumption that Moriarty fell to his death. The fall need not have been fatal, if he could have arranged to contract vampirism beforehand."

"And what makes you think he did this terrible thing?" I said, in a state of horror. I could not, for the life of me, imagine anyone willing this fate upon himself.

"For the very simple reason," Holmes said, "that the Count has had dealings with Moriarty no less than two weeks ago."

"When I first came to London," the Count said, "I required a good many agents to serve my needs, agents that remained here when I returned to my homeland. It was through these agents that I had some inkling of the new self-styled mastermind of the London underworld that my former mistresses were keeping company with. This assisted me upon seeking out Mina after her abduction and I was able to induce a few of Moriarty's henchmen, men with whom I was previously acquainted, to provide me the location of her whereabouts." Dracula gave the barest hint of a smile and I shuddered inwardly when I thought of the nature that the Count's nocturnal visitation and inducement might take.

"While I was not able to recover Mina, I was able to surprise Adaliene, one of my previous wives, and leave a reminder to those that should know better what it means to anger one such as Count Dracula."

"Please forgive me," Holmes said, "but I feel a necessity to interrupt with some explanation, for it was Dracula's work that we found out at the property of Lady Carfax. I was nearly certain then that the remains we found there did not match the finger we had in our possession. That was an entirely different woman, one two inches taller with somewhat longer fingers. What we found was the Count's method of retribution."

"Your face," the Count said, "betrays your thoughts, Doctor. You disapprove? Do not forget yourself. I am a monarch in my own land. In any case, I can hardly expect a British police officer or court to protect me from no less than a murderous assault upon both me and my loved ones. I can assure you that I intend to make sure that this is a lesson they will learn at some cost."

I could not argue most of those points, but still I could not reconcile myself to allowing Holmes to work with such a bloodthirsty and savage creature as this Count Dracula.

"There is more to consider, Watson," Holmes said, clearly divining my thoughts. "While I will concede the point that the vampire represents quite a danger to the common man, it is not so great as one might think. First, the vampire in its natural state, is a solitary creature and no two male vampires will willingly share even quite vast territories such as sprawling London. I have it on Count Dracula's word that he merely desires to rescue his bride and return with her to his estate near the Borgo Pass, and will present no further danger to Britain or any of her citizens. We have an accord on this, and a few other small matters which I do not have the time to go into.

"Now as to Moriarty," he went on implacably. "Moriarty's powerful intellect has allowed him to rise above the natural model of the solitary tendency of the vampire in much the same fashion that your moral code has remained intact. Thus, he has managed to put aside the natural traits and patterns of the solitary predator in a way that no other vampire before him has accomplished, and with terrifying results. The Count assures me that vampires working in collusion, even for a short time, is nearly unheard of and no predator wants to create another such vampire as this would be creating your own competition, to the detriment of your own survival. Evidence supports this, otherwise we would very shortly be overrun with teeming cities of vampires. Do you follow so far?"

"I believe so," I said.

"Very good, then," he went on. "Now, Moriarty has been arranging the creation of new vampires at an alarming rate. I have encountered no less than a dozen in my investigation so far, and have every reason to believe

THE ADVENTURE OF THE SOLITARY GRAVE

that there may be more. He has been replacing his old network of spies and criminals, disdaining the instinctual model of most vampires, even our esteemed Count, in favor of a more encompassing one. He has even gone so far as to release and infect Col. Sebastian Moran in order to set him up once again as his right hand man.

"In short, he is setting up a criminal empire twice as dangerous as the master creation he had previously, and peopled with as many vampires as he requires. It is the conversion of his empire and many of its lieutenants that has delayed him this considerable time from seeking me out and putting an end to any interference I might represent. I also imagine that with a veritable army of vampires at his disposal, he considers me far less a threat than he had in the past. For he now has an army, an army headed by a general that has the most dangerous characteristics of both Dracula and myself. Unchecked, he has all the tools he needs for infecting or overthrowing all of London society and becoming a world power in his own right. Do you see now?"

"Good Lord, Holmes," I cried, "we cannot let this happen!"

"My thinking precisely," Holmes said, "and it is for this very purpose that I have had you brought here, for things are coming to a head this very evening and I wanted to offer you a chance to strike back at the foul monster who has so wronged you. I confess no small amount of personal guilt in this matter, since I'm quite certain that your fate was actually an indirect attack on myself, with the effort of distracting me from pursuing the case."

Holmes put a hand on my shoulder and I could see that my otherwise austere comrade was quite shaken with that deep emotion that I had always known lay underneath the cool exterior. "If not for me," he said, "your dear wife would most surely be alive."

"But for how long?" I said. I felt a weight sink in my heart, but still felt compelled to speak in his defense. "If not for you, a revived Moriarty with all the powers of darkness at his disposal would overrun London in a matter of months, and then the rest of London would join her in Damnation."

"And they still may," he said gravely. "It may be more prudent in your weakened condition for you to stay here, but I have delayed our departure just long enough to offer you the opportunity. Do you feel strong enough to come?"

"To strike a blow at Moriarty?"

"A most telling blow, if all goes according to plan."

"Then a block and tackle should not hold me back," I said, "whatever my condition."

"Most remarkable," Dracula said. "Great faith. It can be a most blessed benediction."

"I have always said," my friend remarked, "that there are great unplumbed depths to Watson. You would do well not to underestimate him, I should think. But come! We have spent too much time already for comfort. We must be off to Blessington's!"

Our short journey began with amazing alacrity. Count Dracula had paused before the cab to stroke the roan mare's neck and whisper some words to her in his native tongue. Then he leapt with startling agility into the carriage and bodily lifted the driver out of the seat as if that robust man were nothing more than a small parcel. The driver picked himself up off the road and began to protest, but Dracula's wrathful countenance and Holmes' hastily flung sovereigns closed any objections he might have had.

"We are ready," Dracula said and clicked his tongue at the horse even as Holmes and I stepped into the cab. The horse leapt like a creature on fire and Holmes and I barely avoided tumbling out with the sudden motion.

I had second thoughts as to my ability to participate in the adventure as we rattled down Baker Street at truly frightening speed. The trap was just two padded benches and wheels, open all around, so I could see that Dracula did not seem to be using the reins at all, or if he did, he used such a light pressure as to be undetectable to my eye. But never did any horse on road or track run with the speed and unerring step as did our roan. Even more bizarrely, the other carriages and even people had an uncanny tendency to stop in their tracks as we drew near and with these obstacles much maneuvered out of our way, we flew through the streets like a veritable bullet.

Holmes braced himself well forward, so that he could whisper directions into Dracula's ear and with his unparalleled knowledge of London and Dracula's uncanny driving and the roan's ceaseless efforts, we had reached the hospital district and passed out of it again before I even realized it. Dracula led the horse briskly around obstacles with seemingly no regard for the safety of anyone, including ourselves. Once we even came to a small channel of water, some man-made tributary of the Thames, and our horse hurled herself into it without breaking stride. Holmes and I had to cling to the seats of the trap like fleas on a dog, or else be left in the water. We emerged dripping and sodden, into the night air. I realized that it must be cool because of the smell, but realized with a shock that the chill did not touch my skin in any sense. Those days were gone to me. It was scarce an hour that passed before we pulled up to the grounds of Blessington University.

When we reached the grounds, our poor and faithful mare shuddered

THE ADVENTURE OF THE SOLITARY GRAVE

in her traces and fell in a total collapse. I rushed to her side, but the Count was there ahead of me.

His face was still as he knelt in the muddy street next to her still form. "She is quite dead," he said. His voice was strangely sad, something I had not expected. He lay his hand on her neck for a moment, and then stood up. "She gave her life nobly. Let us hope that her sacrifice was not a vain and empty one."

The grounds were expansive for such a small school. A low stone wall and many rows of elms ran all around a well-tended lawn, screening the property from outside view. I could smell the cut grass and the trees, but also a small body of water which had a distinctly different smell than the Thames, which lay some distance behind us. Over all of that, though, a much stronger smell pervaded, like ammunition, but different.

"Fireworks," I said. "Up ahead in the park. Near the lake."

"So I detect as well," Holmes said, but he looked at me in some surprise. "I can see that you shall now keep me on my toes. Tell me, can you hear anyone? Perhaps the chatter of young voices?"

I shook my head, "I hear nothing." I turned to ask the Count, assuming him to be possessed of the same frighteningly keen senses I had, but he was nowhere to be seen! "But he was right here!" I said in a shocked voice.

"Come, Watson," Holmes said, going over the wall with easy grace. "Dracula has his methods, and we have ours. We shall have need of both, I am quite sure, before the night is out. Pray that we are not too late!"

We made our way easily over the wall and rushed toward the lake. The moon was partially visible, and it was quite bright out and easy to navigate. A short distance in, we both found a great number of tracks—me by scent and Holmes by sight.

These led us to a most horrifying sight, at least two dozen young men sprawled in haphazard postures like the grisly conclusion of a death march. They were in school clothes with warm coats thrown overtop and a few had the hats and long gowns of a class celebrating its recent graduation. It was with a great deal of relief that I found them all still breathing, albeit shallowly. Now that I concentrated on the sounds, I could hear it clearly. Still the long habits of a surgeon prompted me to go through the sleepers and check their pulses.

"Thank God," I said. "They're only sleeping."

"Drugged, I should expect," Holmes said, leaning over to smell about the lips of one slumbering lad. "And . . . unmarked." He lifted the chin to reveal the clean neck of the boy.

"Surely you don't mean . . . ?"

"But that is exactly what I mean, Watson," Holmes said. "For Moriarty's

261

plan was cunningly simple. With the expedient of an old confederate to administer the drug during a post-graduation expedition of fireworks at the beach, Moriarty meant to infect and thus gain power over some of the very scions of society's finest. This lad, if I'm not mistaken, is Lord Soren's boy. I know of three major bankers, four members of Parliament, two American coal magnates and three European nobles that have children in this graduating class. Should Moriarty have gained control of them through infection, there would be no end to the damage he could cause, and no geographical boundary to stop him. But where is the confederate and why is Moriarty not here yet to complete the deed?"

Our answer to the first question was a loud whooshing sound and the impact of something heavy on the tree next to us, and I realized that we were being shot at. Holmes and I flung ourselves to the ground behind the tree, a large oak. Holmes immediately bounced back up, peered in the uncertain light at the front side of the tree for a brief moment, and then quickly dropped back down beside me.

"As I feared," Holmes said, "It is Moran's air gun and they are using silver bullets. The soft bullet preferred by the air gun is unmistakable, as is the gleam of the bullet upon the torn-up bark and wood. I had hoped that they might not be prepared, but whether it was Dracula or yourself that they have made extra measures for, they are ready. Moriarty misses nothing!"

I tasted the blood in the air. "Holmes! You're injured!" Moran had not completely missed. I cursed myself for a fool that should have known better. I strained my ears and caught the unmistakable grinding and click I remembered so well. Moran had already reloaded his gun.

"Yes," Holmes said. "One point for Moran, but the wound is only minor, and we cannot pause to tend to it. The visibility is poor even for vampire eyes and it is well that we did not carry a lantern. I'm only grateful that I have no susceptibility to silver poisoning. It makes me a comparatively durable target. Such a scrape as this would be much more harmful to you or the Count. It appears that Moriarty and Moran have expected vampire adversaries and consider a human one, even one such as myself, to be a lesser threat. Otherwise, I am sure he should have waited for a better shot. From the direction of the bullet, I have no doubt that he has taken that small building there as his station, either inside or possibly on the roof."

I risked a glance in the direction he indicated, where a small gardener's shed of fieldstone sat at the top of a small hill. The vantage point would cover our entire area, an excellent stake out. I thought, too, of the altered vampire eyesight, that would not be kind to long distances. A fact to which Holmes may have owed much.

THE ADVENTURE OF THE SOLITARY GRAVE

"Come," Holmes said. "I want to make for that copse of trees. We have an ace in the hole that may enter play, if given time. We should be able to provide enough temptation to keep our good Colonel busy! Come, Watson!"

Before I could protest, Holmes jumped up and dashed off. In the flash of moonlight that fell on him, I could see the slick of blood that covered his left shoulder. Even so, with the dauntless will and energy of my friend, I was hard-pressed to keep up. It was only a short run to the trees that Holmes had pointed out, but knowing that Colonel Moran was sitting on the roof of that building, aiming that powerful air gun at Holmes or myself made that run last an eternity. I felt deeply the scrutiny of Moran's gaze peering over the sights, drawing a bead on us like the prize hunter that he was. He had bagged more large game than any man in Europe, Holmes said, and now he hunted us. The hairs on my neck crawled to think on it.

Midway through the run, another whoosh sang out just past my ear, but we kept moving. Then another whoosh, and Holmes stumbled. I could smell more blood, and I helped my stumbling friend the rest of the way. I heard Moran reload once just as we hit the trees, and heard the sounds again just after we dived into shelter. I was sure now that Moran was on the roof and not inside the shed.

"Blast that man!" I said. "He has two of those guns! Holmes! How badly are you hurt?"

He had collapsed into the hollow behind the trees, his face a rictus of pain, but he waved off my further questions.

"Quiet! We must hear!"

I did not know what he was listening for, but knelt beside my friend and looked at the blood spreading around his wound. I had earlier today feared that the temptation of blood would forever make my Doctor's profession impossible for me, but I did not even stop to consider it now. I tore open Holmes coat which was slick with red wetness. He had been hit in the chest.

A blood-curdling scream tore through the night from on top of the hill, more inhuman than any sound I'd ever heard before. I could not help but shudder and pity the poor wretch that might have cause to make that sound.

"Moran," Holmes breathed. "Dracula got to him. Good." And he passed out.

Dracula found us shortly thereafter while I attended to Holmes' wound. One look was all he needed to inform me that Moran would never shoot another air gun. I would have shuddered if I could have spared the motion.

The master vampire's face was an impassive mask as he watched me with my hands drenched in Holmes' blood, desperately performing the necessary field surgery to remove the bullet from his chest. It had not penetrated the lung, but was deep in the muscle, lodged against bone in such a way as to make me fear for my friend's life. For the first time since my transformation, I thanked Providence for my new gifts. The feeble moonlight was more than enough light for me to see clearly, and my fingers had a new sensitivity and deftness that astounded me. Before my change, I should have had to wait until light or transportation to a hospital. Still, I had only a small kit in my coat for tools and the wound was frighteningly dangerous.

"He will not survive," Dracula said. "Not without the transformation."

I had thought Holmes unconscious from the pain, but his thin fingers closed weakly over mine.

"No," he said, his voice hoarse and low. It took all of my keen hearing to make out his words. "I will not be a blight to the world, not . . . undo all that I have done. Promise me that you will not allow it."

"It will not come to that, Holmes," I said, fear and despair rising up in me. I felt a desperate liar as I said it. "I can feel the bullet. I can get it! You shall survive this."

He did not answer me. Holmes had finally passed out.

Dracula shook his head and turned away. I bent back to my task.

Sunlight streamed through the open window back at Baker Street. It would be many years, I now knew, before those rays would be a sure-fire death to me, but even now their light lanced to the back of my head any time I looked directly at them and I instinctively avoided their touch.

I stirred in the silent room, picked up the morning newspaper, and then listlessly dropped it back on the table. Even the warm teapot filled with another delivery from the butcher's shop could not provide a distraction for me.

It took until mid-afternoon before the response to our telegrams came, and I took them into Holmes' room at once. Holmes was irritable, having been bedridden for the past week, but he was growing stronger each day. He snatched the envelopes from my hands and tore them open with shaking fingers. He read the contents of all three and then dropped them on the bedcovers with a disgusted sigh.

"This convalescence has proved to be catastrophic, Watson! If only you could have handled that bullet without tearing so much tissue around it.

THE ADVENTURE OF THE SOLITARY GRAVE

This delay is intolerable!"

"The bullet had to come out," I said mildly. I was privately pleased with the result. The bullet had come out fairly cleanly, and I thought the job a very neat one considering the unfavorable conditions. Furthermore, I had been meticulous about the dressing and was very pleased to see no sign of infection. But I knew my friend could never rest easy with Moriarty's continued freedom. No wound short of a fatal one could change that.

I longed to know the exact contents that distressed him so, but, as ever, my friend divulged details only in his own time and fashion.

"Perhaps a late dinner would help?" I said. "Mrs. Hudson has mentioned a brace of Cornish hens she might bring up no less than seven times."

"Oh, very well," he said, waving his hands in dismissal. "If only to prevent further distracting inquiries. Any news from Count Dracula?"

"Not yet," I said. "It is still another few hours until the sun sets."

Dracula arrived a short time after dusk, and to my great surprise, brought the Countess with him. Holmes was feeling strong enough to move about a little and I helped him into a chair by the fire so that we might receive company.

Countess Mina Dracula was a pale, exquisite creature with dark hair and an outwardly mild demeanor compared to her starkly proud and barbaric husband. Still, every quietly enunciated word and polite smile the delicate featured woman made revealed signs of a pride and savagery every bit as formidable as her Count's. This became especially apparent when they related that it had been Mina who had executed Dracula's two remaining cast-out wives during her rescue. She seemed unbowed from her captivity, though she wore a padded glove to hide the mauling of her finger. Dracula assured us that it would heal in time, and she seemed otherwise unaffected by her imprisonment.

I have since confirmed this from my own experience. Surprisingly, vampire healing is a great deal slower than the human equivalent. A wound such as Holmes received would take much longer to close and heal. However, given many years and an ample supply of blood, there is virtually nothing that cannot be re-grown and eventually made whole in a way far surpassing human biology, as long as the heart and head remain intact.

Still, I shall not soon forget the burning light I saw in the eyes of Count Dracula's wife, and it made me uneasy. Partly this was because of what it displayed about her own soul, and possibly my own. Count Dracula was visibly proud of his terrible wife, and I believe their love was strong, despite the horrific nature of our nocturnal existence. Holmes, in assisting in her recovery, had won a great and terrible force over to his cause. I was forever humbled at how nations, sovereigns and even such as Dracula found themselves indebted to the faculties of Sherlock Holmes.

"But how did you find her?" I asked. Holmes had not seen fit to enlighten me as to any of the details of his dealings with the Count these past few days.

"It was as Holmes predicted," Dracula explained. "With our combined forces arranged against him, and Moran gone, Moriarty has fled. His organization is in disarray without his leadership, making it vulnerable. Holmes gave me a list of several intermediaries that might be involved in Mina's incarceration. These individuals were easy enough to question."

"I confess," Holmes said, "to some pangs of guilt. The men on this list were all headed for the gallows, but still it might be a kinder fate than what befell them at your hands."

If Dracula was insulted by Holmes judgment, he gave no sign. In fact, he gave the smallest of smiles that quite confirmed Holmes' statement and sent a cold chill into the pit of my stomach.

"In any case," Dracula said, "many of them had already been converted and a gallows would not have sufficed. Console yourself with the fact that London's citizens are better off without them."

"Vampires?" I asked. "I should think that vampires would be difficult to force cooperation from."

"Then you would be incorrect, Doctor," Dracula said. "My people are a superstitious lot. You have retained your civilization through the transformation, but this is not the usual case. For most, it is a movement away from reason, towards primal intuition. Examine the primitive hunters among your own people, and you will find no atheists. It may not be a religion that you recognize, but it is the same with us."

I found this to be a shocking statement, and had the sudden urge to ask the Count, if he, too, had foresworn reason in this manner, but his forbidding expression warned me that such a question would not be welcome.

"But what of Moriarty himself?" Holmes said. "His empire can be rebuilt. Even Colonel Moran can be replaced. As long as Moriarty walks free, the danger to England is paramount! I must be out of this confounded bed!"

"I'm afraid that there is little immediate need," the Countess said. "Professor Moriarty has already fled or gone into hiding."

Holmes had a matter which he wished to discuss with Count Dracula in private, leaving me in the decidedly uncomfortable position of private conversation with the Countess Mina Dracula. To my utter discomfort,

THE ADVENTURE OF THE SOLITARY GRAVE

she moved over to my chair and took both of my hands in hers.

"I have heard about your recent loss," she said to me, "and wish to express my deepest regret and sincerest gratitude, since you have suffered all this on my behalf. The transformation can be a curse, but it can also be a blessing. We are not monsters, Doctor, no matter how many people choose to see us that way. I speak from some experience, but also from compassion. Your new life can be rewarding, if you let it be so."

"This affliction has cost me the dearest woman in the world," I said heavily, "also my very way of life. So much that I hold dear is gone to me. And it very nearly cost me much more," I said heavily. "I thank you for your kind words, but I do not believe I can see things the way you do."

"Moriarty took those things from you," she said gravely. "And your wife has made her own choices. But you yourself are a kind man, like my husband."

"Madam . . ." I said, at loss for words.

"Oh, he is hard, too, as the wolf is hard," she said. "Stark and violent, just as the wolf, as life itself is. But he is never cruel. I wonder if most men can say the same?"

I had nothing to say to such an extraordinary statement. I was saved from answering when the door opened and Holmes and Count Dracula himself came back into the common room. I immediately went to help Holmes back into his chair by the fire. I was worried that this might be too taxing in his condition. He shooed me away with an annoyed wave, though his expression of relief when he made it to the chair was unmistakable.

"Come, my love," Count Dracula said. "It is time we depart. Our world awaits." The Countess glided across the room and gave her husband her hand. Dracula's expression was surprisingly tender as he took his wife's damaged hand in his own, but then he turned back to us with his enigmatic predator's expression. "Mr. Holmes, I thank you, and shall do precisely as we discussed. I bid you farewell. I do not think we shall meet again."

"No," Holmes said. "I considered the possibility a highly unlikely one, as things stand."

Dracula turned to face me and nodded. "Doctor." The Countess shot back one long look at me, filled with meaning, and then they were both gone.

◆ ◆ ◆

Once Holmes recovered enough to leave the house, he spent the next few weeks attempting to trace Moriarty's escape. He came back from his last such expedition in a furious and dejected mood, claiming that Moriarty had eluded him once again.

"It is fiendishly simple," Holmes said bitterly after coming back from an information-gathering mission on the lower docks. "And yet I can devise no stratagem to defeat it!"

"Where on Earth has he gone?" I asked.

"He has taken to ship and left London altogether," Holmes said, collapsing into his armchair and despondently tapping on the armrest. I was deeply alarmed. Never had I seen him looking so defeated.

"We must give chase," I said. "Wherever he is heading, we must book passage at once. Have you discovered it?"

"His plans are quite known to me, yes," Holmes said, but the fact did not seem to cheer him.

"Then when do we depart? What is his destination?"

"That is just it, Watson. He has no destination."

"No destination, but how?"

"He has taken a boat and gone to sea, but with no destination at all. He has ample supplies and a loyal and partly eternal crew. At sea, he need fear very little in the nature of discovery. Any ship that comes across them will play the victim and provide fresh supplies and is hardly any threat to a crew of vampires. They need only have enough of a human crew, in proper submission to get them through the days and they can live indefinitely at sea, with much less need for provisions and water than your average ship and every opportunity through piracy to meet any further needs. These are small obstacles to one of Moriarty's intellect. They will be impossible to trace and will leave no clues except the occasional shipwreck. And Moriarty knows that I cannot take to life at sea, even should I be so inclined. The forced idleness of such quarters would be quite intolerable to me. Moriarty has the perfect refuge. He need only wait."

"He has some plan coming to fruition here in London for his return?" I asked.

"You misunderstand me, Watson," Holmes said. "You forget, everything we know, every ploy or stratagem must be cast in a new light based on the vampire's outlook. You yourself are too stolid of moral character to fully see the brilliance of his plan."

"But what are they waiting for?" I asked.

"For my death," Holmes said. "No, do not be alarmed, Watson. I do not mean to say that I should expect another assassination attempt. Moran was always their best hope for that, and he is gone. No, no, Moriarty has only to wait. What is a few decades or more to one who is immortal? Time will remove Moriarty's greatest obstacle, and there is no denying it."

I sat silent in thought while Holmes filled his clay pipe and puffed furiously at it until the entire room was shrouded in smoke.

THE ADVENTURE OF THE SOLITARY GRAVE

"Holmes," I said.

"Watson, Watson," he said with a rueful smile. "I thought you might come around to this suggestion again, but it will hardly serve. I cannot allow myself to contract vampirism, even to confront Moriarty. Come now, don't be so surprised. Your thoughts are apparent to any trained observer. You glance at the darkness outside, then at the specially filled tea kettle at your left elbow and back to the new painting you have gotten of the sunset and it is quite easy to follow the track of your thoughts. At any rate, I have expected this suggestion for some time. But I'm afraid you do me rather too much credit with this one, Watson. I have all the makings of a terrible vampire; I would become a greater threat to London, over time, than Moriarty would ever be. Oh, I know you have adapted rather admirably, but I'm afraid that I possess the antithesis of the qualities that preserve your outlook."

"But Holmes," I said, "if death is the only other option . . ."

"You know how I abhor boredom, Watson, it would be my undoing. You frown now, and with some justification, upon my use of cocaine, but imagine how much worse the addiction to *blood* would be. It would only be a matter of time before my need for stimulation brought about the worst results, and there would be nothing *but* time. You see?"

I nodded miserably, the horror of my new situation come down fully upon me once again. To sit idly by while the truest companion in the world suffered and died, I did not think I had it in me to do this.

Holmes had correctly divined Moriarty's plan, and though we had many interesting cases over the next few years, the mere existence of Sherlock Holmes proved an ample deterrent. Moriarty did not return to England in Holmes' lifetime. There were still many cases of interest, such as the Adventure of the Nordic Octopus, the Adventure of the Elephantine Sculpture, and the Adventure of the Crawling Cadaver, not to mention the strange affair of the Unshaven Clergyman and the strange Case of the Three Island Doctors. However, Moriarty was never entirely gone from Holmes' thoughts, and I could tell that knowledge of the terrible menace waiting for England haunted the detective.

Eventually, Holmes retired, as he had once predicted, to the solitary pursuit of bee keeping. Even then our adventures were not entirely at an end and my friend continued to utilize his amazing gifts in service of England well into his old age.

But eventually the time came, as I knew it must, when I stood on a lonely hill top in Sussex Downs in the dark of night and regarded with deepest sorrow the resting place of the greatest detective and truest friend that this world has ever known. I stayed near the Downs for some weeks, attending to Holmes' grave nightly, per his request. One night during the third such week, I stooped and pulled up a scrap of cloth with a shaking hand. Holmes' old deerstalker cap. Holmes had left specific instructions to me, and I understood that there were a number of provisions of his will, including the release of many of his more secret and sensational cases, that awaited me at the end of his unorthodox instructions. I had been visiting his grave every fortnight, as requested, and the deerstalker cap was the sign that I should proceed to the next phase of his instructions. I was not at all sure how the deerstalker cap came to be here, and who might be Holmes' agent in this. I went home to open the next envelope he had left me, unread all this time. His instructions were unfathomable to me, but I had been in the habit of following them so long, that it did not occur to me to do otherwise. Even if the promised papers had not been an avid goal of mine, I should have done no less than follow his directions to the letter, as always.

The following evening, I arranged for the transportation of my personal effects to be moved back into our old quarters at 221B Baker Street, remarkably preserved just as he had kept them. I had not been here since Holmes had moved to the Sussex Downs—it hadn't felt right without Holmes. I had no idea that they had been preserved all this time, or how Holmes had made these arrangements. I was to understand, again from Holmes' cryptic instructions, that a solicitor should meet me with the box of secret cases, presumably kept in a storage vault, secreted away all this time. I immediately deduced that it must be this same solicitor that had either himself, or through agents, placed the deerstalker hat on Holmes' grave as an unconventional sign that things were in order. Certainly this had been a provision of Holmes' most unusual will.

I sat each night, as instructed, with the windows open and the electric lights burning, so that the solicitor should know that I was awake and at his disposal. Holmes had made arrangements for this transaction to happen after sunset, a courtesy I deeply appreciated. Even my diet was taken care of, through some agent that left anonymous deliveries from the local butcher shop.

I sat for nearly three weeks, letting the smells and sounds of London flow over me. It had been almost three months since Holmes' death, but still his name repeated over and over through the London fog was all that I heard. Three months was enough time for even the most sensational news to blow over, but not enough time for London to forget her most accomplished defender. All the street talk, the conversation in pubs and breweries, the chatter among drivers, all of it filled with the passing of Mr.

THE ADVENTURE OF THE SOLITARY GRAVE

Sherlock Holmes. I put the time to good use, putting my records in order and penning, almost in its entirety, this record of the case that my readers now peruse.

It was a somewhat blustery night in November when a soft voice interrupted my musings.

"I did not expect to find you here, Doctor. This shortcut is a delight, after such a long wait."

I looked up from my papers, expecting no one other than the promised solicitor, since to my knowledge no other man could possibly expect to find me here.

I did not know this man, but the dragon-like countenance, the high-domed forehead and sloping shoulders, while conveying an attitude of profound intelligence, did not make a favorable impression on me in any other regard.

He took out a small notebook. From this notebook he took a news clipping. "I have here an obituary for Mr. Sherlock Holmes," he said, "and know that he can no longer be of any protection to London. He would be a very slight obstacle at this advanced age, being still human, as my agents report, but I had wanted to verify both of these facts and there can no longer be any doubt."

He flashed me a smug smile. "I have examined the corpse myself, you see, and I am now satisfied that there is no mistake on either of these points. I shall grant you passage from England providing that you leave London in the next twenty-four hours and that you leave the country itself in the next three days. This is convenient for me as I have certain other matters to attend to in this time. Their progress is inexorable with proper supervision, but not yet fully complete as I have just arrived home. After the stipulated time, you will not find it safe here and I promise you that there is ample enough space next to the grave of my most hated adversary, the only man to outmatch me, Sherlock Holmes."

"Moriarty," I said, with a breath of wonder. Despite the great conflict between this man and my friend, I had never actually laid eyes on him before and had only Holmes' account of their previous encounters.

"In short," Moriarty said, snapping shut his notebook. "London is mine. By this time tomorrow, I will have certain agents—both human and vampire—in key positions and no one in London will have the strength or means to oppose me. Nothing can stop my ascension. I have come to tell you all this because I thought it appropriate, in the detective's absence, that the only audience remaining should fully understand how thoroughly Holmes' defeat has come to pass."

"Mr. Holmes was quite right," Count Dracula said from the corner. "I had not understood why you might wish to address yourself to the Doctor. I did not think you would come." I was in shock. I had not been surprised in such a manner for decades, but then vampires always have difficulty sensing others of their own kind.

Moriarty stumbled backwards, visibly shaken by the Count's sudden appearance. "You! How could he have known?" Moriarty said, dazed. "All these years at sea . . . wasted. How could he have known?" He spoke to himself, seemingly speaking to Holmes himself and all but ignoring us.

"Count . . ." I said, astounded. "I never thought to see you again. Holmes . . . he arranged all this? There never was to be any solicitor?"

"Forgive the intrusion into your home," Dracula said. "But Holmes' instructions were quite clear, and Count Dracula is a man who honors his debts. I have this letter which he bade me give to you." The Count handed over an ancient looking envelope, yellowed and dirty. "Also, my wife sends her regards."

"Thank you," I said, still half disbelieving this remarkable turn of events.

"No!" the professor snarled. "This cannot be!" In a blur, too fast for me to react, he leapt for the window and neither Dracula nor I did anything to stop him.

"Have no fear, Doctor," Count Dracula said to me. "My dearest wife has been waiting a long time to redress the wrongs done to her by Moriarty in the past. His confederates outside have already been dealt with and I see no difficulty in applying ourselves to a boat full of fledgling vampires once they are without Moriarty's guidance."

"You," I said, "you left Holmes' hat at the grave sight?"

Count Dracula nodded. "Yes, per Holmes' careful instructions. And now, you will excuse me, Doctor, I have but one last portion of my debt to discharge. We shall depart England immediately after our task is complete, so I shall bid you farewell now."

He let slip his civilized demeanor for only the briefest of moments, but my last clear impression of Dracula was a predatory smile that revealed stark white teeth and a smoldering fire in his eyes. Then, with a subtle motion like a patch of darkness falling out of the window, Count Dracula was gone.

I opened the envelope with shaking hands and found both a letter and a smaller slip of paper.

My Dear Watson, (the letter said)
Please forgive this last peccadillo, but I thought it absolutely essential that nothing occur to tip our hand in this endeavor. Also, I could think of no one else trustworthy enough to carry out such instructions without deviation,

THE ADVENTURE OF THE SOLITARY GRAVE

regardless of their bizarre and unexplained nature. I once stated that, should I be able to rid society of Moriarty's evil presence, even at the cost of my own life, it would be a conclusion most congenial to me. Well, I have had both this opportunity and the chance to live out the rest of my life to its natural end, the best of both possible outcomes. Please remember me fondly, and know that I shall live on, in all the ways that matter to me, predominantly through your literary efforts, for which I thank you.

If Count Dracula is a man of his word—and I have observed no less than twenty-seven indications about his person that he is—then you shall hold this letter at the conclusion of my life's work, a tale I should greatly like to be passed on, when you think the world is ready.

I remain,
Very sincerely yours,
Sherlock Holmes

P.S.—The promised box of extraordinary cases lies at the Bank of London Commerce on the corner of Dover and Patterson. I shall include the recovery slip with this letter and trust to your judgment on the proper time to release them.

The rest of the stories were exactly where Holmes' letter said they would be, and I recovered them, through an intermediary, without incident. Some I was present for, events that occurred after Moriarty's flight from London, but a great many more were new to me. These too, have been held in abeyance because of their spectacular nature.

Until now . . .

PLAGUE OF FIRE

LEE CLARK ZUMPE

BEN CARTER WENT HOME early Thursday afternoon.

His coworkers had hounded him all morning, insisting that he seemed lethargic and quiet. One of the girls in the customer service center—a pudgy twenty-year old who normally flirted with him—wandered over to his bench just before lunch and told him he looked pale and "icky." She suggested he take the day off once he had finished repairing the VCR sitting dissected on the counter before him. She patted his head teasingly and wandered back to her cubicle.

While he found the incessant concern for his well being mildly annoying, he finally took his co-workers' advice and punched the time clock.

On the drive home, Ben sat in a pool of sweat. He cursed the car's inefficient air conditioner repeatedly before finally giving up on it and rolling down the windows. Even the breeze seemed dry and scorching. August in Florida could be worse than a descent into Hell. No matter what he did, he could not escape the late-summer heat.

When he got home, he made a beeline to the wall thermostat and turned the central air conditioner down ten degrees; then he went from room to room turning on the ceiling fans. Next month's power bill would be costly . . . it was worth it.

Ben eased himself into his favorite recliner and started reviewing his notes for his class on Western Civilization. He drifted in and out of sleep for an hour before finally dozing off.

He awoke roughly two hours later, panting and sweating. Winds howled outside, heralding the late afternoon storms. Ben's skin felt like he had spent a day on the Gulf of Mexico without the security of sun block. A sledgehammer battered the inner lining of his skull. His eyes burned.

He staggered into the bathroom, cupped his hands under the faucet and splashed water over his face. His flesh was scarlet red, his eyes a knot of bulging, crimson capillaries. He had to prop himself against a wall as he sucked on a thermometer, fearful he might collapse.

He had developed a raging fever.

He stumbled back out into the living room and called the community college, hoping to catch Prof. Allen in her office. He left the instructor a voice mail message apologizing for the fact that he would be missing class that night. He mumbled a garbled theory implicating an unnamed viral infection as the culprit and dazedly wondered if the professor might have an opening in another class the following week he could attend so he could catch up on his notes.

Ben nibbled sparingly at a turkey sandwich later that evening while staring at the local news on his television. Occasionally, a lightning flash from a passing squall line would draw his attention to the sliding glass door. Looking out across the patio and into the backyard, he watched the low black clouds brewing above the swaying palm trees. Rain came in quick, torrential downpours which rattled the awnings and sent waterfalls surging over the rims of inadequate storm gutters.

Aspirin did little to combat the fever, and Ben debated whether or not he should make a trip into the emergency room at Bayshore General. He sat in his recliner, a cold, damp washcloth draped over his forehead, munching on crushed ice he plucked from a bowl in his lap. The house was dark—as though the heat from the lights would be an unbearable condition—and silent and still. Flashes of lightning still danced across the sky, but the rain had stopped.

Ben felt his flesh begin to blister. He felt blood begin to boil in his veins, and the surface of his tongue cracked and seeped blood. He opened his eyes, but he could see nothing but an awful, pulsing red glow.

He struggled for an instant as the fever burning through his body erupted into intense heat. His arms and legs thrashed violently as he tried to drag himself from the recliner to the bathroom, to the bathtub where he could possibly find relief. In an instant, though, all such rational thought had evaporated. Smoke filled his lungs, and he realized that flames were consuming him.

The inferno lasted only a matter of seconds, not even long enough to permit Ben Carter one single wail of agony. Had anyone happened to be passing by his house at the moment of his death, they might have seen the flare of green light as it engulfed the room and poured through the windows onto the lawn.

Silence and darkness followed.

♦ ♦ ♦

Obaid Mutawwa sat at the table across from his friend Ross Damann. He sipped from a cup of black and bitter coffee, flavored with cardamom. The fingers of his left hand fidgeted restlessly with his short white beard.

"I've seen this before. St. Petersburg, many years ago—before you were born; back in the Middle East, too; although I was too young to realize it at the time."

"Spontaneous combustion?" Ross frowned. He had been one of the first investigators to inspect the remains of Mr. Ben Carter of 2211 Coral Ridge Road. His examination left him more perplexed than he had been when a patrol officer phoned in and described the scene. "It all seems so unreal."

"Your description of the remains leaves me with no doubt. The fact that the ashes were confined to a very limited area, the smoke stains lining the ceiling, the overwhelming stench: These are all classic signs. The slightly shrunken skull is evidence enough for me." Obaid scanned the diner. A couple of teenagers sat at the counter sharing a plate of fries and a soda. The lone waitress sat in a booth reading a tabloid. "You can't expect anyone to believe the story, though; so, stick with the lightning theory. It will be questioned, but I'm sure that you can get it to pass as the cause of death."

"There's something more, isn't there?" Ross had known Obaid for more than a decade. The older man had never spoken of his past in the Middle East, and Ross had never asked him to discuss it because he feared it might dredge up bad memories. It seemed now that something from that past might be surfacing, triggered by the strange death of Ben Carter. "What is it that you aren't telling me, Obaid?"

"Nothing, nothing of importance." Obaid shrugged. He turned and stared out the window of the diner. Across the street, and beyond a short stretch of beach, rolling whitecaps dotted the Gulf of Mexico. The sun had already set, leaving the sky awash in fading hues of orange and red. "It is an isolated incident, one which should be forgotten as quickly as possible. Sometimes it is best that we do not explore the unknown; sometimes it is best we live in ignorance."

"That sounds peculiar coming from a teacher, Obaid." Ross smiled slightly, threw some bills on the table. He watched his old friend staring at a dozen pelicans patrolling the waters offshore. One suddenly broke from formation, spiraling down toward the surface of the water hastily.

It crashed into the surf, sending spray and sea foam sailing on the breeze. In an instant, it resurfaced, a fish wiggling down its baggy throat. Finally, Ross continued, "I thought you academic-types were supposed to part the dark veils of ignorance to reveal wisdom, or something . . ."

"Did you know," Obaid said, rubbing his eyes, "that the earth passed through the tail of a comet a few nights ago?"

"Yeah, I read about it in the newspaper. I understand there was a spectacular meteor shower Monday night, sometime after midnight."

"Comets have traditionally been harbingers of doom. Medieval scholars blamed famines and plagues upon them." Obaid noticed that the sky had filled with sea gulls, each plucking fish from the water near where the pelican had made its catch. "They obviously didn't understand the nature of the cosmic event, the dynamics which caused comets to pass near the planet, or what materials comprised a comet; they simply knew that bad things happened in the wake of a comet."

"Superstition."

"Sure . . ." Obaid said uneasily. "Science defined comets for us, banished all of our primitive misconceptions. Now it is widely believed that comets are nothing to fear—unless, of course, the trajectory of one of them causes it to impact the planet."

"Are you saying that we have more to fear now that we understand comets?"

"Maybe," Obaid said, scowling. "Although I'm not even sure we have learned everything there is to know about them, anyway."

Within a week of their conversation, a dozen more incidents had left Chief Detective Ross Damann fending off criticism and answering questions with misinformation. South Florida watched as dozens of specialists arrived from all over the world. The Centers for Disease Control sent in a team hoping to identify whether or not the deaths could be attributed to some rare new viral contagion.

The military manifested itself in units trained to combat biological terrorism.

Religious fanatics crisscrossed the peninsula spreading the word that the situation certainly seemed to be of some unholy origin, and might well portend the coming Apocalypse.

Late on Monday night, Obaid heard his phone ringing. He listened as Ross left another plea for advice on his answering machine.

"If there is anything you know that might help stop this . . . please, call me."

Obaid cradled his head in his hands. Upon the table before him lay a voluminous old tome, a remnant of his heritage in Oman—a nameless text shackling him to a hidden world. When he fled the Middle East more than a half century ago, Obaid carried little more than this and the memories of the awful things he had seen both in the desert and in the shadowy alleyways and subterranean chambers of Dilbai.

He had awoken from dreams spawned by those memories on many nights, and he had wept until the dawn banished them once more.

Guilt weighed heavily upon him. He might have tried to tell his friend what he believed to be the cause of Ben Carter's death, knowing Ross would listen out of respect. But in the end, Ross could not give credence to Obaid's theory. No one would, no one could.

Obaid returned to the manuscript, painstakingly reviewing line after line of text. The ancient Arabic script almost defied translation. The words—scratched onto parchment more than a thousand years ago—mocked the anxious student from across the centuries.

This series of seemingly inexplicable, fiery deaths sprang from events relegated to the dim haze of prehistory—from the dark designs of contemptible beings exiled to remote corners of the cosmos. Plagues of Fire had beset humanity throughout time, but remained cloaked behind the façades of warfare, volcanic cataclysms, and other such catastrophes. Chroniclers of history often disguised the infiltration of outside forces within theological rhetoric or epic literature or dubious memoirs.

A few ancient narratives provided clues to the dreadful truth—often at the cost of the author's sanity.

Somewhere in this ancient tome, hidden amongst the cryptic verses, lay the secrets which would enable Obaid to find the nest of creatures responsible for the current scourge. Their destruction had to be complete, or they would simply move to another area and begin to feed once more.

Obaid shuddered when he thought of the victims who had already fallen prey to the vile beasts his ancestors called Fthagguans. In his youth, he had seen the malignancy of their very existence; he had seen the direct results of an extensive infestation. They constituted an epidemic unlike any other, and they left utter devastation and carnage in their wake.

He had little time to find their source and destroy them. With each new victim, the nest would grow more powerful. The plague would spread unchecked. Hundreds, thousands would die. Should their sphere of influence grow inclusive enough to encompass a large city like Miami, civilization itself might not survive.

Outside, the twilight shuddered with bursts of sporadic lightning. Spidery bolts erupted from beyond the horizon, scattered across the sky and invaded Obaid's apartment in flashes of crimson and blue. The thunder growled with the whisper of the hidden horrors.

A pack of tormented sirens howled through the dusk, scrambling toward a dull, red glow smoldering in the besieged Florida night. Obaid temporarily abandoned his studies and peered through the breach in the curtains covering the window. In the distance, some vast conflagration illuminated the sky, reminding him of burning oil rigs in the desert.

Chief Detective Ross Damann picked through the charred ruins of the Beach Theater, skirting the periphery of destruction. An army of military examiners and CDC pathologists had cordoned off the area and had begun sifting through the debris searching for human remains. Down the street toward the beach, journalists stood in front of transmitter vans broadcasting live updates. Seagulls crowded the tranquil, blue morning sky.

Officially relieved of his responsibilities by the Federal Bureau of Investigation, Ross reluctantly kept his distance. Although there had been no formal condemnation of his inquiry, he felt oddly denigrated. He felt the eyes of the world upon him, categorizing him as an incompetent and a failure.

Overnight, fourteen buildings burned in the county. Early estimates said the death toll would exceed one hundred.

Here alone, some twenty to thirty moviegoers had perished.

Ross watched as CDC personnel in protective gear plucked shrunken skulls from the rubble, depositing them into separate canisters inscribed with biohazard icons. The sea breeze stirred the ashes, spread the stench of burnt flesh amidst the bewildered townsfolk shambling along the sidewalks glaring at the tragedy.

By mid-morning, the seaside community had been quarantined. Soldiers patrolled the island carrying machine guns, and military vehicles sat on the center span of the drawbridge connecting the barrier island with the mainland, blocking traffic. In other towns along the coast, similar actions had been taken since the mysterious fires had begun to spread. Authorities had declared martial law, and had asked for cooperation from the local law enforcement agencies to maintain order and peace.

The media had been effectively silenced. A government spokesperson had been assigned to give news conferences every twelve hours—no additional reports could be filed without the consent of the FBI.

Ross crossed Bayshore, approaching the command post. By now, dozens of governmental organizations had arrived, each one setting up a center of operations on the grassy expanse of the Boca Ciega Municipal Park. Ross recognized the FBI agents in their stylish business suits. Affiliates with the CDC and the World Health Organization mostly wore white lab suits—and more than a few donned accompanying face masks. Army personnel patrolled the beach and the streets; Navy and Coast Guard ships took up positions offshore, and occasionally fighters from the MacDill Air Force Base in Tampa swept low over the horizon.

Other military units had arrived, too—Special Ops groups, wearing heavy armor and sporting strange weapons. They kept a low profile, huddling on the fringes, creeping along rooftops, submerging themselves in shadowy alcoves.

Civilians had been banished from the streets.

Fearing another night of widespread infernos, Ross suggested sending out a plea for firefighters from across the Sunshine State—a proposal that failed to earn the respect of FBI or the CDC.

"As you know, Detective Damann, most of the county is under quarantine as of this morning." The middle-aged bureaucrat scarcely took her eyes off the laptop screen while her index finger stroked the trackball. She sat at a table amidst a forest of tents, surrounded by swarms of unfamiliar people scurrying about like demented insects. Sweat beaded upon her upper lip, dangled in droplets from each earlobe. "We do not want to add to the impacted population."

"But if tonight is anything like last night, we won't have the manpower . . ." Ross regretted the politically incorrect choice of words immediately. He paused, regrouped. "We won't have the number of firefighters needed to control the fires."

"Right now, battling fires is a secondary issue—something each town will have to deal with individually. Speak to the local authority . . ."

"But, ma'am," Ross slapped the table with his hand, and the woman jumped. "I am the local authority, and I'm telling you we'll need help." The sun dipped low behind a row of palm trees lining Bayshore Boulevard. To the east, the gray, anvil-shaped battlements of hulking thunderstorms pressed westward toward the Gulf Coast. Flashes of crimson lightning blossomed along the approaching squall line. "I understand you have to concentrate your resources on finding the cause of all this—but you can't ignore the victims. If a sniper shoots a hundred people in the street, you must dedicate some of your energy to tending to the dead and dying even while you're trying to take down the shooter . . ."

"In that scenario, Detective Damann," the agent said, staring coldly at Ross, "One hundred percent of the Bureau's resources would be spent on the hundred people the sniper hadn't shot yet."

♦ ♦ ♦

As the Gulf of Mexico swallowed the setting sun, the winds began to howl. Blowing ashore off choppy waters, the gale swept torrents of sand across Bayshore Boulevard, lashed the tents dotting Boca Ciega Municipal Park, and sent the Feds reeling in a state of pandemonium.

The squall line inched toward the inter-coastal waterway, its thunder imitating the roar of an army advancing on enemy lines. Lightning now blasted the mainland, and Ross eyed each crimson flash anxiously as he drove toward the southern tip of the island in his patrol car. Each night, the storms had gotten progressively worse—each night, the number of fires had grown.

As he pulled into the parking lot of the apartment complex, the first raindrops struck the windshield.

Obaid answered the door with a grim expression. Wordlessly, he unlatched the chain and opened the door to welcome his friend.

Ross choked on a heady mix of pungent incense and perfumed oils permeating the air of the apartment. Thin strands of smoke slithered through the air like opaque serpents, and candles burned in every corner. An oil lamp sat upon the kitchenette pulsing with a peculiar emerald radiance. Within its glowing warmth sat a book of considerable age.

"I am sorry I have not responded to your phone calls," Obaid said, forcibly closing the door against the stubborn wind. "But I have been trying to find a solution to this problem."

"So, there is more than you were letting on . . ."

"I am only beginning to understand it myself. What is happening here is something that has happened before, many times. These cases of human combustion are caused by entities—things folklorists would call fire elementals." Obaid and Ross sat down at the table. Outside, the storm engulfed the island, and lightning bolts stuck indiscriminately with the ferocity and venom of a cornered viper. "There is more . . . but you would not believe."

"There are soldiers and government lackeys out there ready to wipe this island off the map given enough justification. They don't say that's why they're here, but I can tell." Ross listened to himself. He heard unfamiliar paranoia in his voice, and it surprised him. Severed from the loop, relieved of his authority and discounted by the Feds, he realized for the first time he had no control of his own fate. "I am willing to listen to any theory at this point."

"These things—the Fthagguans—are the minions of more powerful creatures. They've come seeking knowledge, wisdom contained in this book." Obaid's hand rested on the ancient text. "This book has been passed down for generations in my family. We were chosen to protect it from those who would use it to destroy the world."

"Why not simply destroy the book?"

"No—to destroy the book would be to unleash horror upon the world. The book details the methods by which these evils may be kept at bay. Without that knowledge, I and my kind could not protect earth from incursions such as this one." Obaid hesitated, eyeing the lantern. "Besides, they won't gain the knowledge from the book itself—they'll seek it from one who has read it—ultimately, I am what they are here for."

"All right," Ross said, growing impatient, "How do we stop them, then?"

"We must find the nest—if we can destroy the nest, the infestation will end."

The front window of the apartment shuddered as lightning struck a nearby palm tree. Thunder deafened both men, and frantic crimson flashes flooded the room. The door burst open, and wind and rain surged into the chamber. Ross ducked beneath the table, urging his friend to take shelter with him. Outside, a tornado waltzed down Bayshore Boulevard, overturning cars and trucks and plucking pines out of the sandy ground as if they were weeds.

"They've found me!" Obaid stood, staggering backwards a few steps into the living room. He thrust an arm beneath a cushion on the sofa, grasped for the gun he had hidden there days earlier. "You must find the nest, Ross—you must protect the book—do not let them learn the secrets!"

"No, wait," Ross screamed against the riotous howl of the storm, but Obaid could not hear his pleas. "Obaid! Get back here!"

As Ross watched, Obaid flew across the room against the far wall—his eyes bulging from their sockets. The pistol fell from his blackened hands. His flesh bubbled with blisters, and smoke billowed from his mouth. In the weird glow of the oil lantern, Ross watched as a horde of sparkling, spectral lights surrounded his old friend.

"Obaid!" Ross cowered beneath the table, powerless to end his friend's suffering. The Fthagguans overwhelmed their prey, inserting themselves into every pore, igniting every molecule, draining him of both life and knowledge.

Between the flashes of light and the crash of angry thunder, Ross heard the sound of gunfire. Instantly, glass shattered as a barrage of bullets rained into the apartment from an assault squad hidden from view outside in the storm. Obaid's chest exploded, and flames burst forth. Fire swallowed the sofa, crept across the carpet, scaled the drapery. Thick smoke obscured the ceiling and swirled around the open door.

On his knees, Ross took possession of the ancient text and crawled deeper into the apartment.

Two months later, Bayshore Hospital released Chief Detective Ross Damann after an extensive series of reconstructive surgeries. In the fire that leveled the Villa Nova Apartments, he had suffered broken bones, third degree burns, and lung damage due to smoke inhalation. Dozens had died in the blaze, which burned out of control for hours because the local fire engines could not pass tornado damage blocking Bayshore Boulevard. Ross might have died, too, had he not managed to pull himself from the ruins and drag himself to hospital.

Several fires swept the community that same evening, including one at an abandoned paper mill on the northeastern tip of the island. Although the origin of the blaze could not but determined, nearby residents initially reported hearing jets and seeing explosions shortly before the flames stretched into the night sky.

Ross resigned from the police force before he checked out of the hospital. He had trouble accepting the version of the story reported by the FBI. In particular, he dismissed the accusation that his friend Obaid Mutawwa had headed an international terrorist group responsible for the deaths of hundreds of Floridians. The rest of the country believed the tale, and Congress approved a budget increase to study ways to combat the newest weapon in the terrorists' arsenal: The so-called Infectious Spontaneous Human Combustion Agent.

A new cinema multiplex replaced the Beach Theater, opening its doors less than a year after its predecessor went up in smoke. Investors purchased the land where the Villa Nova stood, and began construction on condominiums for wealthy northerners looking for winter homes. The government purchased the paper mill property, allegedly intending to build a Coast Guard substation; however, to date, the land remains untouched, surrounded by tall barbed wire fences.

Ross spends his days studying Arabic at the community college.

OUT OF THE
SHADOWS

GERARD HOUARNER

KENDRA SAT IN A window booth looking out through her own darkskinned reflection at mountains looming over the diner parking lot and the lonely stretch of road beyond. A single green trailer truck was lined up alongside her rental Taurus and a ragged gathering of older, American cars and trucks and recent-model sport utility vehicles, looking like a little boy's collection of toys in the shadow of ancient, rounded, tree-shrouded peaks. The interstate she had driven on all night through slumbering suburban sprawl had shrunk to two lanes in the foothills and was now a fragile tar ribbon tossed casually over convenient folds and crevasses in the earth, with only an occasional passing car to confirm it was still open. Her destination, the town of Tendleton, was only a few miles further along the serpentine highway, nestled between protected National Park land and undeveloped private tracts. She wondered if the road would last the distance she had yet to go, or if anything would be left of the place when she got there. The trip, like her young life, felt like it had reached an ending from which there were no new beginnings.

Kendra shivered. The country air, tangy with the smell of sausages and coffee, chilled her even in the diner, under her zipped up black hooded sweatshirt and black and purple ski vest. Even more than the air, she admitted to herself, it was the foreign territory she found her self in that was seeping into her mind and spirit. She was not a country person. She missed the city, the compression of time and people and space that created the excitement, the buzz, the life she was accustomed to having around her. Only the sizzle of eggs on the grill was familiar and vaguely comforting in the mix of diner sounds that included a static-filled country-western song playing on the radio, the waitress calling orders to the cook with a slurred accent, and the urgent mumbling rising from a couple of tables filled with local workmen. Outside, the quiet was as much a living presence as the city's drone; but it was a presence that brought to the forefront her constant background awareness that she was an alien presence in the place and culture around her.

A sudden rush of anxiety made her skin crawl, vision spin, stomach lurch. Kendra took a deep breath and gripped the edge of the table. Steady, she told herself. Don't be ridiculous. This isn't your first time out in the big bad world.

People avoiding eye contact with her, like the locals, the trucker at the counter, even the waitress who had taken her order, was nothing new. But their studied oblivion to her among them, like she was an error they refused to acknowledge, like the color of her skin was as much of an outrage as the burgundy tinting her short-cropped hair, made her feel even more conspicuous. She loathed this part of the game between her and strangers, the black and white game, when hostility was hidden either behind a thin veil of courtesy or a thick curtain eliminating the threat of her presence. She wished someone would make a remark, give her a look, anything to set off the side of her personality she always relied on to get her out of bad situations.

"Your order, m'am," the waitress said, appearing suddenly, white-streaked auburn hair in a sloppy bun and weathered skin framing dead blank eyes. She set down a steaming plate of pancakes and sausage, and re-filling Kendra's coffee cup without asking, without even a glance at her face. Kendra opened her mouth to say, Don't get many Black folks up here, do you? in her sharpest sarcastic tone, but the waitress withdrew before the coffee had a chance to settle in the cup. She picked up the knife and fork to start in, but her throat constricted at the thought of eating and she put the utensils down and sipped water instead, trying to relax. It's only a job, she told herself. Even if it is your first. You're still in America, it's not like you were sent to the middle of Russia. Of course, the reaction to her might not have been so layered with history had she simply left the country. Simple, naked fear was so much easier to deal with.

The waitress re-appeared, dropping matchbooks across the table, in the side pocket of Kendra's purse and shoulder bag, even in her lap. Kendra batted the woman's hand away, saying, "Excuse me, what the hell is wrong with you?" The waitress scurried away.

What is this supposed to mean, Kendra wondered, brushing away the cardboard packages with "Tendleton Diner" printed on the covers. Was this the mountain version of burning crosses on the lawn? She looked for a reaction, snickers, smiles, anything, from the other patrons, but found none. Maybe the woman was just a little crazy, the local flake holding on to a pity job. Kendra's mood softened.

A rattling, blue and white van pulled in behind one of the trailers and several men came out through the side door to stand by the cab. The men were dressed in jeans, boots and jackets like the workmen in the diner, half wearing baseball caps emblazoned with the bright orange V that was Simon-Verner-Lenard's tri-point corporate logo. The company was Tendleton's largest employer, its only reason for continuing to exist, but Kendra still had no clear idea what business the corporation was in. The computer consulting firm she worked for had won a bid for emergency services for the company, and she had drawn the assignment of being sent into the boondocks to perform the work because, in the game of office politics, she lacked the necessary playing pieces of seniority and political support. Her supervisor had tried to soften the blow by saying the bidding process had included the submission of potential consultants to be assigned to the work, and Simon-Verner-Lenard had requested her. As if she would actually swallow the sugar coating.

She smirked at the ironic justice in her own vague, directionless life being cast into the murky waters of a company so obscure it operated out of backwood towns. A contract in the city, in an established or up-and-coming corporation, might have been just the thing to give her life focus. Meeting new people, getting out more in the city, was the kind of excitement she needed to stimulate her dulled imagination and blunted spirit. But here she was, being pulled deeper into the nowhere of her missing life.

Kendra started turning her attention back to breakfast when a residual image stopped her. A spike of terror punctured the familiar, almost comforting traps of thought her therapist was always pointing out to her. The stew of negative emotions and anxiety drained away, leaving her mind clear and focused on a single, urgent question:

What the hell was that?

Heart beating faster, she looked to the passenger side of the van, but it was empty. Immediately, her mind kicked into an adrenaline-frenzied rush to explain the glistening shape she had glimpsed: a worker in a wet plastic rain coat; a skinned animal carcass brought back from a hunt; a hallucination brought on by the all-night ride to a rush consulting job so she could prove herself equal to a staff who had, no doubt, refused the emergency assignment.

Kendra shook her head.

That had not been a naked, skinless man sitting in the passenger seat staring and grinning at the diner while the blood on his raw, exposed musculature brightened under the sunlight breaking through the tree cover to the east.

Kendra's attention was drawn to one of the men from the van climbing up the cab and looking into the truck while the rest tested the trailer's locked side and rear doors. She glanced at the other locals in the diner and the truckers at the counter. Action. That was what everybody, from teachers to family to lovers to her therapist, was always telling her to take: action. She sucked in a deep breath and shouted: "Hey, mister, your rig's drawing a lot of attention." The shock of what she thought she had seen was washed away by the wave of relief that passed through Kendra as she heard her voice cut through the noise in the room and leave a wake of momentary silence.

The waitress froze for a moment, then lowered her head as she picked up plates and cups from one of the tables. The locals glanced in her direction, quickly looked away. The trucker at the counter turned and craned his neck to look out the window. Cursing, he threw his fork down and bolted out the front door.

Kendra smiled to herself. The ice had been broken, inside of her and in the room.

After the trucker was gone, the locals at one of the tables stood, a small ripple of laughter passing through them. Two wore V hats. They slowly made their way to the door, never looking in Kendra's direction. One of the younger men broke away suddenly, as if rushing to the bathroom. He passed Kendra, turned on his heels and ran up to her, stopping a foot away to brace himself with a hand on the back of her chair, the other on the table. He swooped down and closed the distance between them until she could see the pores on his face.

"Are you the one?" he whispered, smiling, his lips trembling. His breath startled Kendra. It did not smell of coffee or bacon, but was sour, as if a gallon of milk lay curdling in his belly. "Your dark skin glistens, your eyes are pools of otherness. I can hear the drums beat, so close to you, just tell me, are—"

Hands gripped his shoulders and pulled him away as Kendra was rising, the table knife in her lower left hand ready to be thrust into his throat, the cup of hot coffee in her right already in an arc to be tossed into his face. A white-haired man in a suit and tie appeared, one spotted hand on Kendra's shoulder pushing her gently back into her seat, the other directing the men dragging Kendra's assailant to the door.

"Please ignore our friend," the man said, the paper-thin, yellowed skin around his eyes crinkling as he smiled.

Kendra recoiled, startled as much by the man as by the image of what she had seen in earlier in the front of the van returning to her with the suddenness of a fireworks shell accidentally exploding. A toothy grin, like a demonic Cheshire cat's, filled her mind for a second, a close-up of the skinless figure's grin, before the bizarre reality of the young man and his senseless question came crashing back to claim the moment. Kendra shook her head, put a finger to her eyebrow, struggling to settle on what was real and what was not.

"You know how young men are in the presence of a beautiful woman," the man continued, exuding charm through his glittering eyes and slick, tailored suit. She was reminded of fast-talking booking agents and club managers assessing how much they could get out of a hungry musician coming to them for work.

The man bowed, stepped away, made his way to a corner table diagonally across from Kendra's window booth. The remaining table of locals nodded and waved to him, and the cook called out jovially. The last of the locals leaving the diner joined the others outside, formed a tight circle around the man who had spoken to her, and headed for an old Ford pick-up and a Toyota SUV parked beside one another. The young man struggled to look back at Kendra, but the men around him, apparently laughing and playfully slapping his shoulders and the top of his head, kept a tight grip on him. He disappeared into the Toyota with one of his companions on either side of him.

While she watched, the older man who had intervened on her behalf haunted her. She did not remember seeing him come into the diner, nor did she recall him being there when she entered. Perhaps he was the owner who had been working in a back office and had only just come out, though he seemed overdressed to be involved in a diner. She stopped herself before allowing her imagination to speculate in bizarre directions. He was only an old man, and this was not the city.

Kendra remembered the knife and coffee cup she had picked up, old survival skills from public school and poor neighborhoods as well as private schools in wealthy neighborhood, taking over in time of danger. She went to put them down, realized she had already done so.

The shoulder touched by the charming elderly man tingled, returning to life from a brief numbness.

She started to give the diner's latest visitor a long look, but motion drew her attention to the window. The trucker was gesticulating wildly while the local men stood near the truck, some with their hands in their pockets or behind their backs like sheepish boys caught misbehaving, others with arms crossed or by their sides, waiting for the trucker to finish. A few from the last group to come out had joined them. She sensed the need for the local police, and wondered if the arrival of authority would make her feel more secure, or make her afraid again.

Her mind blanked, as if blinded by a psychic flare, and she lost touch with the inner landscape of her mind. For a moment, she forgot who she was, what she was doing in a diner, why she was up in the mountains. The last few minutes, from mountains to vision to trucker to a pair of strangers intruding on her solitude, burst out of the blankness and slammed through her in a series of out-of-context, blown up and cut-edited cinematic fragments of fear, disorientation, alienation that left her feeling stunned. Overwhelmed.

Kendra leaned back on the padded bench, closed her eyes, breathed. Flesh on flesh, finger rubbing skin against bone, generated enough concrete sensual reality to clear away some emotional smoke and she was able to tick off the who, what, and where's of her life. Words tumbled into place: delayed stress syndrome. She laughed at the idea of declaring war on herself, and then suffering a delayed stress reaction over the conflict. What would her therapist think.

So much for the big city girl, she thought, with a snort of amusement. Flustered by the country and its bumpkins.

Searching for something normal to do, she picked up the fork and knife again. Her hands hovered over the pancakes as she judged whether or not her stomach was ready.

Her cell phone rang. Even muffled by the surrounding items she had in her shoulder bag sitting beside her on the booth bench, the sound startled her. She looked up, almost guiltily, as if her beeper had gone off during a dramatic pause at a concert or play.

The old man in the corner smiled at her again, keeping his lips pressed together this time, and nodded his head.

Kendra pulled out the phone, thoughts shifting gears once again as she wondered what emergency waited to ambush her when she turned it on. It was only when the cool plastic device was in her hand that she realized the phone should not be working. Not in these mountains, in a sparsely populated county with limited resources and infrastructure. Developing strategies to cope with local limitations was the reason Simon-Verner-Lenard wanted her in the first place. Unless they had lied about their limitations, and their needs.

She clicked the phone on, rolling her eyes at her melodramatic paranoia. "Hello?" she said, expecting the radio's static to be amplified in her ear. No one answered. She wondered if some local signal had triggered the phone.

Then someone said, "Hello?' and she thought it was an echo of her own voice. "Kendra?" the voice asked, and she knew it was not an echo.

"Maurice." She put her face in her hand.

"Aren't you gone, yet? I thought I'd give you call to see if you'd left, but you sounded so rushed yesterday I wasn't expecting anyone to answer." The connection was poor, filled with a high-pitched background whistle and a deeper hum, like the lower register of other conversations being transmitted on the same frequency.

"I *am* gone. I'm outside Tendleton, up in the mountains already." Already, she knew where their dance was heading.

"Bullshit. If you were in the mountains we wouldn't be talking. See? I busted you and we haven't even started a conversation, yet. What else have you been lying about, Kendra? What's his name? Is he over there right now?"

She welcomed her anger rising, fresh and bracing, like a cold shower. "So what if I was home with a guy. Why would you do, punch him out? Or me? You think you're street or something, you think you own me? It's over. What part of goodbye didn't you understand?"

"The part where you throw out three years, and all that talk about family, and getting a business going for us. The part where you leave for no reason, none at all."

Kendra looked out the window. There was no one left in the parking lot. She assumed the trucker and the locals had gone to the other side of the truck, and she glanced at the waitress to draw her attention to a possible problem. The waitress fled behind the counter and into the kitchen. "Things changed and so did I. Now I just want to do my job and think about what I want out of my life. It isn't a business or a family or a house in the suburbs with you, or with anyone else, that much I know."

"Yeah, well, don't think you're going to run away to live the artsy life. I talked to Darryl and he said no one in your family is going to help you get any gigs or support you if you quit your job. You're going to have to starve and struggle like your old street and college friends who dropped you when they found out you couldn't help with money or connections."

The familiar moves of their personal contest veered into new territory. "You've been talking to my brother?"

"What, you think you own me? Tell me who I can and can't–"

Kendra clicked the phone off and speed-dialed Darryl's number. The smell of pancakes and syrup turned her stomach. She was surprised when the connection was made and the phone rang at the other end. If the town of Tendleton and the surrounding county had such a sophisticated communications network, what did they need with her?

For that matter, what did Maurice need with her? Why couldn't everybody just leave her alone?

Like they did in the diner. Except for the old man, who could not stop glancing at her with a wan smile every few seconds. To the workmen at the other table, it didn't seem to matter if she was talking loudly to herself or to someone on a phone that shouldn't be working this far from a network. They were no more interested in what she had to say than in what she looked like.

"Yeah?" Darryl's voice boomed.

"I heard from Maurice." Kendra worked to keep her voice low, to express her rage in tone alone.

"Good. You guys set a date to tie the knot, yet?"

"I'm not with him, anymore, Darryl."

"Don't tell me you went back to that white boy."

"I'm not going with anybody, Darryl. I want you to stay out of my business. If you're not going to help me, then don't interfere–"

"I *am* helping you, little sister. Whether you know it or not. You have a good thing going with Maurice. A Black man, proud, educated, intelligent—not bad looking, if Mom's a judge, and a nice guy, as far as I can see. So what the hell are you waiting for? You're no corporate slave, you don't have to work for them–"

"Oh, but I can let Maurice work, right? I'm not good enough to make my own way, in business, or in music–"

"Of course, you're good enough for business, like that thing you were talking about with Maurice. Make money for yourself, not for other people. As for music, sister, let's face it. You can't play. How many times do you have to hear us say that, Kendra? You manage to hit the right notes, with a lot of practice. But you have no ideas, no feelings. You can't just pick up your instrument and play. Even the stuff you write is stiff."

Kendra wanted to say, I have feelings. But her brother's electronic ghost, along with the long shadows of the rest of her siblings, her mother and her father, cut her off. And it was better, she thought, not to admit to feelings. Never give the enemy ammunition. Then she might really get hurt. Instead, she said, "Everybody's a critic. Besides, I never said I wanted to go back to music."

"No, you don't say it, you just set yourself up for doing it. I know. I can see it happening. This little break-up with Maurice is just another sign. Running away from responsibility, from what you *can* do, from people trying to help you. You're not going to stop until you're playing in some mongrel band with a bunch of people who can't even read music or play a scale or hit a note, and there you'll be trying to show them what we do as a family, as a people, and all you'll do is embarrass yourself and us. You'll turn everything that's intimate and precious into a cartoon, and you know what'll happen if by some miracle you succeed and make money doing it? You'll make people laugh at us. And that's just what we need, right? It's not enough that we've been bought and sold, that our raped spirit sells stuff for them and makes more money for them, no, now they're going to laugh—"

Kendra screamed and threw the phone down on the floor, stomping on it twice for good measure. Her purse and breakfast flew off the table, and hot coffee stung her fingers as it splattered on her. Tears burned her eyes, and she felt ashamed at her own hurt, at old wounds picked raw and left bleeding so easily by a few casual words. Why did those phone calls have to get through? Like intercontinental missiles, they had traveled impossible distances to deliver devastation with pin point accuracy.

She took money out of her purse, threw it on the table, refusing to linger for the waitress hovering behind the counter as if waiting for a storm to clear. Kendra bolted through the door, still not catching the attention of the workmen at the table, though she was sure she'd left them with something to talk about.

Two steps from the diner, she ran into the trucker heading back inside. He grunted as he absorbed her bump. His glazed eyes tried to focus on her, and after a second he stopped and looked past her at the door.

"Everything okay?" Kendra asked, drawn out of her own frenzy momentarily by the trucker's subdued mood. Automatically, she checked him for signs of violence: torn clothing, bruises, scratches, skinned knuckles.

His face twisted into a grimace. He opened his mouth, shut it, forced a sound out that was a cross between brakes squeaking and gears rattling. As he passed her, she realized the noise came from his lungs, as if he had breathed in a toxic cloud of gas which had ravaged him internally. "Had another load to take on," he said, voice cracking, not looking at her as he spoke. He continued on, walking steadily towards his seat at the counter, where the waitress stood with dish rag in hand, like a mother watching her wayward child come home.

The parking lot came alive with cars and trucks starting up, doors closing, horns blowing farewell beeps. The tractor trailer was free of any sign of damage.

Kendra put her head down and started off toward her car, determined to check into her hotel and give the local Simon-Verner-Lenard office a call to confirm she was in town, and then get some sleep before she met with anyone. Having people tell her who and what to be was the last thing she'd needed. Clearing her head was the priority. Sleep, an afternoon meeting with the people in charge of the project she was working on, and then more sleep, and she'd be ready for anything. Tomorrow.

She was half way to her car when a familiar voice called out over the noise of car engines, "Miss . . . Miss?"

Turning, she knew it was the white-haired man coming up behind her before she saw him. He held out a hand, long fingers curled around her phone.

"I"m sorry for your troubles," he said, passing his burden to her.

She checked it, found the phone undamaged. She glanced at the tractor trailer truck, uncertain why she felt compelled to look there again.

"At least you only lost your peace of mind and not your equipment," the man said, bathing her in the radiance of his smile. With the sun breaking over the mountains and through thin cloud cover, the surrounding countryside brightened as if by magic from the power of his good humor. Birds fluttered away from nearby trees, and a breeze brought life to still and silent trees. Even the smell of exhaust cleared, replaced for an instant by scents of fresh meadow grass and green wood, flowers, rain, and damp earth.

"What?" Kendra shook her head, intoxicated by the sudden richness of the surroundings, and put the phone in her shoulder bag. She caught herself clutching her purse close to her chest, as if threatened by a mugger. She was definitely not in the city, anymore. "Oh, I'm just surprised someone's paying attention to my little drama." She was embarrassed at the man's attentiveness and apparent sympathy. Dire warnings from her father and oldest brother about strangers, and worse, white people, echoed in her head. "Sometimes it seems you can't choose your family *or* your friends.'

"It's not always bad to be chosen, though," the man said. "I'm Tom. Tom Pittens. Can you give me a ride into town?"

Half-joking, taking a backward step to her car, she said, "I don't pick up hitchhikers."

"How about employers?" He handed her a business card with a tri-point corporate logo over the name Simon-Verner-Lenard in raised letters, and his own name and phone number below. He showed her the company ID badge with his picture he wore on the inside of his suit jacket.

"What are you doing out here?" Kendra asked, still half-turned away, the keys in her hand protruding between the closed fingers of her fist.

"Waiting for you."

The answer did not comfort her. "How'd you know I'd be at the diner?"

"I knew whoever was sent had to have driven all night, given our requirements. This is the only stop before town after the thruway, and I thought it might be a good place to rest and gather one self before entering new territory. It's human nature."

"Seems like quite a risk to take. Waiting at the hotel might've been a safer bet. Where's your car?"

"A colleagues from my office dropped me off earlier this morning. If I missed you, he would have returned to pick me up."

"Nice way to spend the working day, if you can get it." She relaxed a little and went to the car, turned off the alarm, opened the door. The security chirp sounded ludicrous in the open air of the countryside. The line of cars and trucks leaving the parking lot were all turning toward the town. "I wanted to stop by the hotel, first, though."

"Of course. You'll need to sleep, and freshen up. And have yourself a decent meal, since you weren't able to enjoy your breakfast."

He walked to the other side of the car as Kendra shut the door on her side, opened the lock on the passenger side. She felt a pang of regret when the door opened, a chill when it slammed shut and the Tom Pittens buckled himself into the seat. She started the car and drove out of the lot.

"This'll give us a little time to get acquainted. There's only one road to town, but I can still lead the way."

"Look, I'm sorry about what happened in there," Kendra said, trying to place the nature of her discomfort with the company representative. She turned in the direction of the town on the main road. There was no traffic going either way. The other cars had vanished around the turn ahead of them.

"You have to forgive folks around here. Many of them were swept up by a cult a few years ago. Victims of an existential plague, you might say. It fell apart, the leader ran off with all their money, but for some of them, that's all they had to hang on to. The company did the best it could, expanding operations, providing more jobs, but really, some of them were too stupid to go over a few valleys and work for a resort. In these small towns and poor counties, there's not always a lot to choose from as an employer."

"Yeah, I suppose that's why I'm here."

"It wasn't always like that, from what I understand of the local history. Tendleton was a hardy little colony when it was founded in the late 18th century as a kind of resort for a certain class of people. Really, a sanatarium for the rich, far enough from polite society to be considered another country. The place was wiped out when tuberculosis hit it early in the 19th century. Some logging and mining concerns took over but failed, and during the second World War there was a small intelligence and training community established here. Since the war, the place has drawn more modern resort facilities; military, university and bio med research concerns, even someone interested in drilling through valley floors for oil to prove a theory of hydrocarbon upwelling from the earth's mantle feeding a bacterial biosphere beneath the earth's surface. We—that is, Simon-Verner-Lenard—seem to be the only ones that have staying power in this region."

Shoot me, Kendra thought, bored with irrelevant recitations reminding her of those still fresh in her mind from her college days. How much was left unsaid, how many more layers of lies, and bodies, were sandwiched between the truth and what Mr. Pittens passed off as quaint local history? And neither the truth nor the lies had anything to do with her, or why she was here. "I don't mean to be rude, but I'm not really interested in Tendleton except as someplace I have to work in right now. But I am curious about what exactly it is your company does?"

"Turn off here," Mr. Pittens said, pointing to a paved, but narrow, unmarked road leading away from the two lane highway and deeper into greening woods. "Of course, your own problems are far too important."

Kendra gave him a quick look as she navigated the steeply sloped, deeply shadowed road. Mr. Pittens gave no indication of being annoyed with her, his slight smile constant, his brows relaxed, his skin a little pale and hairless, perfect for displaying emotional flushes. She returned her attention to the road, hazy with a thin cloud of dust from the caravan that preceded her.

"Well?" she said, pushing him with her tone.

"Oh yes, what do we do. Well, now, that is an interesting question, one perhaps best replaced by a more appropriate one, which would be, what don't we do. We started out manufacturing and distributing a variety of consumer goods, of course, from cosmetics to clothing to, more recently, electronics. Lately, we've contracted with foreign factories and imported for various specialty markets. Our transportation and delivery services date back to the days of the Pony Express, and we still provide discrete and specialized transport, particularly in under-served regions like this one. Over time, our corporate values and decision metrics have evolved, and now we see emerging technologies and their commercial applications as opportunities to broaden our market. We fund unique technological ventures incubating in El Ghazala, Bangalore, Kuala Lumpur, Sao Paulo, Bangkok, Dublin, Santa Fe. We're even taking steps in the arena of games and amusement parks. In short, I think it sums us up to say that with our special vision, we fill niches not occupied by larger, cost-conscious and short-term profit-oriented companies. We have a long-term perspective, and believe diversity sustains the experimentation necessary for the evolutionary process. And as you know, time and evolution can often bring surprising reversals, bringing light to darkness, and making light dark. We are prepared for both."

"I'd love to see your prospectus."

"We don't have one. We're privately owned."

"Really. The three names?"

"Family names. Lenard is my great-uncle."

Again, she checked him, this time for his age, as well as for what he might be trying to tell her with body language and facial expressions. But both were neutral, and did not explain how a man his age might have a living great-uncle.

The road visibility cleared as they passed even darker roads shooting off from either side of the one they drove on. "And what kind of work will I be doing? I have your preliminary specs—something about your information management system?"

"Related to that, yes. The world of computers is changing so quickly, and we need to adapt or lose the capacity to fulfill our evolutionary niche."

"Yeah, you and everybody else." Kendra decided she did not like Mr. Pittens, despite his charm and kindly, paternal manner. Perhaps because of those characteristics. Or, she considered, because of the faint but inescapable odor, slightly sharp, like a trace of ammonia, that made her open her window to let the chilly morning mountain air into the car.

They drove on for another five minutes before the woods fell away, the road stopped climbing, and they emerged into a high clearing crowded with brick and wooden buildings on either side of the central, tree-lined road. Clean, with new windows and doors, behind fresh concrete sidewalks, shiny street lights and manicured patches of greenery, the small town looked like a model for a larger development rather than a lived-in community. They passed a block of modern-looking shops, though there was no supermarket or franchise fast food restaurants. Kendra glanced at the display windows, expecting a run of tourist-trap antique and sporting good stores, but found only basic stores like a grocery, a hardware store, a barbershop with candy-striped pole apparently catering to both men and women, an appliance store, and a clothing merchant, again serving both men and women with fashions in its window so basic, Kendra thought she had slipped into a time warp and landed in a 50's TV sitcom. Other things were missing, but Kendra could not catch them specifically in her mind. Mr. Pittens pointed out the hotel, a three storey, sprawling wood-frame dominating the center of town and Kendra headed for its rear lot. A sign with antique lettering declared the building as the Hotel Tendleton.

"Let me guess," Kendra said, "that was the sanatarium."

"Completely refurbished, now, of course, with state of the ⸺ ence rooms and dining facilities. It's always been the heart of from its first days to its resort era to now."

Kendra popped the trunk and took out her garment bag and thick laptop equipment. Mr. Pittens waited a few feet off, in the direction of the hotel. Kendra wondered if he had forgotten to offer to help her with the bags, if he had a medical condition that prevented him from lifting, or if he was sending her a message.

As she began walking toward him, wheeling the equipment case behind her and shifting the garment and shoulder bags across her shoulder, a wild-haired woman in an enormous, tightly zippered parka containing the multiple layers of clothing the woman wore beneath, sprung from behind one of the other parked cars. She blinked, as if surprised in a delayed reaction to the noise of their arrival. She flinched and jerked her gaze away at the sight of Mr. Pittens, then fixed herself on Kendra.

"We don't want your kind around here," she said, drawing nearer, pointing at Kendra with a stiff forefinger. "You don't belong. Go back where you come from."

Kendra's blood rose to warm her neck and cheeks. She dropped her bags and squared her shoulders to face the woman. "And where are you from, exactly?"

"Now, now, Mrs. McElroy," Mr. Pittens called out, "why don't you spare our young guest your rambling and go back to the clinic. It should be open by now, and I'm sure they'll have a nice hot breakfast for you."

Mrs. McElroy searched in the pockets of her outer coat, keeping a wary eye out for Mr. Pittens.

"I was just trying to figure out what Native American tribe Mrs. McElroy here belonged to," Kendra said, "since she seems to feel she belongs here and I don't. But you know what? I don't think she belongs here, either."

"None of us do, Kendra. None of us do."

Mrs. McElroy squealed, grinned maniacally at Mr. Pittens, produced a lighter, flicked it on and waved the flame in the elderly man's direction.

Kendra almost burst out laughing at the absurdity of the image.

Mr. Pittens turned abruptly and walked toward the hotel. Mrs. McElroy scowled and scurried behind the parked car, where she remained in hiding. Kendra hesitated a moment, amusement gone, digesting the moment's intimacy with the woman's hatred and Mr. Pittens' familiarity. Though she was not sure which she wanted to do more, stay and not give in to such mindlessness or leave the ignorant to their own devices, she knew she could not imagine herself ever calling her guide and apparent employer Tom.

A half-dozen men and women, young and in ill-fitting business suits, emerged from the hotel and surrounded Mr. Pittens. Kendra passed them, overhearing breathless plans for a company marketing conference, including the construction of a helipad, trucking in enough food for the event, arranging entertainment. She was impressed by Mr. Pittens' handling of the commotion, as he anticipated questions, provided advice as well as instructions, and dispatched the band before she was through the hotel's front door. As they wandered off to their assignments, Kendra could not help noticing the young corporate executives did not appear healthy—pasty white, hair too oily or dry and badly cut, backs sagging slightly as if carrying an invisible burden, eyes drawn from too many late nights. In the city, she might have considered them drug and party addicts, though in this wilderness she could not conceive of anything to do except work. She bumped up her estimate of the sleep she would need, if this was an example of how the company treated its employees, and how the town treated people like her.

Mr. Pittens caught up to her at the registration desk. "As you can see, we're a bit busy at the moment. We're in the midst of a massive re-conceptualization of our sales presentations. We need to translate our new paradigms into language and images people can understand. The next few weeks should be very exciting. And you'll be with us, in the background, helping us deliver our message."

"In the background, of course." Kendra signed herself in, surrendered her company's credit card, let a porter take the bags. As she started to follow, Mr. Pittens gently placed a hand under her upper arm and led her back to the door. She tried to draw back, but her arm did not respond, and suddenly she felt compelled to follow Mr. Pittens instead.

"I must go on to the office," he said, his voice like syrup pouring through her, sticking to thoughts and slowing her perceptions, "but I'll send a car for you after you've rested. Say, three-thirty? We'll look over some of the facilities we'll need you to work in, have dinner, and then you can have a nice long rest before starting in tomorrow."

She was at the front entrance to the hotel when Mr. Pittens released her. "Don't let Mrs. McElroy upset you. She's from an old town family and her adjustment to changes during the past few years has been much worse than usual for the locals, though she's not alone in her condition. The waitress at the diner, for example, poor soul. Strange, how some people are immune to what's best for them. But people adapt in varying degrees, most content to move with the times, and the cream rises to take on responsibilities and leadership. Needless to say, Mrs. McElroy lost everything to that cult and benefits greatly from the local mental health clinic funded by the company. You know, every little town has its troubles, and you seem to have run into a couple during your short stay. But I'm sure you understand."

A black plastic bag blew with the breeze across the sidewalk, dancing with the jerky abandon of a marionette controlled by a drunken puppeteer. It shifted shape, snapping and rolling, as air filled and buffeted plastic, until it seemed to breathe with independent life, assuming a new identity with every gust.

And then the plastic, dark and shiny, was something else. Alive, restless, eager. Alien.

Kendra drew her breath in sharply, tried to step back.

"It's nothing, nothing really, to be afraid of," Mr. Pittens said, holding her in place with his tone.

A group of a dozen pre-adolescent boys and girls drifted by, laughing and playing among themselves, and waved to Mr. Pittens. They ignored her, as if a dark-skinned stranger in their midst was not enough to provoke their curiosity, at the very least. As if she did not exist. The plastic bag flew to them like a wounded bird, jerked in one direction then another, following a crazed but deliberate flight path until it was in their midst. Kendra wanted to cry out a warning, afraid the bag, or whatever it really was, would devour the children. But she choked on her own voice, and could not take in air until she stopped trying to speak. The bag darted around the children, dipped between their legs, bumped against their laughing faces and bolted through their eager grasping hands. It was a part of them, and they were a part of it.

The group passed one of the trees along the roadside, and for a moment the tree was also something else: a thick, ropey column of whirling tentacles, like a hundred giant octopuses genetically merged into one entity, each frantic appendage spotted with what at first she took for a kind of grasping sucker, and then realized it was an opening. A lipless mouth, opened, silently in frequencies she could not hear.

Kendra staggered forward, drawn into the unraveling layers of a world she had never before experienced: vague figures moved in windows, mist flowed along the road like a stream, corners and shadows were filled with movement she could not quite discern. A stench like raw petroleum mixed with sewage spilled into the sea turned her stomach. The chirping of birds and the fading laughter of children turned into the angry buzz and clicking of insects seething just beyond sight, behind her head, underground, inside her. The finished painting of the world she knew had regressed into a sketch, a creation in progress, seen from the edge of her vision. The firm musical score of sensory information devolved into poor improvisation.

"Not yet," Mr. Pittens said, drawing her back into the hotel. "Not here. That would be wasting a precious resource."

One of the young women who had rushed to Mr. Pittens upon his arrival reappeared from one of the lobby doors. Hair bangs dropping over her face, a thin patina of sweat giving her face an sickly shine, she said to Mr. Pittens, "Another truck just stopped by the diner. Do we have any shipments ready to go out?"

Mr. Pittens went to a lobby phone, and while they waited for him to return the young woman brushed shoulders with Kendra and whispered, "Are you the one?"

The question rallied Kendra, gave her something familiar and provocative to hang on to, a cause with which to energize herself. One what? she wanted to ask, though her tongue felt thick in her mouth, and the world spun slowly around her head as if she was drunk. She was the focus of something in the community, though what, she could not tell. If they were stereotyping her, it was not as the usual whore, drug addict, criminal, or other demonic nightmare from their fear of anything other than themselves. Something else was going on, beyond her understanding. What kind of trip are these people on? she thought. What kind of trip am I on?

"Are you the one?" the woman asked again, with greater urgency as Mr. Pittens glanced at them. "Do you dance with swords in your hands, and skulls around you neck? Did you worship Ahtu in the jungle from which you came? The God of the Bloody Tongue? Are you here to bring in the new age? Do you have hooves? Where are your hooves?"

Kendra shoved the woman away. Adrenaline rushing through her, she balled and cocked her fists and sank into a crouch, slipping into street mode, eager to vent the frustration that had been building since she was assigned this job. "If you don't stop asking me if I'm the one, I'm going to be the one who's going to bust you up, you hear me?"

Mr. Pittens appeared between them, spoke to the woman, who nodded at the softly spoken instructions and withdrew, her gait unsteady, as if she was not used to walking in even low heels, or as if the floor was shaking.

Mr. Pittens turned to her, put his hands over her lead fist. At the touch of his flesh, exhaustion sucked the energy from her limbs, her body. The reason for her anger evaporated, and the threads of her thoughts flapped uselessly in her head, eluding her attempts to concentrate and weave them into a coherent view of what was happening. She nearly collapsed, but pulled herself together and straightened, basic human instinct driving her not to show vulnerability.

"They are so eager, sometimes too much so," Mr. Pittens said, leading Kendra back into the hotel, through the halls and stairs up to her room. "Like broken vessels, they need to be constantly refilled in order to feel useful. Things were simpler in the days when all there was to count on was the limbic system. But the rewards are so much richer through the neo cortex. Two or three more levels of consciousness, perhaps another organ of perception, and your race will be ready for the work that must be done. But for now, your kind serve well enough. Some better than others, which is why you, in particular, are so welcome here.

"You understand what it is to be alien, to be out of your time and place, to be perceived as something you are not. You understand the world as it is, within the narrow limitations of your awareness, not as the majority, the shapers of illusion, wish you to see reality. You understand the necessity of questions; your survival depends on them. And if you have not directly asked yourself the most dangerous, painful, debilitating question—why?—that is only because you are still young. Inexperienced in the broader world, much less the vastness of the universe. You still play the music others have put inside you, rather than the songs that beg for release within you. You don't know who you are, yet.

"But I do not believe you will be broken when the question is asked, when meaning is broken and the crawling chaos beneath the structure of everyday life is revealed. Adversity has made you strong. You will find your own answer. And that answer will lead you back to us, will make you one of us, rather than one of the broken puppets staggering across our little stage."

Mr. Pittens shook her hand and left. A bell boy appeared and offered to show Kendra to her room. Minutes later, she was sitting on the bed of her third floor room, staring out the window at the town of Tendleton. She felt like she was floating several inches off of the bed, her feet not touching the floor. Slowly, her head cleared, but exhaustion crashed through her body. She started to lay down, saw her cell phone on the room's desk, willed herself to walk over and pick it up. She dialed a familiar number. Her mother picked up. In the background, a choir sang.

"Hello?" her mother said sharply. Her practice was being interrupted.

"Mom, it's me. Sorry to bother you but–"

"Hello! Who is this?"

"Mom, it's Kendra. I'm out in the sticks, mom, and I just needed to talk to some–"

"I don't have time for this nonsense." The phone went dead, became just another lifeless piece of plastic and metal.

"Mom?" Kendra called out, before letting the phone drop. She collapsed on to the bed, squirmed out of half her clothes before she surrendered to her need to rest. As she drifted off into the dizzying blackness of unconsciousness, she realized at least one thing Tendleton lacked: A sign of faith. There were no churches or temples, no imprint of sacredness. Even signs of the cult that had devastated the town had been surgically removed, though she was certain its headquarters had been at the hotel. She could almost feel the desperate need to believe in something, anything, emanating from the walls of the room.

Or was that her own feeling as she lay cut off from the world, a stranger in a strange land.

She'd stepped on too many emotional land mines, today. Too many changes and surprises had hit her, and she could not pull out of her daze to reason anymore.

She welcomed the darkness that came to swallow her.

When the knock on the door came, Kendra started, realized she had been sleeping and bolted upright, knowing she was not showered or dressed yet to go down to the car Mr. Pittens promised to send for her.

And yet when she stood, she was freshly washed, dressed in one of her pressed skirt suits and low heels, made up, subtly perfumed, burgundy curls tight against her skull, her thick briefcase ready by the door with copies of her company's contracts, preliminary job specs, and a notebook computer.

The knock came again. Kendra picked up her purse beside her on the bed, went to the door, thinking she was in a dream and that she'd find her father in the doorway, scowling his disapproval at her, and next would come the naked-in-the-choir episode, and forgetting how to play piano and flute at an audition. But it was Mr. Pittens who stood in the hall waiting for her. He took the briefcase from her when she walked out and lightly touched her elbow as they walked downstairs.

"We took the liberty of upgrading your laptop with our programs so you can interface with our systems. No sense delaying the inevitable. Time for you to do what you must."

Stairs flowed beneath Kendra's feet. "What is it exactly that you want me to do?"

"Why, lead your people from existential terror and the doom of inertia, of course. Give them a reason to continue to exist. Give them purpose. Guide them into raising us from our hidden temples, from our graves between the stars. The cult was an unfortunate experiment to that end, but it placed too many limitations on the people who fell under its spell. There was nothing but disaster."

They were in the car, the countryside draped in late afternoon flowing past the windows. "You shouldn't touch my equipment," Kendra said.

"It doesn't matter. You've already been exposed."

They were deep in the mountains, under the trees. They passed through gates in fences. A group of men loading a tractor trailer stopped to watch them pass.

"Consider it an information virus. A demonic meme. It alters your perception of the world, existence, and your place in it. Subsequently, your awareness changes the world's perception of you."

They stopped in front of a three-storey, windowless cement building built into the face of a mountain. A two-storey rolling metal door opened, and a miniature train of open cars pulled out.

"God knows I exist?" Kendra asked.

"Something knows. Call it God, if you find comfort in that name."

They were sitting side by side in an open train car that reminded her of something from Disney World. She remembered Mr. Pittens talking about amusement parks, but could not place the phrase in the context of her situation.

"What is this place?" she asked.

"A lightning rod. We have places like this throughout the world, drawing power from the land, from the sky. Drawing remarkable young people like yourself. You see? You won't be alone. The burden will not rest entirely on you."

The train moved through the building, into the mountain, rattling on tracks elevated on a wooden trestle that carried them over plunging, invisible depths through a natural cavern descending into the earth. A string of lights hung from jagged rock outcrops and stalactites above, providing faint illumination for workers clustered around ducts, pipes, metal-enclosed work stations. Machinery whined and clanged along with echoing voices. The cool, damp breeze of their gentle downward ride blew against Kendra's skin. She felt as if she were being swallowed by a mythical snake god that had its coils wrapped around the Earth's core. She wondered what enormous beast the snake fed on that required such a gullet; or what creatures it disgorged from the burning engines of creation and destruction in its belly.

"Here is where we would like you to work," Mr. Pittens said, waving his hand at a large window embedded in the wall. Behind it, a gaseous cloud billowed, obscuring banks of machinery. He dropped her briefcase by the side of the train, where it stood as the train inched forward, alone, waiting for her return.

An electric buzz vibrated in the cavern. Kendra winced at the sound.

Mr. Pittens continued. "We have multiple cooling units and generators for the electronic brain of our complex, as well as microwave, satellite and fiber-optic links to our other operations. What you see is a part-nitrogen atmosphere, maintained for security and fire precaution, and the convenience of the guards inside, who are nitrogen breathers. Other gases are mixed in, for other visitors." As they went around a bend, a pair of figures wearing rubber suits, masks and air tanks approached an air locker. Dark shapes moved behind the window, making the gas clouds roil. "As you can see, we still need your particular touch to clear the pathways of our thoughts. Clarity is essential if we are to communicate."

The train passed over an underground stream. A thin, sickly yellow mist clung to the surface of the slow moving water. "Communication is so important," Mr. Pittens said. "Nothing, of course, can replace the flitter of quarks coming and going inside the atoms of our forms, carrying our prayers, thoughts, desires, the flavors of our souls, the scent of our thoughts, from one end of the universe to the other. But you are not prepared to communicate on that level, and so we have struggled to guide you through the garbled translations that have come down over your ages: Greek texts, translated by Jews in Toledo under Muslim supervision into Arabic, with the occasional madman infusing his own Christian, Arabic, Jewish, even Egyptian and Hindu viewpoint into what was once simple truths. The names they've given us, the titles and powers . . .." Mr. Pittens shook his head. "Nyarlathotep, Azathoth—as if your minds could hold even the shadows of what we are."

The train stopped and she was no longer sitting on it, but standing on the edge of a chasm illuminated by floodlights. Drilling equipment groaned at the bottom, cooled by water from chugging pumps. An oily sheen covered the surrounding rock, catching the bright light and shimmering with countless colors.

Not all the colors she recognized. Some danced in her mind, elusive, alien, ultimately escaping the cage of definition.

"As if your bodies could hold more than the dregs of our discharges. What you see in Tendleton, in this lump of flesh, is just a tidal pool left over from the vast sea beneath us, trapped fragments waiting to rejoin the larger host. That is the work that must be done. Now, while there are servants available, while the currents between the stars run in our favor. Now is the time, but," Mr. Pittens said, his cold hand gliding over Kendra's cheek in a gentle caress, "now for us is a million of your years."

And then she was in the pit, the drilling machinery and pumps shut down, the handful of workers going back up stairs carved into stone walls. The stench of petroleum was thick enough to choke Kendra, burning in her stomach and the back of her throat. A wet, mechanical breathing sound bubbled up from the drill hole, as if a worker, the air in his tanks gone, lay slowly suffocating, buried alive.

Between the raspy breaths, another sound echoed. Someone, something, was playing a flute. Thin, faint, airy, Kendra still heard it, hung on every note, hungered for more, though the song invaded her, breaking through the corrupted edifice of her psyche like a worm burrowing into a corpse, intruding into barely formed thoughts, leaving her bloated, sluggish, engorged. Nausea blossomed like a poisoned midnight flower in her belly, ran cold down her guts and up into her throat, though she could not throw up.

She looked for Mr. Pittens, but he was gone. Beside her stood the image she had seen in the van passenger seat outside the Tendleton Diner: a man, flayed, glistening with the blood dripping from his exposed, spots of a yellowish fungus rooted in the tracts of his musculature.

"Look down," the figure said. "Accept the depths."

Kendra concentrated on her feet. Made them step back. Her arms, crossed over her chest, shook with the effort. Her fingers ached as they dug into the leather of the purse she clutched against her breasts. "No," she said.

The flayed man turned, facial muscles twitching, settling into a pattern that might have registered surprise on a patina of skin. "Why are you hanging on to the responsibility of consciousness?" the thing asked. "Or awareness? Unclouded by faith or delusion, you know you are alone in a dying universe, a cosmic aberration, a pointless speck. Why not sacrifice these futile moments of yours for the good of your betters?" Its voice rose, challenging her, as it asked: "Are you afraid? We expected better of you."

"We're not alone," Kendra said, forcing the words out. "There's you."

"But we know our place. You know nothing of yours. You are children asking questions whose answers you cannot understand. Baryonic accidents, ghosts flickering in the storm of neutrinos coursing through the universe."

Low chanting joined the flutist, and the music insinuated itself deeper into Kendra, changing what she wanted to say, inspiring, insisting on responses in languages foreign to her tongue. Hunger stirred in the empty places she had tried to forget, even as she tried to hang on to what she was. Old wounds bled, making her flinch, stoking her hunger to join the choir, to learn the song and its meaning, its changes, and play a mad duet with the subterranean flutist. She felt the warmth of acceptance, a surging, alien joy in her desire to throw away the past, with all its pain and disappointments, and surrender to the thing that wanted her. Here was her family, said the words forming in her mind. Here was love, appreciation, recognition for what she was and what she did.

"Life is symptomatic of your physical laws, but your physics are a transitional phase from one state to another. We exist beyond your laws. We always have, we always will."

The flayed man's arrogance, his absolute, invulnerable superiority, resonated within Kendra, breaking through the sweet horror of the harmonies rising to ensnare her.

Laws. The word hung in her mind, refused to be subsumed by the seductive song invading her, urging her to join its players.

Books of matches scattered across a diner table. A woman holding a lighter like a cross against a vampire. Mr. Pittens turning away.

Kendra sank to her knees, no longer able to stand with the effort required to keep from losing herself to the music. Her stockings and knees tore on the rocky ledge, her shoes slipped off. She barely felt the pain shooting through her legs. An oily film covered her knees, calves, and hands as she put first one and then the other out to find her balance. She thrust fingers into the side pocket of her purse, pulled out several books of matches.

Everywhere, there were rules. In games on the street, in family, in corporations, in the murky borderlands between black and white. Inside her own head. There were rules, and there was the real Kendra, naked, in the center of all the games, alone, a human being. Rules were there to keep her, control her, force her along one path or another. Control her. Keep her from what she truly wanted, what she really needed. But laws worked both ways, and if there were rules to keep her under another's power, there were rules for those in power, as well. Not many, perhaps, but if they played in this world, in this universe, with human minds and bodies, they were subject to some kind of law. Whether they wanted to admit it or not.

Kendra lit a match with shaking hands, fired up the book, threw it at the flayed man.

The flaming match book arced through the air. Fell, spinning, landed. Sputtered on the rocks.

She lit another book of matches. The flayed man hissed. She flung the book at him. It landed at his feet.

Tears burning in her eyes, she struggled with oily fingers to light the third, her last, book. It exploded in her hands, turning into a ball of fire. The flames caught at her hands, her legs. She cried out, stood up, batted at herself trying to put out the flames, which seethed over her stockings and snatched at her skirt.

A louder shriek drowned out her cries. Flames, leaping from crags and pockets where fuel had fed Kendra's pitiful offerings, engulfed the flayed man. But unlike Kendra, the flayed man stood perfectly still, arms by his side, black smoke curling into the air above his head as the fire blackened the visible musculature of his body. Within the blackness, other colors, beyond the human spectrum, burned with an incandescence that hurt Kendra's eyes as deeply as the fire savaged her skin.

Kendra fell backward against the pit wall. She screamed for the workers watching from above to help her, but they stood their ground. Pain, unthinkable, beyond madness, stroked every nerve in her body. She closed her eyes, tried to surrender to the pain and black out, but the fire ate through the thin layer of her eyelid and she could not escape the vision of the flayed man, still standing, a pillar of fire, looking at her with his leering, lipless grin.

Welcome, he said, inside her mind. He shrieked again. The sound was not a cry of pain, but a song. He had joined the music coming from below.

Something came for her out of the shadows, from the void around her, the empty places inside her, from the background of the everyday reality she had always known to the foreground of the now. The thing sang, a babbling sound she could not understand, and offered her a flute. She took it, put it to her lips, gave it the breath of her life. The sound she made was the perfect rendition of every hurt she had ever suffered in her life. She stopped, shuddered, took another breath and gave it to the flute. Her vision of the world expanded beyond the stillness of her moment between one existence and another. She saw, touched, lived in the multiplicity of the entity that had sought her out. She was the workers looking down at her skin being consumed by fire in the cavern pit; she was the clerk registering incoming Simon-Verner-Lenard marketing executives; she was the executives, their drivers and secretaries and assistants, the helicopter pilot who had brought them in, the cooks preparing food in the kitchen, the band rehearsing for the night's show. She was the workers scattered across the countryside on the corporate payroll, truckers on the road, pressed into service, infected with Tendleton's secret, delivering demonic memes and existential plague throughout the country. She was other things, unspeakable, sleeping, lurking, waiting.

She was not the waitress at the diner, Mrs. McElroy, or any of the other town misfits.

The thing from out of the shadows, from deep beneath the earth and beyond the stars, embraced her. Asked her if she knew who she was.

Placing the flute to her lips, Kendra answered.

IF MAMA AIN'T HAPPY

SAM W. ANDERSON

"DON'T BE SCARED OF me. I got no interest that way." The fat man wiped a hand across his sweatshirt and reached inside the bag of pork rinds. "I remember when Stevie P first brought me out here. That's all I worried about—that he was looking for some of that 'man love.'"

Blinking several times, Clive focused on his new surroundings. The limited light and pain pulsing through his skull hindered his sight. Gagging on an overwhelming stench, he struggled with his breathing, the duct tape covering his mouth. Nothing around him appeared familiar, but for certain he hadn't reached Graceland.

"You just relax, partner. We can make this as hard or as easy-peazy as you want." The man gulped off his Nehi, some of the sticky fluid escaping the sides of his mouth and down his chin. Setting the soda on a cinder block coffee table, he clicked on the thirteen-inch Sony resting on a TV tray. An infomercial appeared—make a fortune in real estate with no money down—but the volume was off. "Mama ain't going to be ready 'til midnight or so. She's probably feeding her rug-rats. You just lay low here, and it'll all be over before you can whistle 'Dixie.'"

By the television's glow, the décor of the cramped trailer materialized. Dark faux-wood paneling shrouded the walls, and a worn path ran through the linoleum from the kitchen to the screen door. The irony not lost on Clive, a velvet Elvis painting hung misaligned over the television.

He thought he glimpsed a silhouette of a head peeking through the screen, but when he blinked, nothing was there. The full-moon's shimmer revealed only the strange mounds outside.

"Mama's gonna love you—young, a little meat on your bones. Not like that skinny bastard, Stevie P. I can't believe they ever..." The fat man shook his head and downed the remaining orange drink, tossing the empty bottle into an overflowing bin. "But she's with me now and that's what matters."

A rustling sounded from the kitchen, followed by a crash. Tin cans rolled across the linoleum.

"Get outta there, you little shits and shitters!" The fat man stomped, rocking the trailer like a rusted-out Camero on shot springs.

Feet scurried across the kitchen floor. Clive struggled to sit up, but the tape binding his arms threw him off balance and he toppled sideways with a thud. A shadow, the size of a large dog, motored on all fours, waddling across the doorway. Thrashing about, the tape muffled Clive's screams. What ever drug he'd been slipped was wearing off.

The fat man punched him dead in the forehead. "Don't go getting no ideas. You'll only make this harder on yourself."

Tensing his body, Clive stopped squirming. He inhaled, calming himself as the pain from the blow and his anger hastened his emergence from the drug-induced stupor. Nodding, he acknowledged the fat man's instructions.

"That's better. Don't go doing that again—I don't want to hurt you." The fat man paced the tiny room, shooing away buzzing insects. "I hate this part. Makes it hard to sleep sometimes. I keep tellin' myself, 'Vernon, you gotta get outta this somehow.' But I know I never will. Love makes you do some crazy shit, you know?"

Clive mumbled beneath the duct tape.

"You want that off, do you?"

Clive nodded emphatically.

"S'pose it won't hurt none. Even if you screamed like a school girl at a slasher movie, there ain't much out this way to hear you." The fat man yanked free the tape, ripping away several mustache hairs. "Except for Mama and them damn kids. The crazy ones usually steer clear of my trailer, though. Keep to their own turf." He winked and patted Clive hard on the shoulder before shuffling back to his decaying La-Z-Boy.

"Where am I?" He doubled over, coughing from the heavy stench.

"I'd guess a long way from home. You one of them English pussies?"

"What?" Clive, clenching his hands, glared at his captor. He pictured wrapping them around the fat man's neck blubber. "What is this place? Who the bloody hell are you?"

"Calm down there—don't get your knickers in a knot. That's how you English chaps say it, right?" He removed his worn Atlanta Braves cap from his shaved head and bowed. The motion was exaggerated, mockingly. "Vernon G. Largess at your service. But we met already."

A river of thoughts, anger and confusion rushed through Clive. He nibbled his bottom lip, forcing himself into a calm state. Lately, his emotions had dictated his actions far too much, and going off half-cocked was partially responsible for putting him in this position. That and the promise he made to his mother that someday he'd visit Graceland because she had always dreamed of going herself.

"Guess you probably didn't pay much attention to a local yokel like me, but I picked you up at the airport." A devilish grin crept across Vernon's face. "Remember?"

"I can't recall much of anything." Which was true. He couldn't really recollect boarding the plane in London, but the Bloody Marys accounted for that.

"You called for a cab and I answered. That taxi's the one good thing Stevie P left. Makes it a butt-load easier to get folks when Mama's ready." He dug for another pork rind, popping it in his mouth. "I slipped you a little ether cocktail, and you was agreeable as a drunken prom queen."

Clive struggled to a sitting position, the tape cutting into his wrists. He looked to the screen door. The garbage mounds offered plenty of hiding places, but with his feet and hands bound . . .

"Don't even think about it," Vernon said. "Even if you got past me, Mama's kids would tear you up before you got ten steps out the door. 'Specially if you ran into some of Stevie P's. They's some aggressive fuckers, let me tell you."

Assessing the situation, Clive agreed running—or hopping—away would only aggravate the circumstances. "Vernon, is it? What do you want of me? I'm due for a crucial merger negotiation tomorrow—I'm sure to be missed," he lied. In fact, nobody knew where he was. Once Clive finally decided staying together for the kids was no longer worth enduring Emily's infidelity, he simply up and left. Instead of turning right to the office, he took a left to the pub, and in a drunken rage decided it was time he'd finally seen Elvis' home. No notice to the firm, no note to the family. He wanted to get as far away as possible, and although quite by accident, he'd now succeeded more than he could've imagined.

"They'll be looking for me soon. You won't get away . . ."

Vernon guffawed, spraying Nehi like a sticky sprinkler. "I'll worry about that . . . seems you should have other concerns right about now. But, I don't want nothing from you. Just wanna keep Mama happy." He inhaled another swig. The chorus from "That's Alright Mama" ran through Clive's thoughts

"When her urges start a-flowin', it gets my hackles up a bit, you know?" Vernon bent as far as his flab allowed, lowering his voice. "I wasn't a bad guy, honest. Don't get me wrong. I'm a bad guy now—done some downright awful shit—but I wasn't before Stevie P dragged my ass out here."

Clive squirmed, searching for a comfortable position. "But who's Mama? I assure you I've never met . . ."

"You will." Vernon nestled into the chair, a plume of dust escaping as his weight readjusted. "I wouldn't be in too big a rush if I was you."

Clive recalled seeing a television program claiming the best chance for a kidnap victim to survive was to keep the captor engaged. He grasped for anything to continue the conversation.

"Who's this Stevie P you keep mentioning?"

Vernon chuckled as if the question were too complex to answer. "Sit back there, Nigel . . ."

"Actually it's Clive."

"Whatever. Sit back and I'll tell you a thing or two about Stevie P. Help kill the time anyway." Vernon dusted the pork rind crumbs from his hands. "I'd known Stevie P since we was both sucking titties for breakfast. His real name was Steven SomefuckinIndianname. He was Apache or Seminole, I think. Like I said, some fuckin' Indian. But we all called him Stevie P because that little cuss wet his pants till he was nine or so. Swear to God."

Vernon shifted in the La-Z-Boy, releasing a wet fart. The chair moaned. The sight disgusted Clive, but he maintained his calm demeanor, concealing his desire to break the fat fuck's neck. He hoped he'd get the chance to show what a pissed off "pussy Englishman" could really do.

"Stevie P was a squirrelly little sum-bitch. Strange as a two-headed ass, too—always praying and wearin' all sorts of jewelry. I knew he was queer from the minute I knew what queer was."

Vernon's discharge wafted across the room, its vapors adding to the miasma. The nauseating pall hung over Clive, sharp and repulsive, watering his eyes.

"I'd forgot all about the little fucker until he walks into the Riverside Tavern about twenty years later. He had a wad of cash and started buying me drinks. Next thing I remember, I'm waking up in the back of this cab, tied up right like you. I tell you what, I was glad I came to on my back. I was going to protect my hindquarters at all costs. Exit only, you know."

Outside an uproar erupted. Clive thought it a fight between two alley cats, but the cries consisted of deeper, more boisterous wails. Vernon reached behind his La-Z-Boy and removed a rusted sawed-off shotgun.

"Damn kids," he said. "I'll be right back." He pried himself from the chair and thundered out the door, beyond Clive's sight. A shot exploded. "Stop it, you little fuckers! So help me, if y'all are Stevie P's, I'll skin you half alive."

What have I done? Clive thought. Memories of his girls, Priscilla and Lisa Marie, filled his mind. He mentally kicked himself for following his impulse to leave. If he hadn't, he'd probably be picking the girls up from school now instead of in this crazy predicament.

He stretched, trying to see through the grimy screen, and spied Vernon's elongated shadow in the moonlight with the shotgun resting on a shoulder. Another shadow, similar to the one he'd seen in the kitchen, scampered over the trash heaps. Clive's shoulder popped from the stress. Closing his eyes, he fought the pain, but lost his balance.

Another shot cracked through the night, followed by screeches that burrowed into Clive's spine. He rolled off the couch, his shoulder aching. Like a worm, he slowly inched toward the door.

"Y'all are mighty rambunctious tonight, ain't cha?" Vernon yelled. "You best get more organized if you think you can take me. I'll kill the lot of ya' and fry you up for breakfast—tails and all!"

Clive crossed the grungy linoleum to the door and propped himself up on his elbow. At the base of the garbage mound, a Labrador-sized beast scurried away, a rat-like tail dragging behind through the dirt. It reared up on its back legs and sprinted with an awkward gait into the horizon of waste.

Vernon lumbered back to the trailer, shotgun in tow. Clive rolled back to the couch, his heart thudding. He wasn't sure what frightened him more—the alien animal or Vernon. He rested his head on the cushion, his energy too sapped to get back on the broken-down furniture.

The screen door slammed shut behind Vernon. His smugness revealed itself through his smile as he hovered over Clive.

"Going somewhere?"

"What the hell was that? Is that one of the children?"

Vernon reached down as Clive cowered against the sofa. "Yup, I think that was one of mine. Stevie P's are skinnier." He picked Clive up by his belt and deposited him back on the moldy cushions. "His'n mine got one hell of a turf war going on now."

The blood rushed from Clive's head. He wished the ether had never begun wearing off. Instinctively, he attempted to stand.

Extending a beefy arm, Vernon pointed the shotgun. "I highly recommend you sit your limey ass down. I thought with all them fancy English manners, you'd understand I'm in the middle of a story here. It'd be downright rude to make me kill you before I finish."

Clive gritted his teeth, glaring at his captor. He looked at the barrel and slowly lowered himself back on the couch. Vernon removed a shell from his pocket, reloading the shotgun.

Outside, a call, close to a mewling dropped from the sky and washed over the trailer. Bumps grew on Clive's arms and the hair rose as if excited by static. The call sounded like a train horn in distress, deep and strident.

Vernon rested the shotgun on his shoulder and picked up his half-finished Nehi. "Looks like I'll have to finish our story along the way. You got a date with Mama."

Clive's feet slipped on the linoleum as he backed away into the couch. "Stay away! I don't know what sickness you've been carrying on . . ."

Vernon slammed the shotgun's butt into Clive's abdomen. The blow knocked the air from him, dropping him to his knees.

"I don't think you're in much of a position to judge me. Now, on your feet, sissy-boy." Leaning over him, Vernon pulled him up by one arm. He bent Clive over his shoulder and waddled to the door. "It's time you met Mama."

The taxi was a run-down minivan with balding tires and a crumpled front fender. Vernon threw Clive in the back seat, slamming the door shut. The cab's frame creaked when Vernon entered. It shifted with a series of groans and pops, tilting toward the driver's side.

"Now keep your yapper shut," Vernon whispered. The cab started after several tries, spewing plumes of foul, oil-choked smoke. Pulling a U-turn, Vernon followed a dirt road around the trailer. "We got to go over to the north sector, but we pass through some pretty rough spots. With the turf war and all, this might get hairy. Don't do anything to draw their attention, or we'll be in for a brawl.

"I lost some dumbfuck when I didn't tie his feet good enough. He busted out and ran for it right about here. Little fuckers ripped him to pieces."

"Please, don't do whatever you have planned. I have two girls at home that need me."

Vernon eyed him through the rear-view mirror. Clive believed he detected a hint of mercy. "I can't help you there, Nigel. Mama needs you, too."

Clive's chest hammered and he worried he might suffer a heart attack. He wondered if Emily had reported him missing—or cared at all—but doubted the cavalry was on its way. The landfill's stench burned his lungs. He coughed, his eyes watering.

"Button it up, will ya?" The cab crept along, finding every possible rut.

"These things?" Clive asked in a whisper. "These creatures are your children?"

"Some of 'em. I quit counting 'round two-hundred."

Clive sank against the seat, his head bouncing along with the van. Vernon inserted a cassette into the player, and the one working speaker spat out "In the Ghetto." Shaking his head, Clive couldn't believe he'd been kidnapped by a fellow Elvis devotee. He felt somehow betrayed.

The moon backlit the drifts of garbage. As he focused, Clive saw the outline of several of the "kids" milling over the landscape. He nearly cried from fear.

"But where was I with Stevie P?"

"In the back of the taxi," Clive answered, barely recognizing that he'd spoken.

"Oh yeah—right like you now. Anyways, Stevie P brought me out to the north sector for my meeting with Mama. He tied me all up and shit, but I guess with my size it was a mite harder to cinch down the knots. There was this plywood plank rigged up on some little wheels—he called it an altar, but it looked like a moldy piece of plywood to me. Anyway, he knelt me on this thing, but all I saw was Mama.

"You believe in love at first sight, Nigel?"

"It's Clive, and no, I don't."

"Whatever." Vernon tapped the brakes as the van wound down a hill. "I never gave it no thought, neither, but I fell for Mama right on the spot. I got lost in those big brown eyes like they spoke to me saying all the right things. I felt all dreamy, didn't even remember where I was. I think I just wanted to hold her, you know? When I tried bringing my arms up, the ropes somehow slipped off. I pushed myself up to run, but forgot about the job Stevie P did on my feet. I lost my balance and fell back on that sorry Indian sum-bitch. I think I broke his fucking back.

"Mama got her panties all in a bunch then, screaming and thrashing around like she had a bath in itchin' powder. I felt awful, like I'd hurt her somehow. But, like magic, I understood all what she was saying. She don't speak no English, and I ain't a man of many languages, but I could talk to her—like she put the words right in my head. I just knew, by instinct, what I had to do."

A deafening bang sounded on the roof, and the van shuddered. "You little sum-bitches!" Vernon yelled, slamming on the brakes.

Sliding from the van's roof, the creature's paws scraped across the hood sounding like nails scraping against the metal. It bounced on the hood, buckling the steel, and plunged to the dirt road. Clive smashed into the front seat before recoiling against the back.

The thing rose on its squat hind legs. In the headlights, Clive saw that it was covered in dark matted fur except its face. It appeared human around the ears and eyes, but displayed an elongated snout and needle-like teeth protruded from its mouth. The headlights reflected off the eyes, making them appear as floating, soulless orbs. The creature raised both arms, the rodent-like hands balled in fists with tufts of fur poking through sharp fingers. It stood about four feet and was much thinner than the shadows Clive'd seen before. Rushing toward the cab, it tittered an angry exclamation.

His body frozen with fear, Clive gazed in warped fascination. It seemed like a bad acid trip from college come to life. If not for the pain ripping through his arms, he'd have thought it all a terrible nightmare. And in one of those inappropriate flashes the mind tosses out, he wondered what Emily and the girls were doing.

"That ain't good," Vernon said. He punched the gas. The rat-thing splintered the windshield and bounced out of view.

"What? What's not good?" Clive turned, looking out the back window. Dozens of the creatures chased the van, running with the swift gait of a rodent and pouncing with each step. Clive bit his tongue, repressing a scream.

"That was one of Stevie P's. This is s'posed to be my kids' territory." Clive nearly laughed. Elvis crooned the chorus of "In the Ghetto," through the speaker.

Another creature rammed the front of the van, rocking the vehicle. Swarms emerged from the trash heaps as if the garbage spewed them forth.

A rush of rank wind assaulted Clive as Vernon cranked down the driver-side window. While steering with his right hand, he extended his left arm, pulling the shotgun's trigger. Clive jumped at the piercing blast, seeing one of the creatures drop as the lead shot exploded its skull. The pursuing horde scattered, heading back to the safety of the trash heaps. Vernon drove a while longer before slowing the cab back to a crawl.

"Frisky tonight, ain't they?" Vernon's voice shook. "I told you Stevie P's was some aggressive fuckers."

"What's it mean?" Clive asked, his tone quivering. "Them being in your kids' territory?"

"The turf war's taken a turn. Anything could happen tonight."

Clive granted the pent-up tears a release. He berated himself. Why had he, the steady father, the faithful husband, the even-keeled citizen, suddenly acted on impulse and hopped on a plane to America, not even understanding where Graceland was. *I shouldn't be here at all.*

His wrists struggled against the duct tape. He wanted one shot at Vernon before this ended.

IF MAMA AIN'T HAPPY

"What does Mama want with me?" he asked, knowing he wouldn't like the answer.

"It's the full moon. She needs another man. Not that way—I got her all taken care of there." Vernon put his finger to one nostril, blowing free a hunk of mucus. "I'm not sure why, but that's all she really asks from me. I think Stevie P did something with all that Indian juju to turn her into what she is now. It's the only thing I've come up with that makes any sense. Not that it makes much sense, but it's the best I've been able to figure, anyway. I think it was some down-right evil shit, if you ask me."

Clive struggled for breath, unable to stop the tears. If he hadn't seen the strange offspring, he wouldn't believe a word Vernon had said.

"If it makes you feel any better, they all seem to enjoy it. I can't explain, but even Stevie P flopped around with a big ol' smile across his face. I remember Mama ripping away his insides and him chanting some Indian gibberish all the while. Damnedest thing I ever saw."

The van rounded a bend, revealing another clearing nestled among surrounding piles of garbage. The mounds undulated. Creatures swam over each other making the heaps appear alive.

Clive watched in horror, the events not fully registering in his mind. He still half expected to wake up outside the gates of The King's Memphis home, Vernon, his kids and the impending meeting with Mama all nothing but some alcohol-induced dream.

In the moonlight, he saw the altar. It rested in front of a mound the size of a bi-level house. The mound appeared different, obviously not comprised of trash. The van drawing closer, Clive noticed the enormous attachment at the back of the mound. A good thirty feet long, it tapered to a fine point. The attachment flicked up, and Clive realized it was a tail. Then he saw the elongated nose and the gigantic rodent teeth when Mama tilted her head for a better view of the approaching taxi.

Clive screamed, thrashing about as if trying to escape his own skin. Kicking the front seat, he knocked Vernon into the horn. It blared and startled the brood feeding from Mama. They turned their attention to the van, some raised on hind legs for a better look. Several scrambled about, pacing in skittish steps. Hissing and tittering filled the air as they formed a gauntlet of vermin.

Vernon punched the brakes and slammed the Nehi across Clive's temple. "Stop it! You're gonna make it worse."

Clive leaned his head against the front seat. Blood and sticky soda stung his eyes. His thoughts flashed to images of Priscilla and Lisa Marie. He'd defined himself as a father, but allowed jealousy to cloud what was important. If he'd somehow escape this he vowed he'd return home immediately—Graceland be damned. Surely there was still hope for him and Emily—at least for the girls' sake.

"No. No fuckin' way," Vernon said. He jammed the gearshift into park, opening his door with a great thrust. Waddling around the front of the van, he mumbled "no" along the way, and opened the door with a yank.

"Get out, sissy-boy." Vernon reached inside and pulled Clive out with one arm. He tossed him to the ground as if he weighed no more than a house cat. "Stay here. I'll beat you silly if you don't. You keep quiet while I take care of some business."

He raised the shotgun, firing into the mounds. "This ain't over, you little fuckers! Me and Mama can always make more, ya' hear?" He fired again.

Clive rolled on his side to find a score or more of the fatter children piled in a pyramid—all obviously dead. Tasting bile, he swallowed back the vomit rising in his throat. Vernon continued screaming threats while blubbering in sobs. He backed toward Clive, reaching into his pocket for more shells.

Mama cried again, the mewling reverberating through Clive's skeleton. He heard the melancholy in the call, and it bought an ache to his heart. Grinding his teeth, he let his anger—with Vernon, with himself—rise.

"I'll shoot all of you tonight if I have to!" A shell dropped to the ground. Vernon took two steps back, grunting as he reached for it.

Adrenaline coursed through Clive, his ears ringing. "It's now or never," he sang in his best Elvis voice as he coiled back his legs. With his captor's backside within reach, he sprang both feet into the broad target of Vernon's ass, knocking him forward. Unable to stop his momentum, the American cracked his head against the open van door, collapsing to the ground in a heap of moaning blubber.

Stevie P's brood seized their opportunity, flowing from the heaps like a river of vindictive vermin. Vernon screamed when the first rat-thing pounced. Several others piled on as Mama released another haunting cry. The poignant tones mingled with Vernon's screams, harmonizing into an ungodly chorus.

Clive's body shook as he fixated on the scene. Focusing on the carnage, he barely noticed when one of the kids began gnawing through the duct tape. The sound of blood rushed through his head, thrumming to the beat of an off-kilter drummer. Dizzy, he found calmness when he focused on Mama's mating call. He finally noticed the creature working at the tape around his legs. Hate glared at him through the rat-thing's eyes, but Clive somehow understood he wouldn't be harmed. He heard it in Mama's melodious cries.

When Mama's call stopped, the melee ceased. An eerie silence surrounded the landfill, Clive hearing only the thudding of his heart. The creatures backed away from Vernon, who rolled about languidly. Maintaining eye contact with Clive, the creatures slowly receded, obviously disappointed they were called off before finishing with Vernon. Some backed away on two legs, others on four, back to their turf. Clive felt them evaluating him, summing him up. Empathetic toward them, he understood what it was like to have some strange man wrestle away a valuable part in your life—whether it be stealing your wife or replacing your father.

He turned to Mama. Her eyes were the size of his head, brown and glassy. Staring into their benevolence for a long while, motionless, he saw her pain, her need for somebody—anybody but Vernon. She injected her memories of hate for the fat man, and by instinct, Clive understood what must be done. With his family in tatters, he willingly accepted the role she asked of him.

He rolled Vernon, his body a swollen bag of oatmeal, onto the altar and pushed it closer to Mama. It glided smoothly over the gravel, guided by some other force. Once the altar was close enough, Clive stepped away and gazed at the marvelous creature before him. He smiled, spreading his arms to present the offering.

"Yes, Mama," he answered her unspoken question. "It's Clive. No, not Nigel—Clive."

Mama dug into her meal, proving Vernon right. The fat man massaged his chest, moaning with joy. A delirious smile twisted his face.

A part of Clive's subconscious needled at him like an annoying gnat. He thought there was something else he must do, something he was forgetting. But when he looked at Mama again, the gnat disappeared. He knew he was home.

Hearing the squishing sounds of Mama eating, he ambled toward her distended midsection, whistling "Love Me Tender." He nestled at a teat. An erection grew and he buried it into Mama's flesh. Sucking in her milk, he moaned in ecstasy. He snuggled as close as possible, kicking away some of her feeding offspring.

He would wait for her to finish her meal before consummating their new arrangement.

MOPLEOLI

RICHARD WRIGHT

PROFESSOR CHRISTIAN FARRELL WRESTLED the frustration from his voice. "Miss Stanley, I'm exhausting the ways in which I can politely refuse your request."

The voice on the other end of the phone reached him through a film of tears and mucous. "But you were on the telly . . ."

"For confirming the translation of a 2500 year old Isthmian tablet." The proudest moment of his career was rapidly becoming a millstone around his neck. Pinching the bridge of his nose, he stared resentfully at the carefully ordered shelves of books and papers lining the office walls. A distinguished academic career in ancient languages, several well-regarded papers published, a research and teaching post at Glasgow University— none of it competed with a back page story in the national newspapers. Celebrity, in even the smallest and most obscure dose, versus skill and a hard-won reputation. Apparently, there was no contest.

"Miss Stanley, I can't help you. Good afternoon." Hanging up sharply, he snatched his coat from the chipped stand next to the door. Nicola Stanley was not a quitter, and the best way to avoid her almost hourly calls was to be suddenly elsewhere.

Evening brushed over Glasgow, and from his flat in the Southside of the city, Christian could see across the sparkling murk of the River Clyde to the

University's clock tower in the West End. Cradling the telephone between his neck and shoulder, he waited for Brian Irving to finish.

"That *is* splendid Brian," he finally found a chance to say, "but I'm not prepared to hand my students on to a covering lecturer three weeks before exams, while I jaunt across the Atlantic. I'll happily give the talk, if you can put it back a month."

Christian poured himself a generous glass of red wine before slumping into his leather armchair. The towelling robe he wore was threadbare but deeply comfortable, a gift from an ex-girlfriend that had outlasted her by several years. While Brian continued to coerce him into speaking about the Isthmian translation at Yale, Christian scanned his bookshelves. A lover of fantasy, horror, and science fiction since he was a boy, it was Professor John Ronald Reuel Tolkien's fictional Elvish language that first drew him to his chosen field. The frustration of learning that Tolkien had never completed the rules of grammar or a full vocabulary for his Elven speakers led Christian on to other languages of the world, but it was in the puzzling out of tongues no longer spoken that he found most reward.

Before he could decide whether to next immerse himself in Tolkien's dense *Silmarillion* or Seamus Heaney's translation of *Beowulf*, his buzzer gave a brisk, electronic fart. "Brian, my pizza's here." Grabbing a ten pound note pinned beneath a bookend, he pressed the button next to the door that would let the delivery boy into the block of flats. "We"ll discuss this further tomorrow." Hanging up, he opened his door and waited for his visitor to trudge up three flights of concrete steps.

When Nicola Stanley turned the corner on the landing, his heart sank and his stomach growled. Suddenly, neither seemed due immediate relief.

Christian chewed his cooling pizza as he flicked through the letter, interested despite himself. Taking the pages had been an act of desperation more than generosity. "I promise I'll look at it, and get back to you," he'd said, purely to get rid of her.

Nicola Stanley was heavily built with bad skin, and had shown up in a tightly stretched shell suit and gauche trainers. Perpetually on the verge of tears as she was, Christian could barely understand her thick, nasal Glaswegian accent. Despite having studied regional variations of living languages in his formative years, he still found himself almost professionally offended by the existence of this particular slang. *Class snobbery*, he warned himself. *You're better than that, Christian.*

Latent guilt at his hauteur made him listen to her story one more time, and sheer despondency made him take the handwritten manuscript. When he had done so, the threat of being crushed in an overbearing hug of gratitude caused him to step hastily back into his flat, promising to call her in a few days with his opinion.

Two years ago, Nicola's brother James Stanley had commenced his first year of study at Glasgow University, taking modules in English Language, Divinity, and Ancient Studies. Christian imagined it had been a proud moment for somebody from that social background to gain entry to the University, which at the time was the third highest rated in the country after Oxford and Cambridge. Perhaps it was the pressure of expectation that caused his breakdown, halfway through the academic year, eventually forcing his family to section him. These days James spoke constant nonsense with calm, powerful conviction. Occasionally, he gestured obscenely, and had once bitten off the ear of a nurse in Nicola's presence, but usually he remained calm and certain, often appearing bewildered by people's reactions to his behaviour.

Four weeks ago, James sent Nicola a letter. His previous writings had been gibberish notes on the backs of postcards or envelopes, nothing so involved as this. Nicola had taken it into her head that there was hidden meaning in the nonsensical arrangements of letters, and when the local news had produced a filler story about Christian's recent translation work she had decided to consult his expertise.

Sitting at the reading table in his bedroom, his desk lamp the only illumination, Christian realized with some surprise that she might be right. The letters themselves were from the regular Roman alphabet, and the grammar and syntax conformed to modern standards. A quick comparative study indicated that only the spelling of words was wrong, though the errors were so extreme as to make no sense at all to a casual reader. It looked like all James had done was rearrange the alphabet. If he had done so consistently so that, for example, "a" was always used instead of "u," then deciphering the text would be child's play.

Drawn in by the simple puzzle, Christian poured himself a new glass of wine and found himself a pen.

Hello Nicola. I hope you can read this. There's a chance that writing might work better than trying to tell you, that trapping the words in ink, binding them to paper, might be the key. I'm re-reading this sentence-by-sentence to make sure it's clear. I'm as certain as I can be that it all makes sense.

I've got some stuff to tell you that might not sound very rational. The only thing I want you to promise is not to tell anyone else. Really Nicki. Don't tell anyone, or it will get you too.

I know you all think I've lost my mind. You're wrong. I discovered something remarkable. What I didn't expect was that, at the same time, it was discovering me.

I've got secrets to tell, and I'll continue tomorrow. Taking a break now, because I can hear the cart in the corridor outside. Dinner's coming, and so are the pills, and I can't concentrate for shit when I've taken them.

Uggr dgkfofu Foeao. Oz ol q uggr dgkfofu zgg. O ytts lzkgfu, qfr egfyorefz ziqz O eqf dqat ngx xfrtklzqfr. Eitkt vtkt fg fouizdqktl sqlz fouiz . . .

Christian's head was spinning, partly from the bottle of wine he had drunk, and partly from confusion. The code had changed. The underlying principle appeared to be the same, the simple substitution of one letter with another, but the details were different. "I" was no longer replaced with "K." A first glance made him suspect that "O" could now be fulfilling the same function, but he was too drunk and tired to put the theory to the test.

Giving up for the night, he threw himself on his double bed without bothering to change out of his towelling robe, and let sleep smother him.

Sleeping through his alarm, Christian woke at eight thirty feeling groggy and ill. Throwing on his clothes and making only a token effort to tame his hair, he was almost out of the door when he noticed his bookshelves. Something was different. Turning his head sideways, he realized that the books were in the wrong order.

Christian's obsessive insistence that his books be indexed in strict alphabetical order of author by surname had perplexed lovers and friends alike, but it was an unbreakable habit. Now, everything had been subtly moved around. He ran his finger along the spines of the "L" section. Stephen Laws, Tim Lebbon, Thomas Ligotti, H.P. Lovecraft, Brian Lumley. All wrong.

Christian glanced at his watch. Still an hour before his first lecture started, but it would take him thirty minutes to get there. That gave him half an hour. With his face creased with bafflement, he began to reorder the books.

Lovecraft, Ligotti, Laws, Lumley, Lebbon.

That was better.

Working around the bookshelf to fix the other sections, he decided this was probably an elaborate practical joke. The last people in the flat other than himself were lecturers from his department, Hattie and Jacob, and they often mocked his little obsession. Later he'd give them a call and tell them just how funny he thought it was.

Forty minutes later, running late, he darted out of the door, leaving his bookshelves meticulously alphabetized.

As his students trooped from the seating banks, Christian decided he was going to have a good look at how he was presenting this particular lecture. Last week it had gone well, but his two classes this morning had stared at him in confusion, and he could see them struggle to grasp even the simpler concepts he was outlining.

Feeling irritable, he climbed the stairs of the central aisle, unsurprised to see a small huddle of students waiting for him at the door. The class had been unusually well attended, presumably as he was speaking about the Isthmian translations making his name in linguistic circles, but these few were the diehards who attended every lecture. Smiling, he paused in the doorway and raised his eyebrows. Pink-haired Katy was the first to accept the invitation, but not with the questions he expected.

"Are there going to be lecture notes for that one, professor?"

"Hovi trueble fullowang at?" he asked. There was a pause. Christian frowned. "Ivirythang ukoy?" Another pause. The four students didn't seem to know what to do with themselves. Rebecca smiled uncertainly.

"Um. Is this is a test, sir?"

Christian didn't know how he was supposed to respond to that. Glancing at his watch, he decided to call it a day. "Luuk, A'll be an my uffaci Fradoy oftirnuun. Drup by af yue'ri stall hoving truebli. Ukoy?" Shaking his head, he squeezed past them and made his way outside.

Glasgow was enjoying another warm summer day, and Christian made the most of it, ambling for the tube with his hands in his pockets. Passing the Queen Margaret Union and the crowds of students coming and going from the building, he realized somebody was waving at him. Hattie Connor, his fellow lecturer and likely perpetrator of the book shifting mystery. It wasn't unusual to see her in one of the two student unions—she preferred them to the stuffy staff facilities. Now she was pressed against the window of the notorious Jim's Bar on the first floor, waving.

Christian returned the sentiment, clutching his balls hard with his left hand and thrusting his pelvis violently back and forth while he stuck out his tongue and waggled it slowly up and down.

Normally, Hattie would gesture for him to join her after he waved, but today she simply stared, then jerked back from the window. A group of goths sitting on the steps at the front of the Union were also gawping at him. Two were occasional students of his, and now they whispered cautiously to each other. Christian shrugged playfully, cupping his fingers around an imaginary penis and arcing his hand up and down. Rather than smile, the girls went red, and the whole group stood and hurried into the building.

♦ ♦ ♦

When he got home, Christian checked himself over in the bathroom mirror, looking for something to account for the strange looks he received every time he opened his mouth. While his tongue was a little reddened by last night's wine, nothing accounted for his day so far. People weren't even laughing at him, just staring and shaking their heads.

Perplexed, Christian brewed a coffee to take to the bedroom, deciding that some further work on the letter was the best way to shake the strange, anxious mood that his day was breeding in him. With a little luck, he could finish it off, and get on with reworking his lecture. The reaction this morning had been disconcerting, but he was too unsettled to look at it now.

Drawing the bedroom curtains to shut out the distractions his view offered, he pulled out a pen and began where he had left off.

♦ ♦ ♦

Good morning Nicki. It is a good morning, too. I feel strong, and confident that I can make you understand. There were no nightmares last night, the first time this has happened for as long as I can remember. Am I an idiot, looking for omens and portents? Maybe, but if I can't communicate with the people around me, I'll try the Great Beyond instead.

I'm possessed Nicki.

There, I've said it. I had no idea how to build up to that. Better just to blurt it out.

You saw The Exorcist *when it was re-released, so "possessed" probably has you thinking of projectile vomit, and crucifix masturbation. It isn't like that at all. The creature inside me, doing this to me, isn't some alien, otherworldly thing. Actually, it's more like an old friend, and everybody has one inside them. It hides itself in the most cunning place—in plain sight. It can be categorised in family groupings and subspecies. It evolves, with some species stuck in evolutionary dead ends, and others thriving and spreading.*

It predates mankind by hundreds of thousands of years. Since complex life formed on this world, it has been here too. I suppose you'd call it a parasite.

No, that's not right. It's a symbiote. Sorry Nicki, I'm baffling you with science. I mean it's a creature that needs us to live at the same time as we need it to live. A partner, rather than something that takes without giving back.

I don't know how intelligent the creature is. Clever enough to counter my attempts to expose it. I think that, like any life form, it has evolved natural defenses. It knows enough to neutralize a potential threat, which is what I have been since I discovered it and decided to tell the world.

Enough, I think, for today. I get so tired in here.

I'll continue this tomorrow.

Lk Dkbhk. K hcca rkillfz wsy zssvdkzlu mdv zoccukdz wsy kd ulc fsodkdz . . .

♦ ♦ ♦

Again. It had changed again, and Christian saw the pattern. Whenever James slept, he changed his use of letters on waking. Was it a conscious decision? Surely he would refer to doing it. No, the more he read, the more Christian was certain the man didn't know when it was happening.

The idea of discovering an entirely new medical condition sent a strange, sick thrill through him. Rubbing his temples, he went through to the kitchen. While he waited for the kettle to boil, noticing that the light had faded outside, he marvelled at how complex and specific the disorder was. If he was right though, how did he explain James attacking nurses, even tearing the ear off one with his teeth?

Christian carried his refilled mug past his bookshelves, then stopped dead in his tracks. This morning he had indexed the books fully, from start to finish. Admittedly he had been in a rush, but surely he would have noticed *this*.

"B" and "T" were the wrong way around. "B" was sitting smugly between "A" and "C." "T" had somehow taken its place between "S" and "U." Carefully, Christian rested his mug on the shelf, then walked stealthily to the front door. A swelling tightness in his chest made him breathe deeply and carefully. Kneeling, he checked the lock. Everything seemed in working order. Carefully cracking open the door, he examined the woodwork on the outside. There were no scratches, nothing to indicate the lock had been picked or forced. Christian closed it, locking it behind him and drawing the safety chain for good measure.

A joke was a joke, but this was getting sinister. As he reversed the damage done to his indexing, switching "T" and "B" around on the shelves, he thought of Hattie's strange behavior that afternoon. With both of them spending a great deal of time at the faculty, she had plenty of opportunity to get hold of his keys, copy them, and put them back before he noticed. Was it guilt that had pulled her back from the window when he waved?

Sliding the last of his Campbells and Chizmars into the space he had created after "S" on the shelf, Christian stood back and looked over his work. Perfect. Taking a sip of his coffee, he retrieved his cordless telephone from the couch. Hattie's number was in his speed dial selection. Time to end this particular joke.

"Hello?" She sounded tired.

"Hobbai?"

"I beg your pardon?"

"Luuk, bhas hos gune for inuegh, ekoy. Ab wos fenny ob farsb, teb–"

"Who is this? What do you want?"

"Whu du yue bhank? Chrosbaon. Hobbai, ab's bame bu sbup–"

"Don't call here again." Hattie hung up.

Christian looked at the receiver in his hand. "Feck yue buu," he said to the piece of plastic. Tomorrow, the two of them would have words. Perhaps he had done something to upset her that warranted this strange revenge. Nothing came to mind, but it was always possible.

Putting his irritation aside, he returned to the compelling human story underlying the cracking of a linguistic code. Languages were about living people. In deciphering patterns in written communication you were inevitably introduced to the writer, and he found himself liking James enormously.

So thinking, he bent over the letter and began scanning the next section for patterns.

◆ ◆ ◆

Hi Nicki. I keep wishing you goodnight and greeting you in the morning, forgetting that you"ll probably read this in ten minutes flat. Time's a funny thing, isn't it?

The creature living inside me changed how I communicate. It's hard to explain, because I don't know I'm doing it. People obviously don't understand a word I'm saying, but from this side, people talk to me, I understand them, and I reply in kind. I can't hear myself doing whatever I'm doing.

I wonder too whether the same applies to my body language. We use our bodies a lot to communicate. I remember when I bit the ear off the nurse. Everyone went berserk, and I couldn't understand why. I was flirting, subtly I thought, just because she had always been friendly. At first I assumed the flirtation wasn't welcome. Later, I realized her response was disproportionate, that I'd done something terrible. You see my problem. I've wracked my mind for other ways I could have flirted, but as far as I can see, that's how it's done. At the same time, I recognize now that if somebody severed my ear, I wouldn't interpret it as amorous. I recognize normal behaviour in people around me, but when I try to emulate it, it becomes twisted up.

What the creature inside me has done is rewrite my programming, and built a new language that only I understand. The worse thing is, it's an outgoing curse. I understand what everyone else is doing and saying in the same way as you do. What I can't see is how I'm doing anything different.

I hoped I'd finish this today, but I'm exhausted. Tomorrow I'll tell you about the creature. It's so obvious, Nicki, that I don't see how it's been missed.

Tomorrow, I promise.

Da Panca. Owi zue wiosz bdip? Su zue xopb bu diow? A'xowpapl zue bdueld upni zue cpux, bdiwi'v pu luapl tonc. Zue nop'b nupkipaipbmz ruwlib. Ikiwz afi zue vdwel, uw uyip zuew fuebd, zue'mm fiib bdi nwiobewi. Ops ar zue wz bu vyamm abv vinwibv, bu opztusz, ab xamm sirips abvmir.

Bdi tiovb av mopleoli . . .

Christian scanned the rest of the letter. A new day in James Stanley's life, a new language to express it in. Sitting back in his chair, he rubbed his eyes, wondering whether he should stop for the night. The next section, the final piece of the puzzle, was almost comprehensible to him. Though it would be slow going, he felt that he might even be able to sight-read it. Thinking of James's assertion that a creature lived inside of him, "hiding in plain view," he decided that he wasn't going to be able to sleep before he had the whole story. A faint film of sweat had formed on Christian's forehead, and he wondered whether it came from excitement at what he was uncovering, or nauseous empathy with a man who was no longer master of his own tongue. Was it worse, not being able to hear the mistakes you were making? Christian walked to his sitting room window and stared down at the street lamps reflected in the River Clyde, trying to put himself in the other man's shoes. No wonder everyone thought he was mad.

Somebody knocked on his door. The buzzer hadn't sounded, and his first thought was that this must be Hattie. She had used her copied keys to open the street level security entrance, but hadn't quite dared to let herself into the flat and catch him by surprise.

Smiling, fully prepared to unleash a torrent of smug invective at her, he unlocked the door and yanked it open.

Nicola Stanley stood there.

Surprise must have been etched all over his face. She began to explain before he had a chance to ask the question.

"Look, I'm sorry about coming round early and all that Professor, and I should have buzzed but one of your neighbors was coming out, and I couldn't wait around, see?" Her eyes shone with watery hope, and Christian suddenly decided, yes, he would show her. The need to tell somebody about his discoveries had been building since the afternoon, and why should that not be Nicola? She had more right to his information than any of the academics, psychiatrists, and doctors he had already thought of consulting.

Holding his tongue, he stepped back, and was almost knocked down as she squeezed herself unapologetically past him. Once inside she stopped, gazing uncertainly around the apartment. Christian closed the door behind her and fetched his copy of the transcript, smiling as she snatched it eagerly from him and squinted at the first lines.

Christian had expected tears, or gratitude, or outright glee. When she looked up at him, frowning, he realized she was going to disappoint him.

"I don't get it," she told him dully. "I thought you were going to translate it."

Christian snatched the papers back, wondering if he had given her the original instead of his translation. No, this was it, in his own careful handwriting. James's words, in plain English.

"Wios ab," he told her firmly, holding the papers out to her. "Wios ab bu bdi ips."

Nicola didn't read it though. Instead she froze up, muscles stiffening beneath her pink tracksuit, her eyes going wide. "Professor?" Was she scared, he wondered? Was the truth so hard to face after all this time?

"Boci zuew bafi," he told her gently. There was no rush, after all. "Zue xiwi waldb, Panumo," he reassured her. "Di'v ov vopi ov zue uw A. Ximm, fuvbz."

Nicola raised her hands to her mouth, and then the dam burst and she was crying. When he took a step closer, his own panic and confusion rising, she went more rigid still.

"Diz, diz," he soothed, wondering how he was going to get her out of his flat. Crying women had never been a strong point of Christian's. Stepping awkwardly forward, he resigned himself to comforting her. Raising his fist, he snapped it forward, mashing her nose. Sharp pains flared in his fingers, both surprising him and reminding him why he wasn't normally a tactile person.

Nicola's head snapped back, blood champagning from her nose. Smashing his fist into her face twice more, Christian watched her collapse to the floor. Clutching herself into a ball, blood and snot dripping down her face, her sobbing intensified. Perhaps she wasn't used to the kindness of strangers.

It was almost as though he had made it worse without realizing it. Christian felt a dizzying chasm open in his mind. What if . . . what if . . .

Turning, he looked at his bookshelves, and his jaw dropped at what he was seeing. With Nicola's sobs (of pain?) still blasting out behind him, he closed his eyes. Opened them. The books were still in the wrong order.

Twice today, he had alphabetized them from scratch. Now they were all over the place, and he felt an almost primordial urge to put them in the right order. Swallowing the instinct brought real tears to his eyes.

Trying to make himself heard over the woman's howls, he tried one more time to reassure her as his panic carried him into the bedroom. "Ab'mm ti omm waldb," he called out, no longer believing that it would be.

Picking up the notepad in which he had made his translation, he turned to a new page. Despite the noise, and the sticky mess of blood and snot on his hand (that wasn't right, surely?), he had to concentrate very hard.

The alphabet. The key to the language. *Think it through, slowly.* A, B, C, D, E, F, G . . .

Once he reached the end, he snatched up a pen, took a deep breath, and wrote it down exactly as he had thought it out. O, T, N, S, I, R, L . . .

Only when he had reached the end, comparing the "Z" in his mind with the "J" on the page, did he pause.

Wiped a hand over his tired eyes.

Smiled.

Everything matched up perfectly.

Jim Stanley was insane. Christian Farrell was not.

A particularly resonant sob from Nicola reminded him that he had left a stricken woman to howl out her fear without comfort. Shame rushed him back into the sitting room. "Ab's ucoz, A'f diwi," he said. Standing over her where she lay at the side of the couch, he stamped soothingly on her neck. Three times. As hard as he could.

She was quiet, at last. Now, perhaps, he could explain what he thought the letter meant. "Tibbiv pux?" he asked. Nicola didn't reply, didn't even move. Perhaps she needed a moment to herself. "A'mm ti tonc ap o fapebi," he told her gently. Having nowhere else to go, he retreated to his bedroom once more, and having nothing better to do, he sat himself at his reading desk. Wiping Nicola's blood from his shoe with a tissue, dropping it into the waste basket beneath the desk, he glanced over the letter one more time.

What he saw made him light-headed.

Christian closed his eyes, pictured the letter's final page in his mind, the climactic section still in need of translation. Opening his eyes, he looked down. The end of the letter, explaining all, was written in clear English.

Da Panca. Owi zue wiosz bdip? Su zue xopb bu diow? A'f xowpapl zue bdueld upni zue cpux, bdiwi'v pu luapl tonc. Zue nop'b nupkipaipbmz ruwlib. Ikiwz bafi zue vdwel, uw uyip zuew fuebd, zue'mm fiib bdi nwiobewi. Ops ar zue bwz bu vyamm abv vinwibv, bu opztusz, ab xamm sirips abvimr.

Bdi tiovb av mopleoli, mopleoli av bdi tiovb. Ab'v pub o buum xi nupbwum, teb o nwiobewi xi nuiqavb xabd. Ndwi owi Rofamaiv ur mopleoliv, vetvyinaivm, ikumebaupowz grrvdggbv, omm bdob vuwb ur bdapl. Bdiz ikip apbiwtwiid, ywudenapl urrdywapg.

A epiowbdis bde lwiob vinwib, ops bdi mopleoli dov siripsis abvimr. Nop zue afolapi xbod ab'v maci, cpuxapl bdob bdiwi avp'b o vapmi yiwvup ap bdi xuwmd A mop nuffepanobi xabd?

Sup'b bimm opzupi Panca. Sup'd bwz bu iqyuvi bdif. A muki zue, ops fef, ops Oppai. A muki zue, fuwi bdop A nop voz.

Zuew twubdiw,

Haf.

◆ ◆ ◆

Perfect English. Hadn't Nicola read to the end of the letter? As for what it suggested, the identity of the creature ... well, Christian knew better than most that there was a certain crazy logic to it. Family groupings, evolution, interbreeding—yes, it had a ring of rightness to it. Of course, it was still crazy.

There was silence from the other room, and when he went through he saw Nicola was still on the floor. Part of him had thought she might have sneaked away, shamed by her outburst. Something about the way she lay there, staring blankly at the ceiling, bothered him. Should anybody's head be resting at that angle?

Another knock at his door stopped him from pursuing the thought. Fumbling, he cracked open the door and peered through. Two police officers stood there, a short haired blonde woman and a slightly overweight man.

"Sir," the male officer began, "We've had a complaint about the noise. Could we come in for a moment?"

Christian nodded eagerly, glad to have somebody to help him with his distressed guest. "Ur nuewva," he said, and began to gesture that they should step inside. One of his hands reached out and tightened around the male officer's testicles, his other clutched eagerly at the female officer's left breast.

They didn't respond to the invitation quite as he expected. There was shouting, and confusion, and then for Christian, shock and pain. Only later, curled on the bunk of the police cell, sobbing his frustration that he couldn't make anybody understand him, did he accept that James Stanley had been right.

Mopleoli was their master now, and it enforced their silence.

AND ON THE FOURTH DAY

JAMES ARGENDELI

DAY 1

IT WASN'T HIS FAULT. He would be blamed but it was not his fault. This was the first day of his reign on earth. His eternal reign. As an old philosopher once proclaimed, "It was the first day of the rest of his life." Life everlasting. The war began and ended yesterday. It did not take long. The earth could only bottle up so much hatred before it erupted in its own destruction. He did not even know who started it, or why, but with the end of man's existence he was truly born. He walked through the dust of the ruins of a city. Not one of their big cities, but now all cities were one and the same. There was no difference—no more culture, no more anything. Sure, there would be pockets of surviving people, but eventually, they would all die out, leaving him to enjoy what was left. All alone.

His travel took him to a park. His park now. An homage to the world he created. Did he create this? The trees that were standing were black and misshapen into obscene skeletons. No plant life at all. What passed for grass was burnt and actually cracked as he walked on it. On a melted swing set, he noticed a trail of ants blindly searching their world for survival. So, the meek really did inherit the earth. He stepped on the ants, then stood there in that park next to the swing set as the sky turned dark and the cold silent night eagerly devoured the gray featureless day.

DAY 2

What passed for dawn gradually appeared as the darkness lightened to a numbing dirty yellow mist. He was thinking on day two of his reign. He no longer had the hatred of people to make him strong. Before it was so easy. People wanted what they did not have. They could not be happy with their natural environment. Always bigger, better. They sought more land, food, love, and money. Their vices led to this. Some fled to be alone, but their biggest sin was in helping themselves to their own private piece of earth. The few people left would be in a living hell before joining their brothers and sisters in an eternal one. And would he be to blame? He should feel like a king looking onto his land for the first time after a long journey. Instead, he felt . . . nothing. No joy, no rapture, nothing. An empty feeling for an empty world. Why? Was not this what he always wanted? With his victory had come no reward. He looked around. He was still in the park, but again, the night had claimed another victory. It had come on suddenly with no twilight between day and night. No night sounds to announce her arrival. Just blackness.

DAY 3

Another day. His third day in this kingdom of ash. Once the daylight haze had set in, he left the park to venture out into the city. He soon came across a bridge that marked the beginning of the inner city. He could see no proof but he knew that once a river flowed under the bridge. The river was used for business and recreation. Now, all that remained was black sand and soot covering the riverbed. But there was something else. The smell. The smell of decay. The bridge still spanned the trench in the earth; however, the river was now one of man's broken dreams and ambitions. As he wandered the city, the most noticeable absence was that of sound. No noise of any kind. He knew there should be people making noise. No cars, no trolleys, no busses or trucks, no crying or laughing. He should be laughing. He should be crying for joy. All over the world he had inherited this kingdom. But no sound was heard. Except a wail. If anyone could hear it and understand the despair they would have heard a mournful cry. His cry of anguish that said "I did not cause this."

His silent journey took him into the business district. Empty buildings stood like seashells now abandoned of life. Signs of life but all of it empty, like his soul. Did he even have a soul? He was perceived as having a black, twisted soul. A soul no light could escape. But he felt no justification for this. This is not what he wanted.

As darkness lowered its curtain, he came upon the steps of a church.

DAY 4

Darkness gave up its hold to start another day. Which day was this? He did not know. All the days would start and end the same way. Nothing new. No challenge to conquer. No souls to win. Was this his Hell?

He then remembered being on the broken steps of a church. The church was set on a small hill. It was not a big church, rather, a homely one. Four steps led to the front doors of the church, which led to the sanctuary. The church was in decent condition with some of the windows still intact. Out of the two wooded doors entering the church, one was still attached. There was not a sign of the second door. The building was still standing though a thin layer of ash covered it. The windows were now opaque. He walked into the open doorway. The entrance to the church was littered with papers, booklets and melted balls of wax. The narthex stood empty. The pulpit stood untouched. There was no feeling of anything here. Just another empty building. He walked up to the altar. For a small church, this altar was elaborate. The marble table was still intact but had a series of small spider webbed cracks in its base. On the altar was an open bible. To the left of the table was a baptismal font. The doors leading into the altar were adorned with mosaics of saints and apostles.

For eternity, he had lived so others could suffer. For this! He had come full circle. He knelt in front of the table.

You know why I am here. Was this all part of your plan? I did not want to inherit a cold, dead, barren world. This is not what I caused. I wanted glory. I wanted worshippers. I did not want waste. I did not cause this. Yes, I admit I am evil. But man did not need me. They were evil enough to have caused this. If there were any way to go back, to return to the pitiful human frailties, I would accept that. Why don't you answer me?

I did not win. Answer me.

There was no sound. Nothing.

He left the church.

As he walked down the steps, he stopped. Did he hear a noise? No, it was nothing. He continued to descend the church steps but stopped again. From the corner of his senses, he caught the shadow of something on the final step. A shadow but with no sun. He looked at what had caused the now faded shadow. It was a flower. In full bloom—a white flower. As bright as the brightest star. Like a baby fighting for its first breath—a flower. He bent down to . . . but no, leave it be. He looked up to the heavens and smiled.

As the darkness came, he walked back into the church.

ALSO AVAILABLE FROM ELDER SIGNS PRESS

PUBLISHER OF QUALITY DARK FICTION, SCIENCE FICTION, FANTASY & HORROR

Private investigator Teddy London, who has stood firm against vampires, werewolves, and terrors from beyond without flinching, now faces not only an unimaginable god-horror of unlimited power but also the consequences of his own reckless ego. Acting without thinking, he inadvertently opens the doorway of the dreamplane to a beautiful cat burglar, giving her access to the secrets of the universe.

Now, the balance of all time and space has been thrown into chaos, and Teddy will need more than a gun named Betty and a blade named Veronica to save his own skin, let alone the entire world.

Author: C.J. Henderson
Pages: 272
Trade paperback
MSRP: $14.95
ISBN: 1-934501-15-8

The world ends with the flip of a switch. The thundering storms strike across the world, searing the earth, leaving destruction in their wake. Few will survive.

For the folks living in Temperance, Illinois the nightmare is just beginning. When the sky roils in luminous colors, the people of the small town begin to die, and Randall Clay decides to escape. What he didn't expect was the dead to come back to life—or the nightmare that came after that.

Author:s William Jones
and Alexander Grifin
Pages: 336
Trade paperback
MSRP: $14.95
ISBN: 1-934501-11-5

WWW.ELDERSIGNSPRESS.COM

ELDER SIGNS PRESS, INC.   P.O. BOX 389   LAKE ORION, MI   48361-0389   USA
248-628-9711   WWW.ELDERSIGNSPRESS.COM   INFO@ELDERSIGNSPRESS.COM